TOTAL CONTROL

Also by David Baldacci

Absolute Power

David Baldacci

Total Control

SIMON & SCHUSTER
A VIACOM COMPANY

First published in Great Britain by Simon & Schuster, 1997
An imprint of Simon & Schuster Ltd
A Viacom Company

Simon & Schuster
West Garden Place
Kendal Street
London W2 2AQ

Simon & Schuster of Australia Pty Ltd Sydney

A CIP catalogue record for this book is available
from the British Library.

0-684-82075-7

Printed and bound in Great Britain by
Butler & Tanner Ltd, Frome and London

ACKNOWLEDGMENTS

Total Control required a great deal of research and specialized information, which I was fortunate to obtain through the efforts of the following people.

To my friend Jennifer Steinberg, for going above and beyond the line of duty to ferret out answers to all the esoteric and impossibly complex questions I constantly put to her. If there's a better research person out there, I am not aware of her.

To my friend Tom DePont of NationsBank, for his able assistance on complex banking issues and his very helpful suggestions regarding plausible financial scenarios. To my friend Marvin McIntyre of the brokerage firm Legg Mason and his colleague Paul Montgomery, for sound advice and assistance on the Federal Reserve and investment issues.

To Dr. Catherine Broome, a dear friend and scholarly physician, for her advice on general medical issues and specialized cancer treatments. And also for her and her husband David's insightful details about the city of New Orleans.

To Craig and Amy Haseltine and the rest of the Haseltine clan for graciously introducing me to the beauty of coastal Maine.

To my uncle Bob Baldacci, for providing reams of material and patiently answering a flood of queries as to the complex workings of jet airplanes and airport and maintenance operations.

To my cousin Steve Jennings, for guiding me through the maze of computer technology and the fuzziness of the Internet. And to his wife, Mary, who should strongly consider a career as an editor. Her comments were a big help, and many of them have been incorporated into the finished product. And to Dr. Peter Aiken of Virginia Commonwealth University, for helping me to understand the intricacies of e-mail travel over the Internet.

To Neil Schiff, publicity director at the FBI, for arranging a tour of the Hoover Building and for answering my questions about the Bureau.

To Larry Kirshbaum and Maureen Egen and the rest of the wonderful crew at Warner Books, for all their support. You've all changed my life so much, I feel a real duty to acknowledge that in each novel, if only to show my sincere gratitude.

A very special thanks to Frances Jalet-Miller of the Aaron Priest Agency. I'm truly blessed to have her as an editor and friend. She made *Total Control* far better with her right-on-target comments.

TOTAL CONTROL

CHAPTER ONE

The apartment was small, unattractive and possessed of an unsettling musty odor that suggested long neglect. However, the few furnishings and personal belongings were clean and well organized; several of the chairs and a small side table were clearly antiques of high quality. The largest occupant of the tiny living room was a meticulously crafted maple bookcase that might as well have rested on the moon, so out of place did it seem in the modest, unremarkable space. Most of the volumes neatly lining the shelves were financial in nature and dealt with such subjects as international monetary policy and complex investment theories.

The only light in the room came from a floor lamp next to a rumpled couch. Its small arc of illumination outlined the tall, narrow-shouldered man sitting there, his eyes closed as though he were asleep. The slender watch on his wrist showed it to be four o'clock in the morning. Conservative gray cuffed suit pants hovered over gleaming black-tasseled shoes. Hunter-green suspenders ran down the front of a rigid white dress shirt. The collar of the shirt was open, the ends of a bow tie dangled around the neck. The large bald head was like an afterthought, because what captured one's attention was the thick, steel-gray beard that fronted the wide, deeply lined face. However, when the man abruptly opened his eyes, all other physical characteristics became secondary; the eyes were chestnut brown in color and piercing; they seemed to swell to a size that completely engulfed the eye sockets as they swept across the room.

Then the pain wracked the man and he ripped at his left side; actually the hurt was everywhere now. Its origins, however, had been at the spot he now attacked with a fierce, if futile, vengeance. The breaths came in gushes, the face grossly contorted.

His hand slipped down to the apparatus attached to his belt. About the shape and size of a Walkman, it was actually a CADD pump attached to a Groshong catheter that was fully hidden under the man's shirt, where its other end was embedded in his chest. His finger found the correct button and the computer resting inside the CADD pump immediately delivered an incredibly potent dose of painkilling medication over and above what it automatically dispensed at regular intervals throughout the day. As the combination of drugs flowed directly into the man's bloodstream, the pain finally retreated. But it would return; it always did.

The man lay back, exhausted, his face clammy, his freshly laundered shirt soaked with perspiration. Thank God for the pump's on-demand feature. He had an incredible tolerance for pain, as his mental prowess could easily overpower any physical discomforts, but the beast now devouring his insides had introduced him to an altogether new level of physical anguish. He wondered briefly which would come first: his death or the drugs' total and complete defeat at the hands of the enemy. He prayed for the former.

He stumbled to the bathroom and looked into the mirror. It was at that moment that Arthur Lieberman started to laugh. The near-hysterical howls continued upward, threatening to explode through the thin walls of the apartment, until the uncontrollable outburst ended in sobs and then choked vomiting. A few minutes later, having replaced his soiled shirt with a clean one, Lieberman began calmly to coax his bow tie into shape in the reflection of the bathroom mirror. The violent mood swings were to be expected, he had been told. He shook his head.

He had always taken care of himself. Exercised regularly, never smoked, never drank, watched his diet. Now, at a youthful sixty-two, he would not live to see sixty-three. That fact had been confirmed by so many specialists that, finally, even Lieberman's massive will to live had given way. But he would not go quietly. He had one card left to play. He smiled as he suddenly realized that impending death had granted him a maneuverability that had been denied in life. It would indeed be an ironic twist that such a distinguished career as his would end on such an ignoble note. But the shock waves that would accompany his exit would be worth it at this point. What did he care? He walked into the small bedroom and took a moment to glance at the photos on the desk. Tears welled up in his eyes and he quickly left the room.

At five-thirty precisely Lieberman left the apartment and rode the small elevator down to the street level, where a Crown Victoria, its government license plates a gleaming white in the wash of the streetlight, was parked at the curb, its engine idling. The chauffeur exited the car briskly and opened and held the door for Lieberman. The driver respectfully tipped his cap to his esteemed passenger and, as usual, received no response. In a few moments the car had disappeared down the street.

At about the time Lieberman's car entered the on ramp to the Beltway, the Mariner L500 jetliner was being rolled out of its hangar at Dulles International Airport in preparation for the nonstop flight to Los Angeles. Maintenance checks completed, the 155-foot-long plane was now being fueled. Western Airlines subcontracted out the fueling component of its operation. The fuel truck, squat and bulky, was parked underneath the starboard wing. On the L500 the standard configuration had fuel tanks located within each wing and in the fuselage. The fuel panel under the wing, located about a third of the way out from the fuselage, had been dropped down and the long fuel hose snaked upward into the wing's interior, where it had been locked into place around the fuel intake valve. The one valve served to fuel all three tanks through a series of connecting manifolds. The solitary fueler, wearing thick gloves and dirty overalls, monitored the hose as the highly combustible mixture flowed into the tank. The man looked slowly around at the increasing activity surrounding the aircraft: mail and freight cargo were being loaded on, baggage carts were wending their way to the terminal. Satisfied that he wasn't being observed, the fueler used one gloved hand to casually spray the exposed part of the fuel tank around the intake valve with a substance in a plastic container. The metal of the fuel tank gleamed where it had been sprayed. Closer examination would have revealed a slight misting on the metal's surface, but no closer examination would be made. Even the first officer making the rounds on the preflight check would never discover this little surprise lurking within the massive machine.

The man replaced the small plastic container deep within one pocket of his overalls. He pulled from his other pocket a slender rectangular-shaped object and raised his hand up into the wing's interior. When his hand came back down, it was empty. The fueling completed, the hose was loaded back on the truck and the fuel panel on the wing was reattached. The truck drove off to complete work on another jet. The man looked back once at the L500 and then continued on. He was scheduled to get off duty at seven this morning. He did not intend to stay a minute longer.

The 220,000-pound Mariner L500 lifted off the runway, easily powering through the early morning cloud cover. A single-aisle jet with twin high bypass ratio Rolls-Royce engines, the L500 was the most technologically advanced aircraft currently operating outside those flown by pilots of the U.S. Air Force.

Flight 3223 carried 174 passengers and a seven-member flight crew. Most passengers were settling into their seats with newspapers and magazines while the plane climbed swiftly over the Virginia countryside to its cruising altitude of thirty-five thousand feet. The onboard navigational computer had established a flight time to Los Angeles of five hours and five minutes.

One of the passengers in the first-class section was reading the *Wall Street Journal*. A hand played across the bushy, steel-gray beard as large, active eyes scanned the pages of financial information.

Down the narrow aisle, in the coach section, other passengers sat quietly, some with hands folded across their chests, some with eyes half closed and others reading. In one seat, an old woman gripped rosary beads in her right hand, her mouth silently reciting the familiar words.

As the L500 climbed to thirty-five thousand feet and leveled off, the captain came on the loudspeaker to make her perfunctory greetings while the flight attendants went about their normal routine—a routine that was about to be interrupted.

All heads turned to the red flash that erupted on the right side of the aircraft. Those sitting in the window seats on that side watched in the starkest horror as the right wing buckled, metal skin tearing, rivets popping free. Bare seconds passed before two-thirds of the wing sheared off, carrying with it the starboard-side Rolls-Royce engine. Like savaged veins, shredded hydraulic lines and cables whipped back and forth in the fierce headwind as jet fuel from the cracked fuel tank doused the fuselage.

The L500 immediately rolled left over on its back, making a shambles of the cabin. Inside the fuselage every single human being screamed in mortal terror as the plane whipped across the sky like a tumbleweed, completely out of control. Passengers up and down the aisle were violently torn from their seats. For most of them the short trip from the seats was fatal. Screams of pain were heard as heavy pieces of luggage, disgorged from compartments torn open when the shock waves of air pressure gone wild exceeded their locking mechanism's strength limits, collided with soft human flesh.

The old woman's hand slipped open and the rosary beads slid down to the floor, which was now the ceiling of the upside-down plane. Her eyes were wide open now, but not in fear. She was one of the fortunate ones. A fatal heart attack had rescued her from the next several minutes of sheer terror.

Twin-engine commercial jetliners are certified to fly on only one engine. No jetliner, however, can fly with only one wing. The airworthiness of Flight 3223 had been irreversibly destroyed. The L500 settled into a tight nose-to-ground death spiral.

On the flight deck the two-member crew struggled valiantly

with the controls as their damaged aircraft shot downward through the overcast skies like a spear through cotton. Unsure of the precise nature of this catastrophe, they nevertheless were well aware that the aircraft and all lives on board were in significant jeopardy. As they frantically tried to regain control of the aircraft, the two pilots silently prayed they would collide with no other plane as they hurtled to earth. "Oh, my God!" The captain stared in disbelief at the altimeter as it raced on its unstoppable course to zero. Neither the most sophisticated avionics system in the world nor the most exceptional piloting skills could reverse the startling truth facing every human being on the fractured projectile: They were all going to die, and very soon. And as happens in virtually all air crashes, the two pilots would be the first to leave this world; but the others on board Flight 3223 would only be a fraction of a second behind.

Lieberman's mouth sagged open as he gripped the armrests in total disbelief. As the plane's nose dropped to six o'clock, Lieberman was looking face down at the back of the seat in front of him, as if he were at the very top of some absurd roller coaster. Unfortunately for him, Arthur Lieberman would remain conscious until the very second the aircraft met the immovable object that it was now racing toward. His exit from the living would come several months ahead of schedule and not at all according to plan. As the plane started its final descent, one word escaped from Lieberman's lips. Though monosyllabic, it was uttered in one continuous shriek that could be heard over all of the other terrifying sounds flooding the cabin.

"Noooo!"

CHAPTER TWO

Jason Archer, his starched shirt dirty, his tie askew, labored through the contents of the piles of boxes. A laptop sat beside him. Every few minutes he would stop, pull a piece of paper from the morass and, using a handheld device, scan the contents of the paper into his laptop. Sweat trickled down his nose. The storage warehouse he was in was hot and filthy. Suddenly a voice called out to him from somewhere within the vast space. "Jason?" Footsteps approached. "Jason, are you here?"

Jason quickly closed up the box he was working on, shut down his laptop and slid it between a crevice in the stacks of boxes. A few seconds later a man appeared. Quentin Rowe stood about five-eight, weighed perhaps a hundred fifty, with narrow shoulders; slender oval glasses rested above a hairless face. His long, thin blond hair was tied back into a neat ponytail. He was dressed casually in faded jeans and a white cotton shirt. The antenna of a cellular phone sprouted from his shirt pocket. His hands were stuffed into his back pockets. "I happened to be in the area. How's it coming?"

Jason stood up and stretched his long, muscular frame. "It's coming, Quentin, it's coming."

"The CyberCom deal is really heating up and they want the financials ASAP. How much longer do you think it will take you?" Despite his carefree appearance, Rowe looked anxious.

Jason eyed the stacks of boxes. "Another week, ten days tops."

"You're sure?"

Jason nodded and methodically wiped his hands off before resting his eyes on Rowe. "I won't let you down, Quentin. I know how important CyberCom is to you. To all of us." A twinge of guilt hit Jason between the shoulder blades, but his features were inscrutable.

Rowe relaxed somewhat. "We won't forget your efforts, Jason. What with this and the job you did on the tape backups. Gamble was particularly impressed, to the extent he can understand it."

"I think it'll be remembered for a long time," Jason agreed.

Rowe surveyed the warehouse with incredulity. "To think the contents of this entire warehouse could fit comfortably on a stack of floppy disks. What a waste."

Jason grinned. "Well, Nathan Gamble isn't the most computer literate person in the world." Rowe snorted. "His investment operations generated a lot of paper, Quentin," Jason continued, "and you can't argue with success. The man's made a lot of money over the years."

"Exactly, Jason. That's our only hope. Gamble understands money. The CyberCom deal will make all the others look puny by comparison." Rowe looked admiringly up at Jason Archer. "After all this work you've got a great future ahead of you."

Jason's eyes took on a soft gleam and then he smiled at his colleague. "My thoughts exactly."

Jason Archer climbed into the passenger seat of the Ford Explorer, leaned across and kissed his wife. Sidney Archer was tall and blond. Her chiseled features had softened after the birth of their daughter. She inclined her head toward the rear seat. Jason smiled as his eyes fell upon Amy, two years old and dead asleep in her baby seat, Winnie the Pooh automatically clutched in one fist.

"Long day for her," Jason said as he unknotted his tie.

"For us all," Sidney replied. "I thought being a part-time law partner would be a breeze. Now it seems like I cram the same fifty-hour week into three days." She shook her head wearily and pulled the truck onto the road. Behind them soared the world headquarters building of Triton Global, her husband's employer and the world's undisputed leader in technologies ranging from global computer networks to children's educational software and just about everything in between.

Jason took one of his wife's hands in his and squeezed it tenderly. "I know, Sid. I know it's rough, but I might have some news soon that'll let you chuck the practice for good."

She looked at him and smiled. "You devised a computer program that'll let you pick the correct Lotto numbers?"

"Maybe something better." A grin flashed across his handsome features.

"Okay, you've definitely got my attention. What is it?"

He shook his head. "Uh-uh. Not until I know for sure."

"Jason, don't do this to me." Her mock plea brought a broader smile to his lips. He patted her hand. "You know I'm real good at keeping secrets. And I know how you love surprises."

She stopped at a red light and turned to him. "I also like opening presents on Christmas Eve. So come on, talk."

"Not this time, sorry, no way, nohow. Hey, how about we go out to eat tonight?"

"I'm a very tenacious attorney, so don't try to change the subject on me. Besides, eating out is not in this month's budget. I want details." She playfully poked him as she went through the green light.

"Very, very soon, Sid. I promise. But not now, okay?" His tone had suddenly become more serious, as though he regretted bringing up the subject. She looked over at him. He was staring rigidly out the window. A trace of concern came over her face. He turned back to her, caught the look of worry, put a hand against her cheek and winked. "When we got married, I promised you the world, didn't I?"

"You've given me the world, Jason." She stared at Amy in the rearview mirror. "More than the world."

He rubbed her shoulder. "I love you, Sid, more than anything. You deserve the best. One day I'll give it to you."

She smiled at him; however, as he turned to look out the window the look of concern returned to her features.

The man was bent over the computer, his face bare inches from the screen. His fingers were pounding the keys so fiercely they resembled a column of miniature jackhammers. The battered keyboard appeared ready to disintegrate under the relentless attack. Like pouring water, digital images flowed down the computer screen too fast for the eye to follow. A weak light overhead provided illumination for the man's task. Thick droplets of sweat clustered on his face, although the room temperature hovered at a comfortable seventy degrees. He swiped at the moisture as the salty liquid slid behind his glasses and stung his already painful, bloodshot eyes.

So intent was he on his work that he did not notice the door to the room slowly open. Nor did he hear the three pairs of legs as they made their way in, moving across the thick carpet until they stood directly behind him. Their movements were unhurried; the intruders' superior numbers apparently provided them with overwhelming confidence.

Finally the man at the computer turned around. His limbs started to quake uncontrollably, as though he had foreseen what was about to happen to him.

He would not even have time to scream.

As the triggers snapped back simultaneously and the firing pins rammed home, the guns roared in deafening unison.

Jason Archer jerked upright in the chair where he had fallen asleep. Real sweat clung to his face while the vision of violent death clung to his mind. The damn dream, it just wouldn't let go. He quickly looked around. Sidney was dozing on the couch; the TV droned on in the background. Jason rose and covered his wife with a blanket. Then he went down to Amy's room. It was almost midnight. As he peeked in the door he could hear her tossing in her sleep. He went to the edge of her bed and watched the tiny form as it moved restlessly around. She must be having a bad dream, something her father could well relate to. Jason gently rubbed his daughter's forehead and then picked her up and held her, slowly swaying from side to side in the quiet darkness. This normally chased away the nightmares; and in a few minutes Amy was back in a peaceful sleep. Jason covered her up and kissed her on the cheek. Then he went to the kitchen, scribbled a note to his wife, put it on the table next to the couch where Sidney continued to doze and headed to the garage, where he climbed into his old Cougar convertible.

As he backed out of the garage, he did not notice Sidney at the front window watching him, his note clutched in her hand. After his taillights disappeared down the street, Sidney turned from the window and read the note again. Her husband was heading back to the office to do some work. He would be home when he could. She looked at the clock on the fireplace mantel. It was nearly midnight. She checked on Amy and then put a teakettle on the stove. She suddenly slumped against the kitchen counter as a deeply buried suspicion exploded to the surface. This wasn't the first time she had awoken to find her husband backing his car out of the garage, leaving a note behind telling her he had gone back to work.

She made her tea and then on impulse raced up the stairs to the bathroom. She looked at her face in the mirror. A little fuller than when they had first married. She abruptly stripped off her sleeping gown and underwear. She looked from the front, side and, finally, the back, holding up a hand mirror to check this most depressing angle. Pregnancy had done some damage; the stomach had pretty much recovered, but her bottom was definitely not as firm. Were her breasts sagging? The hips did seem slightly wider than before. Not so unusual after giving birth. With nervous fingers she pinched the millimeter of extra skin under her chin as acute depression sunk in. Jason's body was as iron-hard as it had been when they first started dating. Her husband's amazing physique and classic good looks were only part of a very attractive package that included a remarkable intellect. The package would be immensely attractive to every woman

Sidney knew and certainly most of those she didn't. As she traced her jawline she gasped as she realized what she was doing. A highly intelligent, well-respected attorney, she was examining herself like a piece of meat, just as generations of men had routinely done to womankind. She threw her gown back on. She *was* attractive. Jason *loved* her. He *was* going to work to catch up on things. He was building his career rapidly. Soon, both their dreams would be fulfilled. His to run his own company; hers to be a full-time mother to Amy and the other children they expected to have. If that sounded like a 1950s sitcom, so be it, because that's exactly what the Archers wanted. And Jason, she firmly believed, was right this minute working furiously to get there.

At about the time Sidney wandered off to bed, Jason Archer stopped at a pay phone and dialed a number he had memorized long before. The call was answered immediately.

"Hello, Jason."

"I'm telling you this has to be over soon, or I may not make it."

"Bad dreams again?" The tone managed to sound sympathetic and patronizing at the same time.

"You're implying that they come and go. Actually they're always with me," Jason curtly replied.

"It won't be long now." The voice was now reassuring.

"You're sure they're not on to me? I get these funny feelings, like everyone's watching me."

"It's normal, Jason. Happens all the time. If you were in trouble, we'd know it, believe me. We've been through this before."

"I have believed you. I just hope that belief is not misplaced." Jason's voice grew more tense. "I'm not a pro at this. Dammit, it's getting to me."

"We understand that. Don't go crazy on us now. As I said, it's almost over. A few more items and then you officially retire."

"Look, I don't understand why we can't go with what I've already gotten."

"Jason, it's not your job to think about those things. We need to dig a little deeper and you're just going to have to accept that. Keep your head up. We're not exactly babes in the woods on things like this; we've got it all planned out. You just hold up your end and we're fine. Everybody will be fine."

"Well, I'm going to finish up tonight, that's for damn sure. Do we use the same drop routine?"

"No. This time it'll be a personal exchange."

Jason's tone registered surprise. "Why?"

"We're nearing the end and any mistakes could jeopardize the entire operation. While we have no reason to believe they're on to you, we can't be absolutely sure *we're* not being watched. Remember, we're all taking chances here. Drops are usually safe, but there's always a margin of error built in. A face-to-face out of the area with fresh people eliminates that margin, simple as that. It keeps you safer too. And your family."

"My family? What the hell do they have to do with this?"

"Don't be stupid, Jason. These are high stakes. The risks were explained to you from the start. It's a violent world. Understand?"

"Look—"

"Everything will be fine. You just have to follow the instructions to the letter. To the letter." The last three words were said with particular force. "You haven't told anyone, have you? Particularly not your wife."

"No. Who the hell would I tell? Who would believe me?"

"You'd be surprised. Just remember: Anyone you tell is in danger, just as you are."

"Tell me something I don't know," Jason snapped back. "So what are the details?"

"Not now. Soon. The usual channels. Hang in there, Jason. We're almost through the tunnel."

"Yeah, well, let's hope the damn thing doesn't collapse on me before then."

The response drew a small chuckle and then the line went dead.

Jason slipped his thumb out of the fingerprint scanner, spoke his name into the small speaker mounted on the wall and patiently waited as the computer matched his thumb and voice prints to the ones residing in its massive files. He smiled and nodded at the uniformed security guard sitting at a large console in the middle of the eighth-floor reception area. Jason was conscious of the name TRITON GLOBAL spelled out in foot-long silver letters behind the guard's broad back.

"Too bad they don't give you the authority to just let me in, Charlie. You know, one human being to another."

Charlie was a large black man in his early sixties, with a bald head and a quick wit.

"Hell, Jason, for all I know you could be Saddam Hussein in disguise. These days you can't trust outward appearances. Nice sweater, by the way, Saddam." Charlie chuckled. "Besides, how could this big, sophisticated company possibly trust the judgment of a little old security guard like me when they got all these gadgets to tell them who's who? Computers are king, Jason. The sad truth is human beings don't measure up anymore."

"Don't sound so depressed, Charlie. Technology has its good points. Hey, I tell you what, why don't we switch jobs for a while? Then you can see the good stuff." Jason grinned.

"Sure thing, Jason. I'll go play with all those million-dollar toys and you can go sniffing around the rest room every thirty minutes looking for bad guys. I won't even charge you for use of the uniform. Of course, if we switch jobs we also switch paychecks. I wouldn't want you to miss out on a windfall like seven bucks an hour. It's only fair."

"You're too damn smart for your own good, Charlie."

Charlie laughed and went back to studying the numerous TV monitors mounted into the console.

As the massive door opened on whisper-quiet hinges, the smile on Jason's face abruptly disappeared. He moved through the opening. Striding down the hallway, he pulled something from his coat pocket. It was the size and shape of a typical credit card and was also made of plastic.

Jason stopped in front of a doorway. The card slid neatly into the slot in the metal box bolted to the door. The microchip buried within the card silently communicated with its counterpart attached to the portal. Jason's index finger pecked four times at the adjacent numeric pad. There was an audible click. He gripped the doorknob, turned it and the three-inch-thick door swung back into the darkened space.

As the lights came on, Jason was illuminated briefly in the doorway. He quickly closed the door; the twin dead bolts slid back into place. As he looked around the neatly arranged office, his hands were shaking and his heart was beating so hard he was absolutely certain it could be heard throughout the entire building. This was not the first time. It was far from the first time. He allowed himself a brief smile as he focused on the fact that this would be the last time. Regardless of what happened, this was it. Everyone had a limit, and tonight he had reached his.

He moved to the desk, sat down and turned on the computer. Attached to the monitor was a small microphone mounted on a long flexible metal neck that one could speak into for voice commands. Jason impatiently pushed it out of the way so he would have a clear view of the computer screen. His back ramrod straight, eyes glued to the screen, hands poised to strike, he was now clearly in his element. Like a pianist's in full swing, his fingers flashed across the keyboard. He peered at the screen, which fed instructions back to him, instructions so familiar as to be rote. Jason hit four digits on the numeric pad attached to the base of the computer's microprocessor unit, then he leaned forward and fixed his gaze at a spot in the upper right-hand corner of the monitor. Jason knew that a video camera had just that instant electronically interrogated his right iris, transmitting a host of unique discriminators contained within his eye to a central database, which, in turn, compared the image of his iris to the thirty thousand residing in that computerized file. The entire process had taken barely four seconds. As accustomed as he was to the ever-expanding muscle of technology, even Jason Archer had to shake his head occasionally over what was really out there. Iris scanners were also used to closely monitor worker productivity. Jason grimaced. Truth be known, Orwell had actually underestimated.

He refocused on the machine in front of him. For the next twenty minutes Jason worked away at the keyboard, pausing only when more data flashed across the screen in answer to his queries. The system was fast, yet it had a difficult time keeping up with the fluid swiftness of Jason's commands. Suddenly his head jerked around as a noise from the hallway filtered into the office. The damn dream again. Probably just Charlie making rounds. He looked at the screen. He wasn't getting much of anything. A waste of time. He wrote down a list of file names on a piece of paper, shut the computer down, rose and went to the door. Pausing, he leaned his ear against the wood. Satisfied, he slid the dead bolts back and opened the door, turning off the light as he closed the door behind him. A moment later the dead bolts automatically moved back into locked positions.

He moved quickly down the hallway, finally stopping at the far end of the corridor in a little-used section of the office space. This door had an ordinary lock that Jason opened using a special tool. He locked the door behind him. He did not turn on the overhead light. Instead, he produced a small flashlight from his coat pocket and turned it on. The computer console was in the far corner of the room next to a low filing cabinet piled three feet high with cardboard packing boxes.

Jason pulled the computer workstation away from the wall, exposing cables that dangled down from the back of the computer. He knelt down and gripped the cables while at the same time inching aside a filing cabinet adjacent to the worktable, revealing an outlet on the wall with several data ports. Jason attached a cable line from the computer into a port, making sure it was tight. Then he sat down in front of the computer and turned it on. As the computer came to life, Jason perched his flashlight on a box top so that the light shone directly on the keyboard. There was no numeric keypad on which to input a security pass code. Nor did Jason have to stare at the upper right-hand corner of the computer screen waiting to be positively identified. In fact, as far as Triton's computer network was concerned, this workstation didn't even exist.

He slipped the piece of paper from his pocket and laid it in the flashlight's beam atop the keyboard. Suddenly he was conscious of movement outside the door. Holding his breath, he buried the flash-light into his armpit with his hand before hitting the off button. He dimmed the monitor until the images on the screen receded into blackness. Minutes went by as Jason sat in the darkness. A drop of sweat formed on his forehead and then lazily made its way down his nose before settling on the top of his lip. He was too afraid to wipe it away.

After five minutes of silence he turned the flashlight and com-puter monitor back on and resumed his work. He grinned once as a particularly stubborn firewall—an internal security system designed to prevent unauthorized access to computerized databases—col-lapsed under his persistent nudgings. Working quickly now, he made his way to the end of the files listed on the paper. Then he reached inside his coat and withdrew a three-and-a-half-inch micro floppy disk and placed it in the computer's disk drive. A couple of minutes later, Jason withdrew the disk, turned off the computer and left. He walked quietly back through the maze of security, said good-bye to Charlie and moved out into the night.

CHAPTER THREE

The moonlight drifted through the window, giving shape to certain objects in the darkened interior of the large room. On a long, solid pine bureau a number of framed photos stood in three tiers. In one photo, set in the back row, Sidney Archer, dressed in a dark blue business suit, leaned against a gleaming silver Jaguar sedan. Next to her Jason Archer wore a smile along with his suspenders and dress shirt as he looked lovingly into Sidney's eyes. Another photo showed the same couple, dressed casually, standing in front of the Eiffel Tower, their fingers pointing up, mouths opened in spontaneous laughter.

In the middle row of photos, Sidney, some years older, her face bloated, hair wet and clinging to the sides of her head, reclined in a hospital bed. A tiny bundle, eyes scrunched shut, was clutched in her arms. The picture next to that showed Jason, bleary-eyed and unshaven, wearing only a T-shirt and Looney Tunes boxer shorts, lying on the floor. The little one, the eyes now wide open and the brightest of blues, formed a small and contented hump on her father's chest.

The center photo in the front row had clearly been taken at Halloween. The little bundle was now two years old and dressed as a princess replete with tiara and slippers. Mother and father hovered proudly behind, eyes staring into the camera, their hands cradling the little girl's back and shoulders.

Jason and Sidney lay in the four-poster bed. Jason tossed and turned. It had been a week since the last late-night visit to his office. Now the payoff finally was here, making it impossible to sleep. Next to the bedroom door a fully packed, large and particularly ugly canvas bag with blue crisscross stripes and the initials JWA sat next to a black metal case. The clock on the nightstand limped to two A.M. Sidney's long, slender arm reached out from under the covers and glided around Jason's head, slowly pushing his hair around.

Sidney propped herself up on one elbow and continued to play with her husband's hair as she moved closer to him, finally matching his contours with her own. The flimsy nightgown clung to her. "Are you asleep?" she murmured. In the background the muted creaks and groans of the aged house were the only sounds to break the silence.

Jason rolled over to look at his wife. "Not really."

"I could tell—you've been moving around a lot. Sometimes you do it in your sleep. You and Amy."

"I hope I haven't been talking in my sleep. Don't want to give any secrets away." He smiled weakly.

Her hand dropped to his face, which she gently stroked. "Everyone needs to keep some secrets, I guess, although I thought we agreed not to have any." She gave a little laugh, but it was hollow. Jason's mouth parted for a moment as if he were going to speak, but he quickly closed it, stretched his arms and looked at the clock. He groaned when he saw the time. "Jesus, I might as well get up now. The cab will be here at five-thirty."

Sidney glanced over at the bags by the doorway and frowned. "This trip really came out of the blue, Jason."

Jason didn't look at her. Instead he wiped his eyes and yawned. "I know. I didn't even find out about it until late yesterday afternoon. When the boss says go, I go."

Sidney sighed. "I knew the day would come when we'd both be out of town at the same time."

Jason's voice was anxious as he looked at her. "But you worked it out with the day-care center?"

"I had to arrange for someone to stay past the regular closing, but that's okay. You won't be longer than three days, though, right?"

"Three tops, Sid. I promise." He rubbed vigorously at his scalp. "You couldn't get out of the New York trip?"

Sidney shook her head. "Lawyers don't get excused from business trips. It's not in the Tyler, Stone manual of being a productive attorney."

"Christ, you do more in three days than most of them do in five."

"Well, sweetie, I don't have to tell you, but in our shop, it's what did you do for me today, and, more important, what are you going to do for me tomorrow, and the day after that."

Jason pulled himself up to a sitting position. "Same at Triton; however, being in the advanced technology business, their expectations go into the next millennium. One day our ship will come in, Sid. Maybe today." He looked at her.

She shook her head. "Right. So while you're waiting down at the docks for our yacht, I'll keep depositing our paychecks and paying down debt. Deal?"

"Okay. But sometimes you have to be optimistic. Look into the future."

"Speaking of the future, have you given any more thought to working on another baby?"

"I'm more than ready. If the next one's like Amy, it'll be a breeze."

Sidney pressed her full thighs against him, quietly pleased that he voiced no objection to enlarging the family. If he was seeing someone else . . . ? "Speak for yourself, Mr. Male Half of this little equation." She pushed him.

"Sorry, Sid. Typical brain-dead man thing to say. It won't happen again, promise."

Sidney lay back on the pillow and stared at the ceiling as she gently rubbed his shoulder. Three years ago the thought of leaving the practice of law would have been out of the question. Now, even part-time seemed too intrusive on her life with Amy and Jason. She longed for total freedom to be with her child. Freedom they could not yet afford solely on Jason's salary, even with all the cutbacks they had made, constantly fighting the American-consumer compulsion to spend as much as they earned. But if Jason kept moving up at Triton, who knew?

Sidney had never wanted to be financially dependent on anyone else. She looked at Jason. If she was going to tie her economic survival to one person, who better than a man she had loved almost from the moment she had laid eyes on him? As she continued to watch him, a glimmer of moisture appeared in her eyes. She sat up, leaning into him.

"Well, at least while you're in Los Angeles you can look up some of your old friends—just skip the old flames, please." She tousled his hair. "Besides, you could never leave me. My father would stalk you." Her eyes slowly drifted over his shirtless torso: abdominal muscles stacked on top of one another, cords of muscle rippling just beneath the skin of his shoulders. Sidney was once again reminded of how lucky she had been to collide with Jason Archer's life. And she also knew beyond doubt that her husband believed he was the lucky one for finding her. He didn't answer, just stared off. "You know you've really been burning the midnight oil the last few months, Jason. At the office at all hours, leaving me notes in the middle of the night. I miss you." She nudged him with her hip. "You remember how much fun it is to snuggle at night, don't you?"

In response he kissed her on the cheek.

"Besides, Triton has a lot of employees. You don't have to do it all yourself," she added.

He looked at her and there was a painful weariness in his eyes. "You'd think so, wouldn't you?"

Sidney sighed. "After the CyberCom acquisition closes, you'll probably be busier than ever. Maybe I should sabotage the deal. I am lead counsel for Triton, after all." She smiled.

He chuckled halfheartedly, his mind clearly elsewhere.

"The meeting in New York should be interesting, anyway."

He abruptly focused on her. "Why's that?"

"Because we're meeting on the CyberCom deal. Nathan Gamble and your buddy Quentin Rowe will both be there."

The blood slowly drained from her husband's face. He stammered, "I—I thought the meeting was for the BelTek proposal."

"No, I was taken off that a month ago so I could focus on Triton's acquisition of CyberCom. I thought I told you."

"Why are you meeting them in New York?"

"Nathan Gamble is there this week. He has that penthouse overlooking the park. Billionaires get their way. So off I go to New York."

Jason sat up, his face so gray she thought he was going to be sick.

"Jason, what is it?" She gripped his shoulder.

He finally recovered and faced her, his expression an acutely disturbing one to her—dominated as it was by guilt.

"Sid, I'm not exactly going to L.A. on business for Triton."

She took her hand off his shoulder and stared at him, her eyes wide with astonishment. Every suspicion she had dutifully battled during the last several months now shot back to the surface. Her throat went completely dry. "What do you mean, Jason?"

"I mean"—he took a deep breath and gripped one of her hands—"I mean, this trip is not for Triton."

"Then who exactly is it for?" she demanded, her face flushed.

"For me, us! It's for us, Sidney."

Scowling, she sat back against the headboard and crossed her arms. "Jason, you're going to tell me what's going on and you're going to do it right now."

He looked down and played with the bedcovers. She took his chin in her hand and gave him a searching look. "Jason?" She paused, sensing his inner struggle. "Pretend it's Christmas Eve, honey."

He sighed. "I'm going to L.A. to interview with another firm."

She took her hand away. "What?"

He spoke quickly. "AllegraPort Technology, they're one of the largest specialty software manufacturers in the world. They've offered me, well, they've offered me a vice presidency and would be grooming me for the top spot eventually. Triple my salary, huge year-end bonus, stock options, beautiful retirement plan, the whole ball game, Sid. A home run."

Sidney's face instantly brightened; her shoulders slumped in relief. "That was your big secret? Jason, that's wonderful. Why didn't you tell me?"

"I didn't want to put you in an awkward position. You're Triton's counsel, after all. All the late hours at the office? I was trying to finish up my work. I didn't want to leave them in the lurch. Triton is a powerful company; I didn't want any hard feelings."

"Honey, there's no law against your joining another company. They'd be happy for you."

"Right!" His bitter tone puzzled her for a moment, but he hurried on before she had a chance to question him about it. "They'd also pay for all our relocation expenses. In fact, we'd make a nice profit on this place, enough to pay off all our bills."

She stiffened. "Relocation?"

"Allegra's headquarters are in Los Angeles. That's where we'd be moving. If you don't want me to take it, then I'll respect your decision."

"Jason, you know my firm has an L.A. office. It'll be perfect." She sat back against the headboard again and stared at the ceiling. She looked over at him, a twinkle in her eye. "And let's see, at triple your current salary, the profit from this house and stock options to boot, I just might be able to become a full-time mom a littler sooner than I thought."

He smiled as she gave him a congratulatory hug. "That's why I was so surprised when you told me you were meeting with Triton."

She looked at him, confused.

"They think I took some time off to work around the house."

"Oh. Well, sweetie, don't worry. I'll play along. You know there's attorney-client privilege and then there's the much stronger privilege between a horny wife and her big, beautiful husband." Her soft eyes met his and she nuzzled her lips against his cheek. He swung his legs over the side of the bed. "Thanks, babe, I'm glad I told you." He shrugged. "Well, I might as well jump in the shower. Maybe I can accomplish a few things before I leave."

Before he could stand up, her arms clamped around his waist.

"I'd love to help you accomplish something, Jason."

He turned his head to look at her. She was now wearing nothing; the nightgown lay over the footboard. Her large breasts pushed into his lower back. He smiled and slid one hand down her smooth back and gripped her soft bottom appreciatively.

"I've always said, you've got the world's greatest ass, Sid."

She grunted. "If you like a little additional padding, but I'm working on it."

His strong hands slid under her armpits, hoisting her up so they were face-to-face. His eyes looked deeply into hers and his mouth formed a solemn line before he spoke. "You're more beautiful now than the day I met you, Sidney Archer, and every day I love you more and more." The words came out slowly and gently, and made her tremble just as always. It wasn't the words he used that had that effect on her. You could find them in any Hallmark aisle. It was how he said them. The utter conviction in his voice, his eyes, the pressure of his touch against her skin.

Jason looked at the clock again and grinned mischievously. "I've gotta leave in three hours to make my plane."

She crooked her arm around his neck, pulled him down on top of her. "Well, three hours can be a lifetime."

Two hours later, his hair still wet from the shower, Jason Archer walked down the hallway of his home and opened the door to a small room. Set up as a home office with computer, filing cabinets, wood desk and two small bookcases, the space was cramped but tidy. One small window looked out onto the darkness.

Jason closed the door to his office, took a key from his desk drawer and unlocked the top drawer of the filing cabinet. He stopped and listened for any sound. This had become habitual even in the confines of his own house. That revelation was suddenly profoundly disturbing to him. His wife had gone back to sleep. Amy was sleeping soundly two doors down. He reached in the drawer and carefully pulled out a large old-fashioned leather briefcase with double straps, brass buckles and a worn, glossy finish. Jason opened the briefcase and pulled out a blank floppy disk. The instructions he had been given were precise. Put everything he had on one floppy disk, make one hard copy of the documents and then destroy everything else.

He put the floppy disk in the drive slot and copied all the other materials he had collected onto that same floppy. That completed, his finger hovered over the delete key as he prepared to follow his instructions on destruction of all pertinent files on his hard drive.

His finger wavered, however, and, finally, he chose to follow his instincts instead.

It took him only a few minutes to make a duplicate copy of the floppy, after which he deleted the files on his hard drive. After perusing the contents of the duplicate floppy on his screen for several moments, he took a few minutes to perform some additional functions on his computer. As he watched, the text on the screen turned to gibberish. He saved the changes, exited out of the file, slipped the duplicate disk out of the computer and inserted it in a small padded envelope, which he secreted far down in a side pouch of the leather briefcase. As instructed, he then printed out a hard copy of the contents of the original floppy and put the printed pages and the original floppy disk in the briefcase's main compartment.

Next, he took out his wallet and withdrew the plastic card he had used to enter his office earlier. He would no longer be needing it. He flipped the card into his desk drawer and shut it.

He studied the briefcase, his thoughts hovering far away from the little room. He didn't enjoy lying to his wife. He had never done that before and the feeling of prevarication was particularly repugnant to him. But it was almost over. He shuddered when he thought of all the risks he had taken. His body shook again when he dwelled on the fact that his wife knew absolutely nothing about it. He silently went over the plan again. The route he would take, the evasive steps he would employ, the code names of the people who would be meeting him. In spite of it all his mind continued to wander. He looked out the window, seeming to stare across the horizon as, behind the glasses he wore, his eyes seemed to grow larger and larger as the possibilities were swiftly sorted through. After today he could actually say for the first time that the risk had been worth it. All he had to do was survive today.

CHAPTER FOUR

The darkness that enveloped Dulles International Airport would soon be dispelled by the fast-approaching dawn. As the new day began stretching itself awake, a cab pulled up in front of the airport's terminal. The rear door of the cab opened and Jason Archer stepped out. He carried the leather briefcase in one hand and the black metal case, housing his laptop computer, in the other. He put a dark green wide-brimmed hat with a leather band on his head.

Jason smiled as the memory of making love to his wife commanded his thoughts. They had both showered, but the scent of recent sex lingered, and, had there been time, Jason Archer would have made love to his wife a second time.

He put down the computer case for a moment, stretched his arm back inside the cab and pulled out the oversized canvas bag, which he slung over his shoulder.

At the Western Airlines ticket counter Jason exhibited his driver's license, got his seat assignment and boarding pass and checked the canvas bag. He took a moment to smooth down the collar on his camel-hair overcoat, push his hat farther down on his head and adjust his tie, which bore soft swirls of gold, hazel and lavender. His pants were dark gray and baggy. Not that anyone would have noticed, but the socks were white athletic ones and the dark shoes were, in fact, tennis shoes. A few minutes later, Jason purchased a *USA Today* and a cup of coffee along the terminal's vendors' row. He then passed through the security gates.

The shuttle to the midfield terminal was three-quarters full. Jason stood among men and women dressed much as he was: dark suits, touches of color at the neck, rolling racks stacked with bags clenched in many a weary hand.

Jason's hand never left the leather briefcase; his legs straddled the computer case. He occasionally looked around the interior of the shuttle examining its sleepy occupants. Then his eyes would eventually wander back to his newspaper as the shuttle swayed and bumped over to the midfield terminal.

Sitting in the large, open waiting area in front of Gate 11, Jason checked the time. Boarding would begin soon. He glanced outside the broad window, where a row of Western Airlines jets sporting the familiar brown and yellow stripes were being readied for early morning flights. Slashes of pink streaked the sky as the sun slowly rose to illuminate the East Coast. Outside, the wind pushed fiercely against the thick glass; airline workers hunched forward against the invisible thrusts of nature. The full measure of winter would be settling in soon and the winds and icy precipitation would blanket the area until the following April.

Jason pulled out the boarding pass from his inner coat pocket and studied its contents: Western Airlines Flight 3223 from Washington's Dulles International Airport to Los Angeles International Airport with direct, nonstop service. Jason had been born and raised in the Los Angeles area but hadn't been back there in over two years. Across the aisle of the massive terminal a Western Airlines flight destined for Seattle, after a brief layover in Chicago, would also be boarding shortly. Jason licked his lips, a trickle of apprehension playing through his nervous system. He swallowed a couple of times to work through the dryness in his throat. As he finished his coffee, he thumbed through the newspaper, halfheartedly observing the col-

lective aches and miseries of the world that poured forth from every
colorful page.

As he glanced over the headlines, Jason noted a man striding res-
olutely down the middle of the concourse. He was a six-footer with
a lean build and blond hair. He was dressed in a camel-hair overcoat
and baggy gray pants. A tie identical to Jason's peeped out at his
neck. Like Jason, he carried a leather briefcase and black laptop computer case. In the hand holding the computer case he also held a
white envelope.

Jason quickly rose and walked to the men's room. It had just reopened after having been cleaned.

Entering the last stall, Jason locked the door, hung his overcoat
on the door hook, opened the leather briefcase and extracted a large
collapsible nylon bag. He pulled out a four-by-eight-inch mirror.
He pushed it against the wall of the stall and it held due to its magnetized back. He next pulled out a pair of thick black glasses to replace his wire-rimmed pair, and a paste-on black mustache. A
short-haired wig matched the inky darkness of the mustache. The
tie and jacket came off, were stuffed in the bag and replaced with a
Washington Huskies sweatshirt. The baggy pants came off, revealing matching sweats underneath. Now the tennis shoes did not look
so out of place. The overcoat was reversible and, instead of camel, it
became dark blue in color. Jason checked his appearance again in the
mirror. The leather briefcase and the metal case disappeared into the
nylon bag along with the mirror. He left the hat on the hook behind
the stall door. Unlocking the door, he stepped out and walked over
to the sink.

After washing his hands, Jason studied his new bespectacled face
in the mirror. In the reflection the tall blond man he had seen earlier appeared in the doorway, moved over to the stall Jason had just
exited and closed the door. Jason took a moment to carefully dry his
hands and swipe at his new hair. By that time the man had emerged
from the stall, Jason's hat perched on his head. Without his disguise
Jason and the man could have passed as twins. Leaving through the
exit door, they momentarily collided. Jason quickly mouthed an
apology; the man never looked at him. He quickly walked away,

Jason's plane ticket disappearing into his shirt pocket, while Jason tucked the white envelope into his coat.

Jason was about to return to his seat when he looked over at the bank of phones. Hesitating for an instant, he hurried over and dialed a number.

"Sid?"

"Jason?" Sidney was simultaneously dressing and feeding a struggling Amy Archer and stuffing files into her briefcase. "What's wrong? Is your flight delayed?"

"No, no, it leaves in a few minutes." He fell silent as he caught his altered reflection in the shiny face of the telephone. He felt embarrassed to be talking to his wife while disguised.

Sidney struggled with Amy's coat. "Well, is anything wrong?"

"No, I just thought I'd call, to check on things."

Sidney let out an exasperated grunt. "Well, let me give you the rundown: I'm late, *your* daughter is being uncooperative as usual, and I just realized I left my plane ticket and some documents I need at work, which means instead of having thirty minutes to spare I've got maybe ten seconds."

"I'm . . . I'm sorry, Sid. I . . ." Jason's hand tightly gripped the nylon bag. Today was the last day. The last day, he kept repeating to himself. If anything were to happen to him—if for some reason, despite the precautions, he didn't make it back—she would never know, would she?

Sidney was seething now. Amy had just spilled her bowl of Cheerios all over her coat and a good part of the milk had made its way into Sidney's crammed briefcase as she struggled to hold the phone under her chin. "I've gotta go, Jason."

"No, Sid, wait, I need to tell you some—"

Sidney stood up. Her tone allowed for no compromise as she surveyed the damage wrought by her two-year-old, who now stared defiantly up at her mother with a chin sharply reminiscent of her own. "Jason, it's going to have to wait. I've got a plane to catch too. Goodbye." She hung up the phone and snatched up her writhing daughter under one arm. Cheerios and all, they headed out the door.

Jason slowly put down the phone and turned away. He let out a deep breath and for the hundredth time prayed today would end the way it had been planned to. He did not observe a man glance casually in his direction and then turn away. Earlier, the same man had passed by him before Jason had made the change in the rest room, close enough in fact to read the identification tag on his travel bag. It was one small but significant oversight on Jason's part, because the tag set forth his real name and address.

A few minutes later Jason stood in line to board his flight. He pulled out the white envelope he had been given by the man in the rest room and took out the plane ticket that was in it. He wondered what Seattle would be like. He glanced across the aisle in time to see his "twin" get on the flight to Los Angeles. Then Jason caught a glimpse of another passenger in line for the flight to Los Angeles. Tall and lean, the man had a bald pate that topped a square face partially covered by a massive beard. The expressive features looked familiar, but Jason couldn't quite place their owner, as the man disappeared through the doorway on his way to the waiting plane. Jason shrugged, dutifully handed over his boarding pass and walked down the jetwalk.

Barely half an hour later, as the jet Arthur Lieberman was on slammed into the ground and coils of black smoke soared toward white clouds, hundreds of miles to the north Jason Archer sipped a fresh cup of coffee and opened his laptop computer. Smiling, he looked out the plane's window as it rocketed on to Chicago. The first leg of his trip had gone off without a hitch, and the captain had just announced smooth sailing for the duration of the flight.

CHAPTER FIVE

Sidney Archer tapped the horn impatiently and the car in front of her sped through the green light. With a reflex motion she checked the backseat in her Ford Explorer's rearview mirror. Amy, her Winnie the Pooh bear clutched tightly in one tiny hand, was fast asleep in her baby seat. Amy shared her mother's thick blond hair, strong chin and slender nose. Her dancing blue eyes and much of her athletic grace came from her father, although Sidney Archer had in college been a wick-thin power forward on the women's basketball team.

She turned into the blacktop parking lot and pulled into a parking space in front of the low brick building. She got out, opened the rear door of the Ford and gently disengaged her daughter from the confines of the baby seat, taking care to bring Pooh and Amy's day bag. Sidney pulled up the hood of Amy's jacket and shielded her daughter's face from the biting wind with her overcoat. A sign over the double glass doors said JEFFERSON COUNTY DAY-CARE CENTER.

Inside, Sidney removed Amy's coat, taking a moment to wipe off the remains of the earlier cereal incident, and checked the provisions in her carry bag before handing it over to Karen, one of the day-care people. The front of Karen's white jumpsuit was already smeared with red crayon, and a large spot of what looked to be grape jelly was visible on her right sleeve.

"Hi, Amy. We've got some new toys you probably want to check out." Karen knelt down in front of her. Amy still gripped her bear, her right thumb firmly in her little mouth.

Sidney held up Amy's bag. "Beans and franks, and some juice and a banana. She's already had breakfast. Potato chips, and a brownie if she's really good. Let her sleep a little longer at nap time, Karen, she had a rough night."

Karen put out a finger for Amy to take. "Okay, Mrs. Archer. Amy's always good, aren't you?"

Sidney knelt down and pressed a small kiss on her daughter's cheek. "You've got that right. Except when she doesn't want to eat, sleep or do what she's told."

Karen was the mother of a little boy the same age as Amy. The two moms shared a knowing smile.

"I'll be here by seven-thirty tonight, Karen."

"Yes, ma'am."

"Bye-bye, Mommy. I love chu."

Sidney turned to see Amy waving at her. The little fingers floated up and down. The sharp chin had dissolved into a cute little bump and, with it, Sidney's anger from the morning's battle. Sidney returned the wave.

"I love you too. We'll get some ice cream tonight, sweetie, after dinner. And I'm sure Daddy will be calling to talk to you, okay?" A wonderful smile broke across Amy's features.

Thirty minutes later Sidney pulled into her office parking garage, grabbed her briefcase from the passenger seat and slammed the truck door as she raced to the elevator. The chilly wind funneling down the underground garage entrance brightened her thoughts. Soon the old stone fireplace in their living room would be in use. She had come to love the smell of a fire; it was comforting and made her feel safe. The coming of winter had turned her thoughts to Christmas. This would be the first December in which Amy could actually appreciate its very special time. Sidney felt herself growing more and more excited about the approaching holidays. They were going to her parents' place for Thanksgiving, but this year Jason, Sidney and Amy were staying home for Christmas. Just the three of them. In front of the popping fire flanked by a fat-bottomed white pine Christmas tree and a mountain of presents for their little girl.

Although technically only a part-timer, she was still one of the hardest working attorneys at the firm. The senior partners at Tyler, Stone smiled every time they passed Sidney Archer's office as they saw their respective pieces of the partnership pie grow even larger through her efforts. Though they probably believed they were using her, Sidney had her own agenda. The part-time scenario was only an interim measure. Sidney could always practice law; however, she only had one opportunity to be Amy's mother while Amy was still a little girl.

The old stone and brick house had been purchased at roughly half price because of all the renovation work needed. Work that Sidney and Jason and a group of subcontractors had completed at fiercely negotiated prices over the last two years. The Jag had been traded in for the cranky six-year-old Ford. The last of the massive student loans were almost gone, and their monthly living expenses had been reduced by almost fifty percent through common sense and sacrifice. In another year the Archers would be almost completely debt-free.

Her thoughts went back to the early morning hours. Jason's news had been truly stunning. But she felt the tuggings of a smile as she considered the ramifications. She was proud of Jason. He deserved this kind of success, more than anyone. It was shaping up to be quite a good year. All those late nights. He had probably been putting together the details of his job. All those hours of needless worry on her part. She now felt bad about hanging up on him earlier. She would make it up to him when he got back.

Sidney stepped off the elevator, hurried down the richly appointed hallway and opened the door to her office. She checked her e-mail and voice mail; neither revealed any emergencies. She loaded her briefcase with the documents she would need for her trip, grabbed the airplane tickets from her chair where her secretary had left them and slid her laptop into a carry case. She left a stream of voice-mail instructions for her secretary and four other lawyers at the firm assisting her on various matters. Sufficiently weighed down, she managed to stagger back out to the elevator.

Sidney checked in at the USAir shuttle desk at National Airport and a few minutes later was settling into her seat on the Boeing 737. She was confident the plane would take off right on time for the barely fifty-minute trip to New York's La Guardia Airport. Unfortunately, it took almost as long to drive into the city from the airport as it did to traverse the two hundred and thirty or so miles from the nation's capital to the capital of the financial world.

The flight, as usual, was full. As she assumed her seat, she noted that sitting next to her was an elderly man dressed in an old-fashioned three-piece pinstripe suit. A wide-knotted bright red tie shone out from the background of a crisp button-down shirt. In his lap sat a battered leather briefcase. Slender hands nervously clasped and unclasped as he looked out the window. Small tufts of white hair clung around his earlobes. The shirt collar hung loosely around the skinny neck like walls pulling loose from their foundation. Sidney noticed beads of perspiration adhering to his left temple and over his thin lips.

The plane lumbered clumsily to the main runway. The whir of wing flaps settling into the down takeoff position seemed to calm the old man. He turned to Sidney.

"That's all I listen for anymore," he said, his voice deep and rocky and laced with the front-porch drawl of a lifetime spent in the South.

Sidney looked at him curiously. "What's that?"

He pointed out the small window. "Make sure they set the damn flaps on the wings so this thing'll get off the ground. Remember that plane up in Dee-troit?" He said the word as if it were actually two. "Damn pilots forgot to set the flaps right and killed everybody on board except for that little girl."

Sidney looked out the window for a moment. "I'm sure the pilots are well aware of that," she replied. She sighed inwardly. The last thing she needed was to be sitting next to a nervous flier. Sidney turned back to her notes, doing a quick scan for her presentation before the flight attendants made everyone stow their belongings under the seats. As the flight attendants came by for another check, she slipped the papers back in her briefcase and slid it under the seat in front of her. She looked out the window at the dark, choppy waters of the Potomac. Flocks of seagulls scattered across the water; from a distance they resembled swirling pieces of paper. The captain crisply announced over the intercom that the USAir shuttle was next in line to take off.

A few seconds later the plane rose smoothly off the ground. After banking left to avoid flying over the restricted airspace above the Capitol and the White House, the plane raced to its cruising altitude.

Several minutes after the plane leveled off at twenty-nine thousand feet, the beverage cart rolled by and Sidney got a cup of tea and the obligatory bag of salty peanuts. The elderly man next to her shook his head when asked for his beverage request and continued to stare anxiously out the window.

Sidney reached down and pulled her briefcase from underneath the seat in anticipation of doing some work for the next half hour. She settled back in her seat and took some papers out of her briefcase. As she began to go over their contents she noticed the old man still glancing out the window; his small frame was tense as he rode every bump, obviously listening for any out-of-the-way sound that would herald a catastrophe. The veins were tight in his neck; his hands were wrapped around the armrests of his seat. The common plight of the not-so-rare white-knuckler. Her face softened. Being frightened was difficult enough. Believing you are alone in that fear merely compounded matters. She reached out and patted his arm gently and smiled. He glanced quickly over at her and returned the smile in an embarrassed fashion, his face slightly reddening.

"They do this flight so many times, I'm sure they've worked out all the kinks," she said, her voice quiet and soothing.

He smiled again and rubbed his hands to return the circulation.

"You're absolutely right . . . ma'am."

"Sidney, Sidney Archer."

"George Beard is what they call me. Glad to know you, Sidney."
They firmly shook hands.

Beard abruptly looked out the window at the puffy clouds. The
sunlight was sharp and penetrating. He slid the window shade down
partway. "I've flown so many damn times over the years, you'd think
I'd get used to it."

"It can be nerve-racking for anyone, George, no matter how often
you've done it," Sidney replied kindly. "But it's not nearly as frightening as the cabs we're going to have to take into the city."

They both laughed. Then Beard jumped slightly as the plane hit
a particularly stubborn air pocket and his face once again became
ashen. "Do you go to New York often, George?" She tried to hold
his eyes with hers. No mode of transportation had ever bothered her
in the past. But ever since she'd had Amy, little cells of apprehension appeared when she boarded a plane or train, or even got in her
car. She studied Beard's face as the old man tensed again while the
plane bumped along. "George, it's all right. Just a little turbulence."

He took a deep breath and finally eyed her squarely. "I'm on a
couple of boards of companies headquartered in New York. Have to
go up twice a year."

Sidney glanced back at her documents, suddenly remembering
something. She frowned. There was a mistake on the fourth page.
That would need to be corrected when she got into town.

George Beard touched her arm. "I guess we're all right today at
least. I mean, how often do they have two crashes in one day? Tell
me that."

Preoccupied, Sidney did not answer right away. Finally she turned
to him, her eyes narrowing. "Pardon?"

Beard leaned forward in a confidential manner, his voice low.
"Took one of them puddle-jumpers up from Richmond early this
morning. I got to National about eight o'clock. I overheard two pilots talking. Couldn't hardly believe it. They were nervous, I can tell
you that. Hell, I would be too."

Sidney's face evidenced her confusion. "What are you talking
about?"

Beard bent even closer to her. "I don't know if this is public knowledge, but my hearing aid works a lot better now with the new batteries, so those fellows might have thought I couldn't hear." He paused dramatically, his eyes glancing sharply around before settling once again on Sidney. "There was a plane crash early this morning. No survivors." He looked at her, his white, bushy eyebrows twitching like a cat's tail.

For an instant, Sidney's major organs collectively seemed to cease all functioning. "Where?"

Beard shook his head. "I didn't hear that part. It was a jet, though, a pretty big one, I gathered. Fell right out of the sky, apparently. I guess that's why those fellows were so nervous. I mean, not knowing why is just as bad, right?"

"Do you know what airline?"

He shook his head again. "Guess we'll know soon enough. It'll be on the TV when we get to New York, I would bet. I already called my wife from the airport, told her I was okay. Hell, of course she hadn't even heard about it yet, but I didn't want her to start worrying if she saw it on the TV or something."

Sidney looked at his bright red tie. It suddenly took on the image of a large, fresh wound gaping at his throat. The odds—it couldn't be possible. She shook her head and then stared straight ahead. Looking back at her was a quick resolution to her worry. She inserted her credit card in the slot in the seat in front of her, grabbed the plane phone from its niche and a moment later she was dialing Jason's SkyWord pager. She didn't have his new cell phone number; in any event, he normally turned his phone off during flights. He had been reprimanded twice by airline personnel for receiving cell calls during flights. She hoped to God he had remembered to bring the pager. She checked her watch. He would be above the Midwest right about now, but bouncing its signals off a satellite, the pager was easily capable of receiving pages on planes. However, he couldn't call her back on the plane phone; the 737 she was on was not equipped with that technology yet. So she left her office number at the prompt. She would wait ten minutes and call in to her secretary.

Ten minutes passed and she called her office. Her secretary picked up on the second ring. No, her husband hadn't called. At Sidney's

urging, her secretary checked Sidney's voice mail. Nothing there either. Her secretary had heard of no plane accident. Sidney began to
wonder if George Beard had misunderstood the pilots' conversation.
He probably sat around imagining every possible catastrophe, but
she had to be sure. She frantically searched her memory for the airline her husband was on. She called information and got the number for United Airlines. She finally got through to a human being
and was told that the airline did have an early morning flight to L.A.
from Dulles but there had been no reports of any airline crash. The
woman seemed reluctant to discuss the subject over the telephone
and Sidney hung up with fresh doubts. Next she called American
and, after that, Western Airlines. She could not get through to an
actual person at either airline. The lines seemed to be jammed with
calls. She tried again, with the same result. A numbness slowly
coursed through her body. George Beard touched her arm again.
"Sidney . . . ma'am, is everything okay?" Sidney didn't answer. She
continued to stare ahead, oblivious to everything except the certainty that she would race off the plane as soon as it landed.

CHAPTER SIX

Jason Archer looked at the SkyWord pager and the number etched across its tiny screen. He rubbed at his chin and then took off his glasses and wiped them on his lunch napkin. This was his wife's direct office number. Like his wife's plane the DC-10 he was flying on also had cellular phones recessed into the backs of every other seat. He had started to reach for the phone and then stopped. He knew Sidney was in her firm's New York office today, which was why the leaving of her D.C. office number puzzled him. For a terrifying instant, he thought something might be wrong with Amy. He checked his SkyWord pager again. The call had come in at nine-thirty A.M. EST. He shook his head. His wife would have been on a plane halfway to New York at that time. It wouldn't have had anything to do with Amy. Their daughter would have been at day care before eight. Was she calling to apologize for hanging up on him earlier? That, he concluded, was far from likely. That exchange didn't even qualify for minor spat status. It didn't make any sense. Why on earth would she be calling him from a plane and leaving the number of an office at which he knew she would not be?

His face suddenly went pale. Unless it was not his wife who had called. Given the bizarre circumstances, Jason concluded that it was probably not his wife who had placed that call. He instinctively scanned the cabin. The in-flight movie droned on from the pulldown screen.

He sat back in his seat and stirred the remains of his coffee with a plastic spoon. The flight attendants were clearing away meal plates and offering pillows and blankets. Jason's hand curled protectively around the handle of the leather briefcase. He glanced at the case containing his laptop where it was stowed under the seat in front of him. Maybe her trip had been canceled; however, Gamble was already in New York and nobody canceled on Nathan Gamble, Jason knew that. Besides, the CyberCom deal was at a critical stage.

He leaned back farther in his seat, his hand fingering the Sky-Word pager like a ball of putty. If he placed the call to his wife's office, what then? Would he be relayed to New York? Should he call home to check messages? Any communication option at this juncture required him to use a cellular phone. He was carrying a new, sophisticated model in his briefcase, one with the latest security and scrambler capabilities; however, he was prohibited by airline regulations from using it. He would have to use the one supplied by the airline, in which case he would also have to use a credit or phone card. And it was not a secure line. That would allow opportunities, however remote, for his location to be ascertained. At the bare minimum, there would be a discernible trail. He was supposed to be heading to L.A.; instead he was thirty-one thousand feet above Denver, Colorado, on his way to the Pacific Northwest. This unexpected bump was acutely disturbing after all the careful planning. He hoped it was not a precursor of things to come.

Jason looked at the pager again. The SkyWord pager had a headline news service and late-breaking stories came across its screen several times a day. The political and financial data treading across the pager screen did not interest him at the moment. He turned the matter of the supposed page from his wife over in his mind for a few minutes more and then he deleted the page message and put the audio earphones back on. However, his mind was far away from the images drifting across the movie screen.

*   *   *

Sidney darted through the crowded terminal at La Guardia, her two bags clunking against her nylon-stockinged legs. She did not see the young man until he almost collided with her.

"Sidney Archer?" He was in his twenties and dressed in a black suit and tie, a chauffeur's hat perched on top of brown curly hair. She stopped and looked dully at him, fear thudding through her body as she waited for him to deliver his terrible message. Then she noticed the placard in his hand with her name on it and her entire body deflated in relief. Her firm had sent a car to take her to the Manhattan office. She had forgotten. She nodded slowly, her blood beginning to circulate again.

The young man took one of her bags and led her toward the exit. "I got a description of you from your office. Like to do that in case people don't see the sign. Everybody moves fast around here, preoccupied, y'know. You need a good backup system. Car's right outside. You might want to button your coat up, though, it's freezing out there."

As they passed the check-in counter, Sidney hesitated. Long lines streamed out from the busy airline counters as overwrought travelers tried valiantly to keep one step ahead of the demands of a world that seemed more and more to exceed human capacities. She quickly scanned the terminal for anyone who looked like an idle airline employee. All she saw were the skycaps calmly trucking luggage around amid the hysteria of panicked travelers. It was chaotic, but it was the *normal* chaos. That was good, wasn't it?

The driver looked at her. "Everything okay, Ms. Archer? You not feeling well?" She had grown even paler in the last few seconds. "I've got some Tylenol in the limo. Perk you right up. Those planes make me sick too. All that recirculated air. I tell you what, though, you get some fresh air, you'll be A-OK. That is if you can call the air in New York City fresh." He smiled.

His smile suddenly vanished as Sidney abruptly bolted away.

"Ms. Archer?" He sped after her.

Sidney caught up with the uniformed woman whose identifying badges and insignias stamped her as an employee of American Airlines. Sidney took a few seconds to get her question out. The young woman's eyes grew large.

"I haven't heard anything like that." The woman spoke in a low voice so as not to alarm passersby. "Where did you hear that?" When Sidney answered, the woman smiled. By that time, the driver had joined them. "I just got out of a briefing, ma'am. If something like that happened to one of our aircraft, we would've heard. Trust me."

"But if it had just happened? I mean—" Sidney's voice was rising.

"Ma'am, it's all right, okay? Really. There's nothing to be concerned about. It's by far the safest way to travel." The woman took one of Sidney's hands in a firm grip, looked at the driver with a reassuring smile and then turned and walked away.

Sidney stood there a few moments longer, staring after the woman. Then she took a deep breath, looked around and shook her head in dismay. She started to walk toward the exits again and looked across at the driver as if noticing him for the first time. "What's your name?"

"Tom, Tom Richards. People call me Tommy."

"Tommy, have you been at the airport long this morning?"

"Oh, 'bout a half hour. Like to get here early. Transportation headaches are not what businessmen—um, people need, y'know."

They reached the exit doors and the stiff, punishing wind hit Sidney flush in the face. She staggered for a moment and Tommy grabbed one of her arms to steady her.

"Ma'am, you don't look so good. You want I should drive you to a doctor or something?"

Sidney regained her balance. "I'm fine. Let's just get to the car."

He shrugged and she followed him to a gleaming black Lincoln Town Car. He held the door for her.

She lay back against the seat cushions and took several deep breaths. Tommy climbed in the driver's seat and started the engine. He looked in the rearview mirror. "Look, I don't mean to beat a dead horse, but you sure you're okay?"

She nodded and managed a brief smile. "I'm fine, thank you." She took another deep breath, unbuttoned her coat, smoothed out her dress and crossed her legs. The interior of the car was very warm and after the cold burst she had just encountered she actually wasn't feeling all that well. She looked at the back of the driver's head.

"Tommy, did you hear anything about an airplane crash today? While you were at the airport, or on the news?"

Tommy's eyebrows went up. "Crash? Not me, I ain't heard nothing like that. And I been listening to the twenty-four-hour news radio all morning. Who says a plane crashed? That's crazy. I got friends at most of the airlines. They would've told me." He looked at her warily, as if he were suddenly unsure of her mental state.

Sidney didn't answer but lay back against the seat. She took the cellular phone supplied by the car company out of its receptacle and dialed Tyler, Stone's New York office. She silently cursed George Beard. She knew the odds were billions to one that her husband had been in a plane crash, a purported crash that, so far, only an old, terrified man seemed to know about. She shook her head and finally smiled. The whole thing was absurd. Jason was hard at work on his laptop having a snack and a second cup of coffee or, more likely, settling in to watch the in-flight movie. Her husband's pager was probably gathering dust on his nightstand. She would give him hell about it when he got back. Jason would laugh at her when she told him this story. But that was okay. Right now she very much wanted to hear that laugh.

She spoke into the phone. "It's Sidney. Tell Paul and Harold that I'm on my way." She looked out the window at the smooth-flowing traffic. "Thirty-five minutes tops."

She replaced the phone and again stared out the window. The thick clouds were heavy with moisture and even the stout Lincoln was buffeted by powerful winds when they took the bridge over the East River on their way into Manhattan. Tommy again looked at her in the rearview mirror.

"They're calling for snow today. A lot of it. Me, I say they're blowing smoke. I can't remember the last time the weather guys got anything right. But if they do, you might have a problem getting out, ma'am. They shut La Guardia down at the drop of a hat these days."

Sidney continued to look out the tinted windows, where the army of familiar skyscrapers making up the world-famous Manhattan sky-line filled the horizon. The solid and imposing buildings reaching to the sky seemed to bolster her spirit. In the foreground of her mind Sidney could see that white pine Christmas tree holding court in one corner of the living room, the warmth of a cozy fire radiating out-ward, the touch of her husband's arm around her, his head against her shoulder. And, best of all, the shiny, enchanted eyes of their two-year-old. Poor old George Beard. He should retire from those boards. It was clearly all becoming too much for him. She told her-self he wouldn't even have gotten close with his preposterous story if her husband hadn't been flying today.

She looked toward the front of the Lincoln and allowed herself to relax a little. "Actually, Tommy, I'm thinking of taking the train back."

CHAPTER SEVEN

In the main conference room of Tyler, Stone's New York office in midtown Manhattan, the video presentation outlining the latest business terms and legal strategies for the CyberCom deal had just ended. Sidney stopped the video and the screen returned to a pleasant blue. She scanned the large room where fifteen heads, mostly white males in their early to mid-forties, stared anxiously at one man sitting at the head of the table. The group had been sequestered in the tension-filled room for hours.

Nathan Gamble, the chairman of Triton Global, was a barrel-chested individual of medium height, in his mid-fifties, with gray-streaked hair brushed straight back and held rigidly in place with a substantial amount of gel. The expensive double-breasted suit was professionally tailored to his stocky form. His face was deeply lined and carried the remnants of an off-season tan. His voice was baritone and commanding; Sidney could easily envision the man bellowing across conference room tables at quaking underlings. The head of a far-reaching corporate powerhouse, he certainly looked and acted the part.

From under thick gray eyebrows, Gamble's dark brown eyes were glued on her. Sidney returned the stare. "Do you have any questions, Nathan?"

"Just one."

Sidney steadied herself. She could feel it coming. "What is it?" she asked pleasantly.

"Why the hell are we doing this?"

Everyone in the room, except for Sidney Archer, winced as though they had collectively sat on one gigantic needle.

"I'm not sure I understand your question."

"Sure you do, unless you're stupid, and I know you're not." Gamble spoke quietly, his features inscrutable despite the sharpness of his rhetoric.

Sidney bit her tongue hard. "I take it you don't like having to sell yourself in order to buy CyberCom?"

Gamble looked around the table. "I've offered an exorbitant amount of cash for that company. Apparently, not content with making a ten thousand percent return on their investment, now they want to go through my records. Correct?" He looked at Sidney for an answer. She nodded without speaking, and Gamble continued. "I've bought a lot of companies and no one has ever asked for those materials before. Now CyberCom does. Which gets back to my earlier question. Why are we doing this? What the hell's so special about CyberCom?" His eyes made an exacting scope of the table before settling once again on Sidney.

A man seated to the left of Gamble stirred. A laptop computer in front of him had drawn his attention throughout the meeting. Quentin Rowe was the very young president of Triton and subordinate only to Nathan Gamble. While all the other men in the room were entombed in stylish suits, he was dressed in khaki pants, worn deck shoes, a blue denim shirt and a brown vest buttoned up the front. Two diamond studs were lodged in his left earlobe. He looked more suited to appearing on an album cover than stepping into a boardroom.

"Nathan, CyberCom *is* special," Rowe said. "Without them we could well be out of business within two years. CyberCom's technology will completely reinvent and then dominate how information is processed over the Internet. And as far as the high-tech business is concerned, that's like Moses coming down the mountain with the Commandments; there's no substitute." Rowe's tone was a little weary but carried strident undertones. He did not look at Gamble.

Gamble lit up a cigar, casually leaning his expensive lighter up against a small brass sign on the table that read NO SMOKING. "You know, Rowe, that's the problem with this high-tech crap: You're king of the hill in the morning and cow shit by the afternoon. I never should have gotten into the damn business in the first place."

"Well, if money is all you care about, keep in mind that Triton is the world's dominant technology company and generates more than two billion dollars in profits per quarter," Quentin Rowe shot back.

"And cow shit by tomorrow afternoon." Gamble gave Rowe a sidelong glance filled with disgust and puffed away.

Sidney Archer cleared her throat. "Not if you acquire CyberCom, Nathan." Gamble turned to look at her. "You'll be on top for at least the next decade and your profits could well triple within five years."

"Really?" Gamble did not look convinced.

"She's right," Rowe added. "You have to understand that no one, until now, has been able to design software and related communication peripherals that will allow users to take full advantage of the Internet. Everyone's been floundering, trying to figure out how to make it all work. CyberCom has accomplished that. It's why there's been such a furious bidding war for the company. We are now in a position to close that war out. We have to unless we want to be an also-ran."

"I don't like them looking at our records. Period. We're a privately held company of which I'm, by far, the largest stockholder. And cash is cash." Gamble stared hard between Sidney and Rowe.

"They're going to be your partners, Nathan," Sidney said. "They're not taking your money and walking like the other acquisitions you've done. They want to know what they're getting into. Triton isn't publicly traded, so they can't go to the SEC and get the information they want. This is reasonable due diligence. They requested the same things from the other bidders."

"You presented my last cash offer?"

Sidney nodded. "We did."

"And?"

"And they were duly impressed and reiterated their request for financial and operational records on the company. If we give it to them, sweeten the purchase price some and load the back-end with better incentives, I think we've got a deal."

Gamble's face reddened and he lurched to his feet. "There's not a company out there that can touch us and this chickenshit CyberCom wants to check up on *me*?"

Rowe sighed deeply. "Nathan, it's merely perfunctory. They're not going to have any problems with Triton, we both know that. Let's just get it done. It's not like the records are unavailable. They're in the best shape they've ever been in," he said, visibly frustrated. "In fact, Jason Archer recently completed that reorganization and did a superb job. A warehouse full of paper with no rhyme or reason to it. I still can't believe that." He looked at Gamble with contempt.

"In case you forgot, I was too busy making money to piss around with a bunch of paper, Rowe. The only paper I happen to care about is the green kind."

Rowe ignored Gamble's response. "Because of Jason's work the due diligence can be completed very soon." He waved cigar smoke away from his face.

Gamble glared at Rowe. "Really?" Then he scowled at Sidney. "Well, would someone care to tell me why Archer isn't at this meeting, then?"

Sidney paled and for the first time all day she mentally shut down. "Um—"

Rowe stepped in. "Jason took a few days off."

Gamble rubbed his temples. "Well, let's get him on the phone and see where we stand. Maybe we have to give CyberCom some of it, maybe we don't, but what I don't want is us giving them stuff we don't have to. What if the deal doesn't go through? What then?" His fierce eyes swept the table.

Sidney's tone was calm. "Nathan, we'll have a team of attorneys check every document before they are turned over to CyberCom."

"Fine, but is there anybody who knows the records better than her husband?" Gamble looked at Rowe for an answer.

The young man shrugged. "No, not right now."

"Then let's get him on the line."

"Nathan—"

Gamble cut Rowe off. "Jesus Christ, you'd think that the chairman of the company would be able to get a status report from an employee, wouldn't you? And why is he taking time off anyway with the CyberCom deal heating up?" He jerked his head in Sidney's direction. "I can't say that I much like the idea of having husband and wife involved in the same acquisition, but you happen to be the best deal attorney that I know of."

"Thank you."

"Don't thank me, because this deal isn't done yet." Gamble sat down and took a long puff on his cigar. "Let's call your husband. He home?"

Sidney blinked rapidly and sat back down. "Well, actually he's not right now."

Gamble looked at his watch. "Well, when will he be?"

Sidney distractedly rubbed at her brow. "I'm not exactly sure. I mean, I tried him during our last break and he wasn't. In, I mean."

"Well, let's try him again."

Sidney stared at the man. She seemed suddenly all alone in the massive room. Sidney inwardly sighed and handed the TV remote to Paul Brophy, a young New York–based partner. *Dammit, Jason, I hope you really have this new job locked up because it looks like we're really going to need it, honey.*

The door to the conference room opened and a secretary poked her head in. "Ms. Archer, I hate to interrupt, but is there a problem with your plane tickets?"

Sidney looked puzzled. "Not that I know of, Jan, why?"

"Well, someone from the airline is on the phone for you."

Sidney opened her briefcase, pulled out her shuttle tickets and quickly perused them. She looked back at Jan. "It's a shuttle ticket, so it's an open return. Why would the airline be calling me about that?"

"Can we get on with the meeting?" Gamble bellowed.

Jan cleared her throat, looked anxiously at Nathan Gamble and continued speaking to Sidney. "Well, whoever it is wants to talk to you. Maybe they had to cancel the shuttle for the rest of today. It's been snowing for the last three hours."

Sidney picked up another device and hit a button. The automatic blinds covering the wall of windows slowly slid back.

"Christ!" Sidney gasped in dismay. She watched the fat snowflakes pouring down. They were so thick she couldn't see the building across the street.

Paul Brophy looked at her. "The firm still has that condo up on Park, Sid, if you need to stay over." He paused. "Maybe we could grab some dinner." His eyes were quietly hopeful.

Sidney sat down wearily without looking at him. "I can't." She was about to say that Jason was out of town but quickly caught herself. Sidney thought rapidly. Gamble was obviously not going to let this one go. She could call home, confirm what she already knew: that Jason wasn't there. They could all go out to dinner and she could slip away and start calling around L.A., starting with the offices of AllegraPort. They could patch Jason through, he could satisfy Gamble's curiosity, and with a little luck she and her husband could escape with little more than a bruised ego and the beginnings on an ulcer. And if the airports were closed, she could take the last Metroliner train home. She swiftly calculated travel times. She would have to call the day care. Karen could take Amy home with her. Worse-case scenario, Amy could do a sleep-over at Karen's. This logistical nightmare only reinforced Sidney's desires for a simpler existence.

"Ms. Archer, do you want to take the call?"

Sidney snapped out of her musings. "I'm sorry, Jan, just put it through in here. And Jan, see if you can get me on the last Metroliner, just in case La Guardia's closed."

"Yes, ma'am." Jan closed the door. In another moment a red light blinked on the telephone perched on the credenza. Sidney picked it up.

Paul Brophy ejected the video and the TV came back on, voices from the screen filling the room. He quickly hit the mute button on the remote and the room was once again silent.

Sidney cradled the phone against her ear.

"This is Sidney Archer. Can I help you?"

The woman's voice on the other end was a little hesitant, but oddly soothing. "My name is Linda Freeman. I'm with Western Airlines, Ms. Archer. Your office in Washington gave me this number."

"Western? There must be a mistake. I'm ticketed on USAir. On the New York to D.C. shuttle." Sidney shook her head. A stupid mistake. She had enough on her plate right now.

"Ms. Archer, I need you to confirm that you're the spouse of Jason W. Archer, residing at 611 Morgan Lane, Jefferson County, Virginia."

Sidney's tone betrayed her confusion; however, her answer was automatic. "Yes." As soon as the word passed her lips, Sidney's entire body froze.

"Oh, my God!" Paul Brophy's voice cut through the room.

Sidney whirled around to look at him. All eyes were staring at the TV. Sidney turned slowly toward it. She didn't notice the words "Special News Report" flashing across the top of the screen, or the hearing-impaired close-captioned subtitles flowing across the bottom while the news correspondent recounted the tragic story. Her eyes were riveted on the mass of smoky, blackened wreckage that had once been a proud member of the Western Airlines fleet. George Beard's face appeared in her mind. His low, confidential tones assailed her. *There was a plane crash.*

The voice on the phone beckoned to her. "Ms. Archer, I'm afraid there's been an incident involving one of our aircraft."

Sidney Archer heard no more. Her hand slowly descended to her side. Her fingers involuntarily opened and the phone receiver fell to the thickly carpeted floor.

Outside, the snow continued to pour down so forcefully it resembled one of the city's famous ticker-tape parades. The cold winds hurled themselves against the broad array of windows, and Sidney Archer continued to stare in complete disbelief at the crater containing the remains of Flight 3223.

CHAPTER EIGHT

One man, dark-haired, with a cleft chin below chubby cheeks, dressed in a fashionable two-piece suit and clearly introducing himself as William, met Jason Archer at the airport gate in Seattle. The two exchanged a couple of sentences, each composed of seemingly arbitrary words. The coded greeting successfully exchanged, they walked off together. As William went through the exit doors to signal for their ride, Jason took the opportunity to unobtrusively deposit a padded envelope into a U.S. mailbox located to the right of the exit door. Inside the envelope was the copy of the computer diskette he had made before leaving home.

Jason was quickly escorted to a limousine that had pulled up to the curb on William's signal. Inside the limo William presented identification to Jason that revealed his name actually to be Anthony DePazza. A few words of innocuous conversation were exchanged, but nothing further, as the men settled back into the deep leather. Another man, dressed in a conservative brown suit, drove. During the ride, at DePazza's suggestion, Jason took the opportunity to remove the wig and mustache.

The leather briefcase rode on Jason's lap. Occasionally DePazza would eye it and then continue to stare out the window. Had Jason observed a little more closely, he would have noticed the bulge and occasional glint of metal under DePazza's jacket. The Glock M-17 9mm was a particularly deadly piece of ordnance. The driver was similarly equipped. Even if Jason had seen the weaponry, however, it would not have surprised him. Indeed, he expected them to carry guns.

The limo headed east away from Puget Sound. Jason looked out the tinted windows. The sky was overcast, and drops of rain splattered against the window. From his small pool of meteorological knowledge, Jason knew this weather was apparently a fixture for Seattle.

Within half an hour the limo had reached its destination: a collection of warehouse buildings that were accessed through an electric gate where a guard was stationed.

Jason looked around nervously, but said nothing. He had been told to expect unusual meeting conditions. They entered one of the warehouses through a metal overhead door that rose up as the limo approached. Exiting the vehicle, Jason could see the door closing. The only light came from a couple of overhead fixtures that were in need of cleaning. A set of stairs was at one end of the vast space. The men motioned for Jason to follow them. Jason looked around and felt an uneasiness start to wash over him. With an effort he brushed aside the feeling, took a deep breath and walked toward the stairs.

Up the stairs, they entered a narrow doorway to a small, windowless room. The driver waited outside. DePazza hit the light switch. Jason looked around. The furnishings consisted of one card table, a couple of chairs and a battered file cabinet with holes rusted through.

Completely unknown to Jason, a surveillance camera, activated as soon as the light in the small room had been turned on, looked out from one of the file cabinet's rusty apertures, silently recording the events.

DePazza sat down in one of the chairs and motioned for Jason to do likewise. "Shouldn't be long now," DePazza said in a friendly tone. He flipped out a cigarette and offered another to Jason, who shook his head. "Just remember, Jason, don't do any talking. They only want what's in that briefcase. No need to complicate matters. Okay?"

Jason nodded.

Before DePazza could light the menthol, there were three quick knocks on the door. Jason stood up, as did DePazza, who quickly put the cigarette away and opened the door. In the doorway stood a man, small in stature, his hair solid gray, his skin tanned and heavily wrinkled. Behind him were two men, dressed in cheap suits and wearing sunglasses despite the dim light. They both appeared to be in their late thirties.

The older man looked at DePazza, who in turn pointed to Jason. The man looked at him with penetrating blue eyes. Jason suddenly realized he was drenched with perspiration, although the entire warehouse was unheated and the temperature must have been close to forty degrees.

Jason glanced at DePazza, who slowly nodded. Jason quickly handed over the leather briefcase. The man looked inside the bag, briefly perusing its contents, taking a minute to scrutinize one piece of paper in particular. The two others did likewise; smiles sprouted on their lips. The older man smiled broadly and then replaced the page, closed the briefcase and handed it to one of his men. The other one handed him a silver metal case, which he held briefly and then handed over to Jason. The case was secured by an electronic lock.

The sudden roar of the airplane overhead made them all jerk their heads upward. It seemed to be landing on the building. In a few moments it had passed by and the silence returned.

The elderly man smiled, turned, and the door quietly closed behind all three.

Jason slowly let out his breath.

They waited for a minute in silence and then DePazza opened the door and motioned for Jason to walk out. DePazza and the driver followed. The lights were turned out. The surveillance camera instantly shut off as the darkness returned.

Jason climbed back into the limo, holding tightly to the silver case. It was fairly heavy. He turned to DePazza.

"I didn't expect it to go exactly like that."

DePazza shrugged. "However you count it, though, it was a success."

"Yeah, but why couldn't I say anything?"

DePazza stared at him, faintly annoyed. "What would you have said, Jason?"

Jason finally shrugged.

"If I were you, I'd focus my attention on the contents of that." DePazza pointed at the briefcase.

Jason tried to open it but without success. He raised his eyebrows at his companion.

"When you get to where you'll be staying, you can open it. I'll tell you the code when we get there. Follow the instructions inside." He added, "You won't be disappointed."

"But why Seattle?"

"It's doubtful you'd run into anyone you know here. Correct?" DePazza's calm eyes rested on Jason's face.

"And you won't need me anymore. You're sure?"

DePazza almost smiled. "As sure as I've ever been about anything." He shook Jason's hand.

DePazza leaned back in his seat. Jason put his seat belt on and felt something jab him in the side. He pulled his SkyWord pager from his belt and looked guiltily at it. What if it *had* been his wife calling earlier? He looked at the tiny screen and his face suddenly registered disbelief.

Flashing across the screen, the pager's headline feature told the story of a terrible tragedy: Western Airlines' early morning Flight 3223 from Washington to L.A. had crashed in the Virginia countryside; there were no survivors.

Jason Archer couldn't catch his breath. He tore open his black metal case and frantically reached for the phone inside.

DePazza's voice was sharp. "What the hell are you doing?"

Jason handed DePazza the pager. "My wife thinks I'm dead. Oh, Christ. That's why she was calling. Oh, my God." Jason's fingers fumbled over the phone case, trying to open it.

DePazza looked down at the pager. He read the digitized headline and the word "Shit" silently passed between his lips. Well, this would only accelerate the process slightly, he thought. He didn't like to deviate from the established plan, yet clearly he had no choice but to do exactly that. When he looked back up at Jason, his eyes were cold and deadly. One hand reached over and snatched the cellular phone from Jason's trembling hands. The other reached inside his jacket and reappeared, holding the compact shape of the deadly Glock directly at Jason's head.

Jason looked up and saw the gun.

"I'm afraid that you're not calling anybody." DePazza's eyes never left Jason's face.

Transfixed, Jason watched DePazza reach up to his face and tug at his skin. The elaborate disguise came off piece by piece. In another moment, next to Jason sat a blond-haired man in his early thirties with a long aquiline nose and fair skin. The eyes, though, remained the same blue and chilling. His real name, although he rarely used it, was Kenneth Scales. He was a certifiable sociopath, with a twist. He took great pleasure in killing people, and reveled in the details that went into that terrible process. However, he never did it randomly. And he never did it for free.

CHAPTER NINE

It had taken the better part of five hours to contain the fire, and in the end the flames retreated of their own accord after having consumed everything combustible within their long reach. The local authorities were grateful only that the conflagration had raged in an empty, secluded dirt field.

A National Transportation Safety Board "go-team," outfitted in their blue biohazard protective suits, were now slowly walking the outside perimeter of the crash while smoke billowed skyward and small pockets of obstinate flames were attacked by diligent teams of firefighters. The entire area had been cordoned off with orange and white street barricades behind which a number of anxious area residents stood and stared in the typical mixture of horrified disbelief and morbid interest. Columns of fire trucks, police cars, ambulances, dark green National Guard trucks and other emergency vehicles were stacked along both sides of the field. The EMTs stood next to their vehicles, hands in their pockets. Their services would not be needed other than as silent transports of whatever human remains, if any, could be extracted from the holocaust.

The mayor of the nearby rural Virginia town stood next to the farmer whose land had received this most terrible intrusion from above. Behind them, two Ford pickup trucks sported "I survived Pearl Harbor" license plates. And now, for the second time in their lives, their faces carried the horror of sudden, terrible and massive death.

"It's not a crash site. It's a goddamn crematory." The veteran NTSB investigator shook his head wearily, removed his cap emblazoned with the letters NTSB and wiped at his wrinkled brow with his other hand. George Kaplan was fifty-one years old with thinning, gray-edged hair that covered a wide head; he carried a small paunch on a five-foot-seven-inch frame. As a fighter pilot in Vietnam, then a commercial pilot for many years, he had joined the NTSB after a close friend had crashed a two-seater Piper into the side of a hill after a near miss with a 727 during a heavy fog. It was then that Kaplan decided he should do less flying and more work trying to prevent accidents.

George Kaplan was the designated investigator in charge and this was absolutely the last place in the world he wanted to be; but, unfortunately, one obvious place to seek preventive safety measures was at the scene of aircraft accidents. Every night members of the NTSB crash investigative "go-teams" went to bed hoping beyond hope that no one would have need of their services, praying that there would be no reason to travel to distant places, to pick through the pieces of yet another catastrophe.

As he scanned the crash area, Kaplan grimaced and shook his head again. Starkly absent was the usual trail of aircraft and body parts, luggage, clothing and the millions of other items that routinely would be discovered, sorted, cataloged, analyzed and papered until some conclusions could be found for why a 110-ton plane had fallen out of the skies. They had no eyewitnesses, because the crash occurred in the early morning and the cloud cover was low. It would have only been seconds between the time the plane exited the clouds and when it struck the earth.

Where the plane had penetrated the ground, nose first, there now existed a crater that later excavation would determine to be approximately thirty feet deep, or about one-fifth as long as the aircraft itself. That fact alone was a terrifying testament to the force that had catapulted everyone on board into the hereafter with frightening ease. The entire fuselage, Kaplan figured, had collapsed like an accordion, fore and aft, and its fragments now rested in the depths of the impact crater. Not even the empennage, or tail assembly, was visible. To compound the problem, tons of dirt and rock were lying on top of the aircraft's remains.

The field and surrounding areas were peppered with bits of debris, but most of it was palm-sized, having been thrown off in the explosion when the aircraft hit the earth. Much of the plane and the passengers strapped inside would have disintegrated from the terrible weight and velocity of the impact and the igniting of the jet fuel, which would have caused another explosion bare seconds later, before thirty feet of dirt and rubble combined for an airtight mass grave.

What was left on the surface was unrecognizable as a jet aircraft. It reminded Kaplan of the inexplicable 1991 Colorado Springs crash of a United Boeing 737. He had worked that disaster too as the aviation systems specialist. For the first time in the history of the NTSB, from its inception in 1967 as an independent federal agency, it had not been able to find probable cause for a plane crash. The "tin-kickers," as the NTSB investigators referred to themselves, had never gotten over that one. The similarity of the Pittsburgh crash of a USAir Boeing 737 in 1994 had only heightened their feelings of guilt. If they had solved Colorado, many of them felt, Pittsburgh might have been prevented. And now this.

George Kaplan looked at the now clear sky and his bewilderment grew. He was convinced the Colorado Springs crash had been caused, at least in part, by a freakish rotor cloud that had hit the aircraft on its final approach, a vulnerable moment for any jetliner. A rotor was a vortex of air generated about a horizontal axis by high winds over irregular terrain. In the case of United Airlines Flight 585, the irregular terrain was supplied by the mighty Rocky Mountains. But this was the East Coast. There were no Rocky Mountains here. While an abnormally severe rotor could conceivably have knocked a plane as large as an L500 out of the sky, Kaplan could not believe that was what had befallen Flight 3223. According to air traffic control, the L500 had started falling from its cruising altitude of thirty-five thousand feet and never looked back. No mountains in the United States were capable of throwing off the formation of a rotor that high. Indeed, the only mountains nearby were in the Shenandoah National Forest and were part of the relatively smallish Blue Ridge Mountain chain. They were all in the three- to four-thousand-foot range, more hills than mountains.

Then there was the altitude factor. Normally, the roll experienced by planes flying into a rotor or other freakish atmospheric condition is controlled by aileron application. At six miles up, the Western Airlines pilots would have had time to reestablish control. Kaplan was sure the dark side of Mother Nature had not torn the jet from the peaceful confines of the sky. But something else clearly had.

His team would shortly return to their hotel, where an organizational meeting would be held. Initially, on-scene investigative groups would be formed for structures, systems, survival factors, power plants, weather and air-traffic control. Later, units would be assembled to evaluate aircraft performance, to analyze the cockpit voice recorder and the flight data recorder, crew performance, sound spectrum, maintenance records and metallurgical examinations. It was a slow, tedious and oftentimes heart-wrenching process, but Kaplan would not leave until he had examined every atom of what had recently been a state-of-the-art jetliner and almost two hundred very much alive human beings. He swore to himself that probable cause would not escape him this time.

Kaplan slowly walked toward his rental car. An early spring would come to the dirt field: soon, red flags would bloom everywhere, tiny beacons signifying the location of remnants of the flight. Darkness was settling in rapidly. He blew into his frigid hands to warm them. A hot thermos of coffee waited in the car. He hoped the FDR, the flight data recorder—known popularly as the "black box," although it was actually blazing orange—would live up to its reputation of indestructibility. An updated version had just been installed in the plane and the 121 parameters measured by the FDR would tell them one hell of a lot about what had happened to doom Flight 3223. On the L500 the FDR and the cockpit voice recorder (CVR) were located in the overhead hull between the aft galleys. An L500 had never experienced a hull loss before; this crash would certainly test the flight data recorder's invulnerability.

Too bad human beings weren't invulnerable.

As he climbed a small rise in the earth, George Kaplan froze. In the rapidly failing light a tall image stood a bare five feet from him. Sunglasses hid a pair of slate-gray eyes; the six-foot-three-inch frame supported naturally bulky shoulders, meaty arms and a thickening waistline, and featured a pair of telephone-pole-sized legs; an aging middle linebacker was the description that would probably jump to mind. The man's hands were in his pants pockets, the unmistakable silver shield pinned to the belt.

Kaplan squinted in the gathering dusk. "Lee?"

FBI Special Agent Lee Sawyer stepped forward.

"Hello, George."

The men shook hands.

"What the hell are you doing here?"

Sawyer looked around at the crash site and then back at Kaplan. His angular face carried expressive, full lips. Sawyer had thinning black hair heavily laced with silver. His long forehead and slender nose that veered slightly to the right, a relic from a past case, combined with his impressive size to give him a very intense and commanding presence. "When an American plane is downed over American soil by what looks to be sabotage, the FBI gets a little excited, George." The FBI agent looked at Kaplan pointedly.

"Sabotage?" Kaplan said warily.

Sawyer looked over the expanse of the disaster again. "I checked the meteorological reports. Nothing up there that would have caused this. And the aircraft was almost brand-new."

"That doesn't mean it was sabotage, Lee. It's too early to tell. You know that. Hell, even though the odds are probably a billion to one, we could be looking at the in-flight deployment of a reverse thruster that could've knocked the plane right out of the sky."

"There's a part of the aircraft I'm particularly interested in, George. I'd like you to take a very close look at it."

Kaplan snorted. "Well, that crater's going to take some time for us to dig out. And when we do, you'll be able to hold most of the pieces in your hand."

Sawyer's response almost made Kaplan's knees buckle.

"This part isn't in the crater. And it's fairly large: the starboard wing and engine. We found it about thirty minutes ago."

Kaplan stood stock-still for a full minute as his wide eyes took in Sawyer's expressionless features. Then Sawyer hustled him toward the agent's vehicle.

Sawyer's rented Buick sped away as the last flames from Flight 3223 were extinguished. The darkness would soon be gathering around a thirty-foot-deep pit that represented a crude monument to the abrupt termination of 181 lives.

CHAPTER TEN

The Gulfstream jet streaked through the sky. The luxurious cabin resembled an upscale hotel lounge complete with wood paneling, brown leather captain's chairs and a well-stocked bar, bartender and all. Sidney Archer was curled up in one of the oversized chairs, eyes firmly closed. A cold compress curved over her forehead. When she finally opened her eyes and removed the compress, she looked as though she were sedated, so heavy were her eyelids, so sluggish her movements. In fact, she had neither taken medication nor availed herself of the bar's inventory. Her mind had shut down: Today her husband had died in a plane crash.

She looked around the cabin. It had been Quentin Rowe's suggestion that she take Triton's corporate jet home with him. At the last minute, and adding to Sidney's pain, Gamble had accompanied them. He was now in his private cabin in the rear of the aircraft. She hoped to God he would remain there for the duration. She looked up to see Richard Lucas, Triton's in-house security chief, watching her closely.

"Relax, Rich." Quentin Rowe passed in front of the security man and headed over to Sidney. He sat down next to her. "So, how're you doing?" he asked gently. "We have some Valium on board. Carry a constant supply because of Nathan."

"He uses Valium?" Sidney looked surprised.

Rowe shrugged. "Actually, it's for the people traveling with Nathan."

Sidney managed a weak smile in return, a smile that abruptly vanished. "Oh, God, I can't believe it." She looked out the window with reddened eyes. Her hands flew to her face. She spoke without looking at Rowe. "I know this looks bad, Quentin." Her voice was trembling.

"Hey, no law against someone traveling on his own time," Rowe said quickly.

"I don't know what to say—"

Rowe held up a hand. "Look, this isn't the time or place. I've got some things to do. You need anything, just let me know."

Sidney looked at him gratefully. After he disappeared into another part of the cabin, Sidney leaned back in her chair and once again closed her eyes. The waves of tears slid down her puffy cheeks. From the front of the cabin, Richard Lucas continued his solitary watch.

Sidney would sob anew each time she recalled her last exchange with Jason. In anger, she had hung up the phone on him. Here was a stupid little episode that didn't mean anything, an act replicated a thousand times over the life of many successful marriages, and yet was that to be his last memory of their lives together? She shuddered and gripped the armrest. All her suspicions over the last few months. God! He had been working so hard trying to land a terrific new job, and she could only see the absurd image of him bedding more attractive women. Her guilt was numbing. The rest of her life would be forever tainted by that single, terrible misjudgment of the man she loved.

When she opened her eyes, she received another shock. Nathan Gamble was sitting next to her. She was startled to see tenderness in his face, an emotion she had certainly never witnessed in him before. He offered her the glass in his hand.

"Brandy," he said gruffly, looking past her out the porthole at the dark sky. When she hesitated, he took her hand and wrapped it around the glass. "Right now you don't want to be thinking too clearly," he said. "Drink."

She put the glass to her lips and the warm liquid cascaded down her throat. Gamble sat back in the leather and motioned Lucas to leave. The Triton CEO absently rubbed the armrest as he surveyed the cabin. He had removed his suit jacket and his rolled-up shirtsleeves revealed surprisingly muscular forearms. The plane's engines droned deep in the background. Sidney could almost feel the electrical currents running amok through her as she waited for Gamble to speak. She had seen him completely devastate people at all levels of authority with his relentless disregard for personal feelings. Now, even through the veil of utter grief, she sensed the presence of a different, more caring man next to her.

"I'm very sorry about your husband." Sidney was dimly conscious of how ill at ease Gamble seemed. His hands were constantly in motion, as though matching the maneuvers of his very active mind. Sidney glanced at him as she took another swallow of brandy.

"Thank you," she managed to say.

"I really didn't know him personally. Company as big as Triton, hell, I'm lucky if I meet even ten percent of the management-level people." Gamble sighed and, as if suddenly noticing the ceaseless dance of his hands, folded them across his lap. "Of course, I knew him by reputation and he was moving up quickly. By most accounts he would've made very good executive material."

Sidney winced at the words. She thought back to Jason's news that very morning. A new job, a vice presidency, a new life for them all. And now? She quickly finished the brandy and managed to forestall a sob before it broke the surface. When she glanced again at Gamble, he was looking directly at her. "I might as well get this out now, although it's a rotten time to do it, I know." He paused and studied her face. Sidney braced herself again; her fingers instinctively gripped the armrest as she tried hard not to shake. She swallowed an enormous lump in her throat. The chairman's eyes were no longer tender.

"Your husband was on a plane to Los Angeles." He licked his lips nervously and leaned toward her. "Not at home." Sidney unconsciously nodded, as she knew exactly what the next question would be.

"You were aware of this?"

For one brief moment Sidney felt as if she were floating through the dense clouds without the benefit of a $25 million jet. Time seemed suspended, but actually only a few seconds had passed before she uttered her response. "No." She had never lied to a client before; the word had escaped her lips before she knew it. She was certain he didn't believe her. But it was too late to go back now. Gamble searched her features for a few more seconds, then sat back in his seat. For the moment he was motionless, as if satisfied he had made his point. Abruptly, he patted Sidney's arm and stood up. "When we land, I'll have my limo take you home. You have kids?"

"One daughter." Sidney stared up at him, bewildered that the interrogation had ended so suddenly.

"Just tell the driver where to go and he'll pick her up too. She in day care?" Sidney nodded. Gamble shook his head. "Every kid's in damned day care these days."

Sidney thought of her plans to stay home to raise Amy. She was a single parent now. The revelation made her almost dizzy. If Gamble hadn't been there, she would have slumped to the floor in agony. She looked up to find Gamble eyeing her, one hand gingerly rubbing his forehead. "You need anything else?"

She managed to hold up the empty glass. "Thanks, this helped quite a bit."

He took the glass. "Booze usually does." He started to leave, then paused. "Triton takes good care of its employees, Sidney. You need anything—money, funeral arrangements, help with the house or kid, stuff like that—we have people to handle it. Don't be afraid to give us a call."

"I won't. Thank you."

"And if you want to talk anymore about . . . things"—his eyebrows shot up suggestively—"you know where to find me."

He walked off and Richard Lucas quietly resumed his sentry post. Shaking slightly, Sidney once again closed her eyes. The plane raced on. All she wanted to do was hold her daughter.

CHAPTER ELEVEN

Sitting on the side of the bed, the man stripped down to his boxers. Outside, the sun was not yet up. His body was heavily muscled. A tattoo of a coiled snake rode on his left biceps. Three packed bags stood ready by the bedroom door. A U.S. passport, a batch of airline tickets, cash and identification documents had been waiting for him as promised. They were in a small leather pouch on top of one of the travel bags. His name would change once again, not for the first time in his crime-laden life.

He wouldn't be fueling any more planes. Not that he would ever need to work again. The electronic deposit of funds into the offshore account had been confirmed. He now had the kind of wealth that had eluded him his entire life despite all his past efforts. Even with his long experience in criminal matters, his hands still shook as he pulled the hairpiece, oval turquoise-colored eyeglasses and tinted contacts from a small bag. Although probably weeks would pass before anyone could figure out what had happened, in his line of work you always planned for worst-case scenario. That dictated running immediately and running far. He was well prepared to do both.

He thought back to recent events. He had tossed the plastic container into the Potomac River after he had rid it of its contents; it would never be found. There were no prints to pick up, no other physical evidence left behind. If they found anything tying him to the plane sabotage, he would be long gone anyway. Moreover, the name he had been living under for the last two months would lead them to a complete dead end.

He had killed before, but certainly not on such a vast and impersonal scale. He had always had a reason to kill—if not a personal one, then one supplied by whoever had hired him. This time the sheer number and complete anonymity of the murdered people managed to prick even his hardened conscience. He had not stayed around to see who had boarded the aircraft. He had been paid to do a job and he had done it. He would use the vast sums now at his disposal to forget how he had earned that money. He figured it would not take him all that long.

He sat down in front of the small mirror resting on the table in the bedroom. The wig changed his curly dark hair to a wavy blond. A new suit, far removed in its sleek elegance from the clothing he had just discarded, was hanging on the door. He cupped his hand and bent his head low as he concentrated on inserting the contact lenses that would change his low-key brown eyes to a startling blue.

He rose back up to check the effect in the mirror and felt the elongated muzzle of the Sig P229 placed directly against the base of his skull. With the sharpened perception that accompanies panic, he noticed how the attached suppressor almost doubled the barrel length of the compact 9mm.

His absolute shock lasted barely a second as he felt the cold metal against his skin, saw the dark eyes staring at him in the mirror's reflection, the mouth set in a firm line. His own countenance often held a similar look right before a kill. Taking the life of another human being had always been a serious business to him. Now, in the mirror he watched, mesmerized, as another face went through his very own signature ritual. Then he watched with growing surprise as the features of the person about to kill him next turned to anger and then moved to unadulterated loathing, emotions he had never felt in the midst of an execution. The victim's eyes grew wide as he focused on the finger tightening on the trigger. His mouth moved to say something, probably an expletive; however, the words were not formed in time, as the round exploded into his brain. He jerked backward from the impact and then collapsed forward onto the little table. The killer tossed his limp body face down in the small crevice between the bed and the wall and emptied the remaining eleven shots from the Sig's magazine into the dead man's upper torso. Although the victim's heart was no longer pumping, dime-sized drops of dark blood appeared at each point of entrance, like the sprout of tiny oil wells. The auto pistol landed next to the body.

The shooter walked calmly from the room, stopping only to perform two tasks. First, he scooped up the leather bag containing the dead man's new identity. Second, out in the hallway he hit the HVAC switch on the wall and turned the air-conditioning on full blast. Ten seconds later the front door of the apartment opened and closed. The apartment was silent. In the bedroom, the beige carpet was fast becoming an ugly shade of crimson. The balance in the off-shore bank account would be reduced to zero and closed within the hour, its owner no longer requiring use of the funds.

It was barely seven in the morning. Darkness still reigned outside. Sitting at the kitchen table, wearing her battered old house-robe, Sidney Archer slowly closed her eyes and once again tried to pretend this was all a nightmare and her husband was still alive and would be walking through the front door. He would have a smile on his face, a present under his arm for his daughter and a long, soothing kiss for his wife.

When she opened her eyes, nothing had changed. Sidney looked at her watch. Amy would be awake soon. Sidney had just gotten off the phone with her parents. They would be at their daughter's house at nine to drive the little girl to their home in Hanover, Virginia, where she was going to stay for a few days while Sidney tried to make some sense of what had happened. Sidney cringed at the thought of having to explain the catastrophe to her little girl when she was older, at having to relive, years later, the horror she was now feeling. How to tell her daughter that her father had died for no apparent reason other than a plane doing the unthinkable, shedding almost two hundred lives in the process, and killing the man who had helped breathe life into her.

Jason's parents had passed on years before. An only child, he had adopted Sidney's family as his own, and they had happily accepted him. Sidney's two older brothers had already called with offers of help, commiseration and, finally, quiet sobbing.

Western had offered to fly Sidney to the small town near where the crash had occurred, but she had declined. She could not bear to be with other family members of crash victims. She envisioned all of them boarding long, gray buses in silence, unable to make eye contact, exhausted limbs twitching, frail nervous systems ready to crumble from overwhelming shock. Struggling with complicated feelings of denial, grief and sorrow was terrible enough without being surrounded by people you didn't know who were going through the same ordeal. Right now, the comfort of similarly stricken folk did not sound at all appealing to her.

She headed upstairs, walked down the hallway and paused at her bedroom. As she leaned against the door, it halfway opened. She looked around the room, at all the familiar objects, each having a unique history of its own; memories inextricably tied to her life with Jason. Her gaze finally came to rest on the unmade bed. So much pleasure had occurred there. She couldn't believe that that early morning encounter before Jason had boarded the plane was to be the last time.

She closed the door quietly and walked down the hallway to Amy's room. The even breathing of her daughter was comforting, especially now. Sidney sat in the wicker rocking chair beside the trundle bed. She and Jason had recently succeeded in moving their daughter from crib to bed. The effort had required many nights of sleeping on the floor beside the little girl until she grew comfortable with the new arrangements.

While she slowly rocked in the chair, Sidney continued to watch her daughter, the tangle of blond hair, the small feet in thick socks that had kicked free from the blankets. At seven-thirty, a small cry escaped Amy's lips and she abruptly sat up, eyes tightly shut like a baby bird's. Barely a moment passed before mother had daughter in her arms. They rocked for a while longer until Amy awoke fully.

As the sun began its ascent, Sidney gave Amy a bath, dried her hair, dressed her in warm clothes and helped her down the stairs to the kitchen. While Sidney was making breakfast and brewing coffee, Amy wandered into the adjacent living room, where Sidney could hear her playing with an ever-growing pile of toys that had occupied one corner of the room for the last year. Sidney opened the cupboard and automatically pulled out two coffee cups. She stopped halfway to the coffeepot, rocking slowly back and forth on the wood floor. She bit into her lip until the urge to scream subsided. She felt as though someone had cut her in half. She put one cup back on the shelf and carried her coffee and a bowl of hot oatmeal over to the small pine kitchen table.

She looked toward the living room. "Amy. Amy, sweetie, it's time to eat." She could barely speak above a whisper. Her throat was killing her; her entire body seemed to have eroded into one large ache. The little girl hurtled through the doorway. Amy's normal speed was most other kids' top speed. She carried a stuffed Tigger and a photo frame. As she raced toward her mother, her little face was bright and shining, hair still slightly damp, straight on top with curls emerging at the bottom.

Sidney's breath suddenly left her body as Amy held up a photo of Jason. It had been taken just last month. He had been outside working in the yard. Amy had crept up on him and sprayed him with the hose. Daughter had ended up with father in a pile of bright red, orange and yellow leaves.

"Daddy?" Amy's face was anxious.

Jason was to have been out of town for three days so Sidney had already anticipated having to explain his absence to her daughter. God! Three days seemed like three seconds now. She steeled herself as she smiled at the little face.

"Daddy's away right now, sweetie," she began, unable to hide the tremble in her voice. "It's just you and me right now, okay? Are you hungry, you want to eat?"

"My daddy? Daddy working?" Amy persisted, her chubby finger

pointing at the photo. Sidney lifted her daughter onto her lap. "Amy, do you know who you're going to see today?"

Amy's face looked expectant.

"Gramps and Mimi."

The child's mouth formed a large oval and then broke into a big smile. She nodded enthusiastically and blew a kiss toward the refrigerator, where a picture of her grandparents hung with the aid of a magnet. "Gamps, Mimi."

Sidney carefully pulled the photo of Jason from Amy's hand while sliding the bowl of oatmeal over.

"Now you need to eat before you go, okay? It's got maple syrup and butter, your favorite."

"I do it. *I* do it." Amy climbed out of her mother's lap and into her own chair, carefully maneuvering the spoon as she hungrily plunged into the oatmeal.

Sidney sighed and covered her eyes. She tried to hold her body rigid, but several wracking sobs still managed to escape. She finally fled the room, carrying the photo with her. She raced up the stairs to her bedroom, put the photo on the top shelf of the closet and flung herself on the bed, muffling her sobs in the pillow.

A full five minutes went by and the outpouring of sorrow continued. Usually Sidney could lock on Amy's whereabouts like radar. This time she never heard her little girl until she felt the small hand on her shoulder, pulling at her. Amy lay down beside Sidney, burrowing her face into her mother's shoulder.

Amy saw the tears and cried out "Oh, boo-boos, boo-boos," as she touched the wetness. She cupped her mother's face between her two little hands and started to cry too as she struggled to form the words. "Mommy, sad?" Their wet faces touched, tears mixed together. After a while Sidney pulled herself up, held her daughter, rocked her back and forth on the soft mattress. A bit of oatmeal clung to Amy's mouth. Sidney silently cursed herself for breaking down, for making her daughter cry, but she had never experienced such overpowering emotion before.

Finally the spasms stopped. Sidney rubbed at her eyes for the hundredth time and finally there were no new tears to replace the old. After a few more minutes she carried Amy into the bathroom, wiped her face and kissed her.

"It's okay, baby, Mommy's okay now. No more crying."

When Amy finally calmed down, Sidney gathered some toys from the bathtub for her. While she was thus preoccupied, Sidney quickly showered and changed into a long skirt and turtleneck.

When Sidney's parents knocked on the door promptly at nine, Amy's bag was packed and she was ready to go. They walked out to the car. Sidney's father carried Amy's bag. Sidney's mother walked along with Amy.

Bill Patterson put one burly arm around her daughter's shoulder, his sunken eyes and caved-in shoulders revealing how strongly the tragedy had struck him.

"Jesus, honey, I still can't believe it. I just talked to Jason two days ago. We were going to do some ice fishing this year. Up in Minnesota. Just the two of us."

"I know, Dad, he told me. He was very excited about it."

While her father loaded Amy's bag in the car, Sidney strapped her daughter in the baby seat, handed her Winnie the Pooh, squeezed her hard and then kissed her gently.

"I'll see you very soon, babydoll. Mommy promises."

Sidney closed the door. Her mother took her hand.

"Sidney, please come down with us. You don't want to be alone right now. Please."

Sidney gripped her mother's slender hand. "I do need some time alone, Mom. I need to think things through. I won't be long. A day or two, then I'll be down."

Her mother eyed her for several more seconds and then gripped Sidney in a massive hug, her small frame shaking. When she got in the car, her round face was smeared with tears.

Sidney watched the car pull out of the driveway. She stared at the backseat where her daughter clutched her beloved stuffed bear, a thumb stuck firmly in her small mouth. In a few moments the car turned the corner and they were gone.

With the slow, unsteady motions of an elderly woman, Sidney

walked back to her house. A thought suddenly struck her. With renewed energy, she rushed toward the house.

Inside, she dialed information for the Los Angeles area and obtained the number for AllegraPort Technology. Because of the time difference, she had to wait to call. The hours went by with agonizing slowness. As she punched in the number, she wondered why they hadn't called when Jason had not shown up. There had been no messages from them on the answering machine. That fact should have prepared her for AllegraPort's response, but she wasn't.

After speaking with three different people at the company, she hung up the phone and stared numbly at the kitchen wall. Jason had not been offered a vice presidency with AllegraPort. In fact, they had never heard of him. Sidney abruptly sat down on the floor, drew her knees up to her chest and wept uncontrollably. All of the suspicions she had experienced earlier swarmed back; the swiftness of their return threatened to dissolve her remaining ties to reality. She pulled herself up and ducked her head into the kitchen sink. The cold water partially revived her. She stumbled over to the table, where she covered her face in her hands. Jason had lied to her. That was indisputable now. Jason was dead. That, also, was incontrovertible. And, apparently, she would never know the truth. It was with that last thought that she finally stopped crying and looked out the window into the backyard. She and Jason had planted flowers, bushes and trees over the last two years. Working together toward a common goal: They had conducted much of their married lives along that same theme. And despite all the uncertainty she was feeling right now, one truth remained sacred to her. Jason loved her and Amy. Whatever had compelled him to lie to her, to climb aboard a doomed plane instead of remaining safely at home doing nothing more daring than prepping the kitchen walls for painting, she would find out what it was. She knew Jason's reasons would have been completely innocent. The man she knew intimately and loved with all her heart would have been capable of nothing less. Since he had been senselessly ripped from her, she at least owed it to him to track down why he had been on that plane. As soon as she was mentally able, she would take up that pursuit with every bit of energy she could muster.

CHAPTER TWELVE

The airplane hangar at the regional airport was small. On the walls were rows of power tools; stacks of boxes lay all over the floor. The darkness outside was turned into daylight inside by a ceiling full of overhead lights. Wind rattled against the metal walls as the sleet intensified, clanging like buckshot against the structure. The interior of the hangar was filled with the thick, pungent smell of an assortment of petroleum products.

On the concrete floor near the front of the hangar lay an enormous metal object. Bent and grossly distorted, it was the remains of the right wing of Flight 3223, with starboard engine and pylon intact. It had landed in the middle of a densely wooded area, directly on top of a ninety-foot-tall, hundred-year-old oak, which was split in half by the impact. Miraculously, the jet fuel had not ignited. Most of the payload had probably been lost when the tank and lines had been pierced, and the tree had cushioned some of the fall. The pieces had been removed by helicopter and brought to the hangar for examination.

A small group of men gathered closely around the wreckage. Their exhalations formed clouds in the unheated air; thick jackets kept them warm. They used powerful flashlights to probe the jagged edge of the wing where it had been torn loose from the ill-fated airliner. The nacelle housing the starboard engine was partially crushed and the right-side cowling was caved in. The flaps on the trailing edge of the wing had been ripped off on impact, but these had been recovered nearby. Examination of the engine had shown severe blade shingling, clear evidence of a major airflow disturbance while the engine was delivering power. The "disturbance" was easy to pinpoint. A great deal of debris had been ingested into the engine, essentially destroying its functionality even had it remained attached to the fuselage.

However, the attention of the men gathered around the wing was centered on where it had detached from the plane. The jagged edges of the metal were burned and blackened and, most telling, the metal was bent outward, away from the surface of the wing, with clear signs of indentation and pitting on the metal's surface. There was a short list of events that could have caused that; a bomb was clearly on that list. When Lee Sawyer had examined the wing earlier, his eyes had riveted on that area.

George Kaplan shook his head in disgust. "You're right, Lee. The changes in the metallurgy I'm seeing could only have been caused by a shock wave exerting immense but short-lived overpressure. Something exploded here, all right. It's the damnedest thing. We put detectors in airports so some crazy assholes with an agenda can't smuggle a gun or bomb on board, and now this. Jesus!"

Lee Sawyer moved forward and knelt down next to the edge of the wing. Here he was, nearly fifty years old, half of those years spent with the bureau, and again he was sifting through the catastrophic results of human pollution.

He had worked on the Lockerbie disaster, an investigation of mammoth proportion that had brought together a damned near air-tight case culled from what bordered on microscopic evidence unearthed from the shattered remains of Pan Am Flight 103. With plane bombings there were usually never any "big" clues. At least Special Agent Sawyer had thought so up until now.

His observant eyes swept over the wreckage before they came to rest on the NTSB man. "What's your best list of possible scenarios right now, George?"

Kaplan rubbed his chin, scratching absently at the stubble. "We'll know a lot more when we recover the black boxes, but we do have a clear result: The wing came off a jetliner. However, those things don't just happen. We're not exactly sure when it happened, but radar indicates that a large part of the plane—now we know it was the wing—came off in-flight. When that occurred, of course, there was no possibility of recovery. The first thought is some type of catastrophic structural failure based on a faulty design. But the L500 is a state-of-the-art model from a top manufacturer, so the chances of that kind of structural failure are so remote that I wouldn't waste much time on that angle. So maybe you think it's metal fatigue. But this plane barely had two thousand cycles—takeoffs and landings—it's practically brand-new. Besides that, the metal fatigue accidents we've seen in the past all involved the fuselage because the constant contraction-expansion of cabin pressurization and depressurization seems to contribute to the problem. Aircraft wings are not pressurized. So you rule out metal fatigue. Next, you look at the environment. Lightning strike? Planes get hit by lightning more often than people think. However, planes are equipped to deal with that and because lightning needs to be grounded to do real damage, a plane up in the sky may suffer, at worst, some burning of the skin. Besides, there were no reports of lightning in the area on the morning of the crash. Birds? Show me a bird that flies at thirty-five thousand feet and is large enough to take off an L500's wing and then maybe we'll discuss it. It sure as hell didn't collide with another plane. It sure as hell didn't."

Kaplan's voice was rising with each word. He paused to catch his breath and to look once more at the metal remains.

"So where does that leave us, George?" Sawyer calmly asked.

Kaplan looked back up. He sighed. "Next we look at possible mechanical or nondesign structural failure. Catastrophic results on an aircraft usually stem from two or more failures happening almost simultaneously. I listened to the transmission record between the pilot and the tower. The captain radioed in a Mayday several minutes before the crash, although it was clear from what little she said that they were unsure what had happened. The plane's transponder was still kicking the radar signals back until impact, so at least some of the electrical systems were working up until then. But let's say we had an engine catch on fire at the same time a fuel leak occurred. Most people might assume fuel leak, flames from the engine—wham, you got yourself an explosion and there goes the wing. Or there might not have been an actual explosion, although it sure as hell looks like there was. The fire could've weakened and finally collapsed the spar and the wing gets torn off. That could explain what we think happened to Flight 3223, at least at this early stage." Kaplan did not sound convinced.

"But?" Sawyer looked at him.

Kaplan rubbed at his eyes, the frustration clear in his troubled features. "There's no evidence that anything was wrong with the damned engine. Except for the obvious damage caused from its impact with the terrain and ingesting debris from the initial explosion, nothing leads me to believe that an engine problem played a role in the crash. If there was an engine fire, standard procedure would dictate cutting off the fuel flow to that engine and then turning off the power. The L500's engines are equipped with automatic fire detection and extinguisher systems. And, more importantly, they're mounted low, so no flames would fly toward the wings or the fuselage. So even if you have twin catastrophes—a flaming engine and a fuel leak—the design features of the aircraft and the environmental conditions prevailing at thirty-five thousand feet and an airspeed of over five hundred miles per hour would pretty much ensure that the two shall not meet." He rubbed his foot against the wing. "I guess what I'm saying is I wouldn't bet the farm on a bad engine having crashed this bird." He paused. "There's something else."

Kaplan once again knelt beside the jagged edge of the wing. "Like I said, there is clear evidence of an explosion. When I first checked the wing, I was thinking some type of improvised explosive device. You know, like Semtex wired to a timer or altimeter device. Plane hits a certain altitude, the bomb goes off. The blast fractures the skin, you got almost immediate rivet failure. Hundreds-of-miles-per-hour winds hitting it, that wing's gonna open right up at the weakest point, like unzipping your fly. Spar gives way, and bam. Hell, the weight of the engine on this section of the wing would have guaranteed that result." He paused, apparently to study the interior of the wing more closely. "The twist is I don't think a typical explosive device was involved."

"Why's that?" Sawyer asked.

Kaplan pointed inside the wing to the exposed section of the fuel tank near the fuel panel. He held his light over the spot. "Look at this."

A large hole was clearly visible. All around the perforation were light brown stains and the metal was warped and bubbled. "I noticed those earlier," Sawyer said.

"There is no way in the world a hole like this could have been naturally generated. In any event, it would've been caught on routine inspection before the plane took off," Kaplan said.

Sawyer put on his gloves before touching the area. "Maybe it happened during the explosion."

"If it did, it was the only spot it happened to. There are no other markings like this on this section of the wing, although you got fuel everywhere. That pretty much rules out the explosion having caused it. But I do believe something was put on the fuel tank wall." Kaplan paused and nervously rubbed his fingers together. "I think something was put on it deliberately to cause that hole."

"Like a corrosive acid?" Sawyer asked.

Kaplan nodded. "I'll bet you a dinner that's what we find, Lee. The fuel tanks are of an aluminum alloy structure consisting of the front and rear spars and the top and bottom of the wings. The thickness of the walls varies around the structure. A number of acids will eat right through a soft alloy metal like that."

"Okay, acid; but, depending on when it was applied, it was probably slow-acting, to let the plane get up in the air, right?"

Kaplan answered immediately. "Right. The transponder continually sends the plane's altitude to air traffic control, so we know the plane had reached its cruising altitude shortly before the explosion."

Sawyer continued his line of thought. "Tank gets pierced at some point during the flight. You got jet fuel spilling out. Highly flammable, highly explosive. So what ignited it? Maybe the engine wasn't on fire, but how about just the standard heat thrown off from the engine?"

"No way. You know how cold it is at thirty-five thousand feet? It'd make Alaska feel like the Sahara. Besides, the engine housing and coolant systems pretty much dissipate the heat thrown off from the engine. And any heat it does generate sure as hell ain't gonna end up *inside* the wing. Remember you got a damn fuel tank in there. It's pretty well insulated. On top of that, if you got a fuel leak, because of the plane's airspeed, the fuel will flow backward and not toward the front of the wing and below, where the engine is located. No, if I were inclined to take down a plane this way, no way would I count on engine heat being my detonator. I'd want something a lot more reliable."

Sawyer had a sudden thought. "If there was a leak, wouldn't it be contained?"

"In some sections of the fuel tank the answer to that would be yes. In other areas, including where we got this hole, the answer is no."

"Well, if it went down like you say—and right now I'm inclined to think you're right, George—we're going to have to focus on everybody who had access to that aircraft at least twenty-four hours before its final flight. We're going to need to go easy. It looks to be an insider, so the last thing we need is to spook him. If anybody else is involved in this, I want every last sonofabitch."

Sawyer and Kaplan walked back to their cars. Kaplan looked over at the FBI agent. "You seemed to accept my sabotage theory pretty readily, Lee."

Sawyer was aware of one fact that made the bombing theory infinitely more plausible. "It'll need to be substantiated," he replied without looking at the NTSB man. "But, yeah, I think you're right. I was pretty sure it was that as soon as the wing was found."

"Why the hell would someone do that? I mean, I can understand terrorists taking out an international flight, but this was a plain-vanilla domestic. I just don't get it."

As Kaplan was about to get into his car, Sawyer leaned on the door. "It might make sense if you wanted to kill someone in particular, in a spectacular fashion."

Kaplan stared at the agent. "Down an entire plane to get to one guy? Who the hell was on that thing?"

"Does the name Arthur Lieberman ring any bells?" the FBI agent asked quietly.

Kaplan searched his brain but came up empty. "Sounds damn familiar, but I can't place it."

"Well, if you were an investment banker or stockbroker, or a congressman on the Joint Economic Committee, you'd know. Actually, he's the most powerful person in America, maybe the entire world."

"I thought the most powerful person in America was the president."

Sawyer smiled grimly. "No. It's Arthur Lieberman with the big *S* on his chest."

"Who the hell was he?"

"Arthur Lieberman was the chairman of the Federal Reserve Board. Now he's a homicide victim along with a hundred and eighty others. And my hunch is, he's the only one they wanted to kill."

CHAPTER THIRTEEN

Jason Archer had no idea where he was. The limo had seemed to drive around for hours, he couldn't be sure, and DePazza, or whoever the hell he really was, had blindfolded him. The room he was now in was small and bare. Water dripped in one corner and the air was thick with the odor of mold. He sat on a rickety chair across from the one door. There were no windows. The only light came from a naked overhead bulb. He could hear someone on the other side of the door. They had taken his watch, so he had no idea what time it was. His captors brought him food at very irregular intervals, which made it difficult to ascertain how much time had passed.

Once, when food was brought to him, Jason had noticed his laptop computer and cellular phone resting on a small table just on the other side of the door. Other than that the outer room was much like the one he was in. The silver case had been taken from him. There had been nothing in it, he was now reasonably certain. What was going on was beginning to become clear to him. Christ, what a sucker! He thought of his wife and child, and how desperately he wanted to be with them again. What Sidney must be thinking had happened to him. He could barely comprehend the emotions she must be feeling right now. If only he had told her the truth. She would be in a position to help him. He sighed. But the bottom line was that telling her anything would have put her in danger. That was something he would never do, not even if it meant never seeing her again. He wiped the tears from his eyes as the image of eternal separation fixed itself in his head. He stood up and shook himself.

He wasn't dead yet, although the grimness of his captors was far from reassuring. However, they had made one mistake despite their obvious care. Jason took off his glasses, placed them on the concrete floor and carefully scrunched them with his foot. He picked up one jagged piece of glass, positioned it carefully in his hand, then walked over to the door and pounded on it.

"Hey, can I get something to drink?"

"Shut up in there." The voice sounded annoyed. It wasn't De-Pazza, probably the other man.

"Listen, dammit, I've got medication to take and I need something to take it with."

"Try your own spit." It was the same man's voice. Jason could hear a chuckle.

"The pills are too big," Jason shouted, hoping someone else might hear him.

"Too bad."

Jason could hear the pages of a magazine being leisurely turned.

"Great, I won't take them and I'll just keel over dead right here. It's for high blood pressure and right now mine's clear through the roof."

Now Jason could hear a chair scraping the floor, keys jangling. "Step back from the door."

Jason did so, but only a short distance. The door swung open. The man held the keys in one hand, his gun in the other.

"Where are the pills?" he asked, his eyes narrowing.

"In my hand."

"Show 'em to me."

Jason shook his head in disgust. "I don't believe this." As he stepped forward, he opened his hand and held it out. The man glanced at it. Jason swung his leg up, connected with the man's hand and sent the gun flying.

"Shit," the man yelled. He hurtled toward Jason, who met him with a perfect uppercut. The jagged glass caught the man right across the cheek. He howled in pain and staggered back, blood streaming down from the grisly wound.

The man was large, but his muscle had long since started to turn to fat. Jason exploded into him like a battering ram, smashing the older man flat against the wall. They briefly struggled, but the far stronger Jason was able to hurl the man around until he collided face first with the cinder-block wall. One more serious head thrust into the wall and two vicious punches to the man's kidney's and he slumped to the cold floor unconscious.

Jason picked up the gun and ran through the open doorway. With his free hand he scooped up his laptop and cell phone. Stopping for a moment to gauge his surroundings, he spotted another doorway and, pausing to listen for any sound, he hurried through it.

He stopped and let his eyes adjust to the darkness. He swore under his breath. He was in the same warehouse, or one identical to it. They must have been driving in circles. He cautiously slipped down the steps and onto the main floor. The limo was nowhere in sight. He suddenly heard a sound from the direction he had just come. He raced to the overhead door, searching frantically for the switch to open it. His head jerked around as he heard running footsteps. He ran across the warehouse to the opposite end. Hidden in a corner behind some fifty-gallon drums, he carefully placed the gun on the floor and clicked open his laptop.

The laptop was a sophisticated model complete with a built-in phone modem. He turned on the computer's power switch and used a short cable housed in his laptop's case to hook his computer's modem to his cellular phone. Sweat poured from his brow as the machine took a few seconds to warm up. Using his mouse, he clicked through the necessary function screens and then, in the darkness, his fingers guided by strong familiarity with the keys, he typed his message. So intent was he on sending it, Jason did not hear the footsteps behind him. He began to type in the e-mail address of the recipient. He was sending the message to his own America Online mailbox. Unfortunately, like people who couldn't remember their own phone number because they never called it, Jason, who never sent e-mail to himself, didn't have his e-mail address programmed into his laptop. He did remember it, but typing it cost him a few precious seconds. While his finger hovered over the keys, a light flashed over him, a strong arm locked around his neck.

Jason managed to click on the send command. The message leaped electronically off the screen. For one brief moment. Then a hand slashed in front of his face, grabbed the laptop from him, the cell phone dangling precariously in the air at the end of the short cable. Jason could see the thick fingers hitting the necessary keys to cancel the e-mail.

Jason swung a short, brutal punch that connected with his assailant's jaw. The grip relaxed on the laptop and Jason was able to snatch it and the cell phone away. He slammed a foot into his attacker's abdomen and raced off, leaving the man face down on the floor. Unfortunately, he left the 9mm behind as well.

Heading toward a distant corner of the warehouse, Jason now could hear racing feet coming from all directions. There would be no escape for him, that was clear. But he could still do something. He dodged behind some metal stairs, dropped to his knees and started typing. A shout nearby made him jerk his head up. His flying fingers, so accurate now, failed him as his right index finger hit the wrong keystroke when typing the recipient's e-mail address. He began typing the message, the sweat pouring down his face, stinging his eyes. His breath came in big clumps, his neck ached from the stranglehold. It was so dark, he couldn't even see the keyboard. He alternated between staring at the tiny electronic images on the screen to desperately scanning the warehouse as the shouts and running feet came nearer and nearer to his location.

He didn't realize that the small amount of light thrown off by the computer screen was like a laser show in the dark warehouse. The sound of men running hard toward him barely ten feet away made him cut short his message. Jason hit the send button and waited for the confirming signal. Then he deleted both the file he had sent and the name of the recipient. He did not look at the e-mail address as his finger held down the delete key. He then slid the laptop and cell phone across the floor and underneath the steps until they stopped far back in the corner. He had time to do nothing more as multiple searchlights hit him squarely in the face. He slowly stood up, his breathing heavy but his eyes defiant.

A few minutes later the limo pulled out of the warehouse. Jason was slumped over in the backseat, several lacerations and deep bruises on his face, his breathing irregular. Kenneth Scales had the laptop open and was cursing loudly as he stared at the small screen, powerless to reverse what had occurred minutes earlier. In a fit of rage he tore Jason's cell phone free from the cable and repeatedly smashed it against the door of the limo until it dropped to the floor in jagged pieces. Then he pulled a small secured-line cellular phone from his inner jacket pocket and punched in a number. Scales spoke slowly into the phone. Archer had contacted someone, sent some message. There were a number of possible recipients and they would all have to be checked out and appropriately dealt with. But that potential problem would just have to keep. Other matters would now demand his time. Scales clicked off and looked over at Jason. When Jason managed to look up, the pistol's muzzle was almost against his forehead.

"Who, Jason? Who'd you send the message to?"

Jason managed to catch his breath as he gripped his painfully bruised ribs. "No way. Not in a million years, pal."

Scales pushed the muzzle flush against Jason's head.

"Pull the trigger, you asshole!" Jason screamed.

Scales's finger started to press down on the Glock's trigger, but then he stopped and roughly pushed Jason back against the seat.

"Not yet, Jason. Didn't I tell you? You've got another gig to do."

Jason stared up helplessly at him as Scales smiled wickedly.

Special Agent Raymond Jackson's eyes took in the area with one efficient sweep. He moved into the room, shutting the door behind him. Jackson shook his head in quiet amazement. Arthur Lieberman had been described to him as a fortune-builder with a career several decades long. This hovel did not conform to that description. He checked his watch. The forensics team would be here shortly to conduct an in-depth search. Although it seemed unlikely that Arthur Lieberman personally knew who had blown him out of a peaceful Virginia sky, on investigations of this magnitude, every possibility had to be explored.

Jackson went into the tiny kitchen and quickly determined that Arthur Lieberman did not cook or eat here. There were no dishes or pans in any of the cupboards. The only visible occupant of the refrigerator was a lightbulb. The stove, though old, showed no signs of recent use. Jackson scanned the other areas of the living room and then walked into the small bathroom. With his gloved hand he carefully edged open the door to the medicine cabinet. It contained the usual toiletries, nothing of significance. Jackson was about to close the mirrored door when his eye caught the small bottle edged in between the toothpaste and the deodorant. The prescription label had dosage and refill information and the physician who had prescribed it. Agent Jackson was unfamiliar with the name of the drug. Jackson had three kids and was an informal expert on prescription and over-the-counter drugs for a host of ailments. He wrote down the name of the medication and closed the door to the medicine cabinet.

Lieberman's sleeping chamber was small, the bed little more than a cot. A small desk sat against the wall nearest the window. After examining the closet, Jackson turned his attention to the desk.

Several photos on the desk showed two men and one woman ranging in age from what looked to be late teens to mid-twenties. The photos appeared several years old. Leiberman's kids, Jackson quickly concluded.

Three drawers confronted him. One was locked. It took Jackson only a few seconds to open the locked drawer. Inside was a bundle of handwritten letters held together with a rubber band. The handwriting was careful and precise, the contents of the letters decidedly romantic. The only strange part was that they were all unsigned. Jackson muddled over that one for a moment, then replaced the letters in the drawer. He spent a few more minutes looking around until a knock on the door announced the arrival of the forensics unit.

CHAPTER FOURTEEN

During the time Sidney had been alone in her house, she had explored every crevice of the place, driven by a force that she could not come close to identifying. She sat for hours in the small window seat in the kitchen, her mind racing through her years of marriage. Every detail of those years, even moments of relative insignificance, came surging up from the depths of her subconscious. At times her mouth curled in amusement as she recalled a particularly funny memory. Those instances were brief, however, and were always followed by wracking sobs as the realization that there would be no more fun times with Jason came crashing down on her.

Finally stirring, she rose and walked up the stairs, drifted slowly down the hallway and entered Jason's small study. She looked around at the spare contents, then sat down in front of the computer. She moved her hand across the glass screen. Jason had loved computers ever since she had known him. She was computer functional, but, aside from word processing and checking her e-mail, her knowledge of the world of computer hardware and software was extremely limited.

Jason did quite a bit of correspondence by e-mail and normally checked his electronic mailbox every day. Sidney hadn't checked it since the plane crash. She decided it was time to do so. Many of Jason's friends had probably sent messages. She turned the computer on and watched the screen as a series of numbers and words trooped across that were, in large part, meaningless to her. The only one she did recognize was available memory. There was a lot of it. The system had been customized for her husband and was bursting with power.

She stared at the available memory number. With a jolt she realized that the last three digits, 7, 3 and 0, constituted the date of Jason's birthday, July 30. A deep breath prevented a quick relapse into tears. She slid open the desk drawer and idly fumbled through its contents. As an attorney she well knew the number of documents and procedures that would have to be gone through as Jason's estate was settled. Most of their property was jointly held, but there were still many legal hoops. Everyone eventually had to face such things, but she couldn't believe she had to confront them so soon.

Her fingers sifted over papers and miscellaneous office paraphernalia in the drawer, closing over one object, which she pulled out. Although she was unaware of the fact, she was holding the card Jason had thrust there before leaving for the airport. She looked at it closely. It looked like a credit card, but stamped on it was the name "Triton Global," followed by "Jason Archer" and, finally, the words "Code Restricted—Level 6." Her brow furrowed. She had never seen it before. She assumed it was some type of security pass, although it did not have her husband's photo on it. She slipped it into her pocket. The company would probably want it back.

She accessed America Online and was greeted by the computerized voice announcing that mail was indeed present in their electronic mailbox. As she had thought, it contained numerous messages from their friends. She read through them, crying freely. Finally she lost all desire to complete the task and started to exit out of the computer. She jumped as another e-mail suddenly flashed on the screen; it was addressed to ArchieJW2@aol.com, which was her husband's e-mail address. In the next instant it was gone, like a mischievous inspiration scurrying through one's head before disappearing.

Sidney hit some function keys and quickly checked the computerized mailbox again. Her brow tightened into a sea of wrinkles when she discovered it was completely empty. Sidney continued to stare at the screen. A creeping sensation was pushing her to the conclusion that she had just imagined the entire episode. It had happened so damn quickly. She rubbed at her painful eyes and sat there for another few minutes, anxiously waiting to see if the performance would be repeated, although she had no idea of its meaning. The screen remained blank.

Moments after Jason Archer had re-sent his message, another e-mail was announced by the computerized voice saying, "You've got mail." This time the message held and was duly logged into the mailbox. However, this computer mailbox was not located at the old stone and brick house, nor was it at Sidney's desk at the offices of Tyler, Stone. And, currently, there was no one home to read it. The message would just have to keep.

Sidney finally rose and left the study. For some reason the sudden flash across the computer screen had given her an absurd hope, as if Jason were somehow communicating to her, from wherever he had gone after the jet had plunged into the ground. Stupid! she told herself. That was impossible.

An hour later, after another episode of wrenching grief, her body dehydrated, she gripped a picture of Amy. She had to take care of herself. Amy needed her. She opened a can of soup, turned on the stove and a few minutes later ladled out a small quantity of beef barley into a bowl and carried it over to the kitchen table. She managed to ingest a few spoonfuls while she looked at the walls of the kitchen that Jason had planned to paint that weekend after much nagging from her. Everywhere she turned, a new memory, a fresh pang of guilt, battered her. How could it not? This place contained as much of them, as much of him, as was possible for an inanimate shell to hold.

She could feel the hot soup passing through her system, but her body still shuddered as though it were almost out of fuel. She grabbed a bottle of Gatorade from the refrigerator and drank straight from the container until the shakes stopped. Yet even as the physical side started to calm down, she could feel the inner forces building once again.

She jumped up from the table and walked into the living room; she turned on the TV. Numbly channel-hopping, she ran across the inevitable: live news coverage of the crash. She felt guilty about her curiosity regarding an event that had ripped her husband from her. However, she could not deny that she craved knowledge about the event, as if her approaching it from a coldly factual angle would at least temporarily lessen the terrible hurt that tore at her.

The newswoman was standing near the crash site. In the background the collection process was being dutifully conducted. Sidney watched the debris being carried and sorted into various piles. Suddenly she almost fell out of her chair. One worker had passed directly behind the newswoman as she rambled on with her story. The canvas bag with the crisscross pattern barely looked damaged, only singed and dirtied at the edges. She could even make out the large initials written in the bold, black print. The bag was placed in a pile of similar items. For one awful moment, Sidney Archer couldn't move. Her limbs were completely locked. The next moment she was all action.

She ran upstairs, changed into jeans and a thick white sweater, put on low warm boots and hurriedly packed a bag. In a few minutes she was backing the Ford out of the garage. She glanced once at the Cougar convertible parked in the other garage bay. Jason had lovingly kept it running for almost ten years and its battered look had always been underscored by their memory of the sleek elegance of the Jag. Even the Explorer looked brand-new by comparison with the Cougar. The contrast had always amused her before. Tonight it did not, as a new cascade of tears blurred her vision and made her slam on the brakes.

She beat her hands on the dashboard until jarring pain shot up to her elbows. Finally she laid her head against the steering wheel as she struggled to regain her breath. She thought she would be nauseous as the taste of beef barley made its way into her throat, but it finally receded into the depths of her quivering stomach. Moments later she was heading down the quiet street. She looked back briefly at her home. They had lived there almost three years. A wonderful place built almost a hundred years ago with large-proportioned rooms, wide crown moldings, random-width oak plank flooring and enough secret nooks that you didn't have to try very hard to find a quiet place to lose yourself on a gloomy Sunday afternoon. It had seemed a terrific place to raise kids, they had both decided. So much they had wanted to do. So much.

She felt another wave of sobs climbing diligently toward the surface. She sped up and turned on to a main road. In ten more minutes she was looking at the red and yellow colors of the neighborhood McDonald's. She pulled into the drive-through and ordered a large coffee. As she pressed the window button, she was staring into the freckled face of a gangly teenage girl, her long, auburn hair tied back in a ponytail, who would more than likely grow up into a lovely young woman, just as Amy would. Sidney hoped the girl still had her father. It jolted her again to think that Amy was now fatherless.

Within an hour she was headed west on Route 29, a narrow black strip of road that split gentle rolling Virginia countryside as it cut a roughly forty-five-degree angle through Virginia and on across the North Carolina border. Sidney had traveled the road many times while she attended law school at the University of Virginia in Charlottesville. It was a beautiful drive past long-silent Civil War battlefields and old yet still functioning family farms. In the fall and spring the colors of the foliage rivaled any painting she had ever seen. Names like Brightwood, Locust Dale, Madison and Montpelier flashed by on the road signs, and Sidney thought back to the many trips she and Jason had taken to Charlottesville to attend some function or other. Now no part of the familiar road or countryside felt comforting.

The night swept on. Sidney looked at the dashboard clock and was surprised to see it was nearing one in the morning. She accelerated and the truck flew down the empty road. Outside, the temperature continued to drop as she headed into higher elevations. Thick clouds had settled in and the spread of her headlights was the only contrast to the pitch-blackness. She turned up the truck's heat even more and hit her high beams.

An hour later, she glanced at the map resting next to her on the front seat. Her turnoff was coming up. She held her body rigid as she drew nearer to her destination. She started to count the miles on her odometer.

At Ruckersville she headed west. She was now in Greene County, Virginia, rustic and rural, far removed from the pace of life Sidney knew and had thrived in. The county seat was the town of Standardsville, whose emotional climate was now anything but, with an impact crater and scorched earth appearing on television screens all over the world.

Sidney finally pulled off the road and peered around to try to fix her location. The darkness of the countryside enveloped her. She flicked on the reading light and held the map close to her face. Getting her bearings, she continued down the slash of road another mile until she rounded a bend of partially naked slender elms, knotty maples and towering oaks, after which the vista opened up to stark, flat farmland.

At the end of the road, a police cruiser was parked near a rusted, leaning mailbox. To the right of the mailbox was a dirt road that snaked its way back, with full, well-tended evergreen hedges bordering the dirt road on either side. In the distance the earth seemed to glow like a huge phosphorous cave.

She had found the place.

In the swirl of the Explorer's headlights, Sidney noticed that it was lightly snowing. As she pulled up closer, the door of the police car opened and a uniformed officer wearing a neon-orange all-weather slicker stepped from the vehicle. He walked over to the Ford, pointed his flashlight at the license plate and then swept it over the Explorer's exterior before its beam came to rest on the driver's-side window.

Sidney took a deep breath, hit the window switch and the glass slowly slid down.

The officer's face appeared at her shoulder. His upper lip was partially covered by a bushy mustache streaked with gray, the corners of his eyes were heavily stacked with wrinkles. Even under the orange raincoat, the bulky strength of his shoulders and chest were evident. The officer made a perfunctory scan of the interior and then settled on Sidney.

"Can I help you, ma'am?" The voice was tired, and not just physically.

"I . . . I came . . ." She faltered. Her mind suddenly went blank. She looked at him, her mouth moved, but no words came out.

The cop's shoulders sagged. "Ma'am, it's been one helluva long day up here, y'know? And I've had a lot of people just happen on by here that really have no business being here." He paused and studied her features. "Are you lost?" His tone made it clear that he did not believe she had strayed one inch off her intended course.

She managed to shake her head.

He looked at his watch. "The TV trucks finally headed out on down to Charlottesville about an hour ago. They went to get some sleep. I suggest you do the same. You can see and read all you want on the TV and in the papers, believe me." He straightened back up, signaling that their conversation, one-sided as it was, was at an end. "Can you find your way back out?"

Sidney slowly nodded and the cop lightly touched the brim of his cap and headed back to his car. Sidney turned the truck around and started to drive away. She looked in the rearview mirror and abruptly stopped. The strange glow beckoned to her. She opened the truck door and got out. She opened the rear door of the Ford, pulled out her overcoat and put it on.

The cop watched her walk toward the patrol car and he got out too. His slicker was wet from the snow's moisture. Sidney's blond hair was covered by flakes as the winter storm stepped up its intensity.

Before the cop could open his mouth, Sidney held up one hand.

"My name is Sidney Archer. My husband, Jason Archer . . ." Her voice began to waver here as the full effect of the words she was about to speak hit her. She bit her lip, hard, and continued. "He was on the plane. The airline offered to bring me down here, but . . . I decided to come down on my own. I'm really not sure why, but I did."

The cop stared at her. His eyes had softened considerably; the heavy mustache drooped like a weeping willow, his erect shoulders slumped down. "I'm really sorry, Ms. Archer. I really am. Some of the other . . . family have already come by. They didn't stay very long. The FAA people don't want anybody up there right now. They're coming back tomorrow to walk the area looking . . . looking for . . ." His voice trailed off and he looked down at the ground.

"I just came to see . . ." Her voice failed her too. She looked at him, her eyes a blistering red, her cheeks hollow, her forehead frozen into a vertical column of wrinkles. Although tall, she seemed childlike in her overcoat, her shoulders hunched forward, hands plunged deeply into pockets—as though she were disappearing as well, along with Jason.

The cop looked embarrassed, his vacillation evident. He glanced up the dirt road, then down at his shoes and then back at her. "Hold on a minute, Ms. Archer." He ducked back inside his patrol car. Then his head popped back out. "Ma'am, come on in here out of the snow, please, before you catch something."

Sidney climbed inside the patrol car. It smelled of cigarette smoke and spilled coffee. A rolled-up *People* magazine was tucked inside a crevice in the front seat. A small computer screen sat atop a stack of electronic hardware. The cop rolled down his window and swept the patrol car's searchlight across the rear of the Explorer. He rolled the window back up and proceeded to hit a number of keys on the keyboard and then studied the screen. He looked at Sidney.

"Just punching in your license plate. Gotta confirm your identity, ma'am. Not that I don't believe you. I mean, you didn't drive up here in the middle of the night for a vacation. I know that. But I got rules to go by."

"I understand."

The screen filled with information, which the officer quickly studied. He pulled a clipboard off the dash and ran through a list of names. He looked up at her briefly, embarrassment again displayed on his features.

"You said *Jason* Archer was your husband?"

She slowly nodded. *Was?* The word was numbing to her. She felt her hands begin to shake uncontrollably, the vein in her left temple to pulse spasmodically.

"I just had to make sure. There was another Archer on the plane too. A Benjamin Archer."

For a moment her hopes soared, but reality threw her immediately back down. There had been no mistake. If there had been, Jason would have called. He had been on that plane. As much as she had willed him not to be, he had been. She looked over at the distant lights. He was there now. Still there.

She cleared her throat. "I have some photo identification, Officer." She opened her wallet and handed it across.

He noted the driver's license and then his eyes caught on the photo of Jason, Sidney and Amy, taken barely a month ago. He stared at it for several moments. Then he handed the wallet back quickly. "I don't need to check anything else, Ms. Archer." He looked out the window. "There's a couple of other deputies stationed along up the road, and a slew of National Guard all around. Some of the guys from Washington are still up there, that's what all the lights are for." He looked at her. "I really can't leave my post, Ms. Archer." He looked down at his hands. Her eyes trailed his. She saw the wedding ring on his left hand, the ring finger swollen by time so that the simple gold band would never come off without taking the digit with it. The officer's eyes crinkled and a faint bit of moisture appeared on his cheek. He looked away suddenly, his hand quickly rising to his face and then back down.

He started the car and put it in gear. He looked over at her. "I can understand why you came up here, but I don't recommend that you stay long, Ms. Archer. It's not . . . well, it's not that kind of a place." The patrol car swayed and bumped over the dirt road. The officer stared intently ahead, toward the blinding lights. "There's a devil in hell and a Lord God above, and, while the devil had his way with that plane, all those people are with the Lord right now, Ms. Archer, every last one of 'em. You believe that, and don't let anybody ever tell you different."

Sidney found herself nodding at his words, wanting so badly to believe that they were true.

As they approached the lights, Sidney felt her mind recede farther and farther into the distance. "There was . . . a bag, canvas with blue crisscross stripes. It was my husband's. It has his initials on it. JWA. I actually bought it for him for a trip we took several years ago." She briefly smiled as the memory washed over her. "It was really for a joke. We had sort of had an argument and it was the ugliest bag I could find at the time. Of course, as it turned out, he loved it."

She abruptly looked up and caught the officer's surprised look. "I . . . I saw it on the TV. It didn't even look damaged. Is there any way I could see it?"

"I'm sorry, Ms. Archer. Whatever's been collected has already been taken away. The truck came just about an hour ago to take away the last shipment for the day."

"Do you know where it goes?"

The officer shook his head. "It wouldn't matter if I did. They wouldn't let you near it. After the investigation is complete, they'll return it, I expect. But from the looks of this one, that could be years. Again, I'm sorry."

The patrol car finally stopped a few feet away from another uniformed policeman. The officer got out of the car and conferred briefly with his colleague, pointing twice in the direction of the police cruiser while Sidney sat there, unable to take her eyes off the lights.

She was startled when the officer leaned his head in the car. "Ms. Archer, you can get out here."

Sidney opened the car door and got out. She briefly looked at the other officer and he nervously nodded toward her, pain in his eyes. There was pain, apparently, everywhere. These men too would have rather been home with their families. Here there was death; it was everywhere. It seemed to cling to her clothes, much like the snowfall.

"Ms. Archer, when you're ready to leave, you tell Billy over there and he'll radio me. I'll come right up and get you."

As he started to get back in his cruiser, she called to him. "What's your name?"

The officer looked back. "Eugene, ma'am. Deputy Eugene McKenna."

"Thank you, Eugene."

He nodded and touched the brim of his cap. "Please don't stay too long, Ms. Archer."

As the car drove away, Billy led her toward the lights. He kept his eyes straight ahead. Sidney didn't know how much Officer McKenna had told his partner, but she could feel the distress emanating from his body. He was a slender straw of a man, young, barely twenty-five, she thought, and he looked sickened and nervous.

He finally stopped walking. Up ahead Sidney could see people moving slowly across the property. Barricades and yellow police tape were everywhere. Under the artificial daylight, Sidney could see the utter devastation. It resembled a battlefield, the earth seemingly inflicted with a terrible surface wound.

The young police officer touched her arm. "Ma'am, you oughta stay back around here. Those folk from Washington are real particular about people messing around up here. They're afraid somebody might stumble over . . . you know, mess up stuff." He took a deep breath. "There's just things everywhere, ma'am. Everywhere! I ain't never seen anything like it and I hope I never do again so long as I live." He looked off in the distance again. "When you're ready, I'll be down there." He pointed in the direction from which they had come and then headed back down.

Sidney wrapped her coat around her and brushed the snow from her hair. She unconsciously moved forward, then stopped, then started advancing again. Directly under the umbrella of light, mounds of dirt had been thrown up. She had seen that on the news now countless times. The impact crater. They said the entire plane was in there, and though she knew it to be true, she could not believe it was possible.

The impact crater. Jason was in there too. It was a thought that had become so deep, so wrenching, that instead of sending her into hysterics, it simply incapacitated her. She clenched her eyes shut and then reopened them. Thick tears rolled down her cheeks, and she did not bother to wipe them away.

She did not expect to ever smile again.

Even when she forced herself to think of Amy, of the wonderful little girl Jason had left her, not a trace of happiness was able to break through her utter sorrow. She stared ahead as cold winds buffeted her, her long hair swirling around her head.

While she continued to watch, several large pieces of equipment headed over to the crater, engines whining, black, smoky exhaust gushing up from their bowels. Steam shovels and earth movers attacked the pit with great force, lifting up huge mouthfuls of earth and depositing them in waiting dump trucks, which headed out on special routes over terrain that had already been searched. Speed was the overriding concern, even paramount to the risk of further damaging the aircraft's remains. What everyone wanted desperately to uncover was the FDR. That was more important than worrying about turning a quarter-inch fragment into something smaller by the accelerated excavation work.

Sidney noticed the snow was adhering to the ground—an obvious concern to the investigators, she assumed, as she saw a number of them racing around with searchlights, only stopping long enough to stick small flags in the rapidly whitening earth. When she moved closer, she made out the green-clad figures of the National Guardsmen as they patrolled their sectors, rifles slung over their shoulders, their heads turning constantly in the direction of the crater. Like an omnipotent magnet, the crash site seemed inexorably to demand everyone's attention. The price to be paid for the innumerable joys of life, it seemed, was the constant threat of swift, inexplicable death.

As Sidney moved forward again, her foot caught on something covered by the snow. She bent down to see what it was, and the words of the young policeman came back to her. *There are things everywhere. Everywhere!* She froze, but then continued to search with the innate curiosity of human beings. A moment later she was running down the dirt road, her feet fumbling and slipping in the snow, her arms jerking awkwardly forward, violent sobs exploding from her lungs.

She never saw the man until she collided headlong into him, buckling his legs. They both went down, he as surprised as she, perhaps even more so.

"Damn," Lee Sawyer grunted as he landed on a clod of dirt, the wind knocked out of him. Sidney, however, was on her feet in a second and continued sprinting down the twisting path. Sawyer started to go after her until his knee locked, a recurring condition compliments of his chasing down an athletic bank robber on hard pavement for twenty long blocks many years before. "Hey," he yelled after her as he awkwardly hopped around on one foot, rubbing at his knee. He shone his flashlight in her direction.

When Sidney Archer turned her head, he caught her profile in the arc of the light. A second later he snatched a glimpse of her horror-filled eyes. Then she was gone. He gingerly stepped over to the area where he had first spotted her. He shone his flashlight on the ground. Who the hell was she and what was she doing up here? Then he shrugged. Probably a curious area resident who had seen something she wished she hadn't. A minute later Sawyer's light confirmed his suspicions. He bent down and picked up the small shoe. It looked tiny and helpless in his big paw. Sawyer looked back in Sidney Archer's direction and sighed deeply in the darkness. His large body began to tremble in almost uncontrollable rage as he stared at the terrible hole in the earth dead ahead. He fought back an urge to scream at the top of his lungs. There had only been a handful of times in his career with the FBI that Lee Sawyer wanted to deny the persons he had run to ground the opportunity of a trial by their peers. This was one of those times. He silently prayed that when he did find those responsible for this horrendous act of violence, they would try something, anything that would provide him with the tiniest fraction of an opening, allowing him to spare the country the cost and media circus any such trial would entail. He slipped the shoe into his coat pocket and, nursing his injured knee, walked off to check in with Kaplan. Then he would head back to town. He had an appointment in Washington that afternoon. His investigation of Arthur Lieberman would now start in earnest.

A few minutes later, Officer McKenna looked anxiously at Sidney as he helped her out of the patrol car. "Ms. Archer, are you sure you don't want me to call somebody to come get you?"

Sidney, eggshell pale, limbs convulsing, her hands and clothes dirty from where she had fallen, shook her head hard. "No! No! I'm all right." She leaned up against the cruiser. Her arms and shoulders still twitched involuntarily, but at least her balance had somewhat stabilized. She closed the door of the police cruiser and started to walk unsteadily toward her Ford. She hesitated and then turned around. Officer McKenna was beside his cruiser, watching her closely.

"Eugene?"

"Yes, ma'am?"

"You were right. . . . It's not a place where you should stay too long." The words were said in the hollow tone of one entirely vacant of spirit. She turned and slowly walked toward the Ford and got in.

Deputy Eugene McKenna slowly nodded, his prominent Adam's apple sliding quickly up and down as he briefly fought the tears welling in his eyes. He opened the door of the police cruiser and fell rather than sat in the front seat. He closed the door so the sounds he was about to make would go no farther.

As Sidney retraced her route back, the cellular phone in her car buzzed. The totally unexpected sound made her jerk so badly she almost lost control of the Explorer. She looked down at the phone as complete disbelief spread over her features. No one knew where she was. She looked around at the darkness as if someone were watching her. The shorn trees were the only witnesses to her journey back home. As far as she could tell, she was the only living person around. Her hand slowly reached down to pick up the phone.

CHAPTER FIFTEEN

M_y God, Quentin, it's three in the morning."

"I wouldn't be calling unless it was really important."

"I'm not sure what you want me to say." Sidney's hand slightly trembled as she held the cellular phone. Sidney slowed the car; her foot had steadily pressed down on the accelerator as the conversation continued, until she was traveling at a dangerous rate of speed on the narrow roadway.

"Like I said, I heard you and Gamble talking on the trip back from New York. I thought you would have come to me, Sidney, not Gamble." The voice was soft but contained a certain edge.

"I'm sorry, Quentin, but he asked questions. You didn't."

"I was *trying* to give you some space."

"I appreciate that, I really do. It's just that Gamble confronted me. I mean he was nice about it, but I had to tell him something."

"And so you told him you didn't know why Jason was on that plane? That was your answer? That you had no idea he was even on the plane?" She could discern certain unspoken thoughts in his words. How could she tell Rowe something different from what she had told Gamble? And even if she revealed Jason's story for going to

Los Angeles, how could she tell Rowe that she now knew Jason hadn't gone to interview with another company? She was in an impossible situation and right now there seemed to be no way out of it. She decided, instead, to change the subject.

"How did you think to call me in the car, Quentin?" It made her feel slightly creepy that he had been able to trace her.

"I tried the house, then the office. Only place left was the car," he said simply. "To tell you the truth, I was kind of worried about you. And—" His voice abruptly stopped, as if he had decided an instant too late not to communicate the thought.

"And what?"

Rowe was hesitant on the line, but then he quickly finished his thought. "Sidney, you don't have to be a genius to figure out the question we all want answered. Why was Jason going to L.A.?"

Rowe's tone was clear enough. *He* wanted an answer to that question.

"Why would Triton care what he does on his own time?"

Rowe let out a deep sigh. "Sid, everything Triton does is highly proprietary. There are whole industries out there who spend all day long trying to steal our technology and people. You know that."

Sidney flushed. "Are you accusing Jason of selling Triton's technology to the highest bidder? That's absurd and you know it." Her husband was not here to defend himself and she damned sure wasn't going to let that insinuation go by.

Rowe sounded hurt. "I didn't say *I* was thinking it, but others here are."

"Jason would never, ever do anything like that. He worked his butt off for that company. You were his friend. How could you even make that allegation?"

"Okay, explain what he was doing on a plane to L.A. instead of painting the kitchen, because I'm about to make the one acquisition that will allow Triton to lead the world into the twenty-first century and I cannot allow anything or anyone to destroy that opportunity. It will never be repeated."

The tone in his voice was just enough to ignite every molecule of rage in Sidney Archer's body.

"I can't explain it. I'm not even going to try to explain it. I don't know what the hell's going on. I just lost my husband, *goddammit!* There's no body, there's no clothes. There's nothing left of him and you're sitting there telling me you think he was ripping you off? Damn you." The Ford swerved slightly off the road and she had to struggle to bring it back on. She slowed down once again as the vehicle hit a major rut. The jolt went through her entire body. It was getting harder to see in the swirling snow.

"Sid, please, please calm down." Rowe's voice was suddenly panicked. "Listen, I didn't mean to upset you further. I'm sorry." He paused, then quickly added, "Can I do anything for you?"

"Yeah, you can tell every friggin' person at Triton to drop dead. Why don't you go first?" She clicked the off button and tossed the phone down. The tears were pouring so fast she finally had to pull off the road. Shaking as if she had just been plunged into ice, Sidney finally undid her seat restraint and lay across the front seat, one arm covering her face for several minutes. Then she put the Ford back into gear and took to the road once more. Despite her evident exhaustion, her thoughts moved as fast as the V-6–powered Explorer. Jason had been terrified of her upcoming meeting with Triton. He probably had the job interview story ready in case of an emergency. Her meeting with Nathan Gamble and company had qualified as such. But why? What could he possibly have been involved in? All those late nights? His reticence? What had he been doing?

She looked at the dashboard clock and noted the time creeping relentlessly toward four A.M. While her mind was functioning in high gear, the rest of her wasn't. Her eyes would now barely stay open, and she had to address the obvious concern of where she would spend what was left of the night. She was coming up to Route 29. When she turned onto the highway, she went south instead of retracing her route north. A half hour later Sidney cruised through the empty streets of Charlottesville. She drove past the Holiday Inn and other possibilities for lodging and finally turned off Route 29 onto Ivy Road. She soon entered the parking lot of the Boar's Head Inn, one of the area's best-known resorts.

Within twenty minutes she had signed in and was slowly pushing her near-immobile limbs between the sheets in a well-appointed room with beautiful vistas that at the moment she cared nothing about. What a day of nightmares, all of them absolutely real. It was her last conscious thought. Two hours before dawn, Sidney Archer finally fell asleep.

CHAPTER SIXTEEN

At three o'clock in the morning, Seattle time, the thick clouds spilled open and delivered still more rain to the area. The guard huddled in the small guard shack, his feet and hands close to the floor heater. In one corner of the structure a steady stream of water trickled down the wall, forming a puddle on the ragged green carpet. The guard wearily checked the time. Four hours to go before his watch was over. He poured out the last of the hot coffee from his thermos and longed for a warm bed. Each building was leased by different companies. Some of the buildings simply stood empty, but all were secure regardless of their contents, with armed guards on-site twenty-four hours a day. The high metal fence had barbed wire at the top, although not the deadly razor wire favored at prison facilities. Video monitors were discreetly placed throughout the area. It would be a difficult place to break into.

Difficult, but far from impossible.

The figure was clad head to foot in black. It took him less than a minute to climb the fence in the back of the warehouse facility, expertly avoiding the sharp wire. Once over the fence, he slipped in and out of the shadows as the rain continued to pour down, completely covering the slight sounds that his quick-moving feet made. On his left sleeve was a miniature electronic jamming device. He passed three video cameras on the way to his destination; none of them captured his image.

Reaching the side door of Building 22, he pulled a slender wire-like device from his knapsack and inserted it in the sturdy padlock. Ten seconds later the lock hung loose.

He took the metal steps two at a time after making a visual sweep of the building's interior with his night-vision goggles. He opened the door to a room, illuminating the small space with his flashlight. He unlocked the filing cabinet and removed the surveillance camera. He placed the videotape in one part of his knapsack, reloaded the camera and replaced it in the cabinet. Five minutes later, the area was once again quiet. The guard had not yet finished his last cup of coffee.

At the crack of dawn, a Gulfstream V lifted off from the Seattle airport. The black-clad figure was now dressed in jeans and a sweat-shirt and was fast asleep in one of the luxurious cabin chairs, his dark hair falling into his youthful face. Across the aisle, Frank Hardy, head of a firm specializing in corporate security, and counter-industrial espionage, intently read every page of a lengthy report as the plane soared through the now clear morning sky; the last vestiges of the previous night's storm system had finally pushed on. Inside a metal briefcase was the videotape that had been removed from the camera in the file cabinet. The case was within easy reach of his hand. A steward appeared and poured out another cup of coffee for the plane's one awake passenger. Hardy's eyes rested on the metal briefcase. His brow wrinkled and, from long habit, his fingers traced and retraced the worry lines stamped across his forehead. Then Hardy put the report down, leaned back in his seat and stared out the cabin window as the aircraft headed east. He had a lot to think about. He was not a happy man right now. Both his jaw and his gut clenched and unclenched as the sleek jet raced on.

The Gulfstream hit its cruising altitude on a flight that would culminate in Washington, D.C. The rays of the rising sun reflected off the familiar company logo emblazoned on the aircraft's empennage. The soaring eagle represented an organization like no other. More recognized worldwide than even Coca-Cola, more feared than most of the world's largest conglomerates—which, by comparison, were aging dinosaurs awaiting the constant pull of extinction. It was the complete package as the twenty-first century hurtled toward them, just like the bold eagle symbol that was rapidly making its way into the four corners of the world and everywhere in between.

Triton Global would have it no other way.

CHAPTER SEVENTEEN

A uniformed security guard escorted Lee Sawyer through the massive lobby of the Marriner Eccles Building, the Constitution Avenue home of the Federal Reserve Board. Sawyer thought that the premises were in keeping with the enormous clout of their occupant. After walking up to the second floor, Sawyer and his escort stopped at a thick wooden door and the escort knocked. The words "Come in" filtered out to them. Sawyer moved through the doorway to a large, cozily furnished office. The floor-to-ceiling bookcases, dark furniture and ornate moldings made a somber impression. The thick drapes were closed. A green banker's lamp glowed on the large, leather-topped partners desk. The smell of cigars hovered everywhere; Sawyer could almost see gray wisps of smoke hanging in the air like ghostly apparitions. It reminded him of the scholarly studies of some of his old college professors. A small fire burning in the fireplace threw both warmth and light into the room

When a man of massive girth swiveled around in the chair behind the desk, Sawyer's attention was instantly riveted upon him. A corpulent red face housed light blue eyes hiding behind lids reduced to slits by sagging facial skin and the overgrowth of a pair of eyebrows as thick as Sawyer had ever seen. The hair was white and abundant, the nose was wide and the tip was even redder than the rest of the face. For one brief moment, Sawyer jokingly wondered if he was confronting Santa Claus.

The man rose from behind the desk, and his big, cultured voice flowing across the room to envelop Lee Sawyer dispelled all such thoughts.

"Agent Sawyer, I'm Walter Burns, vice chairman of the Federal Reserve Board."

Sawyer moved forward to grip the flabby hand. Burns matched the six-foot-three Sawyer in height, but carried at least a hundred more pounds on his frame than did the powerfully built FBI agent. Sawyer took the leather chair indicated by Burns. When Burns sat back down, Sawyer noted that he moved with a grace that was not uncommon to large men.

"I appreciate your seeing me, sir."

Burns shot the FBI man a penetrating glance. "I take it that your agency's involvement in this matter means it was not merely a mechanical or other similar problem that befell that plane?"

"We're checking through all possible scenarios. Nothing has been ruled out right now, Mr. Burns." Sawyer's features were impassive.

"My name is Walter, Agent Sawyer. Since we're both members of the sometimes unwieldy system known as the federal government, I think that allows us the pleasure of a first-name basis."

Sawyer grinned. "Mine's Lee."

"How can I help you, Lee?"

The clatter of freezing rain assaulted the window and a chill seemed suddenly to pervade the air. Burns rose and walked over to the fireplace, beckoning Sawyer to pull his chair over. While Burns placed some small pieces of kindling taken from a brass bucket onto the fire, Sawyer flipped open his notebook and briefly studied some notes. When Burns sat down across from him, Sawyer was ready.

"I realize that a lot of people have no idea what the Fed does. I mean people outside the financial markets."

Burns rubbed at one eye and Sawyer almost heard a chuckle escape the other man's lips. "If I were a betting man, I would be inclined to lay money on the fact that fully half the population of this country have no idea of the existence of the Federal Reserve System, and that nine out of ten have no clue as to what our actual purpose is. I must confess I find that anonymity enormously comforting."

Sawyer paused and then leaned toward the older man. "Who would benefit from Arthur Lieberman's death? I don't mean personally, I'm focusing on his professional side. As chairman of the Fed."

Burns's eyes widened until the slits reached the shape of half-moons, about the limits of their range. "You're implying that someone blew up that plane in order to kill Arthur? If you don't mind my saying so, that seems awfully far-fetched."

"I didn't say that was the case. That is, we're looking at everything right now." Sawyer spoke in low tones, as though he feared he would be overheard. "The fact is I've combed through the passenger manifest and your colleague was the only VIP aboard. If it was a deliberate sabotage, then one reason that jumps out would be killing the Fed chairman."

"Or just a planned terrorist attack and Arthur simply had the misfortune to be on board."

Sawyer shook his head. "If we are looking at sabotage, then I don't believe Lieberman being on the plane was a coincidence."

Burns leaned back in his chair and slowly put his feet out toward the fire. "My God!" he finally said as he stared into the fire. Although he would have looked quite at home in a three-piece suit replete with watch chain, his current attire—camel-hair sport coat, dark blue crew sweater with a white button-down shirt collar peeking out, gray pleated slacks and comfortable black loafers—did not look so out of place on his frame. Sawyer noted that the man's feet were surprisingly small for his size. Neither man spoke for at least a minute.

Sawyer finally stirred. "I know I don't have to tell you that anything I say to you tonight is extremely confidential."

Burns's head swiveled around to the FBI agent. "Secrets are something I am quite good at keeping, Lee."

"So getting back to my question: Who benefits?"

Burns considered the query for some moments and then took a

deep breath. "The United States economy is the largest in the world. Hence, as America goes, so goes the world. If another country hostile to America desired to damage our economy or disrupt the world financial markets, perpetrating an atrocity such as this could well have that effect. I have no doubt that the markets will take a staggering blow if it turns out his death was premeditated." The vice chairman shook his head sadly. "I just never thought I would live to see the day."

"How about anyone in this country who might like to see the chairman dead?" Sawyer asked again.

"As long as the Fed has existed there have been conspiracy theories painted so vividly about the institution that I'm quite sure there are more than a handful of people in this country who take them, however nonsensical they are, quite seriously."

Sawyer's eyes narrowed. "Conspiracy theories?"

Burns coughed and then loudly cleared his throat. "There are those who believe that the Fed is actually a tool for wealthy families around the globe to keep the poor in their place. Or that we take our marching orders from a small group of international bankers. I've even heard one theory that has us being the pawns of alien beings who have infiltrated all the highest positions of government. My birth certificate says Boston, Massachusetts, by the way."

Sawyer shook his head. "Christ, that's pretty wacko."

"Exactly. As if a seven-trillion-dollar economy employing well over a hundred million people could be secretly run by a handful of waistcoated tycoons."

"So one of these conspiracy groups could have plotted to kill the chairman in retaliation for perceived corruption or injustice?"

"Well, few governmental institutions are more misunderstood and feared out of ignorance than the Federal Reserve Board. When you first mentioned the possibility, I said it was far-fetched. Having thought about it for a few minutes, I have to say my initial reaction was probably not correct. But blowing up a plane . . ." Burns shook his head wearily.

Sawyer jotted down some notes. "I'd like to know more about Lieberman's background."

"Arthur Lieberman was an immensely popular man in the major financial circles. For years he was one of the top moneymakers on Wall Street, before turning to public service. Arthur called things as he saw them and he was usually right in his judgment. With a series of masterful maneuvers, he shook up the financial markets almost from the moment he became chairman. He showed them who was boss." Burns stopped to put another piece of wood on the fire. "In fact, he led the Fed in a way that I would like to think I would if ever given the opportunity."

"Any idea who might succeed Lieberman?"

Burns shook his head. "No."

"Around the time he left for Los Angeles, had anything unusual occurred at the Fed?"

Burns shrugged. "We had our FOMC meeting on the fifteenth of November, but that was a regularly scheduled event."

Sawyer looked puzzled. "FOMC?"

"Federal Open Market Committee. It's our policymaking board."

"What goes on at those meetings?"

"Well, in a shorthand version, the seven members of the Board of Governors and the presidents of five of the twelve Federal Reserve Banks look at all pertinent financial data on the economy and decide whether any actions are required with respect to money supply and interest rates."

Sawyer nodded. "When the Fed raises or lowers interest rates, for instance, then that affects the entire economy. Contracts or expands it."

"At least we think so," Burns replied sardonically. "Although our actions have not always had the results we intended."

"So was there anything unusual at this FOMC meeting?"

"No."

"Nevertheless, could you give me a rundown of exactly what was said and by whom? It might seem irrelevant, but getting a motive could really help us track down whoever did this."

Burns's voice went up an octave. "Impossible. The actual deliberations of FOMC meetings are absolutely confidential and cannot be divulged to you or anyone else."

"Walter, I won't push it now, but with all due respect, if any information discussed at these meetings is relevant to the FBI's investigation, rest assured that we will have access to it." Sawyer stared at him until Burns dropped his gaze.

"A brief report detailing the minutes of the meeting is released six to eight weeks after the meeting is held," Burns said slowly, "but only after the occurrence of the next meeting. The actual results of the meetings, whether any action was taken or not, are released to the news media the same day."

"I read in the paper where the Fed left the interest rates the same."

Burns pursed his lips and then eyed Sawyer. "That's right, we didn't adjust the interest rates."

"How exactly do you adjust rates?"

"There are actually two interest rates that are directly affected by the Fed, Lee. The Federal Funds Rate is the interest rate banks charge other banks who borrow funds to meet reserve requirements. If that rate goes up or down, interest rates on bank CDs, T-bills, mortgages and commercial paper will soon follow. The Fed sets the target Federal Funds Rate at the FOMC meetings. Then the New York Federal Reserve Bank, through its Domestic Trading Desk, buys or sells government securities, which in turn restricts or expands the supply of money available to banks to ensure that that interest rate is maintained. We call that adding or subtracting liquidity. That's how Arthur took the bulls by the horns when he became chairman; by adjusting the Fed Funds Rate in ways the market didn't anticipate. The second interest rate which can be affected by the Fed is the Discount Rate, the rate charged by the Fed to banks for loans by the Fed. However, the Discount Rate is tied to loans for what amounts to emergency purposes; thus, it's known as the 'window of last resort.' Banks who frequent that window too often will come under increased regulatory scrutiny, since it's seen as a sign of weakness in banking circles. For that reason, most banks will borrow money from other banks at the slightly higher Federal Funds Rate, since there is no stigma attached to that channel of credit."

Sawyer decided to change direction. "Okay, had Lieberman been acting strangely? Anything bothering him? Any threats that you know of?"

Burns shook his head.

"This trip to L.A. that Lieberman was taking, was it a regular thing?"

"Very regular. Arthur was meeting with Charles Tiedman, president of the San Francisco Federal Reserve Bank. Arthur was very good about making the rounds of the presidents, and he and Charles were old friends."

"Wait a minute. If Tiedman is head of the San Francisco bank, why was Lieberman flying into L.A.?"

"There is a branch office of the Fed there. Also, Charles and his wife live in Los Angeles and Arthur would stay with them."

"But he would've just seen Tiedman at the November fifteenth meeting."

"That's right. But Arthur's trip to L.A. was planned well in advance. It was only a coincidence that it occurred shortly after the FOMC meeting. However, I do know he was anxious to talk to Charles."

"Do you know what about?"

Burns shook his head. "You'd have to ask Charles."

"Anything else that might help me?"

Burns considered the question briefly and then shook his head again. "I can't think of anything in Arthur's personal background that would have led to this abomination."

Sawyer rose and shook Burns's hand. "I appreciate the information, Walter."

When Sawyer turned to leave, Burns gripped his shoulder. "Agent Sawyer, the information we have at the Fed is so enormously valuable that the slightest slip could reap incredible profits for undeserving individuals. I guess I've become extremely tight-lipped over the years to prevent just such an occurrence."

"I understand."

Burns put a flabby hand on the door as Sawyer buttoned up his coat. "So, do you have any suspects yet?"

The agent turned back to Burns. "Sorry, Walter, we have secrets at the FBI too."

Henry Wharton sat behind his desk, nervously tapping his foot on the carpeted floor. The managing partner of Tyler, Stone was small in stature but large in legal ability. Partially bald with a trim gray mustache, he looked every bit the senior partner in a major law firm. After thirty-five years of representing the elite of American business, Wharton was not easily intimidated. However, if anyone came close, it was the man currently seated across from him.

"So that's all she told you? That she was unaware her husband was on the plane at all?" Wharton asked.

Nathan Gamble's eyes were half closed as he looked down at his hands. He now looked up at Wharton. The movement made the attorney jerk slightly.

"That's all I asked her."

Wharton shook his head sadly. "Oh, I see. Well, I know when I spoke with her she was devastated. Poor thing. Such a shock, right out of the blue like that. And—"

Wharton broke off speaking as Gamble stood up and went over to the window behind the lawyer's desk. He studied the Washington landscape in the late morning sunlight. "It occurred to me, Henry, that further questioning might better come from you." Gamble put one big hand on Wharton's narrow shoulder and gently squeezed.

Wharton quickly nodded. "Yes, yes, I can understand your thinking on that point."

Gamble strolled over to peruse numerous diplomas from prestigious universities neatly lining one wall of Wharton's expansive quarters. "Very impressive. I never finished high school. I don't know if you knew that or not." He looked over his shoulder at the lawyer.

"I didn't," Wharton said quietly.

"I guess I did okay for a dropout." Gamble shrugged his thick shoulders.

"Quite the understatement. Your success is unparalleled," Wharton said quickly.

"Hell, I started with nothing, probably end up that way."

"I hardly think that."

Gamble took a moment to straighten one of the diplomas. He turned back to Wharton. "Getting to particulars, it was obvious to me that Sidney Archer knew her husband *was* on that plane."

Wharton started. "You're saying you think she lied to you? No disrespect, Nathan, but I can't believe that."

Gamble returned to his chair. Wharton was about to speak again, but Gamble fixed the lawyer with a gaze that froze him. Gamble resumed speaking. "Jason Archer was working on a major project for me. Organizing all of Triton's financial records for the CyberCom deal. Guy's a friggin' computer genius. He had access to everything. Everything!" Gamble slowly pointed a finger across the desk. Wharton nervously rubbed his hands together but kept silent. "Now, Henry, you know that CyberCom is a deal I have to have—at least everyone keeps telling me that."

"Absolutely brilliant match," Wharton ventured.

"Something like that." Gamble pulled out a cigar and took a minute to light up. He blew smoke in Wharton's general direction. "Anyway, on the one hand I've got Jason Archer privy to all my stuff, and on the other I've got Sidney Archer heading up my deal team. You following me?"

Wharton's brow collapsed in puzzlement. "I'm afraid, no, I'm—"

"There are other companies out there who want CyberCom as badly as I do. They'd pay a lot of money to get their hands on my deal terms. Then they'd come in and screw me. I don't like to get fucked, at least not that way. You understand?"

"Yes, certainly, Nathan. But how—"

"And you also know that one of the companies who'd like to get their hands on CyberCom is RTG."

"Nathan, if you're suggesting—"

"Your firm also represents RTG."

"Nathan, you know we've taken care of that. This firm is not representing RTG on their bid for CyberCom in any way, shape or form."

"Philip Goldman's still a partner here, isn't he? And he's still RTG's top gun, isn't he?"

"Of course. We couldn't exactly ask him to leave. It was merely a client conflict and one that has been more than adequately compensated for. Philip Goldman is not working with RTG on its bid for CyberCom."

"You're sure?"

"Positive," Wharton said quickly.

Gamble smoothed down the front of his shirt. "Are you having Goldman followed twenty-four hours a day, his phone lines tapped, his mail read, his business associates shadowed?"

"No, of course not!"

"Then you can hardly be positive he's not working for RTG and against me, can you?"

"I have his word," Wharton said curtly. "And we have certain controls in place."

Gamble played with an elegantly shaped ring on one of his fingers. "Much the same, you can't know what your other partners are really up to, including Sidney Archer, can you?"

"She has the highest integrity of anyone I've ever met, not to mention one of the sharpest minds." Wharton was bristling now.

"And yet she's completely ignorant of her own husband climbing on a plane to Los Angeles, where RTG happens to have its U.S. headquarters. That's quite a coincidence, don't you think?"

"You can't blame her husband's actions on Sidney."

Gamble took the cigar out of his mouth and deliberately removed a bit of fuzz from his suit coat. "What are the Triton billings up to per year now, Henry? Twenty million? Forty million? I can get the exact number when I get back to the office. It's in that ballpark, wouldn't you say?" Gamble stood up. "Now, you and I go back a few years. You know my style. Somebody thinks they got the best of me, they're wrong. It may take me some time, but the knife comes back at you and cuts twice as deep as the hit I took." Gamble put the cigar on Wharton's desk, placed his hands palm down on the leather surface and leaned forward so that he was barely a foot from Wharton's face. "If I lose CyberCom because my own people sold me out, when I come back at the persons responsible it'll be like the big old Mississippi flooding its banks. A whole lot of potential victims out there, most of them entirely blameless, only I'm not going to take the time to sort them out. Do you understand me?" Gamble's tone was low and calm and yet it slammed into Wharton like a giant fist.

Wharton swallowed hard as he stared into the intense brown eyes of the Triton chief. "I believe I do, yes."

Gamble put on his overcoat and picked up his cigar stub. "Have a good day, Henry. When you talk to Sidney, tell her I said hello."

It was one o'clock in the afternoon when Sidney pulled the Ford out of the parking lot of the Boar's Head and quickly made her way back toward Route 29. She drove past the old Memorial Gymnasium where she had once grunted and sweated and hit tennis balls in between the rigors of law school. She pulled her car into a parking garage at the Corner, a favorite hangout of the college crowd, with its numerous bookstores, restaurants and bars.

She slipped into one of the cafés and purchased a cup of coffee and a copy of the day's *Washington Post*. She sat down at one of the small wooden tables and looked over the paper's headlines. She almost fell out of her chair.

The type was bold, thick and marched across the page with the urgency its contents deserved. FEDERAL RESERVE BOARD CHAIRMAN ARTHUR LIEBERMAN KILLED IN AIRPLANE CRASH. Next to the headline was a photo of Lieberman. Sidney was struck by the man's penetrating eyes.

Sidney quickly read the story. Lieberman had been a passenger on Flight 3223. He took regular monthly trips to Los Angeles to meet with the San Francisco Federal Reserve Bank president, Charles Tiedman, and the ill-fated Western Airlines flight had been one of those regular excursions. Sixty-two years old, and divorced, Lieberman had headed the Federal Reserve for the last four years. The article devoted a great deal of space to Lieberman's illustrious financial career and the respect he commanded across the globe. Indeed, the

official news of his death had not been reported until now, because
the government was doing its best to prevent a panic in the financial community. Despite those efforts, the financial markets all over
the world had begun to suffer. The story ended with a notice of a
memorial service for Lieberman the following Sunday in Washington.

There was an additional story about the plane accident farther
back in the front section. There were no new developments, only
that the NTSB was still investigating. It could be over a year before
the world knew why Flight 3223 had ended up in a farmer's plowed-
under cornfield instead of on the tarmac at LAX. Weather, mechanical failure, sabotage and everything in between was being
considered, but for now it was all just speculation.

Sidney finished her coffee, discarded the newspaper and pulled
her portable phone out of her bag. She dialed her parents' house and
spoke for some time to her daughter, coaxing a few words out of
Amy; her daughter was still shy on the phone. Then Sidney spent a
few minutes talking with her mother and father. She next called her
answering machine. There were numerous messages, but one that
plainly stood out from the rest: Henry Wharton. Tyler, Stone had
generously allowed her all the time off she needed to deal with this
personal catastrophe. Sidney was convinced that the rest of her life
would not be long enough. Henry had sounded worried, nervous
even. She knew what that meant: Nathan Gamble had paid him a
visit.

She quickly dialed the familiar number and was put through to
Wharton's office. She tried her best to steady her nerves while she
waited for him to pick up. Wharton could be a holy terror or awe-
inspiring mentor, depending on whether you were in favor or not.
He had always been one of Sidney's biggest supporters. But now?
She took a deep breath when he came on the line.

"Hello, Henry."

"Sid, how are you holding up?"

"I'm still numb, to tell you the truth."

"Maybe that's best. For now. You'll get through this. It might not
seem like it, but you will. You're strong."

"Thanks for the support, Henry. I do feel bad for leaving you in the lurch. What with CyberCom and all."

"I know, Sidney. Don't worry about that."

"Who's taking the lead on it?" She wanted to avoid diving right into the Gamble issue.

Wharton didn't answer right away. When he did, his voice was lower. "Sid, what do you think of Paul Brophy?"

The question caught her by surprise, but it brought some welcome relief. Perhaps she had been wrong about Gamble talking to Wharton. "I like Paul, Henry."

"Yes, yes, I know that. He's a pleasant enough fellow, talented rainmaker, talks a good game."

Sidney spoke slowly. "You want to know whether he can head the CyberCom deal?"

"As you know, he's been involved up until now. But it's stepped up to another level. I want to keep the circle of attorneys with access as limited as possible. You know why. It's no secret about our potential problem with Goldman and his representation of RTG. I don't want even the hint of an impropriety. I also only want guns on that team that can contribute real substance to the process. I'd like your opinion on him under those circumstances."

"This conversation is confidential?"

"Absolutely."

Sidney spoke with authority, grateful to be analyzing, for the moment, something other than her personal loss. "Henry, you know as well as I do that deals as complex as this one are like chess games. You have to see five or ten moves ahead. And you don't get second chances. Paul has a bright future at the firm, but he does not possess the breadth of vision for the deal, or attention to detail. He does not belong on the final negotiation team for the CyberCom acquisition."

"Thank you, Sidney, those were my thoughts precisely."

"Henry, I don't think my comments are exactly earth-shattering news to you. Why was he being considered?"

"Let's just say he expressed a very strong interest in heading the deal. Not hard to see why; it would be a lucrative feather in anyone's cap."

"I see."

"I'm going to put Roger Egert in charge."

"He's a first-rate transaction attorney."

"He was very complimentary of your work on the matter thus far. 'Perfectly positioned,' I think were his words." Wharton paused for a moment. "I hate to ask this, Sidney, I really do."

"What, Henry?"

She heard him let out a long breath. "Well, I promised myself I wouldn't do this—it's just that you're so damn indispensable." He paused again.

"Henry, please, what is it?"

"Could you take a moment to talk to Egert? He's almost up to speed, but a few minutes with you on the strategic and tactical issues would be invaluable. I know that it would. I certainly wouldn't ask it, Sidney, if it weren't vitally important. In any event, you'll also have to provide him with the pass code for the master computer file."

Sidney covered the phone and sighed. She knew Henry meant well, but business always came first with him. "I'll call him today, Henry."

"I won't forget, Sidney."

Her cellular was drowning in static. Sidney walked out of the café to get better reception. Outside, Henry Wharton's tone had changed slightly.

"I received a visit from Nathan Gamble this morning."

Sidney stopped walking and leaned up against the brick wall of the café. She closed her eyes and grit her teeth until they hurt. "I'm surprised he waited so long, Henry."

"He was a little distraught, Sid, to say the least. He firmly believes you lied to him."

"Henry, I know this looks bad." She hesitated and then decided to come clean. "Jason told me he had a job interview in Los Angeles. He obviously didn't want Triton to know. He swore me to secrecy. That's why I didn't tell Gamble."

"Sid, you're Triton's lawyer. There are no secrets—"

"Come on, Henry, this is my husband we're talking about. His taking another job isn't going to damage Triton. And he doesn't have a noncompete."

"Still, Sidney, it hurts me to say this, but I'm not sure you exercised the best judgment in the matter. Gamble suggested quite strongly to me that he suspected Jason of stealing corporate secrets."

"Jason would never do that!"

"That's not the point. It's how the client perceives it. Your having lied to Nathan Gamble does not help matters. Do you know what would happen to the firm if he were to pull the Triton account? And don't think he wouldn't." Wharton's voice was rising steadily.

"Henry, when Gamble wanted to teleconference Jason in, I had maybe two seconds to think about it."

"Well, for God's sake why didn't you tell Gamble the truth? As you said, he wouldn't care."

"Because a few seconds later I found out my husband was dead!"

Neither one said anything for a moment; however, immense friction was clearly present. "Some time has passed now," Wharton reminded her. "If you didn't want to tell them, you could have confided in me. I would've taken care of it for you. Now, I believe I can still patch things up. Gamble can't hold it against *us* that your husband wanted to change jobs. I'm not sure Gamble will be too excited about your working on his matters in the future, Sidney. Perhaps it's good you're taking some time off. It'll pass over, though. I'll call him right now."

When she spoke, Sidney's voice was barely audible. It felt as though a large fist was wedged down her esophagus. "You can't tell Gamble about the job interview, Henry."

"Excuse me?"

"You can't do it."

"Would you mind telling me why not?"

"Because I found out that Jason wasn't interviewing with any other company. Apparently . . ." She paused and forced back a sob. "Apparently he lied to me."

When Wharton again spoke, his tone was one of barely suppressed anger. "I cannot tell you the irreparable damage that this situation may cause and may well already have caused."

"Henry, I don't know what's going on. All I'm telling you is what I know, which isn't much."

"What exactly am I supposed to tell Gamble? He's expecting an answer."

"Put the onus on me, Henry. Tell him I can't be reached. I'm not returning calls. You're working on it and I won't be back at the office until you get to the bottom of the matter."

Wharton thought that over for a moment. "I guess that might work. At least temporarily. I appreciate your taking responsibility for the situation, Sidney. I know it's not of your making, but the *firm* certainly shouldn't suffer. That's my chief concern."

"I understand, Henry. In the meantime, I'll do my best to find out what was going on."

"You sure you're up to that?" Under the circumstances, Wharton felt compelled to ask the question, although he was certain of the answer.

"Do I have a choice, Henry?"

"Our prayers are with you, Sidney. Call if you need anything. We're a family at Tyler, Stone. We take care of each other."

Sidney clicked off her phone and put it away. Wharton's words had hurt her deeply, but maybe she was just being naive. She and Henry were professional colleagues and friends, to a point. Their phone conversation had underscored to her just how superficial most professional relationships are. As long as you were productive, didn't cause waves, kept the sum of the whole thriving, you had nothing to worry about. Now, suddenly a single mom, she had to be careful that her legal career didn't abruptly vanish. She would have to pile that one next to all the other problems she currently had.

She took the brick walkway, cut across Ivy Road and headed over to the university's famed Rotunda building. She made her way through the equally famous Lawn portion of the campus grounds, where the university's elite students lived in one-room quarters that had changed little from Thomas Jefferson's time, with fireplaces the only source of heat. The simple beauty of the campus had enthralled her whenever she had visited before. Now, framed against a pristine late-fall morning, it was barely noticed. She had many questions, and it was time she started getting some answers. She sat down on the steps of the Rotunda and once again pulled her phone from her purse. She punched in the required numbers. The phone rang twice.

"Triton Global."

"Kay?" Sidney asked.

"Sid?" Kay Vincent was Jason's secretary. A plump woman in her fifties, she had adored Jason and had even served as a babysitter for Amy on several occasions. Sidney had liked her from the start, both sharing common perspectives on motherhood, work and men.

"Kay, how are you? I'm sorry I haven't called before."

"How am I? Oh, Lord, Sid, I am so sorry. So damn sorry."

Sidney could hear the tears welling up in the older woman's voice.

"I know, Kay. I know. It's all been so sudden. So . . ." Sidney's voice trailed off, then she steeled herself. She had to know some things, and Kay Vincent was the most honest source she could think of. "Kay, you know that Jason took some time off from the office."

"Right. He said he was going to paint the kitchen and fix up the garage. He'd been talking about it for a week."

"He never mentioned the trip to Los Angeles to you?"

"No. I was shocked to hear he was on that plane."

"Has anyone been in to talk to you about Jason?"

"Lots of people. Everyone's devastated."

"How about Quentin Rowe?"

"He's been by several times." Kay paused and then said, "Sid, why all these questions?"

"Kay, this needs to be kept between us, okay?"

"All right." She sounded very reluctant.

"I thought Jason was going to L.A. for a job interview with another company because that's what he told me. I recently found out that that wasn't true."

"My God!"

While Kay slowly digested the news, Sidney ventured another

question. "Kay, is there any reason you could think of why Jason would have lied about that? Was he acting strange at work?"

There was a considerable pause now. "Kay?" Sidney fidgeted on the steps. The cold from the bricks had begun to chill her. She abruptly stood up.

"Sid, we have really strict rules about discussing any of the company's business. I don't want to get into trouble."

"I know that, Kay. I'm one of Triton's attorneys, remember?"

"Well, this is a little bit different." Kay's voice abruptly disappeared from the line. Sidney wondered if she had hung up, but then the voice reappeared. "Can you call me later tonight? I don't really want to talk on company time about this. I'll be home around eight. You still have my home phone?"

"I've got it, Kay. Thanks."

Kay Vincent hung up without saying anything else.

Jason rarely discussed Triton's business with Sidney, although, as an attorney at Tyler, Stone, she was immersed in numerous matters for the company. Her husband took the ethical responsibilities of his position very seriously. He had always been careful not to put his wife in an awkward situation. At least until now. She slowly walked back to the parking garage.

After paying the attendant, she started toward her car. Suddenly she turned, but by then the man had disappeared around the corner. She walked rapidly back to the street next to the garage and peered down it. No one was in sight. There were numerous shops along there, though. Someone could have disappeared into any one of them in a few seconds. She had first noticed him looking at her while she was seated on the steps of the Rotunda. He had been standing behind one of the many trees sprinkled around the Lawn. Busy talking to Kay, she had quickly dismissed him as some guy just checking her out for the obvious reason. He was tall, at least six feet, lean and dressed in a dark overcoat. His face had been partially covered by sunglasses and the overcoat's collar had been turned up, further hiding his features. A brown hat had covered his hair, although she had managed to note that it was light in color, reddish blond, perhaps. For a brief moment she wondered if paranoia had been added to her growing list of problems. She couldn't worry about it right now. She had to get home. Tomorrow she would pick up her daughter. She then remembered that her mother had mentioned a memorial service for Jason. The details of that would have to be gone over. Amid all the mystery surrounding her late husband's last day, the recollection of the memorial service had brought back the crushing knowledge that Jason was indeed dead. No matter how he had deceived her, or for what reason he had done so, he was gone. She headed back home.

CHAPTER EIGHTEEN

Under drifting cloud cover that was quickly overtaking the razor-blue sky, a chilly wind whipped through the crash site. Armies of people walked the grounds, marking debris with red flags, forming a mass of crimson in the cornfield. Near the crater sat a crane with a dangling bucket large enough to hold two grown men. Another such crane hovered over the crater, its long cable and bucket disappearing into the depths of this shallow hell. Other cables connected to motorized winches set on flatbed trucks snaked down into the pit. Heavy equipment was lumbering nearby in preparation for the final excavation of the impact crater. The most critical piece, the flight data recorder, had not yet been unearthed.

Outside the yellow barricades a number of tents had been raised. They served as depositories of collected evidence for on-site analysis. In one such tent George Kaplan was pouring hot coffee from his thermos into two cups. He briefly scanned the area. Luckily the snow had stopped as quickly as it had started. However, the temperature had remained cool and the weather forecast called for more precipitation. He knew that was not good. Snow would make a logistical nightmare even more daunting.

Kaplan handed one of the steaming cups to Lee Sawyer, who had followed the NTSB investigator's gaze around the crash site.

"That was a good call on the fuel tank, George. The evidence was very slight, but lab results show it was an old reliable: hydrochloric acid. Tests indicated that it would've eaten through the aluminum alloy in about two to four hours. Faster if the acid was heated. Doesn't look like it was accidental."

Kaplan grunted loudly. "Shit, like a mechanic would be walking around with acid and just accidentally smear it on the fuel tank."

"I never thought it was an accident, George."

Kaplan threw up his hand in apology. "And you can carry hydrochloric acid in a plastic container, could even use a squirt bottle with a modified tip so you can gauge how much you're applying. Plastic won't trip a metal detector. It was a good choice." Kaplan's face twisted in disgust.

He looked out at the crash site for a few more seconds and then stirred, turning to Sawyer. "Nailing down the timing that close is good. Cuts down the list of possible suspects who would've had access."

Sawyer nodded in agreement. "We're following that up right now." He took a long sip of the coffee.

"You really think somebody blew up an entire planeload of people to take out one guy?"

"Maybe."

"Christ Almighty, I don't mean to sound callous, but if you want to kill the guy, who not just grab him off the street and put a bullet in his head? Why this?" He pointed at the crater and then slumped back in his seat, his eyes half closed, one hand rubbing viciously at his left temple.

Sawyer sat in one of the folding chairs. "We're not sure that's the case, but Lieberman was the only passenger on the plane warranting that kind of special attention."

"Why the hell go to all this trouble to kill the Fed chairman?"

Sawyer pulled his coat tighter around him as the cold wind swirled inside the tent space. "Well, the financial markets took a tremendous beating when the news broke of Lieberman's death. The

Dow lost almost twelve hundred points, or about twenty-five percent of its total. In two days. That makes the Crash of 1929 look like
a hiccup. The overseas markets are being battered too." Sawyer
stared pointedly at Kaplan. "And wait until news leaks that the
plane was sabotaged. That Lieberman might have been deliberately
killed. Who the hell knows what that will trigger?"

Kaplan's eyes widened. "Jesus! All that for one guy?"

"Like I said, somebody killed Superman."

"So you got a lot of potential suspects—foreign governments, international terrorists, crap like that, right?" Kaplan shook his head
as he contemplated the number of bad people on the increasingly
small sphere they all called home.

Sawyer shrugged. "Let's just say it's not going to be your run-of-
the-mill street criminal."

The two men fell silent and again stared over at the crash site.
They watched the crane's cable reverse its direction, and within two
minutes a bucket carrying two men appeared above the pit. The
crane swung around and gently rested the bucket on the ground.
The two men clambered out. Sawyer and Kaplan watched with
growing excitement as the pair raced toward them.

The first to arrive was a young man whose white-blond hair partially obscured a choirboy's features. In his hand was clenched a plastic baggie. Inside the baggie was a small, metallic, rectangular
object, heavily charred. The other man lumbered up behind him. He
was older, and his red face and labored breathing spoke of the rarity
of his finding himself racing across wide cornfields.

"I couldn't believe it," the younger man almost shouted. "The
starboard wing, or what was left if it, was sitting right on top, pretty
much intact. I guess the left side took the brunt of the explosion
with the full tank. Looks like when the nose burrowed into the
ground, it created an opening slightly larger than the circumference
of the fuselage. When the wings hit the sides of the pit, they crumpled back and over the fuselage. Damn miracle, if you ask me."

Kaplan took the baggie and stepped over to the table. "Where'd
you find it?"

"It was attached to the wing's interior side, right next to the access panel for the fuel tank. It must have been placed inside the wing on the inboard side of the starboard engine. I'm not sure what it is, but I can damn sure tell you it doesn't belong on a plane."

"So it was placed to the left of where the wing sheared off?" Kaplan asked.

"Exactly, Chief. Another couple inches and it would've been gone too."

The older man spoke. "From the looks of it, the fuselage shielded the starboard wing from a good deal of the initial postcrash explosion. When the sides of the crater collapsed, all the dirt must've cut off the fire almost immediately." He paused and then added solemnly, "But the forward section of the cabin's gone. I mean nothing's left, like it was never there."

Kaplan handed the baggie over to Sawyer. "Do you know what the hell this is?"

Sawyer's face broke into a dark scowl. "Yeah, I do."

CHAPTER NINETEEN

Sidney Archer had driven to her office and was now seated at her desk; her office door was closed and locked. It was a little after eight in the evening, but she could hear the faint buzz of a fax machine in the background. She picked up the phone and dialed Kay Vincent's number at home.

A man answered.

"Kay Vincent, please. It's Sidney Archer."

"Just a minute."

As Sidney waited, she looked around the confines of her office. A place normally of deep comfort to her, it looked strangely out of focus. The diplomas on the wall were hers, but at this moment she could not seem to remember when or where she had earned them. She had become purely reactive, battered by one shock after another. She wondered if a new surprise was awaiting her at the other end of the phone line.

"Sidney?"

"Hello, Kay."

The voice sounded ashamed. "I feel so bad, I didn't even ask you this morning about Amy. How is she?"

"She's at my parents' right now." She swallowed hard and then added, "She doesn't know, of course."

"I'm sorry I acted the way I did at work. You know how that place is. They get uptight if they think you're taking personal calls on their time."

"I know, Kay. I didn't know who else to talk to over there." She didn't add, *whom she could trust.*

"I understand, Sid."

Sidney took a deep breath. She might as well get right down to it. Had she looked up, she might have noticed the doorknob on her door slowly turn and then stop as the locking mechanism prohibited further movement.

"Kay, is there something you wanted to tell me? About Jason?"

There was a perceptible pause on the other end of the line before Kay answered. "I couldn't have asked for a better boss. He worked real hard, was moving up fast. But he still took the time to talk to everybody, spend time with them." Kay stopped talking, perhaps trying to collect her thoughts before plunging ahead, Sidney wasn't sure. When Kay didn't say anything, Sidney floated a question. "Well, did that change? Was Jason acting differently?"

"Yes." The word was blurted out so quickly, Sidney almost didn't catch it.

"How so?"

"It was a bunch of little things, really. The first thing that had me concerned was Jason ordering a lock for his door."

"A lock on an office door isn't so unusual, Kay. I have one on mine." Sidney glanced over at her own office door. The doorknob was now motionless.

"I know that, Sid. The thing is, Jason already had a lock on his door."

"I don't understand, Kay. If he already had a lock, why did he order another one?"

"The lock he had on his door was a pretty simple one, a pop-out lock on the doorknob. Yours is probably one of those."

Sidney again glanced at her door. "That's right, it is. Aren't all office door locks pretty much the same?"

"Not these days, Sid. Jason had a computerized lock put on his system that required a smart card."

"Smart card?"

"You know, a plastic card with a microchip thing in it. I'm not sure exactly how it works, but you need it to get into the building here, and certain restricted access areas, among other things."

Sidney fumbled through her purse and pulled out the plastic card she had taken from Jason's desk at home.

"Does anyone else at Triton have those kinds of locks on their office doors?"

"About a half dozen. Most of them are in finance, though."

"Did Jason tell you why he had ordered the additional security for his office?"

"I asked him, because I was concerned that maybe there had been a break-in and nobody told us. But Jason said he had taken on some additional responsibilities with the company and had some items in his keeping that he wanted additional protection for."

Tired of sitting, Sidney stood up and paced. She looked out the window into the darkness. Across the street, the lights of Spencers, a posh new restaurant, gleamed back at her. A stream of taxis and luxury cars disgorged elegantly dressed parties who sauntered into the establishment for a night of fine food, drink and the latest city gossip. Sidney pulled the blind down. She let out her breath and sat on her credenza, slipping out of her shoes and absently rubbing sore and tired feet.

"Why didn't Jason want you to tell anyone that he had taken on additional responsibilities?"

"I don't know. He's been promoted three times already in the company. So I know it wasn't that. You wouldn't be secretive about something like that anyway, would you?"

Sidney pondered this information for a few seconds. Jason hadn't mentioned a promotion to her and it was inconceivable that he would not. "Did he tell you who had given him the additional responsibilities?"

"No. And I really didn't want to pry."

"Did you tell anyone else what Jason had told you?"

"No one," Kay said firmly.

Sidney tended to believe her. She shook her head. "What else had you concerned?"

"Well, Jason kept a lot more to himself lately. He also made excuses for missing staff meetings, things like that. This had been going on for at least a month."

Sidney stopped rubbing nervously at her foot.

"Jason never mentioned testing the waters with another company?"

"Never." Sidney could almost feel the firm shake of Kay's head through the phone line.

"Did you ever ask Jason if anything was bothering him?"

"I did once, only he wasn't real receptive. He was a good friend, but he was also my boss. I didn't want to push it."

"I understand, Kay." Sidney slid off the credenza and replaced her shoes. She noticed a shadow pass under her door and then it stopped. She waited for a few more seconds, but the shadow did not budge. She clicked the button on her receiver to portable use and disconnected the cord. A thought had occurred to her.

"Kay, has anyone actually been into Jason's office?"

"Well . . ." Kay's hesitation allowed Sidney to come up with another inquiry.

"But how could they, with all the extra security measures on his office door?"

"That's the problem, Sid. No one had the code or Jason's security card. The door's three inches of solid wood set on a steel frame. Mr. Gamble and Mr. Rowe haven't been in the office this week and I think no one else really knew what to do."

"So no one's been in Jason's office since it . . . it happened?" Sidney looked down at the smart card.

"Nobody. Mr. Rowe was in late today. He's having the company that installed the lock come tomorrow to open it."

"Who else has been around?"

Sidney could hear Kay let out her breath. "They had someone over from SecurTech."

"SecurTech?" Sidney shifted the phone receiver to her other ear as she continued to eye the shadow. She inched toward the door. She was not concerned that it was an intruder. Plenty of people were still working at the office. "That's Triton's security consultant, isn't it?"

"Yes. I was wondering why they were called in. The word is it's pretty normal procedure when something happens like this."

Sidney was now to the right of the door, her free hand inching toward the doorknob.

"Sidney, I've got some things of Jason's at my workstation. Photos, a sweater of his he let me borrow one time, some books. He tried to get me interested in eighteenth- and nineteenth-century literature, although I'm afraid I never did."

"He did the same thing with Amy until I pointed out it would probably help to have her learn her ABCs before she plunged headlong into Voltaire."

The two women laughed together, which felt very good under the awful circumstances.

"You can come by whenever you want to pick them up."

"I will, Kay, maybe we can have lunch . . . and talk some more."

"I'd like that. I'd like that a lot."

"I really appreciate what you've told me, Kay. You've been a big help."

"Well, I cared a lot for Jason. He was a good, decent man."

Sidney felt the tears start to bubble to the surface, but when she looked at the shadow under her door again, her nerves hardened. "Yes, he was." The last word she uttered contained a dead-cold finality.

"Sid, you need anything, and I mean anything, you just call, you hear me?"

Sidney smiled. "Thank you, Kay. I may just take you up on that." As soon as she clicked off the phone and laid it down, Sidney yanked her office door open.

Philip Goldman did not appear startled. He stood there calmly staring at Sidney with his balding head, expressive face, protruding eyes, slender, rounded shoulders and the beginnings of a belly. His clothing appeared to be and was indeed very expensive. Standing in her shoes, Sidney was taller than Philip by two inches.

"Sidney, I was passing by and noticed the light on. I had no idea you were here."

"Hello, Philip." Sidney eyed him closely. Goldman was a slender notch below Henry Wharton in the Tyler, Stone partnership pecking order. He had a substantial client base and his life was focused on his own professional career enhancement.

"I must say I'm surprised to see you here, Sidney."

"Going home right now isn't such an appealing idea, Philip."

He slowly nodded his head. "Yes, yes, I can well understand that." He glanced over her shoulder at the phone receiver lying on the shelf of one of the bookcases. "Talking with someone?"

"Personal. There are a lot of details I need to go over now."

"Of course. Death is terrible enough to confront. Sudden death even more so." He continued to stare pointedly at her.

Sidney felt her face flushing. She turned away, grabbed her bag off the couch and pulled her coat from behind the door, partially closing the door on Goldman, who had to step back quickly to avoid being struck.

She put on her coat and poised her hand over the light switch. "I've got an appointment I'm late for."

Goldman stepped back into the hallway. Sidney made a show of locking her office door before shutting it.

"This may be an awkward time, Sidney, but I wanted to congratulate you on your handling of the CyberCom transaction."

She jerked her head around. "I'm certain we should not be discussing that subject, Philip."

"I know, Sidney," he said. "However, I still read the *Wall Street Journal* and your name has been mentioned several times. Nathan Gamble must be very pleased."

"Thank you, Philip." She turned to face him. "I have to go now."

"Let me know if there's anything I can do for you."

Sidney quickly nodded and then moved past Goldman. She walked down the hallway toward the firm's main entrance and disappeared around the corner.

Goldman strode quickly down the hallway in time to see Sidney enter the elevator. He then walked casually back down the corridor to Sidney's office. After looking in both directions, he pulled out a key, inserted it in the lock, opened the door and went inside. The lock clicked into place, and then there was silence.

CHAPTER TWENTY

Sidney pulled the Ford into Triton's vast parking lot and got out. She buttoned up her coat against the chilly wind, checked her purse once more to make sure the plastic card was there and walked as normally as she could to the fifteen-story building that housed Triton's world headquarters. She identified herself into the speaker located next to the entrance. A video camera mounted over the doorway was pointed directly at her head. Then a compartment next to the speaker swung open and she was directed to insert her thumb into the fingerprint scanner that was now revealed. Triton's after-hours security measures probably matched those of the CIA, she surmised. The glass and chrome doors slid noiselessly open. She walked into the building's lobby, which featured a soft waterfall, soaring atrium and enough polished marble to have emptied a good-sized quarry. When she walked toward the elevator, the lighting automatically illuminated her path. Gentle music also followed her and the elevator doors opened as she approached them. Triton's headquarters building had received the full benefit of the company's immense technological muscle.

She rode the elevator to the eighth floor and got off.

The security officer on duty there rose and walked over to her, grasping her hand. There was pain in the man's eyes.

"Hello, Charlie."

"Sidney, ma'am. I am so sorry."

"Thank you, Charlie."

Charlie shook his head. "On his way to the top. Worked harder than anybody here. A lot of times it was just him and me in the whole building. He'd bring me coffee and a little something to eat from the lunchroom. Never asked him to, he just did it. Wasn't like some of the big shots here who think they're better than you are."

"You're right, Jason wasn't like that."

"No, ma'am, he wasn't. Now what can I do for you? You need something? You just tell old Charlie what it is."

"Well, I was wondering if Kay Vincent was still here."

Charlie stared blankly at her. "Kay? I don't think so. I come on duty at nine. She's usually gone around seven so . . . I wouldn't have seen her leave. Let me check."

Charlie strode over to the console. The holster housing his revolver flapped against his side and the keys clipped to his gun belt jangled as he walked. He put on a headset and punched a button on the console. After a few seconds he shook his head. "I'm just getting her voice mail, Sidney."

"Oh. Well, she had some things . . . some things of Jason's that I wanted to pick up." Sidney looked down at the floor, apparently unable to continue speaking.

Charlie walked back over to her. He touched her arm. "Well, maybe she has them at her desk."

Sidney looked up at him. "She probably does, I would think."

Charlie hesitated. He knew this was against all the rules. But then, rules shouldn't always apply. He went back over to the console, hit a couple of buttons and Sidney watched as the red light next to the door leading into the office corridor turned to green. He walked back over and, pulling keys from his belt, unlocked the door.

"You know how they freak out over security here, but I think this situation is a little different. Nobody's back there anyway. Usually this place is buzzing up until about ten, but it's the holiday week and all. I've gotta make rounds now on the fourth floor. You know where she sits, right?"

"I do, Charlie. I really appreciate this."

He gave her hand another squeeze. "Like I said, your husband was a good man."

Sidney moved down the softly lit corridor. Kay's cubicle was about halfway down, with Jason's office diagonally across from it. While Sidney walked down the hallway, she looked carefully around; all was quiet. She turned the corner and saw Kay's darkened cubicle. In a box next to her desk chair was a sweater and some framed photos. She probed underneath and lifted out a finely bound book with gilt edges. *David Copperfield.* It was one of Jason's favorites. She put the things back in the box and placed it next to the chair.

She looked around again. The corridor was also empty. Charlie had said everyone was gone, but then again, he hadn't been certain about Kay. Satisfied that she was alone at least for now, Sidney reached her husband's office door. Her hopes sank when she spied the numeric keypad. Kay hadn't mentioned that device. She thought for a moment, pulled the plastic card out of her pocket, looked around once more, and then slid it into the slot. A light on the keypad clicked on. Sidney read the word "Ready" next to the light. She thought quickly and punched in some numbers; however, the light didn't budge from its position. She became frustrated. She didn't even know how many digits to punch in, much less what they were. She tried a few more combinations without success.

She had almost decided to give up when she noted that there was a small digital screen in one corner of the numeric keypad. Apparently it was a time counter and it was now on eight seconds. The alarm light on the pad started to glow a brighter and brighter crimson. "Oh, shit," she hissed. An alarm! The counter was now at five seconds. She stood frozen. Flashing across her mind were all the results that would occur were she found here attempting to infiltrate her husband's office. None of them rated less than a complete disaster. As her eyes locked on the counter, which was now at three seconds, she broke out of her inertia. One more possible combination rocketed across her brain. Mouthing a silent prayer, her fingers punched in the numbers 0-6-1-6. She hit the last digit right as the counter clicked to zero. Waiting for the piercing alarm to explode, Sidney held her breath for one long instant.

The alarm light turned off and the door's locks clicked free. Sidney steadied herself against the wall as she slowly started breathing normally again. June 16 was Amy's birthday. Triton probably had a policy about not using personal numbers for security codes: too easy to crack. For Sidney, it was proof positive that the little girl was never really out of her father's thoughts.

She removed the plastic card from the slot. Before grasping the doorknob, she pulled a handkerchief from her purse and wound it around her hand to avoid leaving any prints. Acting the part of an intruder both exhilarated and terrified her. She felt her pulse hammering in her ears. She entered the office and quickly closed the door behind her.

The flashlight she pulled from her bag was small but effective. Before turning it on, she checked to make sure that the window blinds were all the way down and completely closed. The thin light swept around the office. She had been here before, several times in fact, to have lunch with Jason, although they had not stayed long in his office. Usually it was just to snatch a quick kiss behind closed doors. Her light skipped to bookcases filled with technical tomes far beyond her realm of comprehension. The technocrats really did rule, she mused for a moment, if only because they were the only ones who could fix the damn things when they broke down.

The light fell upon the computer and she quickly went over to it. It was off and the presence of another keypad made her decide not to push her luck in attempting to turn it on. She would be hopelessly lost even if she was fortunate enough to log on, since she had no idea what she was looking for or where to search. It wasn't worth the risk. She noted the microphone attached to the computer monitor. A number of desk drawers were locked. The few that weren't revealed nothing of interest.

In stark contrast to her office at the law firm, there were no diplomas on the walls or other personal touches in her husband's office.

She did note, with a glistening eye, that a photo of Jason and his family held a prominent position on his desk. As she looked around the office, it suddenly occurred to her that she had taken enormous risks for nothing. She whirled around at a sudden noise from somewhere within the office space. The flashlight collided with the microphone and, to her horror, the slender device bent in half. She stood completely still, listening for the sound to be repeated. Finally, after a minute of sheer terror, she turned her attention back to the slender microphone. She spent a couple of minutes trying to return it to its original shape without much success. Finally she gave up, wiped her prints from it, retreated to the door and turned off her flashlight. Using the handkerchief to grip the doorknob, she listened at the door for a moment and then exited the office.

She heard the footsteps coming as soon as she reached Kay's desk. For an instant she thought it might be Charlie, except there was no jangling of keys against his gun belt. She looked quickly around to determine which way the sounds were coming from. Clearly the person was back farther in the office. She slipped across to Kay's cubicle and knelt down behind her desk. Trying to breathe as quietly as possible, she waited as the footsteps came closer. Then they stopped. A minute went by and they did not resume. Then Sidney heard a slight clicking sound, as though something was being rotated back and forth, but only in a limited radius.

Unable to stop herself, she cautiously peered around the corner of Kay's cubicle. A man's back was barely six feet away from her. He was slowly turning the doorknob on Jason's office door back and forth. The man took a card out of his shirt pocket and started to insert it into the slot. Then he hesitated over the keypad as if deciding whether to chance it or not. Finally his courage failed and he put the card back in his pocket and turned away.

Quentin Rowe did not look pleased. He retreated down the hallway the way he had come.

Sidney slipped out from her hiding place and walked in the opposite direction. She was moving rapidly when she rounded the corner and her purse hit the wall. The noise, while not loud, seemed to echo like an explosion through the quiet hallways. Her breath caught in her throat when she heard the retreating footsteps stop and then turn as Quentin Rowe started to head rapidly in her direction. She hurried as fast as she could down the hallway, reached the main office door, was through it in an instant and found herself back in the reception area, staring at Charlie, who looked back at her anxiously.

"Sidney, you okay? You look white as a ghost."

The footsteps were nearing the door. Sidney put one finger to her lips, pointed in the direction of the door and motioned Charlie to go behind his console. He rapidly caught both the sounds of the footsteps and her meaning and quickly followed her instructions. Then Sidney slipped over to the rest room door that stood to the right of the entrance to the lobby. She opened her purse, poised herself at the door to the ladies' room, which she held partially open with one hand, and kept an eye on the door to the hallway. As soon as it opened and Rowe appeared, Sidney pretended to stroll out of the ladies' room, fumbling with something in her purse. When she looked up, Rowe was staring at her. He held the door to the secured area open with one hand.

"Quentin?" She said it with as much surprise as she could muster.

Rowe looked from Sidney to Charlie, suspicion written all over his features.

"What are you doing here?" He did not try to hide his displeasure.

"I came to see Kay. We had talked earlier. She had some things of Jason's. Some personal effects she wanted me to have."

Rowe snapped back, "Nothing can leave the premises without prior authorization. Certainly nothing having to do with Jason."

Sidney looked at him squarely. "I know that, Quentin."

Her response surprised him.

She looked at Charlie, who stared at Rowe with unfriendly eyes. "Charlie already informed me of that, though in a much less offensive way than you just did. And he wouldn't let me back into the office area because we all know that's against the company's security policy."

"I apologize if I was little abrupt. I've been under a lot of pressure lately."

Charlie's voice was tense with a mixture of anger and incredulity. "And *she* hasn't? She just lost her husband, for God's sake."

Before Rowe could answer, Sidney cut in. "Quentin and I have already covered that topic, Charlie, in an earlier conversation. Haven't we, Quentin?"

Rowe seemed to dissolve under her withering gaze.

He decided it best to change subjects. "I thought I heard a noise." He again looked accusingly at Sidney.

Sidney answered immediately. "So did we. Right before I went to the ladies' room, Charlie went to check it out. I guess he heard you and you heard him. He didn't think anyone was still in the office. But you were." Her tone matched his in its accusatory implications.

Rowe bristled. "I'm the president of this company. I can be here at any time of the day or night and it's nobody's business but my own."

Sidney stared him down. "I'm sure you can. However, I would think that you would be working late on their behalf rather than conducting personal business, even though it's long after regular business hours. I'm just speaking as a legal representative of the company, Quentin." Under normal circumstances, she never would have uttered those words to a client's senior executive.

Rowe started to sputter. "Well, of course, I meant I was working for the company. I know all—" Rowe stopped abruptly when Sidney walked over to Charlie and took his hand.

"Thank you very much, Charlie. I understand that rules are rules." Rowe could not see the look she gave the elderly security guard, but it brought a grateful smile to Charlie's face.

As she turned to leave, Rowe said, "Good night, Sidney."

She didn't answer him, nor did she even look at him. After she disappeared into the elevator, Rowe looked angrily over at Charlie, who was getting up to head out the door.

"Where are you going?" he demanded.

Charlie's expression was calm. "I've got rounds to make. That's part of *my* job." He bent down to the smaller man's height when he said it. Charlie started out the door and then turned back. "Oh, it might help avoid confusion in the future if you let me know you're still around." He touched his sidearm. "We don't want no unfortunate accidents, you know?" Rowe went pale at the sight of the gun. "You hear any more noises, you come get me, okay, Mr. Rowe?" After Charlie turned away, he broke out in a broad smile.

Rowe stood at the doorway for a minute longer, thinking intently. Then he turned and went back into the office.

CHAPTER TWENTY-ONE

Lee Sawyer eyed the small three-story apartment building, which was located about five miles from Dulles International Airport. Residents enjoyed a complete fitness center, Olympic-size pool and Jacuzzi, and huge party room. It was home to mostly young single professionals who got up early to make the traffic-stifling trek into downtown. The parking lot was littered with low-end Beemers, Saabs and the occasional Porsche.

Sawyer was interested in only one of the occupants of this community. He was not a young lawyer, marketing executive or holder of an MBA. Sawyer briefly spoke into his walkie-talkie. Three other agents were seated in the sedan with him. Stationed around the area were five other teams of FBI agents. A black-clad squadron of the elite FBI Hostage Rescue Team (HRT) was also zeroing in on Sawyer's target. A battalion of local authorities was backing up the federal lawmen. A lot of innocent people were around, and great pains were being taken to ensure that if anyone was going to get hurt, it would be only the man whom Sawyer believed had already killed almost two hundred people.

Sawyer's plan of attack was textbook FBI. Bring overwhelming force to a completely unsuspecting target, force so overpowering, in a situation so totally controlled, that resistance was useless. Controlling the situation completely meant you could control the outcome too. Or so the theory went.

Every agent carried a 9mm semiautomatic pistol with extra clips. Each team of agents also had one member with an appropriately named Franchi Law-12 semiautomatic shotgun and another member sporting a Colt assault rifle. The HRT members all carried heavy-caliber automatic weapons, most with electronic laser sights.

Sawyer gave the signal to move in and the teams moved forward. In less than one minute members of the HRT had reached the door of apartment number 321. Two other teams covered the only other possible escape, the two back windows of the apartment that overlooked the pool area. Snipers had already set up there, their laser sights fixed immovably on the twin apertures. After listening intently at the door of 321 for a few seconds, the HRT members exploded through the opening. No gunfire disturbed the peaceful stillness of the night. Within a minute, Sawyer received the all-clear signal. He and his men hurried up the stairs of the apartment building.

Sawyer was met by the leader of the HRT.

"Nest empty?" Sawyer asked.

The HRT man shook his head. "Might as well be. Someone beat us to it." He jerked his head in the direction of the small bedroom at the rear of the apartment.

Sawyer walked quickly back there. A shiver hit him right between the shoulder blades; the place was like the insides of a freezer. The overhead light in the bedroom was on. Three HRT members looked down at the small space between the bed and the wall. Sawyer followed their gaze and his spirits sank.

The man was lying face down. Multiple gunshot wounds in the back and head were plainly visible; so were the firearm and the twelve pieces of brass that littered the floor. Sawyer, with the aid of two HRT members, carefully lifted the body, turning it sideways before returning it exactly to the spot where it had been before.

Sawyer rose, shaking his head. He barked into his walkie-talkie.

"Tell the state guys to get a medical examiner out here and I want the forensics team here yesterday."

Sawyer looked down at the body. Well, at least the guy wouldn't be sabotaging any more planes, although a full clip into his body didn't seem like nearly enough punishment for what the sonofabitch had done. But a dead man couldn't talk either. Sawyer moved out of the room, his walkie-talkie squeezed tightly in his hand. In the empty hallway he noted that the air-conditioning had been turned on full blast. The apartment's temperature hovered around thirty degrees. He quickly jotted down the precise temperature setting and then, using the point of a pencil so as not to destroy any possible fingerprints, he turned the heat back on. He wasn't about to let his men freeze to death while they investigated the crime scene. He slumped against the wall, momentarily depressed. While he'd known the odds were long that they would find the suspect at his apartment, the fact that they had found him murdered clearly indicated that someone was a couple of steps ahead of the FBI. Was there a leak somewhere, or had this murder been part of some master plan?

He gripped the walkie-talkie and headed back to the bedroom.

CHAPTER TWENTY-TWO

Sidney exited the Triton building and started across the parking lot. She was so deep in thought she didn't see the black stretch limousine until it careened to a halt directly in front of her. The rear door opened and Richard Lucas stepped out. He was dressed in a dark blue conservative single-breasted suit. His face was chiefly distinguished by a pug nose and a pair of small eyes that were too close together by about an inch. His breadth of shoulders and the omnipresent hump under his suit coat made him an imposing physical presence.

"Mr. Gamble would like to meet with you." His tone was even. He held the door open and Sidney could see the holstered pistol under his coat. She froze, swallowed hard and then her eyes blazed. "I'm not sure that fits into my schedule right now."

Lucas shrugged. "As you wish. However, Mr. Gamble thought it best to speak directly with you. To get your version of the facts before he decides upon any type of action. He felt the sooner the meeting took place the better for *all* concerned."

Sidney took a deep breath and looked at the limo's black-tinted windows. "Where is this meeting to take place?"

"Mr. Gamble's estate in Middleburg." He checked his watch. "Our ETA is thirty-five minutes. We will, of course, take you back to your car after the meeting is concluded."

She eyed him sharply. "Do I really have a choice?"

"A person always has choices, Ms. Archer."

Sidney pulled her coat tighter around her and climbed in. Lucas sat across from her. She didn't ask any more questions and he ventured nothing further. His eyes, however, remained squarely upon her.

Sidney was dimly aware of an enormous house of stone surrounded by meticulously landscaped and tree-lined grounds. *You can make it through this,* she thought. Interrogation was often a two-way street. If Gamble wanted answers from her, she would do her best to get some from him. She followed Lucas through a double-door entryway, down an impressive hallway and into a large chamber of polished mahogany and comfortable seating. Original oil paintings portraying distinctly masculine subjects covered the walls. A small fire burned in the hearth. On a table situated in one corner a dinner with two settings was laid out. Although she had no appetite, the aroma was enticing nevertheless. In the center of the table a bottle of wine was chilling. The door closed behind her with a click. She went over and confirmed that it was indeed locked. She whirled around as she heard a slight movement behind her.

Nathan Gamble, dressed casually in an open-collared shirt and cuffed slacks, came around the corner of a high-wingback chair that had been turned toward the far wall. His penetrating gaze made her draw her coat more closely around her. He moved over to the food. "You hungry?"

"Not really, thanks."

"Well, if you change your mind, there's plenty to eat. I hope you don't mind if I do."

"It's your house."

Gamble sat down at the table and started fixing his plate. Then she watched as he poured two glasses of wine. "When I bought this place it came with a wine cellar and two thousand very dusty bottles of wine. Now, I don't know crap about wine, but my people tell me it's a first-rate collection, not that I intend on collecting. Where I come from, you collect stamps. This stuff you drink." He held up a glass for her.

"I really don't think—"

"I hate to drink alone. Makes me think I'm the only one having fun. Besides, it worked for you on the plane, right?"

She finally nodded, slowly removed her coat and took the glass from him. The room was soothingly warm, but she remained on her guard; it was SOP when in the vicinity of active volcanoes and people like Nathan Gamble. She sat down at the dinner table and eyed him while he started eating. He looked at her and motioned at the food. "You sure you're not interested?"

She held up her glass. "This is fine, thanks."

He shrugged, gulped his wine and then proceeded to slice up a hefty piece of steak. "I talked to Henry Wharton recently. Nice guy, always looking out for his people. I appreciate that in an employer. I look out for my people too." He sopped gravy onto a roll and bit a chunk off.

"Henry has been a wonderful mentor to me."

"That's interesting. I never had a mentor, coming up. That might've been nice." He chuckled lightly.

Sidney glanced around the elegant room. "It doesn't look like it hurt you any."

Gamble raised his wineglass, tapped it to hers and then resumed eating. "You holding up? You look like you've lost some weight from the last time I saw you."

"I'm doing okay. Thanks for asking." She flicked at her hair while watching him carefully, trying to keep her nerves in check. She was waiting for the inevitable moment when the small talk would abruptly end. She would have preferred to have gotten right down to business. Gamble was merely playing with her. She had seen him do it dozens of times with other people.

Gamble poured himself another glass of wine and despite her protests, he topped off Sidney's glass. Twenty minutes of innocuous conversation later, Gamble wiped off his mouth with his napkin, stood up and led Sidney over to an oversized leather sofa in front of the fire. She sat down and crossed her legs and took an invisible deep breath. He remained standing by the fireplace mantel and looked at her from under hooded eyelids.

She studied the fire for a moment, sipped the wine and then looked up at him. If he wasn't going to start, she decided she would. "I spoke with Henry too, apparently soon after you did."

Gamble nodded absently. "I thought Henry might give you a buzz after our little talk." Underneath her opaque exterior, Sidney felt herself growing angry at how Gamble manipulated and bullied people to get what he wanted. Gamble produced a cigar from a humidor perched on the mantel. "You mind?"

"As I said, it's your house."

"Some people say cigars aren't habit-forming; I'm not so sure about that. You have to die from something, right?"

She took another sip of wine. "Lucas said you wanted to meet. I'm not privy to the agenda, so would you like to begin?"

Gamble took several short puffs on his cigar to get it going before answering. "You lied to me on the plane, didn't you?" His tone was not one of anger, which surprised her. If anything, she had assumed that a man like Nathan Gamble would have exhibited unbridled fury at such an offense.

"I wasn't completely truthful, no."

A faint twitch moved across Gamble's features. "You're so damned pretty, I keep forgetting you're an attorney. I guess there's a difference between lying and not being completely truthful, although, frankly, I'm not all that interested in the distinction. You lied to me, that's all I'm going to remember."

"I can understand that."

"Why was your husband on that plane?" The question shot out of Gamble's mouth, but his features remained impassive as he stared at her.

Sidney hesitated, then decided to answer fully. It was going to come out at some point. "Jason told me he had been offered an executive position at another technology company based in Los Angeles. He said he was going out for a last round of meetings."

"What company? RTG?"

"It wasn't RTG. It wasn't a direct competitor of yours at all. That's why I didn't think it important to tell you the truth. But as it turns out, it really doesn't matter which company it was."

"Why not?" Gamble looked surprised.

"Because what Jason told me wasn't the truth. There was no job offer, no meetings. I just found that out." She said this as calmly as she could.

Gamble finished his wine and made considerable progress on his cigar before he spoke again. Sidney had noted this trait with other clients who possessed vast wealth. Nothing hurried them. Your time was their time.

"So your husband lied to you and you lied to me. And I'm now supposed to accept what you're telling me as the gospel?" His tone remained even, but his incredulity was unmistakable. Sidney remained silent. She couldn't actually blame him for not believing her. "You're my lawyer; advise me on how I should handle this situation, Sidney. Do I accept what the witness is saying, or not?"

Sidney spoke hurriedly. "I'm not asking you to accept anything. If you don't believe me, and you probably have reason not to, then there's nothing I can do about that."

Gamble nodded thoughtfully. "Okay. What else?"

"There is no 'what else.' I've told you all I know."

Gamble flicked his cigar into the fire. "Come on! In the course of my three divorces I've found, much to my dismay, that pillow talk does happen. Why should you be any different?"

"Jason doesn't . . . didn't discuss Triton business with me. What he did at your company was confidential as far as I was concerned. I don't know anything. I have a lot of questions myself but no answers." Her tone was suddenly bitter, but then she quickly calmed down. "Has anything happened at Triton? Anything that involved Jason?" Gamble didn't say anything. "I'd really like an answer to that."

"I'm not inclined to tell you anything. I don't know whose side you're on, but I doubt if it's mine." Gamble was eyeing her so severely that she felt her face growing red. She uncrossed her legs and looked up at him. "I know you're suspicious—"

Gamble broke in heatedly. "You're goddamned right I'm suspicious. With RTG breathing down my neck. With everybody telling me my company will be an also-ran unless I do a deal with Cyber-Com. How would you feel?" He didn't allow her to answer. He swiftly sat next to her and gripped one of her hands. "Now, I'm really sorry your husband is dead, and under any other circumstances his getting on a plane wouldn't be any of my business. But when everybody starts lying to me at the same time my company's future is blowing in the wind, then it very much becomes my business." He let her hand drop.

Tears pulled at the corners of Sidney's eyes as she jumped up and grabbed her coat. "Right now I don't give a damn about your company or you, but I can tell you that neither my husband nor I have done anything wrong. You got that?" Her eyes blazed at him, her chest heaving. "And now I want to leave."

Nathan Gamble studied her for a long moment, then went over to a table in the far corner of the room and picked up the phone. She couldn't hear what he said. In a moment the door opened and Lucas appeared.

"This way, Ms. Archer."

Walking out, she looked back at Nathan Gamble. He lifted his wineglass in a salutary manner. "Let's keep in touch," he said quietly. The delivery of those four simple words sent a shiver through her entire body.

The limousine reversed its trek and less than forty-five minutes later Sidney was deposited in front of her Ford Explorer. She quickly got in and drove off. She punched a speed dial on her portable phone. A sleepy voice answered.

"Henry, it's Sidney. Sorry if I woke you."

"Sid, what time . . . Where are you?"

"I wanted you to know that I just met with Nathan Gamble."

Henry Wharton was fully awake now. "How did that come about?"

"Let's just say it was at Nathan's suggestion."

"I've been trying to cover for you."

"I know, Henry. I appreciate it."

"So how did it go?"

"Well, probably as well as it could have, under the circumstances. In fact, he was pretty civil."

"Well, that's good."

"It might not last, though, but I wanted you to know. I just left him."

"Maybe this whole thing will just blow over." He added hurriedly, "Of course, I don't mean about Jason's death. I don't mean in any way to minimize that horrible tragedy—"

Sidney quickly cut him off. "I know, I know, Henry. No offense taken."

"So how did you leave it with Nathan?"

She took a deep breath. "We agreed to keep in touch."

The Hay-Adams Hotel was only a few blocks from Tyler, Stone's offices. Sidney awoke early. The clock showed it to be barely five in the morning. She quietly reassessed the progress of the night before. The visit to her husband's office had yielded nothing useful and the meeting with Nathan Gamble had badly scared her. She hoped she had appeased Henry Wharton. For now. After grabbing a quick shower, she called room service and ordered a pot of coffee. She had to be on the road by seven to pick up Amy. She would discuss the memorial service with her parents then.

By the time she was dressed and packed, it was six-thirty. Her parents were habitual early risers and Amy did not ordinarily sleep past six. Sidney's father answered the phone.

"How is she?"

"Your mother's got her. She just finished getting a bath. Just came marching in our bedroom this morning pretty as you please like she owned the place." Sidney could hear the deep pride in her father's voice. "How you holding up, sweetie? You sound a little better."

"I'm holding, Dad. I'm holding. Finally got some sleep, I'm not sure how."

"Well, your mother and I are coming back up with you and we're not taking no for an answer. We can take care of stuff around the house, field calls, run errands, help with Amy."

"Thanks, Dad. I'll be at your place in a couple of hours."

"Here comes Amy looking like a baby chick caught in the rain. I'll put her on."

Sidney could hear the receiver being coddled by the small hands. A few chortles drifted over the line.

"Amy, sweetie, it's Mommy." In the background, Sidney could hear gentle coaxing coming from her mother and father.

"Hi. Mommy?"

"That's right, sweetie, it's Ma-ma."

"*You* talking to me?" Then the little girl laughed uncontrollably for a moment. This was a favorite phrase right now. Amy always hopped off the ground when she said it. Her daughter proceeded to cradle the phone and rattle off her own version of life, in a language most of which Sidney could easily decipher. This morning it was pancakes and bacon and a bird that she had seen go after a cat outside. Sidney smiled. Her smile abruptly vanished with Amy's next words.

"Daddy. I want my daddy."

Sidney closed her eyes. One of her hands moved across her forehead, brushing some hair back. She felt a painful mound of air muscling its way to her throat. She held her hand over the phone so the sound would not carry.

Recovered, she again spoke into the phone. "I love you, Amy. Mommy loves you more than anything. I'll see you in a little while, okay?"

"Love chu. My daddy? Come over, come over now!"

Sidney heard her father tell Amy to say bye-bye.

"Bye-bye, baby. I'll be there soon." The tears fell freely now, their salty taste very familiar to her.

"Honey?"

"Hello, Mom." Sidney rubbed her sleeve across her face. The wetness sprung back immediately, like a stubborn layer of old paint seeping through the fresh coat.

"I'm sorry, honey. I guess she can't talk to you without thinking about Jason."

"I know."

"She's been sleeping all right, at least."

"I'll see you soon, Mom." Sidney hung up the phone and sat with her head in her hands for a few minutes. Then she drifted over to the window, where she pulled open the curtains a notch and peered out. A three-quarters moon together with the multiple streetlights illuminated the area exceedingly well. Even with that, Sidney didn't see the man standing in an alleyway across the street, a small pair of binoculars held in his hands and pointed in her direction. He was dressed in the same coat and hat he had been wearing in Charlottesville. He dutifully watched as Sidney absently scanned the streets below. From years of pulling this kind of duty, his eyes took in every detail. Her face, her eyes in particular, was weary. Her neck was long and graceful, like a model's, but her neck and shoulders were arched back, obviously filled with tension. When she turned away from the window, he lowered his binoculars. A very troubled woman, he concluded. After having observed the suspicious actions of Jason Archer at the airport the morning of the plane crash, the man felt Sidney Archer had every reason to be worried, nervous, perhaps even fearful. He leaned up against the brick wall and continued his sentinel.

CHAPTER TWENTY-THREE

Lee Sawyer was staring out the window of his small apartment in southeast D.C. In the daylight he would be able to see the dome of Union Station from his bedroom window. But daylight was still at least thirty minutes away. Sawyer had not arrived home from investigating the plane fueler's death until almost four-thirty in the morning. He had allowed himself ten minutes under a hot shower to work out the kinks and grogginess. Then he had quickly dressed, put on a pot of coffee, cooked up a couple of eggs and a slice of ham that he probably should have tossed a week ago and toasted some bread. He ate the simple meal on a TV tray in his living room, a small table lamp the only light. The soothing darkness allowed him to sit quietly and think. With the wind rattling against the windows, Sawyer turned his head to study the simple configurations of his home. He grimaced. Home? This was not really his home, although he had been here over a year. Home was in the tree-lined Virginia suburbs: a split-level with vinyl siding, a two-car garage and a brick barbecue in the backyard. This small apartment was where he ate and occasionally slept, mainly because, after the divorce, it was really the only thing he could afford. But it was not and never would be his home, despite the few personal effects he had brought with him, chief of which were the photographs of his four children that peeked out at him from everywhere. He picked up one of the photos. Looking back at him was his youngest. Meg—Meggie, she was called by nearly everyone. Blond and good-looking, she had inherited her father's height, slender nose and full lips. His career as an FBI agent had taken off during her formative years and he had been on the road for much of her adolescence. Paybacks were hell, though. They were not speaking now. At least she wasn't. And he, big as he was, and despite what he did for a living, was too terrified to try anymore. Besides, how many different ways could you say you were sorry?

He rinsed off the dishes, wiped the sink clean and threw some dirty laundry in a mesh bag for deposit at the cleaners. He looked around for anything else that needed to be done. Really there was nothing. He cracked a weary smile. Just killing time. He checked his watch. Almost seven. He would leave for the office shortly. Although he had regular duty shifts, he was typically there at all hours. Not too difficult to understand, since being an FBI agent was really the only thing he had left. There would always be another case. Isn't that what his wife had said that night? The night their marriage had disintegrated. She had been right, though, there would always be another case. In the end, what more could he really ask for or expect? Tired of waiting, he put on his hat, holstered his gun and walked down the stairs to his car.

Barely a five-minute ride from Sawyer's apartment sat the FBI headquarters building on Pennsylvania Avenue between Ninth and Tenth Streets, northwest. It was home to approximately seventy-five hundred employees of the FBI's total workforce of twenty-four thousand. Of the seventy-five hundred, only about one thousand were special agents; the rest were support and technical personnel. In the headquarters building one prominent special agent was sitting at a large conference room table. Other FBI personnel were scattered around the table dutifully going over stacks of files or screens on their laptops. Sawyer took a moment to look around the room and stretch his limbs. They were in the Strategic Information Operations Center, or SIOC. A restricted access area composed of a block of rooms separated by glass walls and shielded from all known types of electronic surveillance, the SIOC was used as the command post for major FBI operations. On one wall was a line of clocks delineating different time zones. A cluster of large-screen TVs lined another wall. The SIOC had secure communications to the White House Situation Room, the CIA and a myriad of federal law enforcement agencies. With no external windows, and thick carpeting, it was a very quiet place used to organize mammoth investigations. A small galley kept the personnel here functioning through exhaustive work hours. Presently, fresh coffee was brewing. Caffeine and brainstorming seemed to go hand in hand.

Sawyer looked across the table to where David Long, a longtime member of the FBI's Bomb Squad, sat staring at a file. To the left of Long was Herb Barracks, an agent from the Charlottesville resident agency, the closest FBI office to the crash site. Next to Barracks was an agent from the Richmond office, the FBI field office in nearest proximity to the disaster. Across from them were two agents from the Washington metropolitan field office at Buzzard Point, which, until the late eighties, had been simply the Washington field office until the Alexandria, Virginia, field office had been collapsed into it.

The director of the FBI, Lawrence Malone, had left an hour earlier after being briefed on the murder of one Robert Sinclair, most recently employed as an aircraft fueler at Vector Fueling Systems and now an occupant of a Virginia morgue. Sawyer felt sure that a fingerprint run through the FBI's Automated Fingerprint Identification System, or AFIS, would give the late Mr. Sinclair another name. Conspirators in a scheme as large as Sawyer figured this one was rarely used their real names in securing employment positions they would later use to down an airliner.

More than two hundred and fifty agents had been assigned to the bombing of Flight 3223. They were following up leads, interviewing family members of the victims and undertaking an excruciatingly detailed investigation of all persons having the motive and opportunity to sabotage the Western Airlines jet. Sawyer figured

Sinclair had done the actual dirty work, but he wasn't taking any chances on overlooking an accomplice at the airport. While rumors had been floating in the press for some time, the first major story actually declaring the downing of the Western flight as being caused by an explosive device would be in the next morning's edition of the *Washington Post*. The public would demand answers and they would want them soon. That was fine with Sawyer, only results weren't always obtained as fast as one would like—in fact, they almost never were.

The FBI had latched on to the Vector line soon after the NTSB team members had found that very special piece of evidence in the crater. After that it was a simple matter to confirm that Sinclair had been the fueler on Flight 3223. Now Sinclair was dead too. Someone had made sure he would never have an opportunity to tell them why he sabotaged the plane.

Long looked at Sawyer. "You were right, Lee. It was a heavily modified version of one of those new portable heating elements. The latest rage in cigarette lighters. No flame, just intense heat from a platinum coil, pretty much invisible."

"I knew I'd seen it before. Remember that arson case involving the IRS building last year?" Sawyer said.

"Right. Anyway, this thing is capable of sustaining about fifteen hundred degrees Fahrenheit. And it wouldn't be affected by wind or cold, even if doused by the jet fuel, or anything like that. Five-hour supply of fuel, rigged so that if it went out for any reason it would automatically relight. One side was affixed with a magnetic pad. It's a simple but perfect way to do it. Jet fuel comes spewing out when the tank gets penetrated. Sooner or later, it's going to get within range of the flame, and then boom." He shook his head. "Pretty damn ingenious. Carry it in your pocket; even if it's detected, on the surface it's a damned cigarette lighter." Long sifted through some more pages as the other agents closely watched him. He ventured a further analysis. "And they didn't need a timer or altimeter device. They could roughly gauge the timing by the acid's corrosiveness. They knew it would be up in the air when it went. Five-hour flight, plenty of time."

Sawyer nodded. "Kaplan and his team found the black boxes. The casing on the flight data recorder was split open, but the tape was relatively intact. Preliminary conclusions indicate that the starboard engine, and the controls running through that section of the wing, were severed from the plane seconds after the CVR recorded a strange sound. They're doing spectrum sound analysis on it now. The FDR showed no drastic change in cabin pressure, so there was definitely no explosion *inside* the fuselage, which makes sense, since we now know the sabotage occurred on the wing. Before that, everything was operating smoothly: no engine problems, level flight, ordinary control surface movements. But once things went bad, they never had a chance."

"The pilots' recording on the CVR give any clues?" Long asked.

Sawyer shook his head. "Usual expletives. The Mayday they radioed in. The FDR showed the plane was in a ninety-degree dive for almost thirty thousand feet with the left engine going at almost full power. Who knows if they could even have remained conscious under those conditions?" Sawyer paused. "Let's hope none of them were," he said solemnly.

Now that it was clear that sabotage had downed the plane, the FBI had officially taken over the investigation from the NTSB. Because of the complexities of the case and its massive organizational challenges, FBI headquarters would be the originating office and Sawyer, his first-rate work on the Lockerbie bombing still fresh in the minds of FBI leadership, would be the case agent, meaning he would run the investigation. But this bombing was a little different: It had occurred over American airspace, had left a crater on American soil. He would let others at the bureau handle the press inquiries and issue statements to the public. He much preferred doing his work in the background.

The FBI devoted large resources of personnel and money to infiltrate terrorist organizations operating in the United States, ferreting out plans and grand schemes to wreak destruction in the name of some political or religious cause before they had a chance to come to fruition. The bombing of Flight 3223 had come right out of the blue. There had been no trickles of information from the FBI's vast network that anything of this magnitude was on the horizon. Having been unable to prevent the disaster, Sawyer would now devote every waking moment, and probably suffer through many a nightmare, in his quest to bring those responsible to justice.

"Well, we know what happened to that plane," Sawyer said. "Now we just have to find out why and who else is involved. Let's start with motive. What else did you dig up on Arthur Lieberman, Ray?"

Raymond Jackson was Sawyer's young partner. He had played college football at Michigan before hanging up his cleats and eschewing an NFL career for one in law enforcement. A shade under six feet, the thick-shouldered black man possessed intelligent eyes and a soft-spoken manner. Jackson flipped open a three-ring notebook.

"A lot of info here. For starters, the guy was terminal. Pancreatic cancer. It was in an advanced stage. He had, maybe, six months. *Maybe.* All treatment had been discontinued. Dude was on massive painkillers, though. Schlesinger's Solution, a combo of morphine and a mood elevator, probably cocaine, one of its few legit uses in this country. Lieberman was outfitted with one of those portable units that dispense drugs directly into the bloodstream."

Sawyer's face betrayed his astonishment. *Walter Burns and his secrets.* "The Fed chairman has six months to live and nobody knows? Where'd you get the info?"

"I found a bottle of chemotherapy drugs in the medicine cabinet at his apartment. Then I went right to the source. His personal physician. Told him we were just doing routine background inquiries. Lieberman's personal calendar evidenced a lot of doctor visits. Some visits to Johns Hopkins, another to the Mayo Clinic. Then I mentioned the medication I'd found. The doc was nervous when I asked him about it. I subtly suggested that not telling the whole truth to the FBI could land his keister in a shitload of trouble. When I mentioned a subpoena, he cracked. He probably figured the patient was dead, what the hell would he care."

"What about the White House? They had to know."

"If they're playing straight with us, they were in the dark too. I talked with the chief of staff about Lieberman's little secret. I don't think he believed me at first. Had to remind him FBI stands for fidelity, bravery and integrity. I also sent over a copy of the medical records to him. Word is the president went ape-shit when he saw them."

"That's an interesting twist," Sawyer said. "I always understood Lieberman was some financial god. Solid as a rock. And yet he forgets to mention he's about to check out with cancer and leave the country in the lurch. That doesn't make much sense."

Jackson grinned. "Just reporting the facts. You're right about the guy's abilities. He's a bona fide legend. However, personally, he wasn't in such great shape financially."

"What do you mean?" Sawyer asked.

Jackson turned the pages of his fat notebook and then stopped. He flipped the notebook around and slid it across to Sawyer. Sawyer stared down at the information while Jackson continued his report.

"Lieberman was divorced about five years ago after twenty-five years of marriage. Apparently he was a naughty boy caught fooling around on the side. The timing could not have been worse. He was just about to go through Senate confirmation hearings for the Fed position. His wife threatened to shred him in the papers. The Fed chairmanship, which I'm told Lieberman coveted, would've gone bye-bye real quick. To get rid of the problem, Lieberman gave just about everything he had to his ex. She died just a couple of years ago. To complicate matters, rumor has it his twenty-something girlfriend had expensive tastes. The Fed job is prestigious, but it doesn't pay the Wall Street bucks, not anywhere near. Fact is, Lieberman was up to his ass in debt. Lived in a crummy apartment over on Capitol Hill while trying to crawl out of a financial hole the size of the Grand Canyon. The stack of love letters we found at the apartment apparently came from her."

"What happened to the girlfriend?" Sawyer asked.

"Not sure. It wouldn't surprise me if she'd walked out when she found out her little pot of gold was full of the big C."

"Any idea where she is now?"

Jackson shook his head. "From all accounts, she's been out of the picture for some time now. I tracked down several colleagues of

Lieberman's back in New York. The woman was beautiful but brain-less according to them."

"It's probably a waste of time, but make some more inquiries on her anyway, Ray."

Jackson nodded.

Sawyer looked at Barracks. "Any word from the Hill on who's going to take Lieberman's slot?"

When Barracks answered, Sawyer was rocked for the second time in less than a minute.

"General consensus: Walter Burns."

Sawyer stared at Barracks for several moments and then wrote the name "Walter Burns" in his notebook. In the margin next to it he scribbled the word "asshole" and then the word "suspect" with a question mark next to it.

Sawyer looked up from his notebook. "Sounds like our Mr. Lieberman was riding a streak of particularly bad luck. So why kill him?"

"Lots of reasons," Barracks spoke up. "The Fed chairman is the symbol of American monetary policy. Make a nice little target for some third world crap-can of a country with a big green monster on its shoulder. Or pick from about a dozen active terrorist groups who specialize in plane bombings."

Sawyer shook his head. "No group has claimed responsibility for the bombing yet."

Barracks snorted. "Give 'em time. Now that we've confirmed it was a bombing, whoever did it will be phoning in. Blowing Amer-icans out of the sky to make a political statement, that's what those assholes live for."

"Goddammit!" Sawyer slammed his massive fist down on the table, stood up and started pacing, his face a sheet of vivid red. It seemed as though every ten seconds the image of the impact crater swept across his thoughts. Added to that now was the smaller but even more devastating vision of the tiny, singed shoe he had held in his hand. He had cradled each of his children in one big hand upon their birth. It could have been any of them. Any of them! He knew that vision would never fully leave his thoughts for as long as he remained on this earth.

The agents eyed him anxiously. Sawyer had a well-deserved reputation as being one of the sharpest agents among a legion of them at the bureau. Through twenty-five years of seeing fellow humans gallop a crimson path through the country, he had continued to attack each case with the same zeal and rigor he had shown from day one on the job. He ordinarily chose carefully worded analysis over scattergun hyperbole; however, most of the agents who had worked with him over the years understood crystal-clearly that his temper was contained by a very slender catch.

He stopped his pacing and looked at Barracks. "There's a problem with that theory, Herb." His voice was once again calm.

"What's that?"

Sawyer leaned against one of the glass walls, crossed his arms and rested them on his broad chest. "If you're a terrorist looking to make a big splash, you sneak a bomb on the plane—which, let's face it, isn't all that hard to do on a domestic flight—and you blow the plane into a million pieces. Bodies pouring down, crashing through roofs, interrupting Americans eating breakfast. Leave no room for doubt that it was a bombing." Sawyer paused and intently looked at the face of each agent. "That did not happen here, gentlemen."

Sawyer resumed his pacing. All eyes in the room followed his progress. "The jet was virtually intact on its way down. If the right wing hadn't come off, *all* of it would be in that crater. Mark that point. The fueler from Vector is presumably paid to sabotage the plane. Surreptitious work performed by an American who is not, at least as far as we know, linked to any terrorist group. It would be hard for me to believe that Middle Eastern terrorist groups have started admitting Americans into their ranks to perform their dirty work.

"We had the damage on the fuel tank, but that could as easily have been caused by the explosion and fire. The acid was almost all burned away. A little more heat and maybe we would have found nothing. And Kaplan has confirmed that the wing didn't have to come off the fuselage in order to crash the plane in the same manner. The starboard engine was destroyed from debris ingestion, critical flight control hydraulic lines were severed by the fire and explosion, and the aerodynamics of the wing, even if it had remained intact, was destroyed. So if we hadn't found the igniter in the crater, this thing might've gone down as some horrific mechanical failure. And make no mistake about it, it was a damned miracle that the igniter was found."

Sawyer looked through one of the glass walls and continued. "So you add that all up, and what do you have? Arguably, someone who blows up a plane but maybe doesn't want it to look that way. Not your typical terrorist MO. But then the picture gets even more cloudy. The logic starts to cut the other way. First, our fueler ends up with a full clip in him. His bags were packed, half a disguise on, and his employer presumably changes the plan on him. Second, we have Arthur Lieberman on the same flight." Sawyer glanced at Jackson. "The man went to L.A. every month, like clockwork, same airline, same flight each month, right?"

Jackson, eyes narrowed to slits, nodded slowly. Each agent was unconsciously leaning forward as they followed Sawyer's logic.

"So the odds of the guy being on the flight by accident are so high it's not worth debating. Looking at it cold, Lieberman had to be the target, unless we're missing something really big. Now put the two pieces together. Initially, our bombers may have tried to make it look like an accident. Then the fueler ends up dead. "Why?" Sawyer looked sharply around the room.

David Long finally spoke up. "Couldn't risk it. Maybe the chances are it goes down like an accident, and maybe not. They can't wait around until the papers report it one way or another. They have to take the guy out right away. Besides, if the original plan was to have the guy take a hike, him not showing for work would raise suspicion. Even if we didn't think sabotage, the guy skipping town would sure as hell turn us in that direction."

"Agreed," Sawyer replied. "But if you want the trail to end there, why not make it look like the fueler's some fanatical zealot? Put a bullet into his temple, leave the gun and some BS suicide note behind filled with I-hate-America language and let us think the guy's a loner. You fill him full of holes, leave behind evidence pointing to the guy getting ready to run, now we know there are others involved. Why the hell bring yourself that kind of trouble?" Sawyer rubbed his chin.

The other agents leaned back in their chairs, looking confused.

Sawyer finally looked at Jackson. "Any word from the ME on our dead guy?"

"They promised a top priority. We'll know soon."

"Anything else turn up at the guy's apartment?"

"One thing that didn't turn up, Lee."

Sawyer flashed a knowing look. "No I.D. docs."

"Yep," Jackson said. "Guy getting ready to hit the road after blowing up a plane will not be running as himself. Way this was probably planned out, he had to have phony docs, *good* phony docs ready."

"True, Ray, but he could've had them stashed someplace else."

"Or whoever killed him might've taken them too," Barracks ventured.

"No argument there," Sawyer said.

On those words the door to the SIOC opened and through it stepped Marsha Reid. Petite and motherly looking, with salt and pepper hair cut short and glasses riding on a chain over her black dress, she was one of the bureau's top fingerprint personnel. Reid had tracked down some of the worst criminals on the planet through the esoteric world of arches, loops and whorls.

Marsha nodded to the other agents in the room and then sat down and opened the file she had carried in.

"AFIS results, hot off the presses," she said, her tone businesslike but laced with a touch of humor. "Robert Sinclair was actually Joseph Philip Riker, currently wanted in Texas and Arkansas on murder and related weapons charges. His arrest sheet is three pages long. His first arrest was for armed robbery at age sixteen. His last was for second-degree murder. He served seven years. Was released five years ago. Since then he's been implicated in numerous crimes, including two murders-for-hire. An extremely dangerous man. His trail went cold about eighteen months ago. Not a peep from him since. Until now."

Every agent at the table looked stunned.

"How does a guy like that get a job fueling planes?" Sawyer's tone was incredulous.

Jackson answered the query. "I spoke with representatives from Vector. They're a reputable company. Sinclair—or, rather, Riker had been with them only about a month. He had excellent credentials. Worked at several aircraft fueling companies in the Northwest and in southern California. They did a background check on him, under the name Sinclair, of course. Everything came out okay. They were as stunned by this as anyone else."

"What about fingerprints? They had to check his fingerprints. That would've told them who the guy really was."

Reid eyed Sawyer. She spoke with authority. "Depends on who's taking the prints, Lee. A borderline competent tech can be fooled, you know that. There's synthetic material out there you'd swear was skin. You can buy prints on the street. Put it all together and a career criminal becomes a respectable citizen."

Barracks piped in. "And if the guy was wanted on all those other crimes, he probably had a new face put on. Five gets you ten the face in that morgue isn't the face on those wanted posters."

Sawyer looked at Jackson. "How did Riker end up fueling Flight 3223?"

"About a week ago he asked to be switched to the graveyard shift, twelve to seven. Flight 3223's scheduled departure time was six forty-five. Same time every day. Log shows the plane was fueled at five-fifteen. That put it on Riker's rounds. Most people don't volunteer for that shift, so Riker got it pretty much by default."

Another question occurred to Sawyer. "So where's the real Robert Sinclair?"

"Probably dead," said Barracks. "Riker took over his identity."

No one commented on that theory until Sawyer pursued the issue with a startling query. "Or what if Robert Sinclair doesn't exist?" Now even Reid looked puzzled. Sawyer looked deep in thought when he spoke. "There are a lot of problems with taking over a real person's identity. Old photos, co-workers or friends who show up unexpectedly and blow your cover. There's another way to do it." Sawyer pursed his lips and raised his eyebrows as he thought his idea through. "I've got a gut feeling on this one that's telling me we need to redo everything that Vector did when they performed their background check on Riker. Get on that, Ray, like yesterday."

Jackson nodded and jotted down some notes.

Reid looked at Sawyer. "Are you thinking what I think you are?"

Sawyer smiled. "It wouldn't be the first time a person was invented out of whole cloth. Social Security number, job history, past residences, photo identification, bank accounts, training certifications, fake phone numbers, dummy references." He looked at Reid. "Even false prints, Marsha."

"Then we're talking some pretty sophisticated guys," she replied.

"I never doubted they were anything less, Ms. Reid," Sawyer rejoined.

Sawyer looked around the table. "I don't want to stray from SOP, so we'll still continue to conduct interviews of family members of the victims, but I don't want to waste too much time on that. Lieberman is the key to this whole thing." He suddenly changed gears. "Rapid Start running smoothly?" he asked Ray Jackson.

"Very."

Rapid Start was the FBI's version of the show on the road and Sawyer had used it successfully in the past. The premise of Rapid Start was the veracity of an electronic clearinghouse for every bit of information, leads and anonymous tips involved in an investigation that otherwise would become unorganized and muddled. With an integrated investigation and pretty close to real-time access to information, the chances of success, the bureau believed, were immeasurably increased.

The Rapid Start operation for Flight 3223 was housed in an abandoned tobacco warehouse on the outskirts of Standardsville. Instead of tobacco leaves stored floor to ceiling, the building now housed the latest in computer and telecommunications equipment manned by dozens of agents working in shifts who inputted information into the massive databases twenty-four hours a day.

"We're gonna need every miracle it can produce. And even that might not be enough." Sawyer was silent for a moment and then snapped to attention. "Let's get to work."

CHAPTER TWENTY-FOUR

Quentin?" Sidney stood at the front door of her house, the surprise evident on her face.

Quentin Rowe stared back at her through his oval glasses. "May I come in?"

Sidney's parents were out grocery shopping. While Sidney and Quentin headed toward the living room, a sleepy Amy wandered into the room dragging Pooh. "Hi, Amy," Rowe said. He knelt down and put out a hand to her, but the little girl drew back. Rowe smiled at her. "I was shy when I was your age too." He looked up at Sidney. "That's probably why I turned to computers. They didn't talk back at you, or try to touch you." He paused, seemingly lost in thought. Then he started and looked up at her. "Do you have time to talk?"

Sidney hesitated.

"Please, Sidney?"

"Let me put this little girl down for a much-needed nap. I'll be back in a few minutes." Sidney carried her out.

While she was gone, Rowe slowly walked around the room. He studied the many photos of the Archer family scattered across the walls and tabletops. He looked over as Sidney came back into the room. "Beautiful little girl you have there."

"She is something. A terrific something."

"Especially now, right?"

Sidney nodded.

Rowe kept his eyes on her. "I lost both my parents in a plane crash when I was fourteen."

"Oh, Quentin."

He shrugged. "It was a long time ago. But I think I can understand a little better than most how you're feeling. I was an only child. There really wasn't anyone left for me."

"I guess I'm fortunate in that regard."

"You are, Sidney, keep reminding yourself of that."

She took a deep breath. "Would you like something to drink?"

"Tea, if you have it."

A few minutes later they were settled on the living room sofa. Rowe balanced his saucer on his knee while he sipped delicately at his tea. He put his cup down and looked over at her, his awkwardness apparent. "First, I want to apologize to you."

"Quentin—"

He put up one hand. "I know what you're going to say, but I was way out of line. The things I said, the way I treated you. I . . . Sometimes I don't think before I speak. In fact, I'm often that way. I'm not all that good at presenting myself. I know I come off as geeky and uncaring sometimes, but I'm really not."

"I know that, Quentin. We've always had a good relationship. Everyone at Triton thinks the world of you. I know that Jason did. If it makes you feel any better, I find you far easier to relate to than Nathan Gamble."

"You and the rest of the world," Rowe said quickly. "With that said, I guess I should explain by saying that I was under a great deal of pressure, what with Gamble balking at doing CyberCom, the chance that we could lose it all."

"Well, I think Nathan understands what's at stake."

Rowe nodded absently. "The second thing I wanted to tell you is how truly sorry I am about Jason. It just shouldn't have happened.

Jason was probably the one person I could truly connect to at the company. He was as talented as I was on the technology side, but he was also able to present himself well, an area, as I said, I'm lacking in."

"I think you handle yourself very well."

Rowe brightened. "You do?" Then he sighed. "Next to Gamble, most people, I guess, seem like wallflowers."

"I wouldn't disagree, but I also wouldn't recommend that you emulate him."

Rowe put his tea down. "I know it seems like he and I are strange bedfellows."

"It's hard to argue with the success you two have had."

His tone was suddenly bitter. "Right. The great measuring stick of money. When I first started out, I had ideas. Wonderful ideas, but no capital. Then along came Nathan." His expression was not a pleasant one.

"It's not only that, Quentin. You have a vision for the future. I understand that vision, to the extent a technology neophyte can. I know that vision is what's driving the CyberCom deal."

Rowe smacked his fist into the palm of his hand. "Exactly, Sidney. Exactly. The stakes are so incredibly high. CyberCom's technology is so dramatically superior, so monumental, it's like the second coming of Graham Bell." He seemed to shiver with anticipation as he looked at her. "Do you realize that the one thing holding back the limitless potential of the Internet is the fact that it's so large, so all-consuming that navigating it efficiently is often a horrendous exercise in futility for even the most adept computer users?"

"But with CyberCom, that will change?"

"Yes! Yes. Of course."

"I have to confess, despite working on this deal for so many months, I'm really not certain what exactly CyberCom has come up with. Lawyers rarely get into those nuances, particularly those who never excelled in the sciences, such as myself." She smiled.

Rowe sat back, his slender frame assuming a comfortable tilt when the conversation veered toward technical issues. "In laymen's terms CyberCom has done nothing less than create artificial intelligence, so-called intelligent agents that will initially be used to effortlessly navigate the myriad tributaries of the Internet and its progeny."

"Artificial intelligence? I thought that existed only in the movies."

"Not at all. There are degrees of artificial intelligence, of course. CyberCom's is by far the most sophisticated I've ever seen."

"How exactly does it work?"

"Let's say you want to find out about every article written on some controversial subject, and you also want a summary of those articles, listing those in favor and opposed, the reasons therefor, the analysis behind it and so on. Now, if you attempted that on your own through the unwieldy labyrinth the Internet has become, it would take you forever. As I said, the overwhelming amount of information contained on the Internet is its greatest drawback. Human beings are ill-equipped to deal with something on that scale. But you get around that obstacle and suddenly it's as though the surface of Pluto becomes alive with sunshine."

"And that's what CyberCom has done?"

"With CyberCom in our fold, we will initiate a wireless, satellite-based network that will be seamlessly coordinated with proprietary software that will soon be on every computer in America, and eventually the world. The software is easily the most user-friendly I've ever seen. It asks the user precisely what information is needed. It will ask additional questions as it deems necessary. Then, tapping into our satellite-based network, it will explore every molecule of the conglomeration of computers we call the Internet until it assembles, in picture-perfect form, the answer to every single question you asked, and many more you weren't perceptive enough to think of. Best of all, it's chameleon-like in that the intelligent agents can adapt to and communicate with any network server in existence. That's another drawback to the Internet: systems' inability to communicate with each other. And it will perform this task a billion times faster than any human could. It will be like minutely examining every drop of the Nile River in a few minutes. Even faster. Finally, the vast sources of knowledge that are out there and growing exponentially with every passing day can actually be efficiently linked up to the one entity which really needs them." He looked pointedly at her. "Humanity. And it doesn't stop there. The network interface with the Internet is only one small part of the overall puzzle. It also elevates the encryption standard to unparalleled heights. Imagine fluid responses to attempts to illegally decrypt electronic transmissions. Responses that can not only adjust to fend off a hacker's multithrust attacks, but aggressively pursue the intruder and track *him* down. Do you think that would be popular with law enforcement agencies? This is the next milestone in the technological revolution. This will dictate how all data is transmitted and used in the next century. How we build, teach, think. Just envision computers that are not merely dumb machines reacting to precise instructions keyed in by humans. Picture computers using their vast intellectual muscle to think on their own, to *problem-solve* for us in ways unthinkable today. It will make so much obsolete, including much of Triton's existing product line. It changes everything. Like the internal combustion engine did to the era of the horse-drawn carriages but even more profoundly."

"My God," Sidney exclaimed. "And I guess the potential profits—"

"Yes, yes, we'll make billions from sales of software, the network charges—every business in the world will want to be on-line with us. And that's only the beginning." Rowe sounded distinctly uninterested in this side of the equation. "And yet with all that, Gamble still won't see, is incapable of understanding . . ." He stood up in his anxiety, his arms flailing. He caught himself and sat back down, his face carrying a red sheen. "I'm . . . I'm sorry, sometimes I get carried away."

"It's okay, Quentin, I understand. Jason shared your excitement about the CyberCom deal, I know that."

"We had many pleasant discussions about it."

"And Gamble is acutely aware of the consequences of another company acquiring CyberCom. I have to believe that he will come to his senses over the records issue."

Rowe nodded. "One can only hope," he said quickly. Sidney

glanced at the diamond studs in his earlobe. They seemed to be the only extravagance about the man, and a small one at that. A millionaire several hundred times over, Rowe lived much like the impoverished college student he had been ten years ago. Finally Rowe broke the silence. "Jason and I talked about the future a lot, in fact. He was a very special person." He seemed to share the depths of Sidney's misery whenever Jason's name was mentioned. "I guess you won't be working on the CyberCom matter anymore?"

"The attorney who's replacing me is top-notch. You won't miss a beat."

"Oh, good." He sounded extremely unconvinced.

She rose and gripped his shoulder. "Quentin, this deal *will* get done." She noted his empty teacup. "Would you like some more tea?"

"What? Uh, no, no, thanks." He collapsed back into deep thought, rubbing his thin hands nervously. When he snatched a look at her, Sidney thought she knew what was on his mind.

"I had an impromptu meeting with Nathan recently."

Rowe slowly nodded. "He told me something of it."

"So you know about Jason's 'trip'?"

"That he told you he was going for a job interview?"

"Yes."

"What company?" The question was asked very matter-of-factly.

Sidney hesitated and then decided to answer. "AllegraPort Technology."

Rowe snorted. "I could've told you that was a joke. AllegraPort will be out of business in less than two years. They were on the cutting edge a while back, but they let the industry pass them by. You grow and keep innovating in this field or you die. Jason would never have seriously considered going with them."

"As it turned out, he didn't. They had never heard of him."

Rowe was obviously already privy to this information. "Could it have been something else . . . I don't quite know how to put this . . ."

"Personal? Another woman?"

Like an embarrassed child, Rowe mumbled, "I shouldn't have said that. It's none of my business."

"No, it's all right. I can't tell you that the thought never crossed my mind. However, our relationship recently was the best it's ever been."

"So he never indicated to you that anything was going on in his life? Nothing that would have prompted him to . . . to take a trip to L.A., and not to tell you the truth about it?"

Sidney looked wary. Was this all a fishing expedition? Had Gamble perhaps sent his second-in-command over to glean some information? When she looked at Rowe's troubled expression, she swiftly concluded that he had come here on his own in an attempt to figure out what had happened to his employee and friend.

"Nothing. Jason never really talked to me about work. I have no idea what he was doing. I wish to God I did. It's the not knowing that's killing me." She debated whether to ask Rowe about the new locks on Jason's door and Kay Vincent's other concerns, but finally decided not to.

After an awkward silence, Rowe stirred. "I have those personal items of Jason's you came to the office for in the car. After I was so rude to you, I thought it best to bring them myself."

"Thank you, Quentin. Believe me when I tell you I harbor no hard feelings. It's a rough time for us all."

Rowe thanked her with a smile as he stood up. "I have to be going. I'll go get the box. If you need anything, just let me know." After bringing in the items, Rowe said his good-byes and turned to leave. Sidney touched him on the shoulder.

"Nathan Gamble won't be looking over your shoulder forever. Everyone knows who's really behind the success of Triton Global."

He looked surprised. "You really think so?"

"It's hard to hide genius."

He breathed deeply. "I don't know. Gamble seems to keep surprising me in that regard."

He turned and walked slowly back to his car.

CHAPTER TWENTY-FIVE

It was nearly midnight when Lee Sawyer's head hit the pillow after a hastily eaten dinner. His eyes, however, failed to close, although a massive weariness tugged at him. He looked around the tiny living space and abruptly decided to get up. He padded through the hallway in his bare feet, undershorts and T-shirt and plopped down on a beaten-up recliner in the living room. The typical career of an FBI agent didn't often lend itself to long-standing domestic tranquillity. Too many missed anniversaries, holidays, birthdays. Gone for months at a time, no end in sight. He had been severely wounded in the line of duty, a traumatic situation for any spouse. There had been threats to his family from the human waste he had dedicated his life to eradicating. All for the cause of justice, of making the world, if not better, at least momentarily safer. A noble goal that didn't sound so special when you were trying to explain to your eight-year-old over the phone why Daddy was going to miss another baseball game, another recital or school play. He had known that going in; Peg had too. Being so much in love, they truly believed they could beat the odds, and they had for a long time. Ironically, his relationship with Peg was now better than it had been in years.

The kids, though, were a different matter. He had taken the full brunt of the blame for the breakup and maybe he deserved it, he thought. Only now were his three oldest kids beginning to talk to him on anything approaching a consistent basis. Meggie was completely gone from him. He didn't know what was going on in her life. That's what had hurt the most. The not knowing.

Everyone had choices to make and he had made his own. He had enjoyed a very successful career at the bureau, but that success had come with a cost. He walked to the kitchen, pulled out a cold beer and plopped back down in the recliner. His magical sleeping potion of choice. At least he wasn't into the hard liquor. Yet. He finished the beer in several large gulps, lay back in the chair and closed his eyes.

An hour later, the telephone ringing roused him from a deep sleep. He was still sitting in the recliner. He picked up the telephone receiver on the table next to his chair.

"Yeah?"

"Lee?"

Sawyer's eyelids fluttered briefly, then opened. "Frank?" Sawyer looked at his watch. "You're not with the bureau anymore, Frank, I thought the private sector lets you keep more regular hours."

On the other end of the line Frank Hardy was fully dressed and sitting in a nicely furnished office. On the wall behind him hung numerous mementos depicting a long and distinguished career with the FBI. Hardy smiled. "Too much competition out here, Lee. Just having twenty-four hours in a day doesn't seem fair."

"Well, I'm not ashamed to admit it's about my limit. What's up?"

"Your plane bombing," Hardy said simply.

Sawyer sat straight up, fully awake now, his eyes focusing in the darkness. "What?"

"I got something here you're going to need to see, Lee. I'm not clear on exactly what it all means yet. I'm about to brew a pot of coffee. How long will it take you to get here?"

"Give me thirty minutes."

"Just like old times."

In five minutes Sawyer was fully dressed. He slipped his 10mm pistol into its holster and went down to the street to fire up his sedan. On the drive over he reported in to headquarters to alert them to this recent development. Frank Hardy had been one of the best agents the bureau had ever produced. When he left to start his own security firm, every agent had felt the loss, but no one begrudged Hardy the opportunity after his many years of service. He and Sawyer had been partners for ten years before Hardy made his exit. They had been a prolific team, beating the odds on a number of high-profile cases and bringing to justice criminals who had gone far underground. Many of their targets were now serving life sentences without parole at various maximum-security federal prisons around the country. More than a handful, several of them serial killers, had been executed.

If Hardy thought he had something on the plane bombing, then he did. Sawyer sped up and within ten minutes pulled his car into a vast parking lot. The fourteen-story building in Tysons Corner housed a number of businesses, none of them involved in anything nearly as exciting as Hardy's concern.

Sawyer was cleared through security after showing his FBI credentials and rode the elevator up to the fourteenth floor. Stepping out of the elevator, he found himself in the modern-looking reception area. Soft cove lighting illuminated the otherwise darkened expanse of the area. Behind the receptionist's desk were six-inch-high white letters proclaiming the name of the establishment: SE-CURTECH.

CHAPTER TWENTY-SIX

Sidney Archer watched the methodical rise and fall of the small chest. Her parents were sleeping soundly in the guest bedroom down the hall while Sidney sat in the rocking chair in Amy's room. Finally Sidney rose and went to the window to look out. She had never been much of a night person. Hectic days had demanded that when the time came to sleep, she slept. Now the darkness seemed powerfully soothing to her, like a gentle cascade of warm water. It made recent events seem less real, less terrifying than she knew them actually to be. When the daylight came, though, the calming quiet of the night would leave her again. Tomorrow also would bring the memorial service for Jason. People would be coming to the house to pay their respects, to reflect on what a good life her husband had led. Sidney wasn't sure if she would be up to it, but that was a worry that she would allow to lie for a few more hours.

She kissed Amy on the cheek, quietly exited the room and moved down the hallway to Jason's small study. She reached above the door-jamb and pulled down half a bobby pin, which she inserted in the lock on the door. At two years old, Amy Archer could get into anything: mascara, pantyhose, jewelry, Jason's ties, shoes, wallets and purses. They had once found the title to Jason's Cougar crammed in the pancake mix along with the house keys they had been frantically searching for. Once she and Jason had awoken to find a full box of dental floss wrapped around their four-poster bed. Turning doorknobs was a simple matter for the youngest Archer, hence most doors in the place had a bobby pin or bent paper clip riding above them.

Sidney went in and sat down in front of the desk. The computer screen stared back at her, its flat face dark and silent. A part of her waited for another e-mail to burst on the screen, hoping beyond hope, but it did not happen. She looked around the small room. Being wholly Jason's, it seemed continually to draw her. She touched certain favorite items of his as if they would, by osmosis, reveal to her the secrets her husband had left behind. The phone ringing broke her thoughts. It rang again and she quickly picked it up, not knowing what to expect. For a moment Sidney did not recognize the voice. "Paul?"

"I'm sorry for calling so late. I've been trying to reach you the last few days. I left messages."

She hesitated. "I know, Paul, I'm sorry, there's been so much—"

"Jesus, Sid, I didn't say that to make you feel guilty. I was just worried about you. Finding out about Jason like that, I don't know how you're holding up. You're stronger than I am."

She smiled weakly. "I don't feel so strong right now."

Paul Brophy's voice was earnest. "You've got a lot of people at Tyler, Stone pulling for you. And one New York–based partner in particular who is available twenty-four hours a day to help."

"The support is touching, it really is."

"I'm flying down for the memorial service tomorrow."

"You don't have to do that, Paul, you must be swamped."

"Not really. I don't know if you were aware, but I made a run at taking the helm on the CyberCom deal."

"Really?" Sidney did her best to keep her voice even.

"Yeah, only I didn't get it. Wharton was rather blunt in rejecting my offer."

"I'm sorry, Paul." Sidney felt momentary guilt. "There will be other deals, though."

"I know, but I really thought I could do it. I really did." He paused. Sidney prayed that he would not ask her whether Wharton had sought her advice on the matter. When he finally did speak, she felt more guilty still. "I am coming tomorrow, Sid. I can't think of any place I'd rather be."

"Thank you." Sidney pulled her robe closer around her.

"Is it okay if I come directly to your house from the airport?"

"That's fine."

"Get some sleep, Sid. I'll see you first thing in the morning. You need anything, anytime, day or night, you just have to call, okay?"

"Thank you, Paul. Good night." Sidney put the phone down. She had always gotten along with Brophy, but she was certainly aware that under his ultrasmooth exterior lurked a pure opportunist. She had told Henry Wharton that Paul did not belong on the CyberCom deal and now he was coming down to be with her in her time of grief. Well, she may be grieving, but she didn't believe in coincidences that big. She wondered what his true motive could be.

As he hung up the phone, Paul Brophy surveyed the broad expanse of his luxurious apartment. When you were thirty-four, single and good-looking with a mid-six-figure income, New York City was a great place to be. He smiled and ran his hand through thick hair. Six figures that would, with a little luck, turn into seven. Much in life depended on whom you allied yourself with. He picked up the phone and dialed. The phone was answered after one ring. The voice was quick and businesslike after Brophy identified himself.

"Hello, Paul, I was hoping to hear from you tonight," Philip Goldman said.

CHAPTER TWENTY-SEVEN

Frank Hardy loaded the videotape into the VCR resting under the wide-screen TV in one corner of the conference room. It was almost two o'clock in the morning. Lee Sawyer sat in one of the plush chairs, nursing a cup of hot coffee and admiring the surroundings. "Damn, business must be really good, Frank. I keep forgetting how far you've risen in the world."

Hardy laughed. "Well, if you'd ever take my offer to join me, Lee, I wouldn't have to keep reminding you."

"I'm just so set in my ways, Frank."

Hardy grinned. "Renee and I are thinking of going to the Caribbean over Christmas. You could join us. Maybe even bring somebody else along." Hardy looked at his former partner expectantly.

"Sorry, Frank, there really isn't anybody right now."

"It's been two years. I just thought . . . After Sally walked out, I thought I was going to die. Didn't want to go through the dating process again. Then Renee happened along. I couldn't be happier."

"Seeing as how Renee could pass as Michelle Pfeiffer's twin, I can see how you must be a very happy man."

Hardy laughed. "You might want to reconsider. Renee has some girlfriends who adhere strictly to her level of aesthetics. And the women go nuts over you tall, strong types, I'm telling you."

Sawyer grunted. "Right. Not to detract from you, handsome old buddy, but I don't have the bucks in the bank you do. Consequently, my attraction level has dimmed a little over the years. Besides, I'm still only a government employee. Coach class and Kmart are about my limit and I don't think you travel in those circles anymore."

Hardy sat down and picked up a coffee mug with one hand and the VCR remote with the other. "I was planning on picking up the whole tab, Lee," he said quietly. "Call it an early Christmas present. You're so damned hard to shop for."

"Thanks anyway. Actually, I'm thinking about trying to spend some time with the kids this year. If they'll have me."

Frank nodded. "I hear you."

"Now, what do you have for me?"

Hardy said, "We've been Triton Global's chief security consultant for the last several years."

Sawyer picked up his coffee cup. "Triton Global? Computer, telecommunications. They're a Fortune 500, aren't they?"

"Technically, they don't qualify for the list."

"Why's that?"

They're a nonpublic company. They dominate their field, expanding like crazy, and doing it all without capital from the public markets."

"Impressive. How does that tie in to a plane taking a nosedive into the Virginia countryside?"

"Several months ago Triton suspected that certain proprietary information was being leaked to a competitor. They called us in to verify the suspicion and, if true, to discover the leak."

"Did you?"

Hardy nodded. "We first narrowed down the list of those competitors who were most likely to participate in such a scheme. Once we had those nailed down, we undertook surveillance."

"That must've been tough. Big companies, thousands of employees, hundreds of offices."

"It was a daunting challenge, at first. However, our information led us to believe the leak was fairly senior, so we kept our eye on high-level Triton people."

Lee Sawyer settled farther back in his chair and sipped his coffee. "So you identified some other 'unofficial' places where the exchange might take place and set up your snooping shop?"

Hardy smiled. "Sure you don't want that job?"

Sawyer shrugged off the compliment. "So what happened?"

"We identified a number of these 'unofficial' locations, property owned by our suspect companies and which seemed to have no legitimate operational purpose. At each of these sites we set up surveillance." Hardy smiled sardonically at his former colleague. "Don't read me the riot act over trespassing and other related legal violations, Lee. Sometimes the ends do justify the means."

"Not arguing with you there. I wish we could take shortcuts sometimes. But then we'd have a hundred lawyers screaming 'unconstitutional' and there goes my pension."

"Anyway, two days ago a routine inspection was made of a surveillance camera set up inside a warehouse building located near Seattle."

"What led you to stake out that particular warehouse?"

"Information we developed led us to believe that the building was owned, through a string of subsidiaries and partnerships, by the RTG Group. They're one of Triton's major global competitors."

"What was the nature of the information Triton believed was being leaked? Technology?"

"No. Triton was involved in negotiations for the acquisition of a very valuable software company called CyberCom. We believe that information on those negotiations was being leaked to RTG, information that RTG could use to step in and buy the company itself, since it would know Triton's terms and negotiating position. Based on the video you're about to see, we've made subtle noises to RTG. They've denied everything, of course. They're claiming that the warehouse was leased last year to an unaffiliated company. We checked out the company. It's nonexistent. Meaning RTG is lying or we've got another player in this game."

Sawyer nodded. "Okay. Tell me about the tie-in to my case."

Hardy responded by pushing a button on the remote. The large-screen TV sprung to life. Sawyer and Hardy watched as the scene in the small room in the warehouse was replayed. When the tall young man accepted the silver case from the older gentlemen, Hardy froze the screen. He looked over at Sawyer's puzzled face. Hardy pulled a laser pointer from his shirt pocket to highlight the young man.

"This man is employed by Triton Global. We didn't have him on the surveillance list because he wasn't senior-level management and he wasn't directly involved in the acquisition negotiations."

"Despite that, he's obviously your leak. Recognize anyone else?"

Hardy shook his head. "Not yet. The man's name, by the way, is Jason W. Archer of 611 Morgan Lane in Jefferson County, Virginia. Sound familiar?"

Sawyer concentrated hard. The name did seem to ring a bell. Then it suddenly hit him like a half-ton truck. "Jesus Christ!" He half rose out of his chair, eyes bulging at the face on the screen as the name shot out at him from a passenger manifest that he had scrutinized a hundred times already. At the bottom of the screen, digital images paraded across. The date and time stamp read NOVEMBER 17, 1995 11:15 AM PST. Sawyer's quick eyes took in the information with one glance and he calculated rapidly. Seven hours after the plane had crashed in Virginia, this guy was alive and kicking in Seattle. "Jesus H. Christ!" he exclaimed again.

Hardy nodded. "That's right. Jason Archer was listed as a passenger on Flight 3223. But he obviously wasn't on the flight."

Hardy let the tape run. When the roar of the plane erupted on its sound track, Sawyer jerked his head to the window. The damn thing sounded like it was coming right at them. When he looked back at Hardy, his friend was smiling.

"I did the same thing when I heard it for the first time."

Sawyer watched as the men on the screen looked skyward until the sound of the plane in the background drifted away. Sawyer squinted at the screen. Something caught his eye; he just couldn't put his finger on it.

Hardy was watching him closely. "See something?"

Sawyer finally shook his head. "Okay, what was Archer doing in Seattle on the morning of the Virginia crash if he was supposed to be on a plane to L.A.? Company business?"

"Triton didn't even know Archer was gong to L.A., much less Seattle. They thought he was taking some time off to spend at home with his family."

Sawyer narrowed his eyes, searching his memory. "Help me out here, Frank."

Hardy's answer was prompt. "Archer has a wife and young daughter. His wife, Sidney, is an attorney at Tyler, Stone, Triton's lead outside counsel. The wife works on a number of Triton's business matters, including heading up Triton's pursuit of CyberCom."

"That's real interesting, and maybe convenient for her and her husband."

"Gotta admit, that's the first thought that struck me, Lee."

"If Archer was in Seattle by, say, ten or ten-thirty in the morning, Pacific time, he must've grabbed an early morning flight from D.C."

"Western Airlines had one leaving about the same time as the L.A. departure."

Sawyer stood up and walked over to the TV screen. He rewound the tape and then froze it. He scrutinized every detail of Jason Archer's face, burning it into his memory. He turned to Hardy. "We know Archer was on Flight 3223's passenger manifest, but you say his employer didn't know about the trip. How'd they find out he was on the plane? Supposedly was," Sawyer corrected himself.

Hardy poured out some more coffee and stood up, moved over to the window. Both men seemed innately to crave movement while thinking. "Airline tracks down the wife while she's on a business trip to New York and tells her the bad news. At that meeting are a bunch of people from Triton, including the chairman. They find out then. Pretty soon everyone knew. This videotape has only been shown to two other people: Nathan Gamble, the chairman of the board of Triton, and Quentin Rowe, the second-in-command over there."

Sawyer rubbed a kink out of his neck, picked up the fresh cup of coffee and took a gulp. "Western confirmed that he checked in at the ticket counter and that his boarding pass was collected. They wouldn't have informed his family otherwise."

"You know as well as I do that it could've been anyone checking in there using a dummy I.D. The tickets were probably paid for ahead of time. He checks a bag, goes through security. Even with the FAA's recent heightened security requirements, they don't require photo identification to board a plane, only at check-in or with the skycaps."

"But somebody got on the plane in Archer's place. The airline has his boarding pass, and once on, you do not get off an aircraft."

"Whoever it was, was one very stupid or one very unlucky sonofabitch. Probably both."

"Right, but if Archer was on that Seattle flight, that means he had another ticket."

"He could've checked in twice, once for each flight. He could have used an alias and dummy I.D. for the Seattle flight."

"That's true." Sawyer pondered the possibilities. "Or he could've simply switched tickets with the guy who took his place."

"Whatever the truth is, you've certainly got your work cut out for you."

Sawyer fingered his coffee mug. "Anyone talk to the wife?"

In response, Hardy opened the file he had carried in with him. "Nathan Gamble did, briefly, on two occasions. Quentin Rowe also talked to her."

"And what's her story?"

"Initially she said she didn't know her husband was on the plane."

"Initially? So her story changed."

Hardy nodded. "Next she told Nathan Gamble that her husband had lied to her. Said he told her he was going to L.A. to meet with another company about a job. Turns out he wasn't meeting with any other company."

"Who says?"

"Sidney Archer. I guess she must have called the company, probably to tell them her husband wasn't going to be making it."

"But you verified it?" asked Sawyer. Hardy nodded. "So, any progress with your investigation?"

Hardy's face took on almost a pained expression. "Not much makes sense right now. Nathan Gamble is far from a happy man. He pays the bills and wants results. But it takes time, you know that. Still . . ." Hardy paused and studied the thick carpet. It was easy to see the man did not enjoy being puzzled about anything. "Anyway, according to Gamble and Rowe, at least, Mrs. Archer thinks her husband's dead."

"If she's telling the truth, and right now everything with me is a big *if*." Sawyer's tone was heated.

Hardy looked at him quizzically.

Sawyer caught the look and his shoulders slumped. "Just between you and me, Frank, I'm feeling a little stupid on this one."

"Why's that?"

"I had it pegged for sure that Arthur Lieberman was the target. Structured the whole investigation around that theory, mainly just going through the motions on any other angle."

"It's early on in the investigation, Lee. No harm done yet. Besides, maybe Lieberman *was* the target, in a way."

Sawyer's head jerked back. "How's that?"

"Think about it. You already answered your own question."

Hardy's point suddenly came to him. Sawyer's face grew dark. "You mean you think this guy Archer arranged to blow up the plane because we'd think Lieberman was the target? Come on, Frank, that's a helluva stretch."

Hardy countered. "Well if we hadn't lucked out with this video, that's exactly what you'd still be thinking, isn't it? Remember, there's one unique thing about an airplane crash, particularly one where the aircraft collides with the ground relatively intact, as happened here."

Sawyer's face turned ashen while he thought it through. "No bodies. Nothing to identify, no remains."

"Exactly. Now, if the plane had been conventionally blown up in the air, you'd have a lot of bodies to identify."

Sawyer continued to look stunned at Hardy's revelation. "That issue had been bugging the hell out of me. If Archer sold out, collected his payoff and was planning to run, he'd know at some point the police would be on to him."

Hardy picked up the thread. "So to cover his tracks he sets it up like he gets on a plane which ends up thirty feet under. If evidence of sabotage is discovered, you logically think Lieberman's the target. If evidence of sabotage isn't found, you still won't be looking for a dead man. Everyone stops looking for Jason Archer. End of case."

"But Christ, Frank, why not just take the money and run? It's not that difficult to disappear. And there's another thing. The guy we're pretty sure sabotaged 3223 ended up with a bunch of holes in him."

"Would the time of death have allowed Archer to get back and do the killing?" Hardy asked.

"We don't have the autopsy results yet, but based on what I saw of the corpse, it's possible Archer could've gotten back to the East Coast in time to do it."

Hardy fingered his file while he thought through this new information.

"Come on, Frank, how much you figure Archer got for his info? Enough to bribe a fueler to bring down a plane and hire a hit man to take out the fueler? This one guy who until a few days ago led a respectable life with a family? Now he's some kind of mastermind criminal blowing kids and grandmothers out of the sky?"

Frank Hardy looked at his old friend, his lips set in a thin line. "He personally didn't blow up that plane, Lee. Besides, don't tell me you've started analyzing the depths of a person's conscience. If memory serves me correctly, some of the worst perps we ever tracked down led lives on the surface that looked like something out of *Leave It to Beaver*."

Sawyer did not look convinced. "How much?"

"Archer could've gotten several million easy for the information."

"That sounds like a lot, but you think a guy will kill a couple hundred people to cover his tracks for that? No way!"

"There's another wrinkle to all this. A wrinkle that makes me think Jason Archer was some kind of mastermind despite appearances, or maybe that he was *working* for such an organization."

"So what's the wrinkle?"

Hardy suddenly looked embarrassed. "There's some money missing from one of Triton's accounts."

"Money? How much money?"

Hardy eyed Sawyer squarely. "How does a quarter of a billion dollars grab you?"

Sawyer almost spit his coffee across the table. "What?"

"It looks like Archer wasn't just interested in selling secrets. He was also into raiding bank accounts."

"How? I mean, a company that big, it had to have controls in place."

"Triton did, only those controls were premised on it receiving correct information from the bank where the money was on deposit."

"I'm not following you," Sawyer said impatiently.

Hardy sighed and put his elbows on the table. "In this day and age, moving money from point A to point B involves the use of a computer. The banking and financial worlds are wholly dependent upon them, but that dependence comes with risks."

"Like there might be some glitch, the computers go down, stuff like that?" Sawyer ventured.

"Or that the bank's computers might be penetrated and manipulated for illegal purposes. It's nothing new. Hell, you know the bureau created a whole new section to deal with computer crimes."

"Is that what you think happened here?"

Hardy sat down and reopened his file, rustling through some pages until he found what he wanted. "An operating account for Triton Global Investments, Corporation, was maintained at Consolidated BankTrust's branch here in northern Virginia. Triton Global Investments is Triton's Wall Street investment company subsidiary. The account was funded over time until the total bank balance reached two hundred and fifty million."

Sawyer interrupted. "Was Archer involved in setting up the account?"

"No. He had no access to it, in fact."

"Was there a lot of activity in the account?"

"At first, yes. However, as time went on, Triton didn't require the funds. They were sort of kept as a reserve in case Triton or its affiliated companies were in need of funding."

"What happened next?"

"Turns out a couple of months ago a new account was set up at the same bank in the name of Triton Global Investments, Limited."

"So Triton set up another account?"

Hardy was already shaking his head. "No, that's the catch. It was totally unrelated to Triton. Turns out the company is fictitious, no address, no directors or officers, no nothing."

"Do you know who set the bank account up?"

"There was only one signatory to the account. The name given to the bank was Alfred Rhone, chief financial officer. Our investigation turned up zilch on Rhone. But we did find one interesting piece of information."

"What's that?" Sawyer hunched forward in his chair.

"A number of transactions took place from the phony account. Wire transfers, deposits, things like that. The signature of Alfred Rhone appeared on each of these documents. We checked those signatures against those of all of Triton's employees. We found a match. Care to guess who?"

Sawyer's reply was immediate. "Jason Archer."

Hardy nodded.

"So what happened to the money?"

"Someone infiltrated BankTrust's computer system and did some very careful rearranging of accounts. Turns out that the legit Triton account and the phony account were assigned the same account number."

"Christ! You could drive a semi through a hole like that."

"Right. One day before Archer disappeared, a wire transfer authorization was made moving the two hundred and fifty million from the Triton account to an account set up by the phony company at another major money center bank in New York. BankTrust's wire department already had a standing authorization from our friend Alfred Rhone. The account was fully funded, all the *i*'s and *t*'s dotted and crossed. The money was transferred out the same day." Sawyer looked incredulous. "Bank people accept what the computer tells them, Lee, there's no reason not to. Besides, bank departments don't talk to each other. So long as their ass is covered, they just execute orders. Whoever was involved, they knew banking procedures down cold. Did I mention that Jason Archer used to work in the wire department of a bank a few years before he joined Triton?"

Sawyer wearily shook his head. "I knew there was a reason I don't like computers. I still don't understand how it was done."

"Look at it this way, Lee. It was as if they cloned a rich guy and then walked the fake guy in the front door of the bank, withdrew all the rich guy's money and then walked back out. The only difference is BankTrust thought both guys were rich; however, the bank was looking at the same bank balance for both, only counting the money twice."

"Any trace of the funds?"

Hardy shook his head. "I wouldn't have expected there to be. It's gone. We've already met with members of the bureau's Financial Institutions Fraud Unit. They've commenced an investigation."

Sawyer sipped his coffee and then had a sudden thought. "You think maybe RTG was involved in both schemes? Otherwise, it would seem kind of odd that Archer would risk doing both the bank fraud and selling the secrets."

"In fact, Lee, Archer could have initiated only the theft of the company secrets and then RTG may have put him up to the bank fraud in order to further hurt Triton. He was in a perfect position to do it."

"But the bank has to make good on the loss. Triton wasn't really hurt."

"No, you're wrong there. Triton has lost the use of the money while BankTrust sorts things out and the investigation is continuing. This incident went all the way up to the board of directors. It could take months to unravel, or so Triton was told this morning. As you could imagine, Nathan Gamble is one unhappy man."

"Did Triton need the funds for something?"

"You bet they did. Triton was going to use the funds to put a good-faith deposit down on the acquisition of CyberCom, the company I was telling you about."

"So did the deal fall through?"

"Not yet. The last I heard, Nathan Gamble may provide the funds personally."

"Christ, the guy can write a check that big?"

"Gamble is a billionaire several times over. However, it's not like he wants to do it. That ties up his funds on top of losing two hundred and fifty million of Triton's cash. For him it's a five-hundred-million-dollar swing the wrong way. Even for him, that's a lot of money." Hardy winced slightly as if remembering his last encounter with Gamble. "Like I said, not a very happy man right now. His biggest concern is the secrets Archer sold to RTG, however. If RTG gets CyberCom, then the ultimate loss to Triton will be much more than a quarter billion dollars."

"But now that RTG knows you're on to them, they won't be using the info Archer slipped them."

"It's not that simple, Lee. They've denied any involvement, and while we have the video, it's far from slam-dunk evidence. RTG was already in the bidding for CyberCom. If their deal comes in a little sweeter than Triton's, who's to say how that happened?"

"It does get complicated, I guess." Sawyer wearily studied the remains of his coffee.

Hardy spread out his hands at his old partner and smiled. "Well, that's my story."

"I had faith you wouldn't get me out of bed for a simple purse snatching." Sawyer paused. "Archer must be a certifiable genius, Frank."

"Agreed."

Sawyer suddenly perked up. "Then again, everybody makes mistakes and sometimes you get lucky, like that videotape over there. Besides, it's the hard ones that make the job so gratifying. Right?" A grin spread across his face.

Hardy nodded in weary amusement. "So, where do you go from here?"

Sawyer finished his coffee and hooked the pot for a refill. He seemed reenergized as a number of possibilities on the case had now opened up.

"First, I'm going to use your phone to put out a worldwide APB on Jason Archer. Next, I'm going to pick your brain clean for the next hour. Tomorrow morning I'm going to send a team of agents to Dulles Airport to find out as much as they can about Jason Archer. While they're doing that, I'm going to follow up with a personal interview of someone who may turn out to be truly integral to this whole case."

"Who's that?"

"Sidney Archer."

Chapter Twenty-Eight

P aul Brophy, I'm a partner of Sidney's, Mr. . . . ."

Brophy stood in the foyer of the home, his overnight bag in one hand.

"Bill Patterson. I'm Sidney's father."

"She's spoken of you often, Bill. Sorry we never had a chance to meet until now. Terrible what happened. I had to come here for your daughter. She's one of my closest colleagues. A truly remarkable woman."

Bill Patterson eyed the bag Brophy deposited in one corner of the foyer. Dressed in a dark blue double-breasted suit, the latest in fashionable neckwear and glossy black shoes to go with patterned socks, the tall, lean Brophy cut quite a figure. Something about the smooth manner, though, the way he was casually moving around the stricken household, made Patterson frown. He had spent the better part of his working life with his bullshit radar set on high. His alarm was wailing now.

"She's got a lot of family here for her . . . Paul, was it?" Patterson put particular emphasis on the word *family*.

Brophy looked at him, sizing up the man quickly. "Yes. There's nothing more important than family right now. I hope you don't think I'm intruding. That's the last thing I want to do. I talked to Sidney last night. She said it was okay. I've worked with your daughter for many years. We've been through some legal deals that would send you looking for the ulcer medicine. But I don't have to tell you that. You practically ran Bristol-Aluminum the last five years you were there. Read about you in the *Journal* it seems like every month. And that big spread in *Forbes* a few years ago when you retired."

"Business *is* tough," the older man agreed, relaxing his manner as he briefly recalled past triumphs from his business career.

"Well, I know that's what your competition thought." Brophy flashed the friendliest of grins.

Patterson returned it. The guy was probably okay; after all, he had come all this way. Besides, this was not the morning to start any problems. "You want something to drink, or eat? You flew down from New York this morning you say?"

"First shuttle out. If you've got some coffee, that would be great. . . . Sidney?" Brophy's eyes eagerly settled on the tall presence entering the room.

Dressed in black, her mother by her side and similarly attired, Sidney Archer came down the hallway.

"Hello, Paul."

Brophy walked quickly over to her, gave her a full hug and a peck on the cheek that seemed to linger for a few seconds. A little flustered, Sidney made introductions with her mother.

"So, how's little Amy taking it?" Brophy asked anxiously.

"She's staying with a friend. She doesn't understand what's happened." Sidney's mother stared at him, her eyes unfriendly.

"Right, that's right." Brophy fell back a step. He had never had kids, but that had still been a stupid question.

Sidney unwittingly helped him. She turned to her mother. "Paul flew down from New York this morning."

Her mother nodded absently and then bustled off to the kitchen to start some breakfast.

Brophy looked at Sidney. Her hair was silky, straw-colored, its color made more dramatic by the backdrop of the black dress. He found her gaunt look particularly attractive. Even though he had his own agenda, Brophy was still taken aback. The woman *was* beautiful.

"Everyone else is going directly to the chapel. After the service they'll come here." She sounded overwhelmed by the prospect.

Brophy caught the tone. "You just take it easy and when you want to go off by yourself, I'll be right there making small talk and keeping everyone's plate filled with food. If there's anything I've learned being a lawyer, it's how to use a lot of words and never really say anything."

"Don't you have to get back to New York?"

Brophy shook his head, his smile triumphant. "I'm hanging out at the D.C. office for a while." He pulled out a slender cassette recorder from his inner coat pocket. "I'm all set. Already dictated three letters and a speech I'm giving at a political fund-raiser next month. All of which means I'm here as long as you need me." He smiled tenderly, put the recorder back, reached out and took her hand.

She smiled back, a little embarrassed, while she slowly pulled her hand free. "I need to go finish up before we leave."

"Fine, I'll go make trouble in the kitchen with your parents."

She walked down the hallway to the bedroom. Brophy watched her go, a smile appearing on his face as he thought of his future prospects. A moment later Brophy walked into the large kitchen, where Sidney's mother was busily preparing eggs, toast and bacon. Bill Patterson hovered in the back, tinkering with the coffeemaker. The phone rang. Patterson took off his glasses and picked it up on the second ring.

"Hello?" He switched the receiver to his other hand. "Yes, it is. What? Oh, uh, look, can this wait? Oh, well, hold on just a minute."

Mrs. Patterson looked at her husband. "Who is it?"

"Henry Wharton." Patterson looked at Brophy. "He's the head guy at your firm, right?"

Brophy nodded. Even though his being an apostle of Goldman

was a well-kept secret, Brophy was still not a favorite of Wharton's and Brophy looked forward to the day when Wharton was shoved rudely aside as the leader of Tyler, Stone. "Wonderful man, very caring of his colleagues," Brophy said.

"Yeah, well, his timing's lousy," Patterson said. He put the phone receiver down on the table and walked out of the kitchen. With a conciliatory smile, Brophy moved over to assist Mrs. Patterson.

Her father gently knocked on the door. "Honey?"

Sidney opened the door to the bedroom. Behind her Patterson could see the numerous photos of Jason and the rest of the family spread out on the bed. He took a deep breath and swallowed.

"Sweetie, there's some guy from your firm on the phone. Says it's very important that he talk to you."

"Did he give a name?"

"Henry Wharton."

Sidney's brows plunged together and then her face cleared just as suddenly. "He's probably calling to say he can't make the service. I'm not really on his top ten list right now. I'll take it in here, Dad. Tell him to give me a minute."

As her father started to close the door, he again looked at the photos. He abruptly looked up and caught his daughter staring at him, an almost ashamed expression on her face, as though she were a teenager just caught smoking in her room.

Patterson went over and kissed his daughter on the cheek and gave her a long hug.

In the kitchen Patterson picked up the phone again. "She'll be with you in a minute," he said gruffly. He put the phone back down and was about to return to the intricacies of the coffeemaker when he was interrupted by a knock on the door. All three of the kitchen's occupants looked up. Patterson looked over at his wife. "Expecting anyone this early?"

She shook her head. "It's probably just a neighbor with some more food or something. Go answer it, Bill."

Patterson obediently headed to the front door.

Brophy trailed the older man into the foyer.

Patterson opened the front door. Two gentlemen in suits stared back at him.

"Can I help you?" Patterson asked.

Lee Sawyer deliberately exhibited his credentials. The man beside him did likewise. "I'm FBI Special Agent Lee Sawyer. My partner, Raymond Jackson."

Bill Patterson's confusion was evident as he looked from the official government credentials to the men holding them. They looked steadily back at him.

Sidney quickly put the photos away, lingering over only one: from the day Amy had been born. Jason, dressed in hospital garb, was holding his minutes-old daughter. The look of absolute pride on the new father's face was wonderful to behold. She put that one in her purse. She felt certain she would need it during the course of the day when it all started to become too much, as she knew it would. She smoothed down her dress and went over to the nightstand, sat down on the bed and picked up the phone.

"Hello, Henry."

"Sid."

If she hadn't been sitting down, Sidney would have undoubtedly toppled to the floor. As it was, her entire body collapsed. Her brain felt as though it had been crushed.

"Sid?" The voice said again, more anxiously.

One step at a time, Sidney managed to focus herself. She felt as though she were struggling to the water's surface from some terrible depths where humans could not survive. Her brain suddenly restarted and she struggled up an inch at a time. As she fought an overpowering urge to pass out, Sidney Archer managed to utter one word in a way she never thought she would again. The two syllables struggled out from between trembling lips.

"Jason?"

CHAPTER TWENTY-NINE

While Sidney's mother walked through the living room to join her husband at the front door, Paul Brophy discreetly retreated until he was once again in the kitchen. FBI? This was getting interesting. While he was pondering whether to contact Goldman, Brophy spotted the phone receiver lying on the counter where Bill Patterson had set it down. Henry Wharton was on the phone. Brophy wondered what they were discussing. He could certainly score some significant points with Goldman if he could find out.

Brophy edged over to the kitchen doorway. The group was still huddled in the front foyer. He hurried over to the kitchen counter, put one hand over the lower part of the receiver and lifted the telephone to his ear. His mouth dropped open and his eyes widened while he listened to two very familiar voices. He reached into his pocket. He held the Dictaphone up to the phone receiver and recorded the conversation between husband and wife.

Five minutes later, Bill Patterson again knocked on his daughter's door. When Sidney finally opened the door, her father was surprised by her appearance. The eyes were still red and weary, but there seemed to be a light in them that he had not seen since Jason's death. He was also startled by what he saw on the bed: a half-filled suit- case. Without taking his eyes off the suitcase, Patterson said, "Sweetie, I don't know what they want, but the FBI are here. They want to talk to you."

"FBI?" She suddenly went limp and her father grabbed on to one arm.

Patterson's face was a morass of concern. "Baby, what's going on? Why are you packing?"

Sidney managed to regain her composure. "I'm all right, Dad. I . . . I just have to go somewhere after the service."

"Go? Go where? What are you talking about?"

"Dad, please, not now. I can't go into it right now."

"But Sid—"

"Please, Dad."

Under his daughter's pleading eyes, Patterson finally looked away, disappointment and something akin to fear on his features.

"All right, Sidney."

"Where are the agents, Dad?"

"In the living room. They said they want to talk to you privately. I tried to get rid of them, but, hell, they're the FBI, you know?"

"It's all right, Dad, I'll talk to them." Sidney thought for a mo- ment. She looked over at the phone she had just put down and then checked her watch. "Take them into the den and tell them I'll be there in two minutes."

Her hands clasped together, Sidney went over and closed the suit- case, picked it up and slid it under the bed.

Her father followed her movements, then raised his thick eye- brows to ask, "You sure you know what you're doing?"

Her answer was immediate. "I'm sure."

Jason Archer was handcuffed to the chair. A smiling Kenneth Scales held the Glock against his head. Another man hovered in the background. "Good job on the phone, Jason," Scales said. "You might have had a future in the movies. Too bad you don't have a fu- ture left."

Jason glared up at him, fury in his eyes. "You sonofabitch! You hurt my wife or my daughter and I'll tear you apart. I swear to God."

Scales's smile broadened. "Is that right. Tell me, how you gonna do that?" He smacked Jason across the jaw with the pistol. The door to the small room they were in opened slightly. As Jason recovered from the blow and stared through the cracked door, a snarl escaped his lips. With a burst of strength, he flung himself across the room, chair and all. He made it to the man's feet before Scales and his associate subdued him, dragging him back across the floor.

"Goddamn you, I'll kill you, I'll kill you!" Jason shrieked at the visitor.

The man stepped into the room and closed the door behind him. He smiled while Jason was dragged up and heavy tape was placed across his mouth. "Having bad dreams again, Jason?"

After Bill Patterson had escorted the two FBI agents to the small but comfortably furnished den, he returned to find his wife and Paul Brophy in the kitchen. He stared over at the phone, puzzlement on his features. The receiver had been replaced on the wall. Brophy caught the look. "I hung it back up for you. Figured you had other things to deal with."

"Thanks, Paul."

"My pleasure." Brophy sipped at his coffee, highly pleased with himself as he fingered the small cassette tape tucked safely in his pants pocket. "Jesus"—he looked at the Pattersons—"the FBI. What could they want?"

Patterson shrugged. "I don't know and I know Sidney doesn't know." He was intensely defensive of his daughter. The worry lines were prominent on his forehead. "Lousy timing all around today, if you ask me," he muttered as he sat down at the table to scan the newspaper. He was about to say something else when he saw the front-page headline.

CHAPTER THIRTY

Agents Sawyer and Jackson rose when Sidney entered the room. Sawyer visibly started when he saw her. He made a conscious effort to suck in his stomach and one of his hands flew up to his hair in a feeble attempt to press his stubborn cowlick back into place. When he brought his hand back down, he looked at it for a moment as though it were not part of his body, wondering what the hell had made it do such a thing. Both agents identified themselves and again displayed their credentials. Sawyer was aware that Sidney looked intently at him before sitting down across from them.

Sawyer rapidly sized her up. A real looker with brains and spirit. But there was something else. He could have sworn they had met before. His eyes drifted over her long form. The black dress was tasteful and appropriate to such a solemn occasion; however, it also clung to her figure in several provocative locations. Her shapely legs too, sheathed in black stockings, were equally inspiring. Her face was lovely in its despair. "Ms. Archer, by any chance have we met before?"

Her surprise was genuine. "I don't think so, Mr. Sawyer."

He studied her for another moment, shrugged and quickly

launched into his interview. "As I told your father, Ms. Archer, we understand that the timing of this interview couldn't be worse, but we needed to talk with you as soon as possible."

"May I ask what it concerns?" Sidney's voice was on automatic. Her eyes flitted around the room before coming to rest on Sawyer's face. She saw a big, strong wall of a man who seemed sincere. Under normal circumstances, Sidney would have cooperated fully with Lee Sawyer. Circumstances, however, were far from normal.

Her green eyes were now sparkling and Sawyer had to kick-start his brain when he found himself transfixed by those eyes. In trying to read their depths, he found himself venturing into dangerous waters. "It has to do with your husband, Ms. Archer," he said quickly.

"Please call me Sidney. What about my husband? Is this about the plane accident?"

Sawyer didn't answer right away. He was studying her again without seeming to do so. Every word, every expression, every pause was important. It was always a very tiring, often frustrating, but sometimes incredibly productive task. "It wasn't an accident, Sidney," he finally said.

Her eyes flickered briefly, like the lights in a house do when there's a thunderstorm. The mouth parted slightly, but no words emerged.

"The plane was sabotaged; all the people on board that plane, every last one of them, were deliberately murdered." While Sawyer continued to watch, Sidney shut down completely for about a minute. Her features held real, not feigned, horror. Her eyes suddenly lost their feverish sparkle.

After a minute, Sawyer gently said, "Sidney? Sidney?"

With a jolt, Sidney came back but then was gone again just as quickly. Her breath suddenly came out in a huge burst. For an instant she was certain she would vomit all over herself. She put her head in her lap, clutching her calves. Ironically, her movements mirrored a passenger in crash position on an airliner. When she started moaning and the rest of her body began to shake uncontrollably, Sawyer swiftly rose and sat beside her. One arm clutched her shoulder, steadying her; the other gripped one of her hands tightly.

Sawyer looked up at Jackson. "Water, tea, something, Ray. Pronto!"

Jackson raced off.

With nervous hands, Sidney's mother poured out a glass of water for Jackson. When Jackson turned to leave, Bill Patterson held up the newspaper. "This is what's it's all about, right?" The paper's headlines were big, bold and deadly sounding. WESTERN AIRLINES CRASH BLAMED ON SABOTAGE. FEDERAL GOVERNMENT OFFERS TWO-MILLION-DOLLAR REWARD. "Jason and all the others were victims of a terrorist. That's why you're here, isn't it?" In the background, Mrs. Patterson covered her face in her hands, her quiet weeping pervading the room as she sat down at the table.

"Sir, not right now, okay?" Jackson's tone brooked no opposition. He left the room with the glass of water.

Paul Brophy, meanwhile, had gone into the front yard, ostensibly to smoke a cigarette, despite the cold. If anyone had looked out the living room window, they would have seen the small cellular phone pressed to the side of his face.

Sawyer virtually had to force the water down Sidney's throat, but finally she was able to sit up. After Sidney composed herself and handed back the glass of water with a grateful look, Sawyer did not return to the plane bombing. "Believe me, if this weren't very, very important, we'd leave right now, okay?"

Sidney nodded. She still looked ghastly. Sawyer took a moment to marshal his thoughts. Sidney seemed relieved when he asked a couple of seemingly innocuous questions about Jason's work at Triton Global. Sidney answered calmly enough, although she was clearly puzzled. He looked around the room. They had a nice home. "Any money problems?" he asked.

"Where is this going, Mr. Sawyer?" Sidney's face had regained some of its rigidity. Suddenly she softened; she had just remembered Jason's remark about giving her the world.

"Wherever it happens to lead at this point, ma'am," Sawyer answered, his eyes meeting hers without hesitation. They seemed to burn through her exterior wall, clearly reading the thoughts, the nagging doubts buried deep within. She realized she would have to tread very cautiously with him. "We're talking with all the families of the passengers on that plane. If the plane was sabotaged because of who was on it, we need to find out reasons why."

"I see." Sidney took a deep breath. "To answer your question, we're in better shape financially than we've been in years."

"You're an attorney for Triton, right?"

"Among about fifty other clients. So?"

Sawyer changed tactics. "Okay, you know that your husband had taken a few days off from work?"

"I'm his wife."

"Good, then maybe you'd like to explain why it was, if he was taking a few days off, that he happened to be on a plane to L.A." Sawyer had almost said "allegedly" been on a plane but fortunately caught himself.

Sidney's tone was businesslike. "Look, I have to assume you've already talked to Triton. Maybe you've spoken to Henry Wharton as well. Jason told me he was going to L.A. on business for Triton. On the morning he left, I reminded him that I had a meeting in New York with Triton. That's when he told me he was traveling to L.A. regarding another employment opportunity. He didn't want me to let the fact of his L.A. trip slip to any of the Triton people. I played along. I know it wasn't exactly the most truthful thing to do, but I did it."

"But there was no other job."

Sidney slumped back. "No."

"So, being his wife and all, do you have any idea what he was actually going to L.A. for? Any suspicions?"

She shook her head.

"That's it? Nothing else? You're sure it had nothing to do with Triton?"

"Jason rarely talked about company business with me."

"Why's that?" Sawyer craved a cup of coffee. His body was starting to go down on him after the late night with Hardy.

"My firm represents some other companies who might be perceived as having competing interests with Triton. However, any potential conflict has been waived by the respective clients, including Triton, and we've constructed Chinese walls from time to time when necessary—"

"Come again?" This was Ray Jackson. "Chinese walls?"

Sidney looked at him. "That's what it's called when we cut off communications of any kind, access to files, even shop talk, shooting the breeze in the hallway, about a particular client's matters if an attorney of the firm represents another client with a possible conflict. We even maintain secure computerized databases with respect to pending deals we're handling on behalf of clients. We also do it to ensure that up-to-the-minute negotiation terms are accurately maintained. Deals change fast, and we don't want clients surprised about what the principal terms are. People's memories are fallible; computer memories are a lot better. Access to those files is restricted by use of a password known only to the lead attorneys on the case. The theory is that a law firm can carve itself up, upon occasion, in order to avoid problems like that. Hence the term."

Sawyer leaned in. "So what other clients does your firm represent who could possibly have a conflict with Triton?"

Sidney thought for a moment. A name had come to mind, but she was unsure of whether to give it. If she did, the interview might be hastened to a conclusion.

"RTG Group."

Sawyer and Jackson exchanged quick glances. Sawyer spoke up. "Who at your firm represents RTG?"

Sawyer was sure he caught a twinkle in Sidney Archer's eyes before she answered. "Philip Goldman."

In the front yard of the Archers' home, the cold was beginning to eat through Paul Brophy's very expensive gloves.

"No, I have no clue as to what's going on," Brophy said into the cellular phone. He jerked his head away from the handheld unit when the speaker on the other end unleashed a blistering response to Brophy's professed ignorance. "Wait a minute, Philip. It's the FBI. They carry guns, okay? You weren't expecting that to happen, why should I?"

This deference to Philip Goldman's superior intelligence apparently calmed the man down because Brophy now held the phone normally. "Yes, I'm sure it was him. I know what he sounds like and she called him by name. I've got the whole thing on tape. Pretty damn brilliant on my part, wouldn't you say? What? Yeah, you bet I plan on sticking around, see what I can find out. Right, I'll check back with you in a few hours." Brophy put the phone away, rubbed his stiff fingers together and went back in the house.

Sawyer was watching Sidney Archer carefully as she slid her hand back and forth on the armrest of the sofa. He was debating whether to drop the bombshell on her: to tell her that Jason Archer was definitely not buried in a crater in Virginia. Finally, after much internal conflict, his gut won out over his brain. He rose and offered Sidney his hand. "Thank you for your cooperation, Ms. Archer. If you think of anything that might help us, you can reach me day or night at these numbers." Sawyer handed her a card. "That's my home phone on the back. Do you have a card with numbers where you can be reached?" Sidney picked up her purse from the table, rummaged through it and produced one of her business cards. "Again, I'm sorry about your husband." He truly meant the last part. If Hardy was right, then what the woman was going through right now would seem like a day in the park compared to what was ahead for her. Ray Jackson exited the room. Sawyer was about to join him when Sidney put a hand on his shoulder.

"Mr. Sawyer—"

"You can make it Lee."

"Lee, I would have to be pretty stupid not to realize that this all looks very bad."

"And not for a minute do I think you're stupid, Sidney." They exchanged glances of mutual respect; however, Sawyer's statement was not entirely supportive.

"Do you have any reason to suspect that my husband was involved in anything . . ."—she paused and swallowed hard, preparing to utter the unthinkable—"in anything illegal?"

He looked at her, and the unmistakable sense that he had seen the woman somewhere before began to nag him again until it became a certainty. "Sidney, let's just say that your husband's activities right before he left on that flight are giving us some problems."

Sidney thought back to all those late nights, Jason's trips back to the office. "Is anything amiss at Triton?"

Sawyer watched her squeezing her hands together. Normally the most tight-lipped of FBI agents, for some reason Sawyer wanted to tell her everything he knew. He resisted the temptation. "It's an ongoing bureau investigation, Sidney. I really can't say."

She stepped back a bit. "I understand, of course."

"We'll be in touch."

After Sawyer left the room, Sidney felt a twinge of apprehension as she recalled Nathan Gamble's similar remark about keeping in touch. She suddenly felt enveloped by cold bands of fear. She hugged herself and drew closer to the fire.

The phone call from Jason had initially buoyed her to the highest levels of euphoria. She had never felt such joy, yet the scant details he had provided had brought her plummeting back downward. She was currently in a state of utter confusion, helplessness and unbridled loyalty to her husband; an unwieldy emotional elixir to be carrying around inside. She wondered what surprises tomorrow would bring.

On the way out of the house, the two agents were trailed by a chatty Paul Brophy. "So obviously my firm would be quite anxious to learn of any possible wrongdoing involving Jason Archer and Triton Global." He finally stopped talking and looked hopeful.

Sawyer just kept walking. "So I've heard." The FBI agent stopped behind Bill Patterson's Cadillac, which was parked in the driveway. When he put his foot up on the rear bumper to retie his shoelaces, he saw a MAINE, THE VACATIONLAND STATE bumper sticker. *When was the last time I had a vacation?* he thought. *You know you're in trouble when you can't even remember.* He hitched up his pants and turned to the attorney, who was watching him from the front sidewalk.

"What'd you say your name was again?"

Brophy glanced at the front door and then hurried over. "Brophy.

Paul Brophy." He hurriedly added, "As I said, I'm a New York–based attorney, so I really have little to do with Sidney Archer."

Sawyer eyed him closely. "And yet you flew all the way down here for the memorial service. That's what you said, right?"

Brophy looked at both men. Ray Jackson's eyes narrowed as he took in Paul Brophy. Slick money and bullshit were written all over the man.

"I'm really here as the firm's representative. Sort of by default. Sidney Archer is *only* a part-time attorney, and I was in town on business anyway."

Sawyer stared at a patch of cloud above the house. "Is that right? You know, I had an opportunity to check up on Ms. Archer. From the people I spoke with, she's one of Tyler, Stone's top attorneys. Part-time or not. In fact, I asked for a list of the top five guns in your place from at least three different sources, and you know what? The lady was on every list." He looked at Brophy and added, "Funny, though, your name never came up."

Brophy sputtered for a moment, but Sawyer wanted to move on anyway. "You been here awhile, Mr. Brophy?" He nodded in the direction of the Archer residence.

"About an hour. Why?" Brophy's whiny tone betrayed his hurt feelings.

"Anything unusual happen while you were here?"

Brophy was bursting to tell the agents that he had a dead man's words captured on tape, but that information was far too valuable simply to give away. "Not really. I mean, she's tired and depressed, or at least seems so."

"What do you mean by that?" Jackson asked, taking off his sunglasses and staring at Brophy.

"Nothing. I mean, like I said, I don't know Sidney all that well. So I don't know if she and her husband really got along."

"Uh-huh." Jackson's lip curled and he put his shades back on. He eyed his partner. "You ready, Lee? This man here looks cold. Oughta go in there and warm up," he said, looking at Brophy. "Go pay your respects to your *bare* acquaintance in there."

Jackson and Sawyer turned and headed to their car.

Brophy's face was red with anger. He looked back at the house once more and then called after them. "Oh, that's right, there was the phone call she got."

Both agents turned in perfect unison. "What's that?" Sawyer asked. His temples throbbed from lack of caffeine and he was tired of listening to this jerk. "What phone call?"

Brophy approached them and spoke in a lowered tone, occasionally glancing back at the house. "About two minutes before you showed up. The caller identified himself as Henry Wharton when Sidney's father answered the phone." The agents looked puzzled. "He's the managing partner of Tyler, Stone."

"So?" Jackson said. "The man might be checking in on her. Seeing if she's okay."

"That's what I would've thought too, but . . ."

Sawyer's fuse was about gone. "But what?" he asked angrily.

"I'm not sure if I'm at liberty to say."

Sawyer's voice dropped back to normal, but his words took on an even more menacing tone. "It's a little cold out here for bullshit responses, Mr. Brophy, so I'm going to ask you real nicely to give me the information, and that will be the only time I'll ask real nicely." Sawyer leaned into Brophy's now frightened face while the burly Jackson crowded him from behind.

Brophy blurted out, "I called Henry Wharton at the office while Sidney was talking to you." Brophy paused dramatically. "When I asked about his talk with Sidney, he was completely surprised. He had never called her. And when she came out of the bedroom after taking the call, she was white as a sheet. I thought she was going to faint. Her father noticed it too and was greatly disturbed."

"Well, if the FBI came knocking on my door on the day of my spouse's memorial service, I'd probably look pretty bad too," Jackson responded. One hand curled and uncurled, making a very large fist that he would have given anything at that moment to let fly.

"Yeah, well, according to her father, she looked that way *before* he told her you were at the front door." Brophy had made that part up, but so what? It wasn't the FBI appearing at her doorstep that had thrown Sidney Archer for a loop.

Sawyer straightened up and looked at the house. He eyed Jackson, whose eyebrows clicked up a notch. Sawyer studied Brophy's face. If the guy was screwing with them . . . But no, it was obvious he was telling the truth, or at least mostly the truth. He had evidently been dying to tell them something to bounce Sidney Archer off the ceiling. Sawyer didn't care about Paul Brophy's personal vendetta. He did care about that phone call.

"Thanks for the information, Mr. Brophy. You think of anything else, here's my number." He handed the attorney his card and left him in the front yard.

Driving back into town, Sawyer glanced at his partner. "I want Sidney Archer put under immediate twenty-four-hour surveillance. And I want all calls going into her home in the last twenty-four hours checked, starting with the one Mister Fancy Pants told us about."

Jackson stared out the window. "You think that was her husband on the phone?"

"I think she's been through enough hell to where it would take something pretty big to knock her off her feet like that. Even while we were talking to her, you could see something was off. Way off."

"So she *did* think he was dead?"

Sawyer shrugged. "Right now, I'm not jumping to any conclusions. We'll just watch her and see what happens. My gut tells me Sidney Archer is going to turn out to be a pretty interesting piece to this puzzle."

"Speaking of guts, can we stop and get something to eat? I'm starving." Jackson looked at the long line of eateries they were now passing.

"Hell, I'll even buy, Ray. Nothing's too good for my partner." Sawyer smiled and turned into the parking lot of a McDonald's. Jackson looked over at Sawyer, mock disgust on his face. Then, shaking his head, he picked up the car phone and started punching in numbers.

CHAPTER THIRTY-ONE

The slim Learjet streaked through the skies with power to spare. Inside the luxurious cabin Philip Goldman reclined in his seat and sipped at a cup of hot tea while the remnants of a meal were cleared away by the cabin steward. Across from Goldman sat Alan Porcher, president and chief executive officer of RTG Group, the Western Europe–based global consortium. The tanned, slender Porcher cradled a glass of wine and studied the attorney intently before speaking.

"You know Triton Global claims they have concrete evidence of one of their employees handing over sensitive documents to us at one of our warehouse facilities in Seattle. We can expect to hear from their lawyers shortly, I would imagine." Porcher paused. "From *your* law firm, of course, Tyler, Stone. Ironic, isn't it?"

Goldman put down his teacup and folded his hands in his lap. "And this troubles you?"

Porcher looked surprised. "Why shouldn't it?"

Goldman's reply was simple. "Because, with respect to that claim, you're not guilty." He added, "Ironic, isn't it?"

"Still, I have heard some things about the CyberCom deal that trouble me, Philip."

Goldman sighed and sat forward in his cabin chair. "Such as?"

"That perhaps the acquisition of CyberCom will occur more rapidly than we thought. That perhaps we do not know the latest offer that will be made by Triton. When we make our offer, I must be assured it will be accepted. I will not be allowed to bid again. CyberCom is inclined toward the Americans as it is."

Goldman cocked his head and absorbed the CEO's words. "I'm not so sure of that. The Internet knows no geopolitical boundaries. So who's to say the domination cannot occur from the other side of the Atlantic?"

Porcher took another sip of wine before answering. "No, other things being equal, the deal will land in the western hemisphere. Therefore, we must ensure that conditions are decidedly unequal." There was now a hard glint in Porcher's eyes.

Goldman took a moment to methodically wipe his mouth with his handkerchief before responding. "Tell me, who are your sources for this information?"

Porcher waved his hand distractedly. "It blows in the wind."

"I don't believe in winds. I believe in facts. And the facts are that we do know Triton's latest negotiating position. To the last detail."

"Yes, but Brophy is now out of the loop. I cannot be limited to old news."

"You won't be. As I've told you, I am currently very close to solving that problem. When I do, and I will, you can easily trump Triton and walk away with an acquisition that will ensure your domination of the information superhighway for the foreseeable future."

Porcher looked pointedly at the attorney. "You know, Philip, I have often been curious about your motivation regarding this matter. If, as I hope and you continue to promise, we succeed in acquiring CyberCom, Triton will most assuredly be unhappy with your law firm. They may go elsewhere."

"One can only hope." A faraway look appeared on Goldman's face as he thought of the possibility.

"I'm afraid you have lost me."

Goldman assumed a pedantic tone. "Triton Global is Tyler, Stone's largest client. Triton Global is Henry Wharton's client. That is the chief reason Henry is managing partner. If Triton ceases using the firm as counsel, would you like to guess who becomes the largest rainmaker at the firm and, therefore, the probable successor to Wharton as managing partner?"

Porcher pointed at Goldman. "And I would hope that in such a case RTG matters would be given the highest priority in the firm."

"I think I can safely promise that."

Porcher put down his wineglass and lit a cigarette. "Now tell me exactly how you plan to solve the problem."

"Do you really care about the method, or just the results?"

"Indulge me with your brilliance. I recall you often enjoy doing that. Just don't sound so damn professorial when doing so. I have been out of university many years now."

Goldman raised an eyebrow at the CEO's remark. "You seem to know me all too well."

"You are one of the few attorneys in my acquaintance who thinks like a businessman. Winning is king. Fuck the law!"

Goldman accepted one of the cigarettes from Porcher and took a moment lighting it. "A very recent development has occurred that has given us a golden opportunity to gain firsthand, almost real-time information about Triton's proposed deal with CyberCom. We'll know Triton's best and final offer before they even have a chance to communicate it to CyberCom. Then we march in a few hours earlier, present our proposal and wait for Triton's deal to come in. CyberCom rejects it and you become the proud owner of another jewel in your far-flung empire."

Porcher slowly withdrew the cigarette from between his lips and stared wide-eyed at his companion. "You can do this?"

"I can do this."

CHAPTER THIRTY-TWO

Lee, let me warn you, he can be a little abrasive at times, but that's just the man's personality." Frank Hardy glanced back at Sawyer, and the two men walked down a long corridor after exiting a private elevator onto the top floor of the Triton Global building.

"Kid gloves, I promise, Frank. I don't usually pull out my brass knuckles on the victims, you know."

While they walked, Sawyer reflected on the results of the airport queries about Jason Archer. His men had dug up two airport personnel who had recognized Jason Archer's picture. One was the Western Airlines employee who had checked in his bag on the morning of the seventeenth. The other was a janitor who had noticed Jason sitting and reading the paper. He remembered him because Jason had never let go of his leather briefcase, even while reading the paper or drinking his coffee. Jason had gone into the rest room, but the janitor had left the area and had not noticed him coming back out. The FBI agents could not question the young woman who had actually collected boarding passes from the passengers on the ill-fated plane, since she had been one of the flight attendants on Flight 3223. A number of people recalled seeing Arthur Lieberman.

He had been a regular at Dulles for many years. All in all, not much useful information.

Sawyer refocused on Hardy's back; he was moving quickly down the plushly carpeted hallway. Gaining entry to the technology giant's headquarters had not been easy. Triton's security had been so zealous that they had even wanted to call the bureau to verify the serial number on Sawyer's credentials until Hardy sternly informed them that that would be unnecessary and that the veteran FBI special agent deserved a lot more deference than he was being shown. None of that had ever happened to Sawyer before in all his years with the bureau, and he jokingly let a sheepish Hardy know it.

"Hey, Frank, these guys hoarding gold bullion or uranium 235 in here?"

"Let's just say they're slightly paranoid."

"I'm impressed. Usually we FBI types scare the crap out of everybody. I bet they thumb their noses at the IRS guys too."

"Actually, a former head of the IRS is their top tax guru."

"Damn, they really do have all the bases covered."

An uneasy feeling crept over Sawyer the more he thought about his chosen profession. Information was king these days. Access to information was ruled by and large through computers. The private sector was so far ahead of the government realm that there was no possible way the government would ever catch up. Even the FBI, which in public sectors had state-of-the-art technology, would have existed far down the technological sophistication list in the world where Triton Global did battle. To Sawyer the revelation was not a pleasant one. One would have to be an imbecile not to realize that computer crimes would soon dwarf all other manifestations of human evil, at least in dollar terms. But dollar terms meant a lot. They translated into jobs and homes and happy families. Or not. Sawyer stopped walking. "You mind me asking how much Triton pays you a year?"

Hardy turned around and smiled. "Why? You thinking of hanging out your own shingle and trying to steal my clients?"

"Hey, just testing the waters in case I ever take you up on that offer of a job."

Hardy glanced sharply at Sawyer. "You serious?"

"At my age, you learn never to say never."

Hardy's face resumed its serious look while he pondered his ex-partner's words. "I'd rather not get into specifics, but Triton is well into the seven figures as a client, not counting a substantial retainer they pay us."

Sawyer blew a silent whistle. "Christ, I hope you see a big slice of that at the end of the day, Frank."

Hardy nodded curtly. "I do. And you could too if you'd ever wise up and join me."

"Okay, I'll bite: What are we talking salary-wise if I come on with you? Just ballpark."

"Five to six hundred thousand the first year."

Sawyer's mouth almost hit the floor. "You've got to be shitting me, Frank."

"I never joke about money, Lee. As long as crime is around, we'll never have a bad year." The men resumed walking as Hardy added, "Think about it anyway, will you?"

Sawyer rubbed his chin and thought about his mounting debt, never-ending work hours and his tiny office at the Hoover Building. "I will, Frank." He decided to change the subject. "So is Gamble a one-man show?"

"Not by a long shot. Oh, he's the undisputed leader of Triton; however, the real technology wizard is Quentin Rowe."

"What's he like? A geek?"

"Yes and no," Hardy explained. "Quentin Rowe graduated at the top of his class from Columbia University. He won a slew of awards in the technology field while working at Bell Labs, and then at Intel. He started his own computer company at age twenty-eight. That company was the hottest stock on NASDAQ three years ago and was one of the most sought-after acquisitions of the decade when Nathan Gamble bought it. It's been a brilliant fit. Quentin is the true visionary at the company. He's the one pushing for the CyberCom acquisition. He and Gamble aren't the best of friends, but they've done incredibly well together and Gamble tends to listen to him if the dollars are right. Anyway, you can't argue with the success they've had."

Sawyer nodded. "By the way, we got Sidney Archer under round-the-clock surveillance."

"I take it your interview with her aroused some suspicions."

"You could say that. And something shook her up right when we got there."

"What was that?"

"A phone call."

"From who?"

"I don't know. We traced the call. It came from a phone booth in Los Angeles. Whoever placed the call could be in Australia by now."

"You think it was her husband?"

Sawyer shrugged. "Our source said the person lied about who he was to Sidney Archer's dad when he picked up the phone. And our source said Sidney Archer looked like death warmed over after the call."

Using a smart card, Hardy accessed a private elevator. While they were carried up to the top floor, Hardy took a moment to adjust his fashionable tie and flick at his hair in the reflection of the mirrored elevator doors. His thousand-dollar suit hung well on his lean frame. Gold-plated cuff links glinted at his wrists. Sawyer appraised his former partner's exterior and then looked at his own reflection. His shirt, while freshly laundered, was frayed at the collar, the tie was a relic from a decade ago. Topping it off, Sawyer's perpetual cowlick stuck up like a tiny periscope. Sawyer assumed a mock serious tone as he looked over the very polished Hardy. "You know, Frank, it's a good thing you left the bureau."

"What?" Hardy was rocked.

"You're just too damn pretty to be an FBI agent anymore." Sawyer grinned.

Hardy laughed. "Speaking of pretty, I had lunch with Meggie the other day. Great head on her shoulders too. Getting into law school at Stanford isn't easy. She's going to have a great life."

"In spite of her old man, you probably want to add."

The elevator stopped and they got off. "I don't have the best track record in the world with my two, Lee, you know that. You weren't the only one who missed all those birthdays."

"I think you recovered a lot better with your kids than I did."

"Yeah? Well, Stanford isn't cheap. Think about my offer. Might speed up your recovery. Here we are." Hardy passed through elegant glass doors etched with the shape of an eagle, the glass sliding noiselessly open at their approach. The executive secretary, a nice-looking woman with an efficient, firm manner, announced their arrival into her headset. She pressed a button set in a panel on top of a sleek wood and metal console that looked more like a piece of modern art than a desk, and motioned Hardy and Sawyer to move toward a massive wall of lacquered Macassar ebony wood. A section of the wall opened up when they approached. Sawyer shook his head in amazement, as he had done many times since entering the Triton building.

In a few moments they were standing in front of a desk, although a more apt description would have labeled it a command center, with its wall of TV monitors, phones and other electronic gadgetry neatly built into shining tables and impressive wall units. The man behind the desk was just putting down the phone. He turned to them.

Hardy said, "Special Agent Lee Sawyer of the FBI, Nathan Gamble, chairman of Triton Global."

Sawyer could feel the strength of the grip when Nathan Gamble's fingers closed around his own and the two men exchanged perfunctory greetings.

"Do you have Archer yet?"

Sawyer was halfway to his chair when the question hit him. The tone was clearly that of a superior to a subordinate and was more than sufficient to raise every hair on the agent's thick neck. Sawyer finished sitting down and took a moment to study the man before answering. Out of the corner of his eye, Sawyer caught the apprehensive look on his former partner's face from where he stood rigidly near the doorway. Sawyer took another moment to undo the button on his suit coat and flip open his notebook before resting his steady eyes back on Gamble.

"I'll need to ask you some questions, Mr. Gamble. I hope it won't take all that long."

"You haven't answered my question." The chairman's voice was a notch deeper now.

"No, I haven't and I don't intend to." The two men's eyes locked, until Gamble finally broke it off and looked over at Hardy.

"Mr. Gamble, it's an ongoing bureau investigation. The bureau doesn't usually comment—"

Gamble cut Hardy off with an abrupt wave of his hand. "Then let's get this over with. I have to leave to catch a plane in one hour."

Sawyer didn't know who he wanted to belt more—Gamble, or Hardy for taking this kind of crap.

"Mr. Gamble, perhaps Quentin and Richard Lucas should be in on this discussion."

"Maybe you should have thought about that before scheduling this meeting, Hardy." Gamble punched a button on his console. "Find Rowe and Lucas, right now."

Hardy touched Sawyer on the shoulder. "Quentin heads up the division Archer was in. Lucas is head of internal security."

"Then you're right, Frank, I'll want to speak with them."

A few minutes later the broad portal opened and two men stepped into Nathan Gamble's private domain. Sawyer ran a penetrating eye over them and quickly discerned who was who. His grim demeanor, his look of competitive reproach at Hardy, and the slight hump under his left breast labeled Richard Lucas as Triton's head of security. Sawyer pegged Quentin Rowe as early thirties. Rowe's face held a ready smile underneath a pair of large hazel eyes that were more dreamy than intense. Sawyer concluded that Nathan Gamble could not have had a more unlikely colleague. The expanded group adjourned to the large conference table housed in one corner of Gamble's mammoth office.

Gamble stared at his watch and then looked over at Sawyer. "You have fifty minutes and counting, Sawyer. I was hoping you'd have something important for me. However, I feel disappointment looming. Why don't you prove me wrong?"

Sawyer bit his lip and tensed his shoulders, then decided against taking the bait. He looked over at Lucas. "When did you first suspect Archer?"

Lucas shifted uncomfortably in his chair. Obviously, the security man felt particularly humbled by recent events. "The first definitive event was the videotape of Archer making the exchange in Seattle."

"The one Frank's people obtained?" Sawyer eyed Lucas for confirmation.

Lucas's sullen expression spoke volumes. "That's right. Although I had my own suspicions of Archer before the video was taken."

Gamble spoke up. "Is that so? I don't recall your ever voicing those suspicions before. I don't pay you all that money to keep your mouth shut."

Sawyer eyed Lucas closely. The guy had said too much with probably nothing to back it up. But Sawyer was duty-bound to follow through.

"What sort of suspicions?"

Lucas's face was still frozen on his boss, the fierce reprimand still resonating. Lucas looked dully at Sawyer. "Well, perhaps they were more hunches than anything else. Nothing concrete to go on. Just my gut. Sometimes that's more important, you know what I mean?"

"I do."

"He worked a lot. Irregular hours. His computer log-in times made for some interesting reading, I can tell you that."

Gamble stirred. "I only hire hard workers. Eighty percent of the people here pull seventy-five to ninety hours per week, every week of the year."

"I take it you don't believe in idle hands," Sawyer said.

"I work my people hard, but they're well compensated. Every senior-level manager on up to the executive level at my company is a millionaire. And most of them are under forty." He nodded at Quentin Rowe. "I won't tell you how much he got when I bought him out, but if he wanted to go buy an island somewhere, build himself a mansion, bring in a harem and a private jet, he could do it all without borrowing a dime and have enough left over to keep his great-grandchildren in Ivy League and limos. Of course, I wouldn't

expect a federal bureaucrat to understand the nuances of free enter-
prise. You now have forty-seven minutes left."

Sawyer promised himself he would never allow Gamble an opening of that size again. "Have you confirmed the facts of the bank account scam?" Sawyer eyed Hardy.

His friend nodded. "I'll hook you up with bureau agents handling
it."

Gamble erupted, slamming his fist on the table and glaring at
Sawyer as though he had personally ripped off the Triton chief. "Two
hundred and fifty million dollars!" Gamble was shaking with fury.

An awkward moment of silence was broken by Sawyer. "I understand Archer had some additional protective measures put on his office door."

Lucas answered, his face a shade paler. "That's right, he did."

"I'll need to look over his office later. What sort of things did he
have installed?"

Everyone in the room looked at Richard Lucas. Sawyer could almost see the sweat glistening on the security chief's palms.

"A few months ago he ordered a digital numeric pad and smart
card entry system wired to an alarm for his office door."

"Was that unusual or necessary?" Sawyer asked. He couldn't
imagine it was necessary, considering how many damn hoops one
had to jump through just to get in the place.

"I didn't think it was necessary at all. We have the most secure
shop in the industry." Lucas cringed when this response was met by
a loud grunt from Gamble. "But I'm not sure I could say it was unusual; other people here had similar setups on their office doors."

Quentin Rowe joined in. "Not that you could have missed it, Mr.
Sawyer, but everyone at Triton is terribly security conscious. It's
beaten into the head of every employee here that paranoia is the
proper mind-set to have when it comes to protecting proprietary
technology. In fact, Frank comes in each quarter and lectures the
employees on that very subject. If an employee had a problem or security concern, he or she could go either to Richard or one of his
staff, or Frank. My employees all knew of Frank's illustrious career
at the FBI. I feel confident that anyone with a concern about secu-

rity would have had no hesitation about going to either of them. In fact, employees have done that in the past, nipping some potentially big problems in the bud."

Sawyer looked over at Hardy, who nodded in agreement. "But you had trouble getting into his office after he disappeared. You must have a system to take into account employees who get sick, die or quit."

"There is a system," Lucas proclaimed.

"Jason apparently circumvented it," Rowe said with a trace of admiration.

"How?"

Rowe looked at Lucas and then sighed. "In accordance with company policy, the code to be inputted into any individual security system placed on-site has to be delivered to the head of security," Quentin explained. "To Rich. In addition, all security personnel and key management have master key cards that can access any area of the office."

"Did Archer deliver the code?"

"He delivered the code to Rich, but then he reprogrammed the reader unit at his office door with a different code."

"And that switch wasn't caught before?" Sawyer looked incredulously over at Lucas.

"There was no reason to think he had changed the code," Rowe said. "During office hours Jason's office door was usually kept open. No one other than Jason had any reason to be in there after normal hours."

"Okay, the information Archer allegedly delivered to RTG, how did he get his hands on it? Was he cleared for it?"

"Some of it." Quentin Rowe shifted uneasily in his seat and slid one hand down his ponytail. "Jason was part of the acquisition team for that project. However, there were certain parts, the highest levels of the negotiation, to which he was not privy at all. They were known only to Nathan, myself, and three other senior executives at the company. And outside legal counsel, of course."

"Where was this information kept? File drawer? Safe?" Sawyer asked.

Rowe and Lucas exchanged smiles.

Rowe answered. "We have, to a significant degree, a paperless office. All key documents are stored in computerized files."

"I assume there was some sort of security on these files, then? Like a password."

Lucas said condescendingly, "It was far more than a password."

"And yet Archer broke into it anyway, it seems," Sawyer jabbed back.

Lucas scrunched his mouth up like someone had just jammed a lemon inside.

Quentin Rowe wiped at his glasses. "Yes, he did. Would you like to see how?"

The group of men filled the small, cluttered storeroom. Richard Lucas pushed away the boxes from beside the wall while Rowe, Hardy and Sawyer looked on. Nathan Gamble had declined to join them. Where the boxes had rested, the cable outlet was now exposed. Quentin Rowe moved next to the computer and held up the cables.

"Jason hardwired into our local area network through this workstation."

"Why not just use the computer in his office?"

Rowe was shaking his head before Sawyer had stopped talking. "When he logs on to his own computer," Lucas said, "he has to go through a series of security measures. Those security measures do not merely verify the user, they *confirm* the user's identity. Every workstation in the place has an iris scanner, which takes an initial video image of the user's iris patterns. In addition, the scanner takes periodic sweeps of the operator to continually confirm the user's identity. If Archer had left his desk or someone had sat down in his place, then the system would have automatically shut off to that workstation."

Rowe looked steadily at Sawyer. "The important point in all that is if Archer had accessed any file from his own workstation, we would have known he had done it."

"How's that?" Sawyer asked.

"Our network has a tag feature. Most systems have some attribute of that kind. If a user accesses a file, that access is recorded by the system. By using this workstation"—Quentin pointed at the old computer—"which is not supposed to be on the network and is assigned no number through the network administrator, he bypassed that risk. For all intents and purposes, this was a phantom computer on our network. He may have used the computer in his office to find the location of certain files without accessing them. He could do that at his leisure. That would cut down on the time he needed to spend here, where he could be caught."

Sawyer shook his head. "Wait a minute. If Archer didn't use his own workstation to access the files because it could positively identify him and used this one instead because it couldn't, how do you know it was Archer who accessed the files in the first place?"

Hardy pointed at the keyboard. "An old reliable. We lifted numerous fingerprints from here. They all matched Archer's."

Sawyer finally asked the most obvious question. "Okay, but how do you know this workstation was used to access any files?"

Lucas sat down on one of the boxes. "For a period of time we were getting unauthorized entries onto the system. Although Archer didn't need to go through the identification process to log on through this unit, he would still leave a trail if he accessed files using it unless he electronically erased his trail as he exited. That's possible to do, although tricky. In fact, I think that's what he did. Initially, at least. Then he got sloppy. We finally picked up the trail and, while it took time, we narrowed down the breach until it led us right here."

Hardy folded his arms across his chest. "You know, it's ironic. You put all this time and effort and money into securing your networks against any breaches. You have steel doors, security guards, electronic monitoring devices, smart cards—you name it, Triton has it. And yet . . ." He looked up at the ceiling. "And yet you also have drop-down ceiling panels with exposed cables connecting your entire network together, ripe for penetration." He shook his head in dismay and looked at Lucas. "I've warned you about this risk before."

"He was an insider," Lucas said heatedly. "He knew the system and he used that knowledge to hack it." Lucas brooded for a moment. "And then he took down a planeload of people in the process. Let's not forget that little fact."

Ten minutes later the men were once again in Gamble's office. He did not look up when they reappeared.

Sawyer sat down. "Okay, any further developments on the RTG end?" he asked.

Gamble's face flamed red at the mention of his competitor. "Nobody rips me off and gets away with it."

"Jason Archer's involvement with RTG hasn't been proven. It's all speculation at this point," Sawyer said evenly.

Gamble dramatically rolled his eyes. "Right! Well, you just go and jump through your little hoops so you can keep your little job and I'll take care of the tough stuff."

Sawyer closed his notebook and stood up to his full height. Hardy stood up too, and reached out to grab Sawyer's coat, until his former partner froze him with a stare that Hardy had seen him use on many an occasion at the bureau. Sawyer turned back to Gamble.

"Ten minutes, Sawyer. Since you don't appear to have anything of note to report, I'm going to catch my plane a little early." When Gamble walked past the burly FBI agent, Sawyer tightly gripped his arm and led the Triton chairman outside into the private reception area. Sawyer looked over at Gamble's executive assistant. "Excuse us for a minute, ma'am." The woman hesitated, looking at Gamble.

"I said excuse us!" Sawyer's drill-sergeant tone catapulted the woman out of her chair and she fled the room.

Sawyer turned to the chairman. "Let's get a couple of things straight, Gamble. First, I don't report to you or anyone else at this place. Second, since it looks like one of your people conspired to blow up a plane, I'll ask you as many questions as I want to and I don't give a shit about your travel schedule. And if you tell me one more time how many minutes I've got left, I'll rip that goddamned watch off your wrist and stuff it in your mouth. I'm not one of your lackey boys and don't you ever, ever talk to me that way again. I'm an FBI agent and a damn good one. I've been shot, knifed, kicked and bitten by some seriously demented assholes who would make you look like the biggest pussy in the world on your best day. So if you think your bullshit tough-guy act is gonna make me pee in my pants, then you're wasting everybody's time, including your own. Now get back in there and sit the fuck down."

Two hours later Sawyer had finished interviewing Gamble and company and spent thirty minutes looking through Jason Archer's office, ordering it off limits and calling for a investigative team to methodically analyze every molecule of the place. Sawyer checked out Jason's computer system, but he had no way of knowing that something was missing. The only remnant of the microphone was a small, silver-plated plug.

Sawyer walked to the elevator bank with Hardy.

"See, Frank, I told you there was nothing to worry about. Gamble and I got along just fine."

Hardy laughed out loud. "I don't think I've ever seen his face quite that shade of white before. What the hell did you say to the man?"

"Just told him what a great guy I thought he was. He was probably just embarrassed by my frank admiration."

At the elevators, Sawyer said, "You know, I didn't get much usable info in there. Sure, Archer pulling off the crime of the century might make for fascinating reading, but I'd prefer to have him in a jail cell."

"Well, these guys just got taken to the cleaners and they're certainly not used to that experience. They know what happened and pretty much how it happened, but all after the fact."

Sawyer leaned up against the wall and rubbed his forehead. "You realize there's no evidence tying Archer to the plane bombing."

Hardy nodded in agreement. "I said before that Archer could've used Lieberman to cover his tracks, but there's no proof of that either. If there is no connection, Archer's one helluva lucky guy for not getting on that plane."

"Well, if that's the case, then somebody else out there took down that airliner."

Sawyer was about to hit the elevator button when Hardy touched his sleeve. "Hey, Lee, if you want my humble opinion, I don't think your biggest problem will be proving Archer was involved in the plane sabotage."

"So what's my biggest problem, Frank?"

"Finding him."

Hardy walked off. As Sawyer waited for the elevator, a voice called to him.

"Mr. Sawyer? Do you have a minute?"

Sawyer turned to find Quentin Rowe walking toward him.

"What can I do for you, Mr. Rowe?"

"Please call me Quentin." Rowe paused and looked around the hallways. "Would you like to take a short tour of one of our production facilities?"

Sawyer quickly caught his meaning. "Okay. Sure."

CHAPTER THIRTY-THREE

The fifteen-story Triton office building was hooked to a sprawling three-story structure that covered about five acres of ground. Sawyer pinned on a visitor's badge at the main entrance to the facility and followed Rowe through a number of security checkpoints. Rowe was obviously well-known and well-liked here, as he received a number of cordial greetings from Triton personnel. At one point, through a wall of glass, Sawyer and Rowe watched lab technicians in white coats, gloves and surgical masks working away in a large space.

Sawyer looked at Rowe. "Geez, looks more like an operating room than a factory."

Rowe smiled. "Actually, that room is far cleaner than any hospital operating room."

He watched Sawyer's surprised reaction with amusement. "Those technicians are testing a new generation of computer chips. The environment has to be completely sterile, absolutely dust-free. Once they're fully functional, these prototypes will be able to carry out two TIPS."

"Damn," Sawyer said absently, having no earthly idea what the acronym stood for.

"That means two trillion instructions per *second.*"

Sawyer gaped at the small man. "What in the hell needs to move that fast?"

"You'd be surprised. A litany of engineering applications. Computer-aided designs of cars, aircraft, ships, space shuttles, buildings, manufacturing processes of all types. Financial markets, corporate operations. Take a company like General Motors: millions of pieces of inventory, hundreds of thousands of employees, thousands of locations. It all adds up. We help all of them do their jobs more efficiently." He pointed to another production area. "A new line of hard drives is being tested in there. They'll be by far the most powerful and efficient in the industry when they hit the market next year. Yet a year after that they'll be obsolete." He looked at Sawyer. "What sort of system do you use at work?"

Sawyer put his hands in his pocket. "You might not have heard of it: Smith Corona?"

Rowe gaped at him. "You're kidding."

"Just got a new ribbon in it, baby runs sweet as mother's milk." Sawyer sounded very defensive.

Rowe shook his head. "A friendly warning. Anyone who doesn't know how to operate a computer in the coming years will not be able to function in society. Don't be intimidated. The systems today are not only user friendly, they are idiot friendly, no offense intended."

Sawyer sighed. "Computers getting faster all the time, this Internet thing, whatever it really is, growing like crazy, networks, paging, cellular phones, faxes. Jesus, where's it going to end?"

"Since it's the business I'm in, I hope it never does."

"Sometimes change can happen too fast."

Rowe smiled benignly. "The change we see going on today will pale in comparison to what will take place in the next five years. We're on the cusp of technological breakthroughs that would have seemed unthinkable barely ten years ago." Rowe's eyes appeared to shine ahead into the next century. "What we know as the Internet today will seem boring and quaint very soon. Triton Global will be a huge part of that happening. In fact, if things work out correctly, we will be leading the way. Education, medicine, the workplace, travel, entertainment, how we eat, socialize, consume, produce— everything human beings do or benefit from will be transformed. Poverty, prejudice, crime, injustice, disease will crumple under the sheer weight of information, of discovery. Ignorance will simply dis- appear. The knowledge of thousands of libraries, the sum of the world's greatest minds, all will be readily accessible by anyone. In the end, the world of computers as we know it today will metamor- phose into one enormous interactive global link of limitless poten- tial." He peered at Sawyer through his glasses. "All the world's knowledge, the solutions to every problem, will be one keystroke away. It's the natural next step."

"One person will be able to get all that from a computer." Sawyer's tone was skeptical.

"Isn't that a thrilling vision?"

"Scares the shit out of me."

Rowe's mouth dropped open. "How could that possibly be fright- ening to you?"

"Maybe I'm a little cynical after twenty-five years of doing what I do for a living. But you tell me one guy can get all that informa- tion and you know the first thought pops into my head?"

"No, what?"

"What if he's a *bad* guy?" Rowe didn't react. "What if with one keystroke he wipes out all the world's knowledge?" Sawyer snapped his fingers. "He destroys everything? Or just screws it all up. Then what the hell do we do?"

Rowe smiled. "The benefits of technology far surpass any poten- tial dangers. You may not agree with me, but the coming years will prove me right."

Sawyer scratched the back of his head. "You're probably too young to know this, but back in the fifties, nobody thought illegal drugs would ever be a big problem either. Go figure."

The two men continued their tour. "We have five of these facili- ties situated across the country," Rowe said.

"Must get pretty expensive."

"You could say that. We spend over ten billion dollars per year on R&D."

Sawyer whistled. "You're talking numbers I can't even begin to contemplate. Of course, I'm just a working-stiff bureaucrat who sits around picking his nose on the public dole."

Rowe smiled. "Nathan Gamble delights in making other people squirm. I think he met his match in you, though. For obvious reasons I didn't applaud your performance, but I was seriously thinking about a standing ovation."

"Hardy said you had your own company, hot stock. If you don't mind my asking, how come you hooked up with Gamble?"

"Money." Rowe waved his arm around the facility they were in. "This all costs billions of dollars. My company was doing well, but lots of tech companies were doing well *in the stock market*. What people don't seem to understand is that while my company's stock price went from nineteen dollars a share on the day it hit the market to a hundred sixty per share less than six months later, we didn't see any of that enormous markup. That went to the people who bought the stock."

"You had to keep a chunk of the company's stock, though."

"I did, but with the securities laws being what they are, and our underwriter's requirements, I couldn't really sell any of it. On paper I was worth a fortune. However, my company was still struggling, R&D was eating us up, we had no earnings," he said bitterly.

"So enter Nathan Gamble?"

"Actually he was a very early investor in the company, before we went public. He gave us some seed capital. He also gave us something else we didn't have but desperately needed: respectability on Wall Street, with the capital markets. A good solid business background. A penchant for making money. When my company went public, he held on to his shares as well. Later, Gamble and I discussed the future and decided to take the company back private."

"In retrospect a good decision?"

"From a dollar perspective, an incredibly good decision."

"But money ain't everything, right, Quentin?"

"Sometimes I wonder."

Sawyer leaned up against the wall, folded his beefy arms across his chest and looked directly at Rowe. "The tour is real interesting, but I hope that wasn't all you had in mind."

"It wasn't." Rowe swiped his card through the reader on a nearby door and motioned for Sawyer to follow him in. They sat down at a small table. Rowe spent a moment collecting his thoughts before he started speaking. "You know, if you had asked me before this all happened who I would suspect of having stolen from us, Jason Archer's name would never have entered my mind." Rowe took off his glasses and rubbed them with a handkerchief pulled from his shirt pocket.

"So you trusted him?"

"Absolutely."

"And now?"

"And now I think I was wrong. I feel betrayed, in fact."

"I could see how you might feel that way. You think anybody else at the company might be involved?"

"My God, I hope not." Rowe seemed stricken by the suggestion. "I would certainly rather believe it was Jason on his own or a competitor working with him. That, to me, makes a lot more sense. Besides, Jason would have been perfectly capable of hacking into BankTrust's computer system by himself. It's really not all that hard to do."

"You sound like you speak from experience."

Rowe's face reddened. "Let's just say that I have an insatiable curiosity. Poking around databases was a favorite pastime in college. My classmates and I had quite a good time doing it, although the local authorities, on more than one occasion, voiced their displeasure. However, we never stole anything. I actually helped train some of the police technicians in methods to detect and prevent computer-related crimes."

"Any of those people working on your security detail?"

"You mean Richard Lucas? No, he's been with Gamble it seems like forever now. Again, he's very good at what he does, but not the most pleasant company to have around. However, it's not his job to be pleasant."

"But Archer still fooled him."

"He fooled all of us. I'm certainly in no position to point fingers."

"Did you notice anything about Jason Archer that in retrospect looked suspicious?"

"Most things look different in retrospect. I know that better than most. I've given it some thought and Jason did seem to take a very active interest in the CyberCom deal."

"He *was* working on it."

"I don't mean just that. Even on the segments of the deal he wasn't involved in he asked a lot of questions."

"Like what?"

"Like did I think the terms were fair. Did I think the deal was going to get done. What would be his role once it was done. That sort of thing."

"He ever ask you about any confidential records you kept regarding the deal?"

"Not directly, no."

"He apparently got everything he needed off the computer system?"

"So it would seem."

The two men sat staring off into space for a few moments.

"You have any inkling where Archer might be?"

Rowe shook his head. "I visited his wife, Sidney."

"We've met."

"It's hard to believe he would just up and leave them like that. He has a daughter too. A beautiful little girl."

"Maybe he didn't plan to leave them."

Rowe looked at him oddly. "What do you mean?"

"I mean maybe he intends to come back for them."

"He's a fugitive from justice now. Why would he come back? Besides, Sidney wouldn't go with him."

"Why not?"

"Because he's a criminal. She's an attorney."

"This may come as a big surprise to you, Quentin, but some lawyers aren't honest."

"You mean . . . you mean you suspect Sidney Archer of being involved in this whole thing?"

"I mean I haven't ruled her or anyone else out right now as a suspect. She's an attorney for Triton. She was working on the Cyber-Com deal. Seems like a perfect position to cherry-pick secrets and sell them to RTG. Who the hell knows? I intend to find out."

Rowe put his glasses back on and rubbed his hand nervously across the glass tabletop. "It's so hard to believe Sidney would be involved in all this." Rowe's tone betrayed the conviction of his words.

Sawyer studied him closely. "Quentin, do you want to tell me something? Maybe about Sidney Archer?"

Rowe finally sighed and looked at Sawyer. "I'm convinced that Sidney was in Jason's office at Triton after the plane crash."

Sawyer's eyes narrowed. "What proof do you have?"

"The night before Jason supposedly left for L.A. he and I were working late on a project in his office. We left together. He secured his office door behind me. His office remained locked from that moment until we had the company come to deactivate the alarm and remove the door."

"So?"

"When we entered the office, I noticed immediately that the microphone on Jason's computer was bent almost in half. Like someone had hit it and then tried to straighten it."

"Why would you think that someone was Sidney Archer? Maybe Jason came back later that night."

"If he had there would be a record of it, both electronically and with the on-site security guard." Rowe paused, dwelling on the memory of the night of Sidney's visit. Finally he threw up his hands. "I know of no other way to put it. She was sneaking around. She claimed she was not in the restricted area, and yet I'm sure she was. I think the security guard was covering for her. And Sidney told me some bogus story about meeting Jason's secretary there to get some of Jason's personal things."

"Doesn't that sound plausible?"

"It would have, except I casually asked Kay Vincent, Jason's secretary, if she had spoken to Sidney recently. And she had, from her home, on the very night Sidney went down to the office. She knew Kay wasn't there."

Sawyer sat back in his chair. Rowe continued. "You need a special chip card even to begin the deactivation process on Jason's office door. In addition, you need to know a four-digit password or the alarm will go off. It happened, in fact, when we initially tried to enter his office. That's when we found out Jason had changed the password. I even considered attempting it the night Sidney came by, only I knew it would be futile. I had a master security card, but without the password, the alarm would've just gone off again." He paused to take a breath. "Sidney could've have had access to Jason's security card and he could've told her the password. I can't believe I'm saying this, but she's involved in something, I just don't know what."

"I just looked through Archer's office and I didn't see any microphone. What did it look like?"

"About five inches long, the thickness of a pencil, small speaker at one end. It was mounted directly on the computer's CPU on the bottom left-hand side. It's for voice-activated commands. One day it'll replace the keyboard entirely. It's a godsend for people who can't type well."

"I didn't see anything like that."

"Probably not. I'm sure it was removed from the office because it was so damaged."

Sawyer took a few minutes to jot down notes and asked Rowe a few follow-up questions. Then Rowe escorted him back to the exit. "You think of anything else, Quentin, you let me know." He handed Rowe a business card.

"I wish I knew what the hell was going on, Agent Sawyer. I have my hands full with CyberCom, and now this."

"I'm doing what I can, Quentin. Hang in there."

Rowe slowly went back inside, Sawyer's card clutched in his hand. Sawyer walked to his car; he could hear his cellular phone buzzing. Ray Jackson's voice was agitated. "You were right."

"About what?"

"Sidney Archer's on the move."

CHAPTER THIRTY-FOUR

A half block behind the airport cab were the two FBI tail cars. Two other sedans were running on parallel streets and would cross over at strategic points to take over the chase so as not to alert the person they were tracking. That person swept the hair from her eyes, took a deep breath and stared out the window of the cab. Sidney Archer swiftly ran through the details of her trip once more and wondered if she had just exchanged one nightmare for another.

"She came back to the house after the memorial service, stayed a little while and then the cab came and picked her up. The direction they're heading, my call is Dulles Airport," Ray Jackson said into the car phone. "She made one stop. At a bank. Probably withdrawing some cash."

Lee Sawyer pressed the phone against his ear and fought through rush-hour traffic. "Where are you now?"

Jackson relayed his position. "You shouldn't have trouble, Lee, we're crawling through traffic here."

Sawyer started looking at cross streets. "I can be up with you in about ten minutes. How many pieces of luggage she carrying?"

"One medium suitcase."

"Short trip, then."

"Probably." Jackson eyed the cab. "Oh, shit!"

"What?" Sawyer almost yelled into the phone.

In dismay Jackson watched as the cab abruptly pulled into the Vienna metro subway station. "Looks like the lady just had a change in travel arrangements. She's hopping on the subway." Jackson watched Sidney Archer step out of the cab.

"Get a couple of guys in there right now, Ray."

"Roger that, double-quick."

Sawyer turned on his grille lights and cut around the stalled traffic. When his phone buzzed again, he snatched it up. "Talk to me, Ray, only good news."

His partner's breathing was a little more normal. "Okay, we got two guys on with her."

"I'm one minute from the station. Which way she headed? Wait a minute, Vienna's the end of the orange line. She must be headed into town."

"Maybe, Lee, unless she's gonna double back on us and grab another cab when she exits the subway. Dulles is the other way. And we got a potential problem with our lines of communication. The walkie-talkies don't always work so well on the metro. If she changes trains inside the metro and our guys lose her, she's gone."

Sawyer thought for a moment. "Did she take her luggage, Ray?"

"What? Damn. No, she didn't."

"Get two cars glued to that cab, Ray. I doubt Mrs. Archer is leaving behind her clean undies and her makeup kit."

"I'm on it myself. You want to pair with me?"

Sawyer was about to agree, then abruptly changed his mind. He streaked through a red light. "You hang on it, Ray, I'm gonna cover another angle. Check in every five minutes and let's hope she doesn't give us the slip."

Sawyer did a U-turn and hurtled east.

Sidney had changed trains at the Rosslyn substation and boarded a blue-line train heading south. At the Pentagon metro station, the doors on the subway opened and approximately one thousand people careened off the train cars. Sidney was carrying the white coat she had been wearing. She didn't want to stand out from the crowd. The blue sweater she wore was swiftly lost in the thickening crowds of similarly attired military personnel.

The two FBI agents pushed through the masses as they desperately tried to relocate Sidney Archer. Neither one noticed Sidney reboard the same train several cars down, and she continued on to National Airport. She looked behind her several times, but the train now held no obvious pursuers.

Sawyer pulled to a halt in front of the main terminal at National Airport, flashed his credentials to a surprised parking lot attendant and raced into the building. A few seconds later he stopped dead and his shoulders sagged in frustration as he scanned the wall-to-wall people. "Shit!" The next second he flattened himself against the wall as Sidney Archer passed barely ten feet in front of him.

As soon as Sidney was safely ahead of him, Sawyer started tracking her. The short journey ended in the line at the United Airlines ticket desk, which stood twenty deep.

Out of sight of both Sawyer and Sidney, Paul Brophy rolled his luggage carrier toward an American Airlines departure gate. Inside Brophy's inner suit pocket was Sidney's entire travel itinerary gleaned from her conversation with Jason Archer. He continued on unhurriedly. He could afford that luxury as chaos swirled around him. He would even have time to check in with Goldman.

After forty-five minutes Sidney finally received her ticket and boarding pass. Sawyer watched from a distance and noted the large wad of bills she used for the purchase. As soon as she had disappeared around the corner, Sawyer swiftly sliced through the line, his FBI badge prominently held in his hand as the first wave of angry travelers quickly parted for him.

The ticket person stared at the badge and then at Sawyer.

"The woman you just sold a ticket to, Sidney Archer. Tall, good-looking blond, dressed in blue with a white coat over her arm,"

Sawyer added just in case his prey had used an alias. "What flight is she on? Quick."

The woman froze for an instant and then started punching keys. "Flight 715 to New Orleans. It leaves in twenty minutes."

"New Orleans?" said Sawyer, more to himself than to the woman. Now he momentarily regretted having personally interviewed Sidney Archer. She would recognize him instantly. But there was no time to call in another agent. "What gate?"

"Eleven."

Sawyer leaned forward and spoke in a low tone. "Okay, what's her seat?"

The woman glanced at the screen. "Twenty-seven C."

"Is there a problem here?" The woman's supervisor had drifted over. Sawyer showed her his FBI credentials and quickly explained his situation. The supervisor picked up a phone and alerted both the boarding gate and security, who would, in turn, inform the flight crew. The last thing Sawyer needed was a flight attendant spotting his gun during the trip with the result that the New Orleans police would be waiting for him at the door when the plane landed.

A few minutes later Sawyer, wearing a beat-up hat hastily borrowed from security personnel, his coat collar turned up, strode down the terminal's broad aisle, an airline security officer in tow. Sawyer was escorted around the metal detectors while he scanned the crowds for Sidney Archer. He spotted her at the departure gate already in line to board. He immediately turned around and sat facing away from the gate. Several minutes after the last group of people moved onto the plane, Sawyer walked down the jetwalk. He settled down into first class, in one of the few available seats on the crowded jet, and allowed himself a brief smile. It was the first time he had ever flown in such luxury. He fumbled through his wallet for his phone card. His finger closed around Sidney Archer's business card. There were phone numbers for Sidney's direct office line, pager, fax, and mobile phone. Sawyer shook his head. That was the private sector, for you. Need to know where you are every minute. He pulled out the plane phone and slid his card through it.

*   *   *

The flight to New Orleans was nonstop and two and a half hours later the jet was descending into New Orleans International Airport. Sidney Archer had not budged from her seat the entire flight, for which Lee Sawyer was immensely grateful. Sawyer had made a number of phone calls from the plane and his team was in place at the airport. When the door to the jet opened, Sawyer was the first one off.

When Sidney exited the airport into the mugginess of the New Orleans night, she did not notice the black sedan with the tinted windows parked across the narrow roadway used to pick up or drop off passengers. Settled into her seat in the battered gray Cadillac with CAJUN CAB COMPANY stenciled on the side, Sidney loosened the collar of her shirt and wiped a bit of perspiration from her forehead. "The LaFitte Guest House, please. Bourbon Street."

As the cab drifted away from the curb, the sedan waited a moment, then followed. Inside the sedan Lee Sawyer was filling in the other agents on the situation, his eyes all the time riveted on the dirty Caddie.

Sidney stared anxiously out the cab window. They left the highway and headed to the Vieux Carre. In the background the New Orleans skyline glittered out of the darkness, the massive hump of the Superdome resting in the foreground.

Bourbon Street was narrow and lined with garish edifices of, by American standards at least, the "ancient" French Quarter. At this time of the year, the sixty-six blocks of the Quarter were relatively quiet, although the smell of beer rose powerfully from the sidewalks as casually dressed vacationers staggered around carrying large cups of the stuff. Sidney left the cab in front of the LaFitte Guest House. She took a quick look up and down the street. No cars were in sight. She walked up the steps and pushed open the heavy front door.

Inside, the comforting smell of antiques embraced her. To her left was a large and stylishly decorated drawing room. The night clerk at the small desk raised his eyebrows slightly at Sidney's lack of baggage but smiled and nodded when she explained it was coming later.

She was given the choice of riding the small elevator to the third floor, but chose the broad staircase instead. Key in hand, she went up two flights of stairs to her room. Her room contained a four-poster bed, writing desk, three walls of bookshelves and a Victorian-style chaise lounge.

Outside, the black sedan pulled into an alleyway half a block down from the LaFitte Guest House. A man dressed in jeans and a windbreaker alighted from the rear of the car, walked nonchalantly down the street and went into the building. Five minutes later he was back in the car.

Lee Sawyer leaned anxiously over the front seat. "What's going on in there?"

The man unzipped his windbreaker, revealing the pistol in his waistband. "Sidney Archer checked in for two days. Room's on the third floor right across from the top of the stairs. Said her baggage was coming later."

The driver looked over at Sawyer. "You think she's meeting up with Jason Archer?"

"Let's put it this way: I'd be damn surprised if she flew down here just for some R&R," Sawyer replied.

"What do you want to do?"

"Discreetly surround this place. Jason Archer shows up, we grab him. In the meantime, let's see if we can get some surveillance equipment in the room next to hers. Then see if you can get a tap on her phone line. Use a male and female team so the Archers don't get their radar up. Sidney Archer isn't someone you want to under-estimate." Sawyer's tone was filled with grudging admiration. He looked out the window. "Let's get out of here. I don't want to give Jason Archer any reason not to show up." The sedan pulled slowly away.

Sidney Archer sat in the chair by the bed, staring out the window of her room onto the side balcony of the LaFitte Guest House and awaiting her husband. She rose and nervously paced the room. She was fairly certain she had lost the FBI agents in the subway, but she could not be absolutely sure. If they managed to trace her? She shiv-

ered. Ever since Jason's phone call had thrown her life into a cata-
clysm for a second time, Sidney had felt invisible walls closing in
around her.

Jason's instructions, however, had been explicit and she intended
to follow them. She adhered fiercely to the belief that her husband
had done nothing wrong, which he had assured her was correct. He
needed her help; that was why she had boarded that plane and was
presently pacing a quaint room in the most famous Louisiana city.
She still had faith in her husband, despite events that, she had to
admit, had shaken that faith, and nothing short of death would stop
her from helping him. Death? Her husband had escaped its complicated tentacles one time already. From the sound of his voice, she
had nagging doubts about his present safety. He was unable to give
her many details. Not over the phone. Only in person, he had said.
She so wanted to see him, to touch him, to confirm for herself that
he was not an apparition.

She sat down in the chair and stared out the open window. A refreshing breeze helped to dispel the humidity. She did not hear a
couple in their mid-thirties, courtesy of the FBI's New Orleans field
office, move into the room next to hers. With her phone line tapped
and listening devices set up in the adjoining suite recording every
sound from her room, Sidney Archer finally nodded off in the chair
around one in the morning. Jason Archer had still not come.

The house was dark. A layer of new-fallen snow shone under the
radiant eye of a full moon. The figure alighted from the nearby
woods and approached the home from the rear. A few moments at
the back door and the old lock succumbed to the skillful manipula-
tions of the darkly clad intruder. Snow boots were removed and left
outside the back door. A few moments later a single arc of light cut
through the deserted house. Sidney Archer's parents and Amy had
left to go back to the Pattersons' home shortly after Sidney had departed for her trip.

The intruder went straight to Jason Archer's home office. The
room's window looked out onto the backyard rather than the street,
so the figure risked turning on the desk lamp. Several minutes were

spent thoroughly searching the desk and stacks of computer floppies. Then Jason Archer's computer system was turned on. A search was made of all files on the database. Each floppy was submitted to a detailed review. With that completed, the figure slipped a hand inside the dark jacket and extracted a floppy disk of his own. This was inserted into the computer's disk drive. After several minutes the task was complete. The "sniffer" software now existing on Jason's computer would effectively capture everything coming across its threshold. Within five minutes the house was once again empty. The footprints from the edge of the woods to the back door had been obliterated.

Unknown to the Archers' nocturnal visitor, Bill Patterson had accomplished one task, however innocently, before leaving for his Hanover home. While he backed his car out of the driveway, he had eyed the familiar red, white and blue truck stopping in front of his daughter's house. After the mail truck had departed, Patterson had hesitated and then arrived at his decision. Save his daughter the trouble, anyway. He glanced at a few of the items before depositing the pile of mail in a plastic bag. He turned toward the house and then remembered he had already locked it up and the keys were in his wife's purse. The garage door was unlocked, however. Patterson went in the garage, opened the door of the Explorer and placed the bag on the front seat. He locked the car door and then pulled down the garage door and locked it.

About midway down in the stack of mail and unnoticed by Patterson was a soft-sided package specifically designed with built-in padding to send fragile items safely through the postal system. The handwriting on the package would have been familiar to Sidney Archer at even a passing glance.

Jason Archer had mailed the computer disk to himself.

CHAPTER THIRTY-FIVE

Across the street from the LaFitte Guest House, Lee Sawyer stared at the old hotel through the darkened window of the room he was occupying. The FBI had set up their surveillance headquarters in an abandoned brick building its owner was planning to renovate in a year or so. Sawyer sipped hot coffee and looked at his watch. Six-thirty A.M. Raindrops clattered against the window as a chilly early morning shower invaded the area.

Next to the window stood a tripod with a camera attached. The long-range lens was almost a foot long. The only pictures snapped thus far had been of the LaFitte Guest House's entryway and only to gauge focus, distance and lighting. Sawyer walked over and looked down at the series of photos on the table. The pictures did neither the face nor the emerald eyes justice. Sidney Archer had been photographed by the New Orleans FBI field office upon exiting the airport. Despite her ignorance, she looked almost posed for the camera. Her countenance was lovely, the hair full and luxuriant. Sawyer gently traced the slender nose down to the full lips. With a start he jerked his hand away from the photograph and looked around, embarrassed. Fortunately, none of the other agents in the room had been paying attention to what he was doing.

He surveyed the rest of the room. The long table was set up in the middle of the large and practically empty space with bare brick walls, dark-timbered ceilings and filthy floors. Twin PCs occupied the most prominent space on the table. A tape-recording machine was next to them. Several of the local bureau agents manned the machines. One young agent caught Sawyer's eye and removed his headphones. "Our people are all in place. From the sounds of it, she's probably still asleep."

Sawyer nodded slowly and turned to look back out the window once again. His men had ascertained that five other guest rooms were occupied in the small hotel. All couples. None of the males matched Jason Archer's description.

The next few hours passed slowly. Used to long stakeouts that netted little except a sour stomach and an aching back, Sawyer was unfazed by the tedium.

The young agent was listening intently to his headphones. "She's exiting her room right now."

Sawyer stood up, stretched and again looked at his watch. "Eleven A.M. Maybe she's going for a late breakfast."

"How do you want to handle the surveillance?"

Sawyer considered for a moment. "As we discussed. Two teams. Use the woman from the room next door as one and a pair as the other. They can alternate on the surveillance. Tell them to look sharp. Archer's gonna be on her guard. Keep in radio communication at all times. Remember, she doesn't have any luggage at the hotel. So tell them to be ready for any mode of transportation, including Archer jumping on another plane. Make sure you got vehicles nearby at all times."

"Right."

Sawyer looked out the window again while his instructions were relayed to the teams of agents. He had a feeling about all of this he couldn't quite pin down. Why New Orleans? Why, on the same day the FBI had interrogated her, would she risk something like this? He abruptly stopped his musings as Sidney Archer appeared on the front steps of the LaFitte Guest House. She looked back over her shoulder, her eyes filled with barely concealed fright; that look was instantly familiar to the FBI agent. A quiver went up Sawyer's spine as he suddenly realized where he had seen Sidney Archer before: at the crash site. He raced across the room and snatched up a phone.

Sidney was wearing her white coat, testament to how the temperature had dropped. She had managed to check the guest registry without the clerk observing her. There had been only one check-in after her. A couple from Ames, Iowa, was in the room next to hers. The check-in time must have been near midnight if not after. It didn't strike her as likely that a couple from the Midwest would be checking into a hotel at about the hour they would normally be entering REM sleep patterns. That she had not heard them move into the room raised her suspicions even more. Weary travelers arriving at midnight were usually not so understanding of their fellow lodgers. She had to assume that the FBI was next door to her and probably watching the entire area. Despite her precautions, they had found her. It was hardly surprising, she had to remind herself as she walked along the mostly deserted streets. The FBI did this for a living. She didn't. And if the FBI closed in? Well, she had decided from the moment she learned her husband was alive that his chances of keeping that life intact would be considerably enhanced if he would place himself in the hands of the authorities.

Sawyer paced the room, hands shoved in his pockets. He had drunk so much coffee he could feel his bladder shooting nasty signals at him. The phone rang. The young agent answered it, identified the caller as Ray Jackson, and then handed it over to Sawyer, who took off his headphones.

"Yeah?" Sawyer's voice was vibrating with anticipation. He rubbed at his bloodshot eyes; a quarter century of pulling this kind of duty didn't make it any easier on the body.

"So how's the Big Easy?" Ray Jackson sounded fresh and alert.

Sawyer looked around at the crumbling surroundings. "Well,

from where I'm standing, it's sorely in need of a broom and some paint."

Jackson chuckled. "Well, your tracking down Sidney Archer at the airport is already the stuff of legend around here. I still don't know how you did it."

"Yeah, but I'm afraid I just wore my lucky rabbit's foot clean out with that one, Ray. Tell me you got something for me." Sawyer switched the receiver to his right ear and stretched his left arm until a cramp worked itself loose.

"You bet I do. Want to guess?"

"Ray, I love you, man, I really do, but my bed last night was a sleeping bag on a cold floor, and there's not one part of my body that doesn't ache. On top of that I've got no clean underwear, so unless you want me to shoot you on sight when I get back, start talking."

"Stay cool, big guy. Okay, you were absolutely right, Sidney Archer did visit the crash site in the middle of the night."

"You're sure?" Sawyer was convinced he was right, but years of habit required independent substantiation.

"One of the local cops . . ." Sawyer heard papers being shuffled over the phone line, "Deputy Eugene McKenna, was on duty that night when Sidney Archer pulls up. McKenna thinks she's just a curiosity-seeker and tells her to head on out, but then she tells him about her husband being on the plane. She just wants to look around; she's all broken up. McKenna feels sorry for her, you know, driving all night to get there and all. He checks her out, confirms she is who she says she is and then drives her up near the crash site so she can at least watch what's going on." Jackson paused.

Sawyer was irritable. "So how the hell does that help us?"

"Man, you are grouchy. I'm getting to that. On the drive up, Archer asks about a canvas bag with her husband's initials on it. She had seen it on TV. I guess it had been thrown off in the crash and was found and put with the other collected debris. Bottom line: She wanted to get that bag."

Sawyer sat down, looked out the window and then refocused on the phone. "What did McKenna tell her?"

"That it was evidence and wasn't even on-site anymore. That

she'd probably get it back after the investigation was complete but that that would be a while, maybe years."

Sawyer stood up and absentmindedly poured himself another cup of coffee from the pot on the hot plate while he worked through this latest development. His bladder would just have to deal with it. "Ray, what exactly did McKenna say about Archer's appearance that night?"

"I know what you're thinking. Did she really believe her husband was on that plane? McKenna said if she was faking, she'd make Katharine Hepburn look like the world's worst actress."

"Okay, we'll let that ride for now. What about the bag? You got it?"

"Damn straight. Right on my desk here."

"And?" Sawyer's shoulders tensed, then dropped just as suddenly at his partner's response.

"Nothing. At least nothing we can find. The lab's been through it three times. Just some clothes, a couple of travel books. Notepad with nothing written on it. No surprises, Lee."

"Why would she drive all that way in the middle of the night for that?"

"Well, maybe there was supposed to be something in it, but there wasn't."

"That would figure if her husband was double-crossing her."

"How's that?"

Sawyer sipped his coffee and then stood up. "If Archer is on the run, one would think he is either planning to bring his family along at a later date or dump them. Right?"

"Okay, I'm following you."

"So if his wife thought he was on that plane, maybe on the initial leg of his getaway run, then that would jibe with her being despondent over the plane crash. She really thinks he's dead."

"But the money?"

"Right. If Sidney Archer knew what her husband had done, maybe had even helped him pull it off somehow, she would want to get her hands on the money. It would help get her over her grief, I'm thinking. Then she sees the bag on TV."

"But what could be in the bag? Not the cash."

"No, but it could have been something to point her in the direction of the money. Archer was a computer whiz. Maybe the location of a computer file on a floppy where all the info on the money is stored. A Swiss bank account number. An airport locker key card. It could be anything, Ray."

"Well, we didn't find anything remotely like that."

"It wouldn't necessarily be in that bag. She saw it on TV and thought she could get her hands on it."

"So you really think she was in on this thing from the get-go?"

Sawyer sat back down wearily. "I don't know, Ray. I've got no strong feeling either way on it." That wasn't exactly true, but Sawyer had no desire to discuss certain disturbing thoughts with his partner.

"So what about the plane crash? How does that tie in?"

Sawyer's response was abrupt. "Who knows if it does? They could be unrelated. Maybe he paid to have it sabotaged to cover his tracks. That's what Frank Hardy thinks happened." Sawyer had stepped over to the window while he was speaking. What he saw on the street outside made him want to end the phone call quickly.

"Anything else, Ray?"

"Nope, that's it."

"Good, because I gotta run." Sawyer hung up the phone, manned the camera himself and started clicking away. Then he stepped back to the window and watched while Paul Brophy, looking searchingly up and down the street, climbed the steps of the LaFitte Guest House and went inside.

CHAPTER THIRTY-SIX

The typical noise and merriment usually associated with Jackson Square would have made a stark contrast to the more modest proceedings of the Quarter at this time of the morning. Musicians, jugglers and unicyclists, tarot card readers and artists ranging in talent from superb to mediocre competed for the attention and dollars of the few tourists who had braved the inclement weather.

Sidney Archer walked in front of the triple-steepled St. Louis Cathedral on her way to find food. She was also following her husband's instructions: If he had not contacted her at the hotel by eleven A.M. she was to go to Jackson Square. The bronze equestrian statue of Andrew Jackson, which had lent dignity to the square for the last 140 years, loomed large over her as she made her way to the French Market Place on Decatur Street. She had visited the city several times before, during her college and law school days when she had been young enough to survive Mardis Gras and even to enjoy and participate in its atmosphere of drunken extravagance.

Minutes later she sat near the riverfront sipping hot coffee and biting unenthusiastically into a fluffy, butter-filled croissant, idly watching the barges and tugs along the mighty Mississippi as they made slow progress toward the enormous bridge in the near distance. Within a hundred yards of her, on either side, were positioned teams of FBI agents. Listening equipment discreetly pointed in her direction was capable of capturing virtually every word spoken by or to her.

For a few minutes Sidney Archer remained alone. She quietly finished her coffee and studied the muscular river with its rain-swollen banks and stiff whitecaps.

"Three dollars and fifty cents says I can tell you where you got your shoes."

Sidney collapsed out of her brown study and stared up at the face. Behind her the teams of agents slightly stiffened and edged forward. They would have surged toward her at full sprint when the man began to approach except that the speaker was short, black and close to seventy. This was not Jason Archer. But it still might be something.

"What?" She shook her head clear.

"Your shoes. I know where you got your shoes. Three-fifty if I'm right. A free shine for you if I'm wrong." His snow-white mustache hung over a mouth largely absent of teeth. His clothes were more rags than anything else. She also observed the battered wooden shoeshine kit resting on the bench beside her.

"I'm sorry. I'm really not interested."

"Come on, lady. Tell you what, I'll throw in the shine if I'm right, but you still got to come up with the money. What's to lose? You get a great shine for a very reasonable price."

Sidney was about to refuse him again until she saw the ribs sticking through the worn, gauzy shirt. Her eyes drifted over his own shoes, from which bare and heavily callused toes protruded at several spots. She smiled and reached inside her purse for money.

"Uh-uh, don't do it that way, lady. Sorry. Got to play the game or we don't do business." There was more than a small reserve of pride in his words. He started to pick up his box.

"Wait a minute. All right," said Sidney.

"Okay, you don't think I can tell you where you got your shoes, do you?" he said.

Sidney Archer shook her head. She had purchased them at an obscure store in southern Maine a little over two years ago. It had since gone out of business. There was no way. "Sorry, but I don't think so," she replied.

"Well, I'm gonna tell you where you got those shoes." The man paused dramatically and then almost cackled as he pointed down. "You got them on your feet."

Sidney joined in his laughter.

In the background, the two agents holding listening devices couldn't help but smile.

After performing a mock bow to his audience of one, the old man knelt down in front of Sidney and prepared her shoes for polishing. He chatted away amiably while his dexterous hands soon turned her dull black flats to lustrous ebony.

"Nice quality, lady. Last you a long time if you take care of them. Nice ankles to go with them too. That never hurts."

She smiled at the compliment as he rose and repacked his box. Sidney pulled out three dollars and rummaged in her purse for change.

He looked at her. "That's okay, ma'am, I got plenty of change," he said quickly.

In response she handed him a five and told him to keep the difference.

He shook his head. "No way, no sir. Three-fifty was the deal and three-fifty it is."

Despite her protests, he handed her back a crumpled single and a fifty-cent piece. When her hand closed around the silver, she felt the small piece of paper taped to its underside. Her eyes bulged at him. He merely smiled and tipped the brim of his raggedy cap. "Nice doing business with you, ma'am. Remember, take care of those shoes."

After he moved off, Sidney quickly put the money away in her purse, waited for several minutes and then got up and walked off as casually as she was able.

She made her way back over to the French Market Place and into the ladies' room. In one of the stalls her quivering hands unfolded the paper. The message was short and in block print. She reread it several times and then promptly flushed it down the toilet.

Making her way up Dumaine Street toward Bourbon, she paused and opened her purse for a moment. She made a show of briefly checking her watch. She looked around and noted the pay phone attached to a brick building that housed one of the largest bars in the Quarter. She crossed the street, picked up the phone and, calling card in hand, punched in a series of digits. The number she was calling was her private line at Tyler, Stone. She was bewildered, but the piece of paper had told her to do it, and she had no choice but to follow those instructions. The voice that answered after two rings did not belong to anyone at her law firm, nor was it her recorded voice announcing her absence from the office. She could not know that the call had been diverted from her office to another number located nowhere near Washington, D.C. She was now trying to remain calm while Jason Archer's voice quietly drifted over the telephone line.

The police were watching, she was told. She was not to say anything, especially not mention his name. They would have to try again. She was to go home. He would contact her again. The words were spoken in a supremely tired manner; she could almost feel the incredible strain in the timbre. He ended by saying that he loved her. And Amy. And that everything would be worked out. Eventually.

With a thousand questions assailing her that she was in absolutely no position to ask, Sidney Archer hung up the phone and walked off toward the LaFitte Guest House, deep depression seemingly hitched to every one of her strides. With a supreme effort at self-control, she held her head up and attempted to walk normally. It was incredibly important not to reflect in her physical appearance the utter terror she was feeling inside. Her husband's obvious fear of the authorities had undermined her belief that he was innocent of any wrongdoing. Despite her intense joy at knowing he was alive, she wondered at what price that joy had come to her. In this far, she had to keep going.

*   *   *

The recording machine was clicked off and the telephone receiver was removed from the special receptacle in the machine. Next, Kenneth Scales rewound the digital tape. He hit the start button and listened while Jason Archer's voice once again filled the room. He smiled malevolently, turned off the machine, took out the tape and left the room.

"He climbed in the window from the galleria," Sawyer was being informed by an agent stationed on a rooftop overlooking Sidney Archer's lodgings. "He's still in there," the agent whispered into his radio. "You want me to pick him up?"

"No," Sawyer answered, peering out through the blinds onto the street. The surveillance devices installed next door to Sidney's room had told them what Paul Brophy was up to. He was searching her room. Sawyer's earlier thought of an assignation between the two law partners had obviously been way off the mark.

"He's leaving now. Going out the back way," the agent reported suddenly.

"Good thing," Sawyer replied as he spotted Sidney Archer coming down the street. After she had reentered the LaFitte Guest House, Sawyer ordered a team of agents to tail a disappointed Paul Brophy, who was walking down Bourbon Street in the other direction.

Ten minutes later Sawyer was informed that Sidney Archer had placed a call from a pay phone during her morning breakfast walk. It had gone to her office. For the next five hours nothing happened. Then Sawyer snapped to attention as Sidney Archer walked out of the LaFitte Guest House. A white cab pulled up in front of the building and she got in. The cab quickly pulled away.

Sawyer hurtled down the stairs and in another minute was riding shotgun in the same black sedan in which he had followed Sidney from the airport. He was not surprised to see the cab swing onto Interstate 10, or pull off at the exit for the airport about half an hour later.

"She's heading home," Sawyer muttered to no one in particular. "She didn't find whatever it was she came here for, that's for sure.

Not unless Jason Archer turned himself into the invisible man." The veteran FBI man slumped back in his seat as a new and particularly troubling revelation crossed his mind. "She's on to us."

The driver jerked his head in Sawyer's direction. "No way, Lee."

"She sure as hell is," Sawyer insisted. "She flies all the way down here, hangs out, then makes a phone call and now she's on her way back home."

"I know she didn't spot our cover teams."

"I didn't say *she* did. Her husband and whoever else is involved in this did. They tipped her and she's going home."

"But we checked. The phone call was to her office."

Sawyer shook his head impatiently. "Phone calls can be diverted."

"But how did she know to call? Something prearranged?"

"Who knows? She only had that run-in with the shoeshine guy. You're sure?"

"That's it. Played the usual tourist scam on her and then shined her shoes. He was a street person, clearly enough. Gave her her change and that was it."

Sawyer abruptly eyed the man. "Change?"

"Yeah, it was a three-fifty shine. She gave him a five. He gave her a buck-fifty back. Wouldn't take her tip."

Sawyer gripped the dashboard, leaving indentations on the smooth surface. "Damn, that was it."

The driver looked bewildered. "He only gave her the change back. I got a clear look through my lens. We heard every word they said."

"Let me guess. He gave her a fifty-cent piece instead of two quarters, right?"

The man gaped. "How'd you know that?"

Sawyer sighed. "How many street people you know who would refuse a buck-fifty tip and then happen to have a fifty-cent piece all ready to give as change? And doesn't it strike you as odd in the first place that it was three-fifty for the shine as opposed to three or four bucks? Why three-fifty?"

"So you gotta make change." The driver sounded depressed now that the truth was dawning on him.

"Message taped to the coin." Sawyer stared glumly ahead at the rear of Sidney Archer's cab. "Pick up our generous shoeshine man. Just maybe he can manage a description of whoever hired him." Sawyer wasn't holding out much hope on that one.

The cars sailed toward the airport. Sawyer endured the short ride in silence, staring out the window at brightly painted jets roaring overhead. An hour later he boarded a private FBI jet for the trip back to Washington. Sidney's nonstop flight had already left. No FBI agents boarded her plane. Sawyer and his men had reviewed the passenger manifest and diligently watched every person board the aircraft. Jason Archer was not among them. Nothing could occur on the flight back, they were confident. They didn't want to tip their hand even more to an already alerted Sidney. They would pick up her trail at National Airport.

The private jet carrying Sawyer and several other FBI agents accelerated down the runway and lifted off into the dark sky over New Orleans. Sawyer began to wonder what the hell had just happened. Why the trip in the first place? It just didn't make any sense. Then his mouth dropped open. The muck had suddenly become just a shade clearer. But he had also made a mistake, maybe a big one.

CHAPTER THIRTY-SEVEN

Sidney Archer sipped her coffee while the beverage cart made its way down the rest of the aisle. She was reaching to pick at the sandwich on her tray when the blue markings on the paper napkin caught her eye. She focused on the writing, a jolt went through her, and she almost spilled her coffee.

The FBI are not on the plane. We need to talk.

The napkin was on the right side of her tray and her gaze automatically swerved in that direction. For a moment she couldn't even think. Then recognition slowly came to her. The man was casually drinking his soda while munching on his meal. Thinning reddish blond hair gave way to a long, clean-shaven face that had more than its share of worry lines. The man looked mid-forties and was dressed in chino pants and a white shirt. A six-footer, he had his long legs partly stuck out into the aisle. He finally put down the soda, patted his mouth with a napkin and turned to her.

"You've been following me," she said, her voice barely above a whisper. "In Charlottesville."

"I'm afraid that's not the only place. Actually, I've kept you under surveillance since shortly after the plane crash."

Sidney's hand flew to the attendant button.

"I wouldn't do that."

Her hand stopped, millimeters from summoning assistance. "Why not?" she coldly asked.

"Because I'm here to help you find your husband," he said simply.

She finally managed to answer him, her wariness evident. "My husband is dead."

"I'm not the FBI, and I'm not trying to entrap you. However, I can't prove a negative, so I won't even try. What I will do is give you a telephone number where you can reach me day or night." He handed her a small white card with a Virginia telephone number on it. Otherwise it was blank.

Sidney looked at the card. "Why should I call you? I don't even know who you are or what you're doing. Only that you've been following me. That does not win you confidence points in my book," she said angrily as her fear receded. He couldn't be a threat to her on a crowded plane.

The man shrugged. "I don't have a good answer to that. But I know your husband isn't dead and you know it too." He paused; Sidney Archer stared at him, unable to say anything. "Although you have no reason to believe me, I'm here to help you, and Jason, if it's not too late."

"What do you mean, 'too late'?"

The man sat back in his seat and closed his eyes. When he reopened them, the pain evident there made her suspicions start to fade.

"Ms. Archer, I'm not exactly sure what your husband is involved in. But I do know enough to realize that, wherever he is, he could very well be in grave danger." He closed his eyes again while Sidney's heart sank to a depth she hadn't realized existed within her.

He looked over at her. "The FBI have you under round-the-clock surveillance." His next words chilled her to the bone. "You should be very thankful for that, Ms. Archer."

When she finally spoke, the words were barely audible to the man, who bent toward her so he could hear them. "Do you know where Jason is?"

The man shook his head. "If I did, I wouldn't be sitting on this plane with you." He looked at her hopeless expression. "All I can tell you, Ms. Archer, is I'm not sure of anything." He let out a breath and passed a hand over his forehead. For the first time Sidney noticed that his hand was shaking.

"I was at Dulles Airport the same morning your husband was."

Sidney's eyes grew wide, her hand gripping the armrest. "You were following my husband? Why?"

The man looked over at her. "I didn't say I was following your husband." He sipped his drink to moisten a throat suddenly gone dry. "He was sitting in the departure area for the flight to L.A. He looked nervous and agitated. That's what drew my attention to him in the first place. He got up and went into the men's room. Another man went in after him a few minutes later."

"Why is that unusual?"

"The second man had a white envelope in his hand when he came into the departure area. That envelope was clearly visible, almost like a lantern the way the guy was swinging it. I believe it was a signal to your husband. I've seen that technique used before."

"A signal. For what?" Sidney's breathing had accelerated to such an extent that she had to make a conscious effort to slow it down.

"For your husband to act. Which he did. He went into the men's room. The other man came out a little later. I forgot to mention that he was dressed almost identically to your husband and was carrying the same sort of baggage. Your husband never did come out."

"What do you mean my husband never came out? He had to."

"I meant he never came out as Jason Archer."

Sidney looked totally confused.

He hurriedly went on. "The first thing I noticed about your husband was his shoes. He was dressed in a suit, but he had on black tennis shoes. Do you remember him putting on tennis shoes that morning?"

"I was asleep when he left."

"Well, when he came out of the rest room his appearance had

completely changed. He looked like he was a college student, dressed in a sweatsuit, different hair, everything."

"How did you know it was him, then?"

"Two reasons. First, the rest room had just opened after being cleaned when your husband went in. I watched that door like a hawk. No one remotely resembling the guy who later came out had gone in there. Second, the black tennis shoes were very distinctive. He probably should have worn a more low-key pair. It was your husband, all right. And you want to know something else?"

Sidney could barely get the words out. "Tell me."

"The other guy came out wearing your husband's hat. With the hat on, he could've passed as your husband's twin."

Sidney took a deep breath as this revelation settled in.

"Your husband got in line for the flight to Seattle. He took the same white envelope the other guy had been carrying out of his pocket. In it was the plane ticket and boarding pass for the Seattle flight. The other guy got on the flight to L.A."

"Meaning they made a ticket switch in the rest room. The other man was dressed to look like Jason in case anyone was watching."

"That's right." He nodded slowly. "Your husband wanted someone to think he was on the L.A. flight."

"But why?" Sidney said this more to herself than to him.

The man shrugged. "I don't know. I do know that the plane your husband was supposed to be on crashed. Then I was even more suspicious."

"Did you go to the police?"

The man shook his head. "And tell them what? It's not like I saw a bomb being put on that flight. Besides, I had my own reasons for keeping quiet."

"What sort of reasons?"

The man put up one hand and shook his head. "Let's just leave it at that for now."

"How did you find out my husband's identity? I'm assuming you didn't know him by sight?"

"Never laid eyes on him before. But I made a couple of casual passes by before he went into the rest room. He had a name and address label on his briefcase. I'm real good at reading things upside down. It didn't take me long to find out where he worked, what he did for a living, more info than I'd ever need to know. I also found out the same things about you. That's when I started following you. To tell you the truth, I didn't know if you were in any danger or not." He spoke matter-of-factly; however, Sidney's blood ran cold at this unexpected intrusion in her life.

"Then while I'm down talking to a friend of mine at the Fairfax police, an APB with your husband's photo came over the wire. That's when I took up your trail in earnest. I thought you might lead me to him."

"Oh." Sidney settled back in her chair. Then a thought struck her. "How did you follow me to New Orleans?"

"The very first thing I did was tap your phone." He ignored her surprised expression. "I needed to know quickly where you were going to go. I heard your conversation with your husband. He seemed particularly evasive."

The plane droned on through the dark skies, and Sidney Archer touched the man's sleeve. "You said you weren't FBI. Who are you, then? Why are you involved in this?"

The man scanned the aisle for several seconds before answering. When he looked back at her, he sighed. "I'm a private investigator, Ms. Archer. The case that is now occupying me pretty much full-time is your husband."

"Who hired you?"

"Nobody." He looked around again before continuing. "I thought your husband might try to contact you. Eventually he did. That's why I'm here. But it seems New Orleans was a bust. That was him on the pay phone, wasn't it? The shoeshine guy slipped you a note, right?"

Sidney Archer hesitated, then nodded her head.

"Did your husband give you any clue where he might be?"

Sidney shook her head. "He said he would contact me later. When it was safer."

The man almost laughed. "That might be a long time. A real long time, Ms. Archer."

When the plane was descending into Washington National, the man turned again to Sidney. "Couple of things, Ms. Archer. When I listened to the tape of you and your husband talking on the phone, I picked up some background noise. Like water running. I can't be sure, but I think someone was listening on another line." Sidney's face froze. "Ms. Archer, you had better assume the Feds know Jason is alive too."

A little while later the plane thudded to a landing and the cabin became alive with activity.

"You said you wanted to tell me a couple of things. What's the other one?"

The man leaned down and pulled out a small briefcase from under the seat in front of him. When he sat back up, he looked her directly in the eye. "People who can bring down a jetliner can do just about anything. Don't trust anyone, Ms. Archer. And be more careful than you have ever been in your entire life. Even that might not be enough. I'm sorry if that sounds like shitty advice, but it's all I have to give you."

In another few minutes the man was gone. Sidney was one of the last passengers off the plane. The airport wasn't crowded at this hour. She made her way toward the cab stand. Remembering the man's advice, she looked carefully around, trying not to be too obvious. Her sole comfort was the fact that amid all the people probably tracking her, at least some of them were FBI.

After leaving Sidney Archer, the man boarded an airport shuttle bus that deposited him at the long-term parking lot. It was almost ten o'clock. The area was deserted. He carried a bag that he had checked onto the flight from New Orleans. Its orange sticker proclaimed that it carried an unloaded firearm. As he reached his car, a late-model Grand Marquis, he opened the bag to extract his pistol with the intent of reloading it and placing it in his shoulder holster.

The stiletto blade first hit his right lung, was pulled free, and then the savage process was repeated on the left one, collapsing both and forestalling any cry for help he might otherwise have managed. The third thrust sliced neatly through the right side of his neck. The bag dropped to the concrete floor, the firearm now useless to its dying owner. In another moment he was down on the ground, his eyes already glassing over, staring up at his killer.

A van pulled alongside and Kenneth Scales climbed in. In another moment the dead man was alone.

CHAPTER THIRTY-EIGHT

Lee Sawyer sat at the conference table in the FBI building going over numerous reports. He put one hand through his rumpled hair, tilted back in his chair and put his feet up on the table while he mentally sorted through the new facts. The autopsy report on Riker indicated that he had been dead about forty-eight hours before his body had been discovered. Because the room temperature had hovered around freezing, however, Sawyer knew the postmortem putrefaction of the body was not nearly as accurate as it otherwise would have been.

Sawyer looked at photos of the Sig P229 auto pistol that had been recovered at the crime scene. The serial numbers on the pistol had been sanded down and then drilled out. He next looked at photos of the slugs recovered from the body. Riker had been on the receiving end of eleven more of the hollow-point projectiles than had been necessary to kill him. The lead barrage bothered the FBI agent greatly. Riker's murder had most of the hallmarks of a professional kill. Professional assassins rarely needed more than one shot. The first shot in this case had been instantly fatal, the medical examiner had concluded. The heart had not been pumping when the other bullets had entered the body.

The blood spatters on the table, chair and mirror indicated that Riker had been shot from behind while seated. The killer had apparently dragged Riker out of the chair, thrown him face down in the corner of the bedroom and proceeded to empty his clip into the dead body from directly above at a distance of about three feet. But why? Sawyer couldn't answer that question right now. He turned his thoughts elsewhere.

Despite numerous inquiries and potential leads, nothing had been turned up on Riker's movements for the last eighteen months. No addresses, no friends, no jobs, no credit card bills, nothing. While Rapid Start was processing tons of data a day on the plane crash, they couldn't get a solid lead on anything. They knew how it had been done, they had the body of the damned person responsible for actually doing it, and yet they couldn't get beyond his corpse.

In frustration, Sawyer sat up and thumbed another report. Riker had also had a great deal of cosmetic surgery. Photos taken at Riker's last arrest bore absolutely no resemblance to the man who had met his bloody end in a quiet Virginia apartment building.

Sawyer grimaced. His gut on the Sinclair alias had been right on the mark too. Riker had not taken the place of another person. Sinclair had been created out of broadcloth and computerized records, with the result that Robert Sinclair had been hired as a living, breathing person, with excellent background credentials to be a fueler for a reputable company that had contracts to service several of the major airlines operating out of Dulles International Airport, including Western. However, Vector had made some mistakes in its background checks. They had not verified the phone numbers of Sinclair's previous employers, but had merely used the numbers provided by Riker, aka Sinclair. All the references provided by the dead man had been small fueling operations in Washington state, southern California and one in Alaska. None of those outfits actually existed. When Sawyer's men checked, they found the numbers had been disconnected. The employment addresses given by Riker on his application were phony too. His Social Security number, however, had been run through the system and had come back as valid.

His prints had also been run through the Virginia State Police AFIS. Riker had spent time in a Virginia prison and his prints were supposed to be on file there. Only they weren't. That could only mean one thing. The Social Security Administration's and the Virginia State Police's databases had been compromised. The whole system might as well have burned up. How could you be sure of anything now? Without absolute reliability, the systems were next to useless. And if someone could do that to Virginia and the SSA, who was safe? Sawyer angrily shoved the reports aside, poured himself another cup of coffee and paced around the broad space of the SIOC.

Jason Archer had been way ahead of them. There had only been one reason to have Sidney Archer travel to New Orleans. In fact, it could have been any city. The important point was that she leave town. And when she had, the FBI had gone with her. Her home had been left unguarded. Sawyer had learned from discreet inquiries with her neighbors that Sidney Archer's parents and daughter had left shortly after Sidney Archer had departed.

Sawyer clenched and unclenched his fist. A diversion. And he had fallen for it like the greenest agent in the world. He had no direct evidence supporting it, but he knew as well as he knew his own name that someone had entered the Archer home and presumably taken something from within. To go to all that risk meant that something incredibly important had slipped right through Sawyer's fingers.

It had not been a good morning and it only threatened to grow rapidly worse. He was not used to getting his butt kicked at every turn. He had filled in Frank Hardy on the results thus far. His friend was making inquiries into Paul Brophy's and Philip Goldman's backgrounds. Hardy had been understandably intrigued when he heard of Brophy's clandestine roaming through Sidney Archer's hotel room.

Sawyer flipped open the newspaper and read the headline. Sidney Archer would be heading into the panic zone right about now, he figured. Since Jason Archer was undoubtedly on to their pursuit of him, the consensus at the bureau had been to go public with his alleged crimes: corporate espionage and embezzlement of Triton's funds. His direct involvement in the plane crash was not alluded to, although the story did mention that he was listed as a passenger on the ill-fated flight but had not been on board. People could read the huge gaps between the lines on that one, Sawyer concluded. Sidney Archer's recent activities were also prominently mentioned. He looked at his watch. He was going to pay Sidney Archer a second visit. And despite his personal sympathy for the woman, this time he wasn't leaving until he got some answers.

Henry Wharton stood behind his desk, his chin sunk down on his chest as he moodily contemplated the cloudy sky outside his window. A copy of that morning's *Post* was lying face down on his desk; at least the vastly disturbing headlines were out of sight. In a chair across from his desk sat Philip Goldman. Goldman's eyes were focused on Wharton's back.

"I really don't see that we have any choice, Henry." Goldman paused, a slight look of satisfaction escaping from his otherwise inscrutable features. "I understand Nathan Gamble was particularly upset when he phoned this morning. Who could really blame him? There's talk that he may pull the whole account."

Wharton winced at the remark. When he turned to face Goldman, his eyes remained downcast. Wharton was clearly wavering. Goldman leaned forward, eager to press this obvious advantage. "It's for the good of the firm, Henry. It will be painful for many people, and despite my differences with her in the past, I would have to include myself in that group, not least of which because she is a particularly strong asset for this firm." This time Goldman succeeded in restraining the smile. "But the future of the firm, the future of hundreds of people, cannot be sacrificed for the benefit of one person, Henry, you know that." Goldman leaned back in his chair, placing his hands in his lap, a placid expression on his face. He managed a sigh. "I can take care of it, Henry, if you would prefer. I know how close you two are."

Wharton finally looked up. The nod was quick, short, like the abrupt plunge of the ax it clearly was. Goldman quietly left the room.

Sidney Archer was picking up the newspaper from her front sidewalk when the phone rang. She raced back inside, the unopened *Post* in one hand. She was fairly certain it was not her husband calling, but right now she could be absolutely certain of nothing. She tossed the paper down on top of other editions she had not read yet.

Her father's voice boomed across the line. Had she read the paper? What the hell were they talking about? These accusations. He would sue, her father proclaimed angrily. He would sue everyone involved, including Triton and the FBI. By the time she got him calmed down, Sidney managed to open the paper. The headline took her breath away, as though someone had stomped on her chest. She tumbled into the chair in the semidarkness of her kitchen. She quickly read the cover story, which implicated her husband in stealing immensely valuable secrets and hundreds of millions of dollars from his employer. To top it off, Jason Archer clearly was also suspected in the plane bombing, his motive presumably to convince the authorities he was dead. Now the world knew him to be alive and on the run, according to the FBI.

When she read her own name about halfway down the page, Sidney Archer became violently sick to her stomach. She had traveled to New Orleans, the story said, shortly after her husband's memorial service, which the story made seem highly suspicious. Of course it was suspicious. Everyone, Sidney Archer included, would find such a trip fraught with dubious motives. An entire life of scrupulous honesty had just been irreversibly destroyed. In her distress she hung up on her father. She barely made it to the kitchen sink. The nausea made her dizzy. She poured cold water over her neck and forehead.

She managed to stumble back to the kitchen table, where she sobbed for some minutes. She had never felt such hopelessness. Then a sudden emotion invaded her body. Anger. She raced to her bedroom, threw on some clothes and two minutes later opened the door of the Ford Explorer. "Shit." The mail tumbled out and she bent down automatically to retrieve it. Her hands quickly sorted through the fallen pieces until she abruptly stopped as her fingers closed around the package addressed to Jason Archer. Her husband's handwriting on the package made her legs wobble. She could feel the slender object inside. She looked at the postmark. It had been sent from Seattle on the very day Jason had left for the airport. She involuntarily shuddered. Her husband had many mailing packs like this in his home office. They were specifically designed to send computer disks safely through the mail. She did not have time to think about this latest development. She threw the mail back in the truck, climbed in and roared off.

Thirty minutes later, a disheveled Sidney Archer, escorted by Richard Lucas, entered Nathan Gamble's office. Right behind them was an astonished Quentin Rowe. Sidney marched right up to Gamble's desk and tossed the *Post* in his lap.

"I hope to hell you have some really good defamation attorneys." Her intense fury made Lucas step hastily forward until Gamble waved him off. The Triton chief gingerly picked up the paper and glanced down at the story. Then he looked up at her. "I didn't write this."

"The hell you didn't."

Gamble put out his cigarette and stood up. "Excuse me, but why am I thinking that I should be the one who's pissed off?"

"My husband blowing up planes, selling secrets, ripping you off. It's a pack of lies and you know it."

Gamble stormed around the desk to face her. "Let me tell you what I know, lady. I'm out a ton of cash, that's a fact. And your husband gave RTG everything it needs to bury my company. That's also a fact. What am I supposed to do, give you a goddamned medal?"

"It's not true."

"Oh, yeah!" Gamble wheeled a chair around. "Sit down!"

Gamble unlocked a drawer in his desk, pulled out a videotape and tossed it over to Lucas. Then he hit a button on his desk console and part of the wall moved back, revealing a large TV and VCR combination unit. While Lucas popped the tape in, Sidney, her legs shaking, sank into the chair. She looked over at Quentin Rowe, who stood stock-still in the corner of the office, his wide eyes glued to her. She nervously licked her lips and turned to the TV.

Her heart almost stopped beating when she saw her husband. Having only heard his voice ever since that horrible day, she felt as though he had been gone forever. At first she fixated on his fluid movements, so familiar to her. Then she focused on his face and gasped. She had never seen her husband more nervous, under more strain. The briefcase handed across, the plane roaring overhead, the smiles of the men, the papers examined, all of these things were in the background for her, far in the background; she kept her eyes on Jason. Her eyes drifted to the time and date stamp and her heart took another jolt when the significance of those numbers hit her. When the tape went dark, she turned to find all eyes in the room on her.

"That exchange took place in an RTG facility in Seattle long after that plane went into the ground." Gamble stood behind her. "Now if you still want to sue me for defamation, go right ahead. Of course, if we lose CyberCom you might have trouble collecting any money," he added grimly.

Sidney stood up. Gamble reached behind his desk. "Here's your paper." He tossed it to her. Although she could barely stand, she managed to catch it neatly. In another moment she had fled the room.

Sidney pulled into her garage and listened to the door winding its way back down. Her limbs quivering and lungs expunging air heavily laced with sobs every few seconds, she gripped the newspaper. When it fell open, revealing the bottom half of the front page, Sidney Archer received yet another shock. This one contained a distinct element of uncontrollable dread.

The man's photo was some years old, but there was no mistaking the face. His name was now revealed to her: Edward Page. He had been a local private detective for five years after spending ten years in New York City as a police officer. He had worked solo, his firm bearing the name Private Solutions, the story stated. Page had been the victim of a fatal robbery at a National Airport parking lot. Divorced, he left behind two teenage children, the paper reported.

The familiar eyes stared at her from the depths of the page, and a chill went through her body. It was more obvious to her than to anyone else, other than Page's killer, that his death was not the result of a search for cash and credit cards. A few minutes after talking to her, the man was dead. She would have to be damn foolish to dismiss his death as a coincidence. She jumped out of the truck and raced into the house.

She took out the gleaming silver metal Smith & Wesson Slim-Nine she had kept locked in the metal box in the bedroom closet and quickly loaded it. The Hydra-Shok hollowpoints would be highly effective against anyone wishing to perpetrate a deadly attack. She checked her wallet. Her concealed-weapon permit was still valid.

When she reached up to return the box to the top of the closet, the pistol slipped out of her pocket and hit the nightstand before settling on the carpeted floor. Thank God she'd had the safety on. As she picked it up, she noted that a small corner of the hard plastic grip had broken off from the impact, but everything else was intact. Pistol in hand, she returned to the garage and climbed back into the Ford.

She suddenly froze. A sound floated toward her from inside her house. She flipped off the pistol's safety, keeping one eye and the barrel of the Smith & Wesson on the door leading back into the house. With her free hand she struggled with her car keys. One of the keys slid across her finger, gashing it. She hit the garage door opener clipped to the truck's sun visor. Her heart pounded while she waited for the damn door to finish its agonizingly slow ascent. She kept her eyes glued to the door to the house, expecting any moment for it to burst open.

Her mind darted back to the news story detailing Edward Page's demise. Two teenagers left behind. Her features grew deadly in their own right. She was not leaving her little girl behind. Her grip tightened on the butt of the pistol. She hit a button on the driver's-side armrest and the passenger window slid down. Now she would have an unobstructed firing line at the door leading into the house. She had never used her weapon on anything other than shooting range targets. But she was going to do her best to kill whoever was about to come through that door.

She did not notice the man bending low to come through the garage door as it was opening. He stepped quickly to the driver's-side door, pistol drawn. At that instant, the door from the house into the garage started to open. Sidney's grip tightened even more on her weapon until the veins rode high on her hands. Her finger started to descend on the trigger.

"Jesus Christ, lady! Put it down. Now!" The man next to the car yelled, his pistol pointed right at the driver's window and through it to Sidney's left temple.

Sidney whirled around in the car and found herself eye to eye with Agent Ray Jackson. Suddenly the house door to the garage was thrown open and crashed against the wall. Sidney jerked her head back in that direction and watched the massive bulk of Lee Sawyer hurtle through the door, his 10mm making wide arcs in the direction of the vehicles. Sidney slumped back in her seat, sweat streaming off her forehead.

Ray Jackson, gun still in hand, threw open the door of the Explorer and eyed both Sidney Archer and the gun that had almost taken a considerable hole out of his partner. "Are you crazy?" He leaned across her lap and snatched away the pistol, flipping on the safety. Sidney made no move to stop him, but fury suddenly sprawled across her features. "What are you doing, breaking into my house? I could have shot you."

Lee Sawyer slipped his pistol back into his belt holster and moved over to the Ford.

"Front door was open, Ms. Archer. We thought something might be wrong when you didn't answer our knock." His frankness made the fury evaporate as quickly as it had surfaced. She had left the front door open when she had raced inside to answer the phone call from her father. She put her head down on the steering wheel. She struggled not to be sick. Her entire body was soaked with perspiration. She shivered as a chilly wind invaded the garage from the open door.

"Going somewhere?" Sawyer eyed the Ford and then rested his gaze on the woman who sat back up dejectedly.

"Just for a drive." Her voice was weak. She did not look at him. She ran her hands over the steering wheel. The sweat from her palms glistened on the padded surface.

Sawyer looked over at the stack of mail on the passenger seat. "You always carry your mail in your car?"

Sidney followed his stare. "I don't know how it got here. Maybe my father put it there before he left."

"That's right. Right after you left. How was New Orleans, by the way? You have a good time?"

Sidney stared dully at the man.

Sawyer placed one hand firmly under her elbow. "Let's go have a chat, Ms. Archer."

CHAPTER THIRTY-NINE

Before exiting the car, Sidney carefully gathered up the mail and slid the *Post* under her arm. Out of the agents' sight she slipped the disk into her jacket pocket. Climbing out of the car, she eyed the pistol Jackson had abruptly confiscated. "I have a concealed weapons permit for that." Sidney handed over the authorization.

"Mind if I unload it before I give it back?"

"If it'll make you feel safer," she said, hitting the button on the garage door opener, closing the door of the Ford and heading toward the house. "Just make sure you leave the bullets."

Jackson stared after her, amazement on his features. The two FBI agents followed her into the house.

"Would you like coffee? Something to eat? It's still pretty early." These last words Sidney said in an accusatory fashion.

"Coffee would be fine," Sawyer answered, ignoring her tone. Jackson nodded his assent.

While Sidney poured out three cups of coffee, Sawyer methodically looked her over. Her unwashed blond hair hung limply around her face, which bore no makeup and was more drawn and haggard than the last time he had been here. Her clothes hung loosely on her tall frame. Her green eyes were as bewitching as usual, however. He picked up on the slight shake in her hands while she handled the coffeepot. She was clearly on the edge. He had to grudgingly admire how she was holding up under a nightmare that seemed to metastasize with every passing day. But then everybody had limits. He expected to learn Sidney Archer's before it was all over.

Sidney placed the cups of coffee on a tray with sugar and creamer. She reached into the breadbox and pulled out an assortment of doughnuts and muffins. She loaded the tray and placed it in the middle of the kitchen table. While the agents helped themselves, she took out some Rolaids and slowly crunched them.

"Good doughnut. Thanks. By the way, you usually carry a gun with you?" Sawyer looked at her expectantly.

"There have been some break-ins nearby. I've received professional instruction on how to use it. Besides, I'm no stranger to guns. My dad and oldest brother, Kenny, were in the Marine Corps. They're also avid hunters. Kenny has an extensive firearms collection. When I was growing up, my dad used to take me skeet and target shooting. I've fired just about every type of weapon you can think of and I'm a very good shot."

Ray Jackson said, "You were handling the piece pretty good back there in the garage." He noted the crack in the grip. "I hope you didn't drop it while it was loaded."

"I'm very careful with firearms, Mr. Jackson, but I appreciate your concern."

Jackson looked at the pistol once more before sliding it and the full magazine over to her. "Nice piece of hardware. Lightweight. I use Hydra-Shok ammo too—excellent stopping force. There's still a round in the firing chamber," he reminded her.

"It's equipped with a magazine safety. No mag, no fire." Sidney touched the pistol gingerly. "But I don't like having to keep it in the house, especially with Amy, although it's kept unloaded and in a locked box."

"Not much good, then, in the event of a burglary," Sawyer said between a bite of doughnut and a gulp of hot coffee.

"Only if you get surprised. I try never to be." After the events of the morning, she struggled mightily not to perceptibly wince at that remark.

Sliding the plate of bakery goods away, he asked, "You mind telling me why you took that little trip to New Orleans?"

Sidney held up the morning's newspaper so the headline was fully exposed. "Why? Are you moonlighting as a reporter and need to file your next story? By the way, thanks for ruining my life." She angrily tossed the paper on the table and looked away. A twitch erupted over her left eye. She gripped the edge of the weathered pine table as she felt herself trembling.

Sawyer ran his eye down the story. "I don't see anything here that isn't true. Your husband *is* suspected of being involved in a theft of secrets from his company. On top of that, he wasn't on a plane he was supposed to be on. That plane ends up in a cornfield. Your husband is alive and kicking." When she didn't respond, Sawyer reached across the table and touched her elbow. "I said your husband is alive, Ms. Archer. That doesn't seem to surprise you. You want to tell me about New Orleans now?"

She slowly turned to look at him, her features surprisingly calm. "You say he's alive?"

Sawyer nodded.

"Then why don't you tell me where he is?"

"I was about to ask you that question."

Sidney dug her fingers into her thigh. "I haven't seen my husband since that morning."

Sawyer edged closer to her. "Look, Ms. Archer, let's cut through the crap. You get a mysterious phone call and then you take a plane to New Orleans after you hold a friggin' memorial service for your dearly departed, who, as it turns out, isn't. You jump out of a cab and onto the subway, leaving your suitcase behind. You lose my guys and hightail it south. You check into a hotel, where I'm betting you're waiting for a rendezvous with your husband." Sidney Archer, to her credit, did not even flinch. Sawyer continued. "You take a walk, get a shoeshine from a very amiable old guy who's the only street person in my experience who refuses a tip. You make a phone call, and wham, you're back on a plane to D.C. What do you say to that?"

Sidney took an invisible breath and then stared hard at Sawyer. "You said I got a mysterious phone call. Who told you that?"

The agents exchanged looks. "We've got our sources, Ms. Archer. We also checked your phone log," Sawyer said.

Sidney crossed her legs and leaned forward. "You mean the call from Henry Wharton?"

Sawyer eyed her calmly. "You're saying you talked to Wharton?" He didn't expect her to walk into that easy a trap, and he wasn't disappointed.

"No. I'm saying someone called here identifying himself as Henry Wharton."

"But you spoke with someone."

"No."

Sawyer sighed. "We've got a record of the phone call. You were on that phone for about five minutes. Were you just listening to heavy breathing or what?"

"I don't have to sit here and be insulted by you or anyone else. Do you understand that?"

"All right, my apologies. So who was it?"

"I don't know."

Sawyer jerked upright in his chair and slammed his big fist down on the table. Sidney almost jumped out of her chair. "Jesus Christ, come on—"

"I'm telling you I don't know," Sidney interrupted angrily. "I thought it was Henry, but it wasn't. The person never said anything. I hung up the phone after a few seconds." Her heart started racing as it occurred to her that she was lying to the FBI.

Sawyer looked at her wearily. "Computers don't lie, Ms. Archer." Sawyer inwardly winced at this statement as his mind dwelled for an instant on the Riker fiasco. "The phone log says five minutes."

"My father answered the phone in the kitchen and then laid it down on the counter to come and tell me. You two showed up at about the same time. Do you think it's beyond the realm of possibility that he forgot to hang it back up? Wouldn't that account for the five minutes? Maybe you'd like to call and ask him. You can use the phone right over there." Sidney pointed to the kitchen wall next to the doorway.

Sawyer looked over at the phone and took a moment to think. He felt sure the lady was lying, but what she was saying was plausible. He had forgotten he was talking to an attorney, a highly skilled one.

"Would you like to call him?" Sidney repeated. "I happen to know he's home because he called just a little while ago. The last thing I heard him scream over the phone was his plan to file a lawsuit against the FBI and Triton."

"Maybe I'll try him later."

"Fine. I just thought you'd want to do it now so you couldn't accuse me later of arranging for my father to lie to you." Her eyes dug into the agent's troubled features. "And while we're at it, let's address your other accusations. You said I somehow evaded your men. Since I was unaware I was being followed, it would seem impossible for me to 'lose' anyone. My cab was stuck in traffic. I was afraid I would miss my flight, so I jumped on the subway. I haven't used the subway in years, so I got out at the Pentagon station because I couldn't remember if I had to change trains there to get to the airport. When I realized my mistake, I simply got back on the same train. I didn't take my suitcase with me because I didn't want to have to lug it around on the subway, especially if I had to run to make a plane. If I had stayed in New Orleans, I was going to arrange for it to be sent down on a later flight. I've been to New Orleans many times. I've always had good times down there. It seemed like a logical place, not that I've been thinking very logically lately. I had my shoes shined. Is that illegal?" She looked at the two men. "I hope burying your spouse when you don't even have a body is something neither of you ever have to go through."

She angrily tossed the newspaper on the floor. "The man in that story is *not* my husband. You know what our idea of a wild time was? Barbecuing in the backyard in the winter. The most reckless thing I've ever known Jason to do was occasionally drive too fast and not wear his seat belt. He couldn't have been involved in blowing up that plane. I know you don't believe me, but right now I don't really care."

She stood up and leaned against the refrigerator before continuing. "I needed to get away. Do I really have to tell you why? Do I really have to do that?" Her voice rose almost to a scream before it tapered off and she fell silent.

Sawyer started to reply but then abruptly closed his mouth as Sidney held up her hand and continued speaking, in a calmer tone. "I stayed in New Orleans all of one day. It suddenly occurred to me that I couldn't run away from the nightmare my life has become. I have a little girl who needs me. And I need her. She's all I have left. Do you understand that? Can either of you understand anything?" Tears were starting to trickle out. Her hands clenched and unclenched. Her chest rose and fell unevenly. She abruptly sat back down.

Ray Jackson nervously played with his coffee cup while he looked over at his partner. "Ms. Archer, Lee and I both have families. I can't imagine what you're going through right now. You gotta understand we're just trying to do our job. A lot of things don't make sense right now. But one thing is for certain. A planeload of people are dead and whoever is responsible for that is gonna pay."

Sidney stood up again on unsteady legs, the tears now pouring. Her voice was shrill, near hysterical, her eyes blazing. "Don't you think I know that? I went down . . . there. To that . . . that hell!" Her voice rose to an even higher pitch, the tears streaming down the front of her blouse, her eyes at their widest. "I saw it." She stared fiercely at them. "Everything. The . . . the shoe . . . a baby's shoe." Moaning, Sidney fell back into her chair, the sobs wracking her frame to such a degree that it looked as though her back would erupt like a volcano spewing forth far more misery than human beings had the ability to endure.

Jackson rose to get her a paper towel.

Sighing quietly, Sawyer put his hand on Sidney's and gripped it in a gentle squeeze. The baby's shoe. The one he had held in his hand, and also shed tears over. For the first time he noted Sidney's engagement ring and wedding band. A beautiful if small setting, she would have worn it all these years with pride, he was certain of that. Whether Jason Archer had done anything wrong or not, he had a woman who loved him, believed in him. Sawyer felt himself starting to hope that Jason would turn out to be innocent, despite all the evidence to the contrary. He did not want Sidney to have to confront the reality of betrayal. He wrapped a big arm around her shoulders. His body seemed to jerk and pitch with every convulsion that raced through her. He whispered soothing words into her ear, trying desperately to get her to come around. For a very brief instant his memory skipped back to the time he had held another young woman like this. That catastrophe had been a prom date gone terribly bad. It had been one of the few times he had actually been there for one of his kids. It had felt wonderful to wrap his burly arms around the small, quaking form, letting her hurt, her embarrassment, siphon off into him. Sawyer refocused on Sidney Archer. She had been hurt enough, he decided. The raw pain he was holding on to right now was not capable of being fabricated. Regardless of anything else, Sidney Archer was telling them the truth, or at least most of it. As if sensing his thoughts, her grip tightened on his hand.

Jackson handed him the wet paper towel. Sawyer did not see his partner's worried look as Jackson watched the gentle way in which he slowly brought Sidney around. The things Sawyer said to her, to calm her down, the way he kept his arms protectively around her. Ray Jackson was clearly not happy with his partner right now.

A few minutes later Sidney was sitting in front of a fire that Jackson had quickly prepared in the living room fireplace. The warmth felt good. When Sawyer looked out the broad picture window he noticed that it was snowing again. He looked around the room and his eyes settled on the fireplace mantel, where a procession of framed photographs held forth: Jason Archer, looking anything but a participant in one of the most horrendous crimes ever committed; Amy Archer, as pretty a little girl as Sawyer had ever seen; and Sidney Archer, beautiful and enchanting. A picture-perfect family, at least on the surface. Sawyer had spent the last twenty-five years of his life constantly probing beneath the surface. He looked forward to the day when he would not have to do that. To the time when delving into the motives and circumstances that turned human beings into monsters would be someone else's job. Today, though, that duty was his. He turned his gaze from the photo to the real thing.

"I'm sorry. I seem to lose it every time you two show up." Sidney spoke slowly, her eyes clamped shut. She seemed smaller than Sawyer had remembered, as though crisis on top of crisis were causing her to collapse inward.

"Where's your little girl?" he asked.

"With my parents," Sidney replied quickly.

Sawyer nodded slowly.

Sidney's eyes fluttered open and then closed again. "The only time she's not asking for her father is when she's asleep," she added in a hushed voice, her lips trembling.

Sawyer rubbed tired eyes and drew closer to the fire. "Sidney?" She finally opened her eyes and looked at him, gathered around her shoulders the blanket she had taken from the ottoman, lifted her knees to her chest, and settled back into the chair. "Sidney, you said you went to the crash site. I happen to know that's true. You remember running into somebody out there? My knee still aches."

Sidney started, her eyes seeming to dilate fully and then slowly recede as she stared at him.

Sawyer continued to look at her. "We also have a report from the deputy on duty that night. Deputy McKenna?"

"Yes, he was very nice to me."

"Why did you go there, Sidney?"

Sidney didn't answer. She wrapped her arms tightly around her legs. Finally she looked up. However, her eyes were fixed on the opposite wall rather than on the two agents. She seemed to be looking over a great distance, as though she were reaching back to the painful depths of a great hole in the earth; to a dismal cavern she had thought at the time had swallowed her husband.

"I had to." She abruptly closed her mouth.

Jackson started to say something, but Sawyer stopped him.

"I had to," Sidney repeated. The tears started to tumble again, but her voice remained steady. "I saw it on TV."

"What?" Sawyer leaned forward anxiously. "What did you see?"

"I saw his bag. Jason's bag." Her mouth trembled as she said his name. One shaky hand fluttered to her mouth as though to corral the utter grief concentrated there. Her hand dropped back down. "I could still see his initials on the side." She stopped again and dabbed at a tear with the back of her hand. "It suddenly occurred to me that it was probably the only thing . . . the only thing left of him. So I went to get it. Officer McKenna told me I couldn't have it until the investigation was over. So I went back home with nothing. Nothing." She said the word slowly, as though it summarized the desolate status of the life she had left.

Sawyer leaned back in his chair and looked at his partner. The bag was a dead end. He let the silence persist for about a minute before he began speaking again. "When I said your husband was alive, you didn't seem to be surprised." Sawyer's tone was low and calming, but there was an unmistakable edge to it.

Sidney's response was biting, but the voice was tired. She was obviously running out of steam. "I had just read the article in the paper. If you wanted to see surprise, you should have shown up before the paperboy did." She wasn't about to go into the humiliating experience at Gamble's office.

Sawyer sat back. He had expected that very logical answer, but was still gratified to hear it from her lips. Liars often opted for complicated stories in their effort to avoid detection. "Okay, fair enough. I don't want to drag this conversation out, so I'm just going to ask you some questions and I want some straight answers. That's all. If you don't know the answer, so be it. Those are the ground rules. Are you willing to do that?"

Sidney didn't respond. Her weary eyes swung between the two FBI agents. Sawyer hunched forward some more. "I didn't make up those accusations against your husband. But in all honesty, the evidence we've uncovered so far does not paint a real benign picture of him."

"What evidence?" Sidney asked sharply.

Sawyer shook his head. "I'm sorry, I'm not at liberty to say. But I will tell you it's strong enough for an arrest warrant to have been issued for your husband. If you didn't already know it, every cop in the world right now is looking for him."

Sidney's eyes glistened as the incredible words sunk in. Her husband, a fugitive sought worldwide. She looked at Sawyer. "Did you know all this when you were here the first time?"

Sawyer's expression became slightly pained. He finally said, "Some of it." Sawyer shifted uneasily in his chair while Jackson picked up for his partner.

"If your husband didn't do the things he's accused of doing, then he's got nothing to worry about on our end. We can't speak for anybody else's agenda, though."

Sidney riveted her gaze on him. "What do you mean by that?"

Jackson shrugged his broad shoulders. "Let's say he didn't do anything wrong. We know beyond doubt that he wasn't on that plane. So where is he? If he had maybe missed the plane by accident, he would've gotten on the horn right away to you, to let you know he was okay. That didn't happen. Why? The partial answer to that is that he's got himself involved in something not exactly legit. On top of that, the kind of planning and execution we're looking at on this one leads us to believe that it's more than a one-man show." Jackson paused and looked over at Sawyer, who nodded slightly. Jackson continued. "Ms. Archer, the man we suspect actually sabotaged that plane was found murdered in his apartment. It looked like he was getting ready to leave the country, but somebody had a change in plans for him."

Sidney mouthed the word slowly. "Murdered." She thought of Edward Page lying in a vast pool of his own blood. Dying right after talking to her. She pulled the blanket tighter around her. She hesitated, debating whether to tell the agents about talking with Page. Then, for a reason she could not precisely pinpoint, she decided not to. She drew a deep breath. "What are your questions?"

"First, I'll let you in on a little theory of mine." Sawyer paused for a moment, compiling his thoughts. "For the moment, we'll accept your story that you went down to New Orleans on a whim. We followed you down there. We also know that your parents and your daughter left this house shortly after you did."

"So? Why should they stay here?" Sidney looked around the interior of her once beloved house. *What is here anymore except misery?*

"Right. But see, you left, we left and your parents left." He paused.

"If this has a point, I'm afraid I'm not getting it."

Sawyer abruptly rose and stood with his broad back to the fire while he looked down at Sidney. He spread his arms wide. "There was no one here, Sidney. The place was completely unguarded. Regardless of why you went to New Orleans, it had the effect of drawing us off. And that left no one watching your house. Now do you see?"

Despite the fire's warmth, a sudden chill stalked through Sidney's veins. She had been a diversion. Jason knew the authorities had been watching her. He had used her. Used her to get at something in this house.

Sawyer and Jackson watched Sidney carefully. They could almost see the powerful mental gymnastics flowing behind her forehead.

Sidney looked out the window. Her eyes swept across the gray blazer lying over the rocking chair. The disk resting in the inside pocket. She suddenly wanted to hasten this interview to an end.

"There's nothing here anyone could want."

"Nothing?" Jackson sounded skeptical. "Your husband didn't keep any files or records here? Nothing like that?"

"Not from work. Triton is very paranoid about things like that."

Sawyer slowly nodded. Based on his own experience with Triton, that was one statement he could readily believe. "Nonetheless, Sidney, you might want to give it some thought. You haven't noticed anything missing or disturbed?"

Sidney slowly shook her head. "I haven't really looked, though."

Jackson stirred. "Well, if you don't have an objection, we could search the house right now." He looked over at his partner, who had raised his eyebrows at the request. Then Jackson looked at Sidney, waiting for her answer.

When she didn't deliver one, Jackson took a step forward. "We can always get a warrant. Plenty of probable cause. You could save us a lot of time and trouble, though. And if it's like you say and there's nothing here, you shouldn't have a problem with that, right?"

"I'm an attorney, Mr. Jackson," Sidney said coldly. "I know the drill. All right, help yourself. Please excuse the dirt, I haven't really kept up the household chores." She stood up, slipped off the blanket, reached out for her blazer and put it on. "While you're doing that, I'm going for some fresh air. How long will you need?"

The two agents looked at each other. "A few hours."

"Fine, help yourself to the fridge. Searching can be very hungry work."

After she had walked out, Jackson turned to his partner. "Damn, she's a piece of work, isn't she?"

Sawyer stared after the lithe form as she headed toward the garage. "She sure is."

Several hours later Sidney Archer returned.

"Nothing?" She looked at the two disheveled men.

"Not that we could find, anyway." Jackson's tone was one of reproach.

She stared him down. "That's not my problem, is it?"

The two looked at each other for several moments. "You had some questions?" Sidney finally said.

When the two FBI agents were leaving about an hour later, Sidney touched Sawyer on the arm. "You obviously didn't know my husband. If you had, you would have no doubt that he couldn't . . ." Her lips moved, but no words came out for a moment. "He could never have had anything to do with that plane crash. With all those people . . ." She closed her eyes and steadied herself against the front door.

Sawyer's features were troubled. How could anyone think someone they loved, had a child with, could be capable of anything like that? But human beings committed atrocities every minute of every day; the only living things who killed with malice.

"I understand how you feel, Sidney," the agent said quietly.

Jackson kicked a piece of gravel on the way to the car and looked over at his partner. "I don't know, Lee, things just aren't adding up with that woman. She's definitely holding back."

Sawyer shrugged. "Hell, if I were in her position, I'd do the same thing."

Jackson looked surprised. "Lie to the FBI?"

"She's caught in the middle, doesn't know which way to turn. Under those circumstances, I'd play it close to the vest too."

"I guess I'll go with your judgment on that." Jackson's words did not sound very confident as he climbed in the car.

CHAPTER FORTY

Sidney raced to the phone but abruptly stopped. She looked at the receiver as though it were a cobra about to sink venom into her. If the late Edward Page had tapped her phone, how probable was it that others had? She put the phone back down and looked at her cellular phone, which sat recharging on the kitchen counter. How secure was that? She slammed her fist against the wall in frustration as she imagined hundreds of pairs of electronic eyes monitoring and recording her every action. She slid her alphanumeric pager into her purse, figuring that form of communication was reasonably safe. It would have to do, in any case. She put her loaded pistol in her purse and raced to the Explorer. The disk was safely in her pocket. It would have to wait for now. She had something else to do that at that moment was even more important.

The Ford pulled into the McDonald's parking lot. Sidney went inside, ordered a take-out lunch and went down the hallway toward the rest room, stopping at the pay phone. After dialing, she scanned the parking lot for signs of the FBI. She saw nothing out of the ordinary, which was good—they were supposed to be invisible. But a shiver went down her back as she wondered who else was out there.

A voice came on the other end of the phone line. It took her several minutes to calm her father down. When she stated her request, he began to erupt all over again.

"What the hell do you want me to do that for?"

"Please, Dad. I want you and Mom to go. And I want you to take Amy with you."

"You know we never go to Maine after Labor Day."

Sidney held the receiver away from her mouth and took a deep breath. "Look, Dad, you read the paper."

He started off again. "That's the biggest bunch of bullshit I ever heard. Sid—"

"Dad, just listen to me. I don't have time to argue." She had never raised her voice to her father like that.

They were both quiet for a moment.

When she broke the silence, her voice was firm. "The FBI just left my house. Jason was involved in . . . something. I'm not exactly sure what yet. But if even half of what that story reported is true . . ." She shuddered. "On the flight back from New Orleans a man spoke to me. His name was Edward Page. He was a private investigator. He was investigating something to do with Jason."

Bill Patterson's voice was incredulous. "What was he investigating Jason for?"

"I don't know. He wouldn't tell me."

"Well, I say we go ask him and we don't take no for an answer."

"We can't ask him: He was murdered about five minutes after he left me, Dad."

Stunned, Bill Patterson could no longer find his voice.

"Will you please go to the house in Maine, Dad? Please. As soon as possible."

Patterson didn't answer for a few seconds. When he finally spoke, his voice was weak. "We'll leave after lunch. I'll pack my shotgun just in case."

Sidney's hunched shoulders relaxed in relief.

"Sidney?"

"Yes, Dad?"

"I want you to come with us."

Sidney shook her head. "I can't do that, Dad."

Her father exploded. "Why the hell not? You're up there all alone. You're Jason's wife. You could sure as hell be a target in all this."

"The FBI are watching me."

"You think they're invulnerable? You don't think they make mistakes? Don't be crazy, honey."

"I can't, Dad. The FBI probably aren't the only ones watching me. If I came with you so would they." Sidney's entire body shook as she uttered the words.

"Jesus, baby." Sidney could distinctly hear her father swallowing over the phone line. "Look, why don't I send your mother and Amy up there and I'll come stay with you."

"I don't want them or you getting involved in this. It's enough that I am. And I want you with Amy and Mom. I want you to protect *them*. I can take care of myself."

"I've never lacked for confidence in you, baby girl. But . . . but this is a little different. If these people have already killed . . ." Bill Patterson couldn't finish. He had gone numb at the prospect of losing his youngest to violent death.

"Dad, I'll be fine. I have my pistol. The FBI are out there every minute. I'll check in with you every day."

"Sid—"

"Dad, I'll be fine."

Patterson didn't answer right away. Finally he said resignedly, "Okay, but call twice a day."

"Okay, twice a day. Give Mom my love. I know the paper must have upset her. But don't tell her about our talk."

"Sid, your mother's no fool. She's gonna wonder why we're suddenly taking off for Maine at this time of year."

"Please, Dad. Just make up something."

Bill Patterson finally sighed. "Anything else?"

"Tell Amy I love her. Tell her that me and her dad love her more than anything." Wet clusters were forming around Sidney's eyes as the one thing she desperately wanted to do, be with her daughter, was now firmly beyond her. In order to keep Amy safe, Sidney had to stay away, far away.

"I'll tell her, sweetie," Bill Patterson said quietly.

Sidney devoured her lunch on the ride back home. She dashed through the house and within a minute was sitting in front of her husband's computer. She had taken the precaution of locking the door to the room and bringing her cellular phone with her just in case she had to dial 911. She slid the disk out of her jacket pocket, pulled the pistol out and laid them both down on the table next to her.

She turned on the computer and watched the screen as the computer began to wake up. When she was about to pop the disk into the floppy drive she jolted upright, her eyes transfixed by what was on the screen. The available memory figure had just come up. Something wasn't right. She hit several keys on the keyboard. The available hard disk memory again came across the screen and then held. Sidney read the figures slowly: 1,356,600 kilobytes, or about 1.3 gigs, of hard drive were available. She stared hard at the last three digits. She thought back to the last time she had sat in front of the computer. The last three digits of the available memory had been Jason's birthday—seven, zero, six, a fact that had caused her to cry. To break down once again. She had prepared herself for that again, but there was less memory available now. But how could that be? She hadn't touched the computer since . . .

Oh, Christ!

A knot erupted in her stomach as she jumped up from the chair, grabbed the pistol and put the disk back in her jacket pocket. She almost felt like putting a round right into the damned computer screen. Sawyer had been right and wrong. Right that someone had been in her house while she was in New Orleans. Wrong that they had come to take something. They had *left* something instead. Something that resided on her husband's computer. Something that she was running from now as quickly as she could.

It took her ten minutes to return to McDonald's and get back on the pay phone. Her secretary's tone was strained.

"Hello, Ms. Archer."

Ms. Archer? Her secretary had been with her almost six years and hadn't called her Ms. Archer after the second day. Sidney ignored it for the moment. "Sarah, is Jeff in today?" Jeff Fisher was Tyler, Stone's resident computer guru.

"I'm not sure. Would you like me to transfer you to his assistant, Ms. Archer?"

Sidney finally blurted out, "Sarah, what the hell is it with the Ms. Archer label?"

Sarah didn't immediately answer, but then she started to whisper furiously into the phone. "Sid, that story in the paper is all over the firm. They've faxed it to every office. The Triton people are threatening to pull the entire account from the firm. Mr. Wharton is furious. And it's no secret that all the higher-ups are blaming you."

"I'm as much in the dark as everyone else."

"Well, that story made it seem . . . you know."

Sidney sighed heavily. "You want to transfer me to Henry? I'll straighten this whole thing out."

Sarah's response rocked her boss. "The management committee held a meeting this morning. They teleconferenced in the partners from the other offices. Rumor has it that they're putting together a letter to send to you."

"A letter? What kind of letter?" The astonishment was rapidly growing on Sidney's face.

In the background, Sidney could hear people passing by Sarah's cubicle. After the noise drifted away, Sarah spoke, her voice even lower. "I . . . I don't know how to tell you this, but I heard it was a letter of termination."

"Termination?" Sidney put one hand up against the wall to steady herself. "I haven't even been accused of anything and they've already tried and convicted me and now they're sentencing me? All because of that one story?"

"I think everyone here is worried about the firm surviving. Most people are pointing their finger at you." Sarah added quickly, "And your husband. To find out Jason's still alive . . . People feel betrayed, they really do."

Sidney drew a large breath and her shoulders slumped down. A complete weariness dragged at her.

"My God, Sarah, how do you think I felt?" Sarah didn't say anything. Sidney fingered the disk in her pocket. The pistol made an uncomfortable lump under her jacket front. She would just have to get used to that. "Sarah, I wish I could explain it to you, but I can't. All I can tell you is I haven't done anything wrong and I don't know what the hell's happened to my life. But I don't have much time. Could you discreetly find out if Jeff's in? Please, Sarah."

Sarah paused and then said, "Hold on, Sid."

As it turned out, Jeff had taken a few days off. Sarah gave Sidney his home number. She prayed he was not out of town. Around three o'clock, Sidney finally reached him. Her original plan had been to meet him at the firm. However, now that was out of the question. Instead, she made arrangements to meet him at his home in Alexandria. It didn't hurt that he had not been at the office the last couple of days to hear all the rumors swirling around her. When Sidney told him she had a computer problem, he was eager to assist. He had some business to take care of but would be home around eight. She would just have to wait it out.

Two hours later a knock at the door startled Sidney while she was nervously pacing through the living room. She looked through the peephole and then opened the door in mild surprise. Lee Sawyer didn't wait to be asked in. He strode through the foyer and sat down in one of the chairs next to the fireplace hearth. The fire had long since gone out.

"Where's your partner?"

Sawyer ignored her question. "I checked in at Triton," he said. "You didn't tell me you had paid a call there this morning."

She stood in front of him, her arms crossed. She had showered and changed into a black pleated skirt and white V-neck sweater. Her hair, combed straight back, was still damp. She was in her stocking feet; her pumps lay next to the sofa. "You didn't ask."

Sawyer grunted. "So what did you think of your husband's little video?"

"I really haven't given it much thought."

"Like hell you haven't."

She sat down on the sofa, drawing her legs up underneath her before responding. "What exactly do you want?" she said stiffly.

"The truth wouldn't be bad, to start with. From there we might be able to move on to some solutions."

"Like putting my husband in prison for the rest of his life? That's the solution you want, isn't it?" She slung the words at him.

Sawyer absently fingered the badge on his belt. His stern expression faded. When he looked at her, his eyes were weary, his big body listing to one side. "Look, Sidney, like I said, I was at the crash site that night. I . . . I held that little shoe in my hand too." His voice started to break up. Tears appeared in Sidney's eyes, but she continued to look at him, even as her frame started to shake.

Sawyer resumed speaking, his voice low but clear. "I see photos all over your house of a very happy family. A handsome husband, one of the prettiest little girls I've ever laid my eyes on and . . ." He paused. "And a very beautiful wife and mother." Sidney's cheeks flushed at the words.

Embarrassed, Sawyer hurried on. "It makes no sense to me that your husband, even if he did steal from his employer, would have participated in blowing up that plane." A tear plunged from Sidney's cheek and stained the couch while she listened. "Now, I won't lie to you and tell you that I think your husband is completely innocent. For your sake, I hope to God he is and this whole mess can be explained somehow. But my job is to find whoever brought down that plane and killed all those people." He took a long breath. "Including the owner of that little shoe." He paused again. "And I'm going to do my job."

"Go on," Sidney encouraged him, one hand nervously gripping the hemline of her skirt.

"The best lead I have now is your husband. The only way I know to explore that lead right now is through you."

"So you want me to help you bring my husband in?"

"I want you to tell me anything you can that will help me get to the bottom of this. Don't you want that too?"

It took Sidney a full minute to respond. When the word finally came, it was buttressed by sobs. "Yes." She said nothing else for several moments. Finally she looked at him. "But my little girl needs me. I don't know where Jason is, and if I were to go away too . . ." Her voice trailed off.

Sawyer looked confused for a moment and then it dawned on him what she was saying. He reached across and gently took one of her hands. "Sidney, I don't believe you had anything to do with any of this. I'm sure as hell not going to arrest you and take you away from your daughter. Maybe you didn't tell me the whole story before, but Christ, you're only human. I can't even begin to imagine the pressure you've been under. Please believe me. And trust me." He let go of her hand and sat back.

She dabbed at her eyes, managed a brief smile, and composed herself. She took one last deep breath before taking the plunge. "That was my husband on the phone the day you came by." After having said it, she glanced sharply at Sawyer, as though she were still afraid that he might pull out his handcuffs. He merely hunched forward, his face a mass of wrinkles.

"What did he say? Give it to me as precisely as you can."

"He said that he knew things looked bad, but that he would explain everything as soon as he saw me. I was so thrilled to know he was alive, I didn't ask very many questions. He also called me from the airport before he got on the plane on the day of the crash." Sawyer perked up. "But I didn't have time to talk to him."

Sidney steeled herself for another guilt attack as the memory flooded back to her. Then she recounted to Sawyer Jason's late nights at the office and their early morning conversation before he had left for the airport.

"And he suggested the New Orleans trip?" Sawyer asked.

She nodded. "He said if he didn't contact me at the hotel that I should go to Jackson Square and he would get a message to me there."

"The shoeshine guy, right?"

Sidney nodded again.

Sawyer sighed. "So that was Jason you called from the pay phone?"

"Actually, the message said to call my office number, only Jason answered. He said not to say anything, that the police were around. He told me to go home and he would contact me when it was safe to do so."

"But he hasn't as yet?"

She slowly shook her head. "I've heard nothing."

Sawyer chose his words carefully. "You know, Sidney, your loyalty is admirable, it really is. You've lived up to your marriage vows big-time, because I don't think even God himself envisioned these kinds of 'bad times.'"

"But?" She looked at him searchingly.

"But there comes a time when you have to look beyond the devotion, beyond the feelings you have for someone and consider the cold, hard facts. I'm not very eloquent, but if your husband did something wrong—and I'm not saying he did—then you shouldn't go down with him. Like you said, you've got a little girl who needs you. I've got four kids of my own; I'm not the greatest father in the world, but I can still relate."

"So what are you proposing?" Her voice was hushed.

"Cooperation. Nothing more than that. You give me info, I give you info. Here's some for you. Call it a good-faith deposit. The stuff in the newspaper article pretty much sums up what we know. You saw the video. Your husband met with someone and an exchange took place. Triton is convinced it was information designed to hurt their chances at acquiring CyberCom. They also have pretty strong evidence tying Jason to the bank fraud."

"I know the evidence seems overwhelming, but I can't believe any of it. I really can't."

"Well, sometimes the clearest signposts point in the wrong direction. It's my job to figure out which way they should be pointing. I gotta admit I don't believe your husband is completely clean, but on the other hand, I don't think he's the only one out there."

"You think he's working with RTG, don't you?"

"It's possible," Sawyer frankly admitted. "We're following up that lead along with all the others. It seems the most straightforward, but then again, you never know." He paused. "Anything else you want to tell me?"

Sidney hesitated for a moment as she thought back to her conversation with Ed Page right before he was murdered. When her eyes came to rest on her tweed jacket lying over the chair, she almost jerked. The fact of the disk and her planned meeting with Jeff Fisher came rushing back to her. She swallowed and then reddened. "Not that I can think of. No."

Sawyer continued to watch her for a long moment and then slowly got to his feet. "While we're exchanging information, I thought you might like to know that your buddy Paul Brophy followed you down to Louisiana."

Sidney froze at his words.

"He searched your hotel room while you went out for coffee. Feel free to use that information however you see fit." He started to walk out the door and then turned back. "And just so there's no mistake, we have you under twenty-four-hour surveillance."

"I don't plan on taking any more trips, if that's what you're worried about."

His response surprised her. "Don't keep that pistol locked up, Sidney. Keep it within easy reach, and keep it loaded at all times. In fact . . ." Sawyer opened his coat, undid his clip-on belt holster, removed his pistol and handed the holster to Sidney. "In my experience, guns in purses aren't all that effective. Please be careful."

He left Sidney in the open doorway, her thoughts centered on the brutal fate of the last man to give her that particular piece of advice.

CHAPTER FORTY-ONE

Lee Sawyer looked at the carefully sculpted black-and-white marble walls and floors. They were cut in asymmetrical triangular patterns. He assumed they were supposed to convey a sophisticated artistic statement. However, they only served to give the FBI agent a throbbing headache. Through the gracefully carved lines of a birchwood double doorway with etched-glass panels and buttressed by a pair of faux Corinthian columns, the clink of dishes and silverware filtered out to him from the main dining area. He took off his overcoat, removed his hat and gave both to a pretty young woman in a short black skirt and tight blouse that managed to enhance a body that didn't need much enhancing. He was given a claim check in return, accompanied by a very warm smile. One of her fingernails had slid delicately across his palm when the claim check was passed over, digging just deep enough into his skin to make his body tingle in certain discreet places. She must do damn well in tips, he figured.

The maître d' appeared and eyed the FBI agent.

"I'm here to meet Frank Hardy."

The man again flicked his eyes over Sawyer's rumpled appearance.

The severe appraisal was not lost on Sawyer, who took a moment to hitch up his pants, a duty repeated many times a day by people of Sawyer's healthy dimensions. "How're the burgers here, pal?" he inquired. He took out a stick of gum, wadded it up and popped it into his mouth.

"Burgers?" The man seemed ready to topple over at the thought. "We serve *French* cuisine here, sir. The finest in the city." His accented speech bubbled with indignation.

"French? Great, I bet your fries must be damn good, then."

Turning quickly on his heel the maître d' led Sawyer through the immense dining area, where rows of crystal chandeliers sparkled above a clientele that nearly matched the brilliance of the finely cut light fixtures.

The ever elegantly dressed Frank Hardy rose from a corner booth and inclined his head at his former partner. Their waitress appeared moments after Sawyer did.

"What're you drinking, Lee?"

Sawyer settled his bulk into the booth. "Bourbon and spit," he grumbled without looking up.

The waitress looked at him blankly. "Excuse me?"

Hardy laughed. "In his own crude way my friend means *straight* bourbon. I'll have another martini."

The waitress went off, rolling her eyes.

Sawyer blew into his handkerchief and proceeded to look around the room. "Gee, Frank, I'm glad you picked the place."

"Why's that?"

"Because if I had, we'd be at Shoneys. But maybe it's best. I hear it's tough as hell to get reservations there this time of year."

Hardy chuckled and swallowed the rest of his drink. "You just can't accept even a sliver of the good life, can you?"

"Hell, I can accept it, so long as I don't have to pay for it. I'm figuring dinner for two here would run about what I have in my retirement plan."

The two men chatted for a few minutes while the waitress returned, situated their drinks and then stood ready to take their dinner orders.

Sawyer looked over the menu, which was written very clearly, but unfortunately only in French. He put the menu down on the table. "What's the most expensive item on the menu?" he asked the waitress. She rattled off a dish in French.

"Is it real food? Not snails or crap like that?"

With raised eyebrows and a stern expression, she assured him that snails were on the menu and were excellent, but the selection she had mentioned was not snails.

With a grin at Hardy, he said, "Then I'll have that."

After the waitress departed, Sawyer swallowed his gum, grabbed a hunk of bread from the basket in the center of the table and munched on it. "So, you find out anything on RTG?" he said between bites.

Hardy put his hands on the table, smoothing out the linen cloth. "Philip Goldman is RTG's top counsel and has been for many years now."

"Doesn't that strike you as funny?"

"What?"

"That RTG would use the same lawyers as Triton, and vice versa. I mean, I'm no attorney, but isn't that setting somebody up for a nasty fall?"

"It's not that simple, Lee."

"Gee, why am I not surprised."

Hardy ignored the remark. "Goldman has a national reputation and he's been RTG's top dog for a long time. Triton is a relative newcomer to Tyler, Stone's fold. Henry Wharton brought the account in. At the time, the two companies had no direct conflicts. Since then, there have been some tricky issues as the two companies' businesses have expanded. However, they've always worked through that—full disclosures, written waivers, all papered properly. Tyler, Stone is a top-flight firm and I think neither company wanted to lose that expertise. It takes time to build that continuity and trust."

"Trust. Now, there's a funny word to use in a case like this." Sawyer fiddled with the bread crumbs in front of him while he listened.

"Anyway, with the CyberCom deal, there was a direct conflict,"

Hardy continued. "Both RTG and Triton want CyberCom. Tyler, Stone was barred by the code of legal ethics from representing both clients."

"So they opted to rep Triton. How come?"

Hardy shrugged. "Wharton is managing partner. Triton is his client. Enough said? They sure as hell weren't going to let both companies be represented by someone else on this deal. Too tempting for another firm to walk away with the whole kit and caboodle."

"I take it Goldman was a little upset when the firm dissed his client like that."

"From what I could find out, homicidal was more like it."

"But who's to say he can't work behind the scenes to get RTG the prize?"

"Nothing. Nathan Gamble is no dummy; he's well aware of that. And if RTG beats out Triton, you know what might well happen, don't you?"

"Let me guess. Gamble might find some new lawyers?"

Hardy nodded. "Besides that, you read the headlines. They are mad as hell at Sidney Archer. I think her job security might be a little weak."

"Well, the lady's not too thrilled herself right now."

"You talked to her?"

Sawyer nodded and finished off his bourbon. He debated and then decided not to fill in Hardy on Sidney Archer's confession to him. Hardy worked for Gamble, and Sawyer was pretty sure what Gamble would do with that information: Destroy the lady. He threw out a fact as a theory instead. "Maybe she went to New Orleans to meet her husband."

Hardy stroked his chin. "I guess it makes sense."

"That's the problem, Frank, it *doesn't* make a damned bit of sense."

"How's that?" Hardy looked surprised.

Sawyer put his elbows on the table. "Look at it this way. The FBI shows up on her doorstep asking a bunch of questions. Now, you've got to be a friggin' *zombie* not to get a little nervous when that happens. So on the same day she hops on a plane to meet her husband?"

"It's possible she didn't know she was being followed."

Sawyer shook his head. "Uh-uh. This lady is sharp, like ginzu-knife sharp. I thought I had her dead to rights on a phone call she got the morning of her husband's memorial service and she sidesteps it with a perfectly plausible explanation that she probably thought up right then and there. She did the same thing when I accused her of ditching my cover guys. She knew she had a tail on her. And she still went."

"Maybe Jason Archer didn't know you were watching."

"If the guy did pull off all this shit, you don't think he's smart enough to realize the cops *might* be watching his wife? Come on."

"But she *did* go to New Orleans, Lee. You can't get around that fact."

"I'm not trying to. I think her husband did contact her and told her to hightail it down there despite our presence."

"Why in the hell would he do that?"

Sawyer fiddled with his napkin and didn't respond. Then their meals arrived.

"Looks good." Sawyer eyed his meticulously arranged meal.

"It is. It'll kick your cholesterol to an all-time new high, but you'll die a happy man."

Hardy reached across and tapped Sawyer's plate with his knife. "You haven't answered my question: Why would Jason Archer have done that?"

Sawyer slid a forkful of food into his mouth. "You weren't kidding about this stuff, Frank. And to think I was going to Chef Boyardee-it when you called and asked me to dinner."

"Dammit, come on, Lee."

Sawyer put down his fork. "When Sidney Archer went to New Orleans, we pulled all our guys because we had a number of routes to cover. She still almost gave us the slip. In fact, except for me getting incredibly lucky at the airport, we wouldn't have known where the hell she went. And now I think I know the reason she did go: as a diversion."

Hardy looked incredulous. "What the hell do you mean? A diversion from what?"

"When I said we pulled all our guys, I meant we pulled *all* our guys, Frank. There wasn't anybody watching the Archers' house while we were gone."

Hardy sucked in his breath and collapsed back in his seat. "Shit!"

Sawyer eyed him wearily. "I know. A big-time screwup on my part, but it's too late to bitch and moan about it now."

"So you think—"

"I think somebody paid that house a call while the missus was cooling her high heels in the Big Easy."

"Wait a minute, you don't think it was . . ."

"Let's put it this way: Jason Archer would be on my top-five list."

"What could he have wanted?"

"I don't know. Ray and I searched the place and didn't find anything."

"You think the wife is in on it?"

Sawyer took another bite of food before answering. "If you had asked me that question a week ago, I probably would have said yes. Now? Now I think she has no idea what's going on."

Hardy sat back. "You really believe that?"

"The newspaper shredded her. She's in deep shit with her law firm. Her husband never showed up and she comes home empty-handed. What did she gain except an even bigger headache?"

Hardy started to eat again but continued to look thoughtful.

Sawyer shook his head. "Christ, this case is like a jelly doughnut. Every time you take a bite, sticky shit squirts all over you." Sawyer stuffed a mound of food in his mouth.

Hardy laughed and looked around the dining room. His eyes suddenly focused on something. "I thought he was out of town."

Sawyer followed his gaze. "Who?"

"Quentin Rowe." He discreetly pointed. "Over there."

Rowe was halfway across the dining room, ensconced at a booth in a secluded corner. Soft candlelight gave the table an intimate feel in the expanse of the crowded restaurant. He wore a costly silk blazer, collarless shirt buttoned to the top and a pair of matching silk trousers. His ponytail flopped across the back of his neck as he engaged in an animated conversation with his dinner companion, a man in his early twenties dressed in an expensively tailored suit. The two young men were sitting side by side, their eyes firmly set on one another. They spoke in low tones, and Rowe's hand briefly flickered on top of his companion's.

"Sawyer arched an eyebrow at Hardy. "They make a nice couple."

"Watch it. You're starting to sound politically incorrect."

"Hey, live and let live. That's my motto. Guy can date whoever he wants."

Hardy continued to observe the pair. "Well, Quentin Rowe is worth about three hundred million dollars, and the way things are going he'll be a billionaire well before he's forty. I'd say that makes him a very eligible bachelor."

"I'm sure there's an army of young ladies just kicking themselves over that one."

"You better believe it. But the guy's flat-out brilliant. He deserves the success."

"Yeah, he gave me a little tour of the company. I didn't understand half of what he was talking about, but it was still interesting stuff. Can't say I like where all this technology crap is going, though."

"Can't stop progress, Lee."

"I don't want to stop it, Frank, I'd just like to choose how much I have to participate in it. According to Rowe, it doesn't look like I'm going to get that opportunity."

"It is a little scary. But it sure as hell is lucrative."

Sawyer glanced again in Rowe's direction. "Speaking of couples, Rowe and Gamble sure make an odd one."

"Really, what makes you say that?" Hardy grinned. "Seriously, they just happened to run into each other at an opportune time. The rest is history."

"So I understand. Gamble had the money bags and Rowe brought along the brains?"

Hardy shook his head. "Don't sell Nathan Gamble short. It's not easy making the bucks he did on Wall Street. He is one bright guy and a hell of a businessman."

Sawyer wiped his mouth with his napkin. "Good thing, because the man ain't going to get by on his charm."

CHAPTER FORTY-TWO

It was eight o'clock when Sidney reached Jeff Fisher's home, a restored row house on the outskirts of Old Town Alexandria's elite residential area. Dressed in MIT sweats and battered tennis shoes, a Red Sox cap perched on his nearly bald head, the short, pudgy Fisher welcomed her and led her to a large room crammed top to bottom with computer equipment of all descriptions, cables running all over the hardwood floors, and multiple electrical outlets jammed to capacity. Sidney thought the space looked as though it belonged more in the Pentagon War Room than in this quiet suburban area.

Fisher proudly watched her obvious astonishment. "Actually, I've cut back some. I thought I might be getting out of control a little bit." He grinned broadly.

Sidney pulled the disk out of her pocket. "Jeff, could you put this in your computer and read what's on it?"

Fisher took the disk, a disappointed look on his face. "Is that all you need? Your computer at work can read this floppy, Sidney."

"I know, but I was afraid I might screw it up somehow. It came in the mail and it might be damaged. I'm not in your league when it comes to computers, Jeff. I wanted to come to the best."

Fisher beamed at this ego-stroking. "Okay. It'll just take a second."

He started to pop the disk into the computer.

Sidney put a hand over his, halting him. "Jeff, is that computer on-line?"

He looked at the computer and then back at her. "Yeah. I've got three different services I use, plus my own gateway onto the Internet I got through using MIT as a host. Why?"

"Could you use a computer that isn't on-line? I mean, can't other people get to things on your database if you're on-line?"

"Yeah, it's a two-way street. You send stuff out. Others can hack it. That's the trade-off. But it's a big trade-off. Although you don't have to be on-line to get hacked."

"What do you mean?" Sidney asked.

"Ever heard of Van Eck radiation?" Fisher asked. Sidney shook her head. "It's really electromagnetic eavesdropping."

Sidney's face held a blank look. "What's that?"

Fisher swiveled around in his chair and looked at the puzzled attorney. "All electrical current produces a magnetic field, thus computers emit magnetic fields, relatively strong ones. These transmissions can be easily captured and recorded. On top of it, computers also give off digital impulses. This CRT"—Fisher pointed at his computer monitor—"throws off clear video images if you have the right receiving equipment, which is widely available. I could drive through downtown D.C. with a directional antenna, a black-and-white TV and a few bucks' worth of electronic parts and steal the information off every computer network in every law firm, accounting firm and government facility in the city. Easy."

Sidney was incredulous. "You're saying if it's on someone else's screen you can see it? How is that possible?"

"Simple. The shapes and lines on a computer screen are composed of millions of tiny dots called picture elements—or pixels, for short. When you type in a command, electrons are fired at the appropriate spot on the screen to light appropriate pixels—like painting a picture. The computer screen must be continually refreshed with electrons to keep the pixels lit. Whether you're playing a computer game or doing word processing or whatever, that's how you can see things on your screen. You with me so far?" Sidney nodded.

"Okay, each time electrons are shot at the screen, they give off a high-voltage pulse of electromagnetic emission. A TV monitor can receive these pulses pixel by pixel. However, since an ordinary TV monitor can't adequately organize these pixels to reconstruct what's on your screen, an artificial synchronization signal is used so the picture can be exactly reproduced."

Fisher paused to look at his computer again and then continued. "Printer? Fax? Same thing. Cellular phones? Give me one minute with a scanner and I can have your internal electronics serial number, or ESN, your cell phone number, your station class data and the phone's maker. I program that data into another cell phone with some reconfigured chips, and I start selling long-distance service and charge it to you. Any information that flows through a computer, either through the phone lines or through the air, is fair game. And what doesn't these days? Absolutely nothing is safe.

"You know what my theory is? Pretty soon we'll stop using computers because of all the security problems. Go back to typewriters and 'snail mail.'"

Sidney looked puzzled.

"Snail mail is a techie's derogatory term for the U.S. mail. They may get the last laugh, though. Mark my words. That day is coming."

A sudden thought entered Sidney's head. "Jeff, what about regular phones? How could it be that I call a number, say my firm number, and someone answers who I know for a fact cannot be at my firm?"

"Somebody hacked into the switch," Fisher said immediately.

"The switch?" Sidney looked completely bewildered.

"It's the electronics network over which all communications from pay phones to cellular phones travel across the United States. If you hack into it, you can communicate with impunity." Fisher turned back to his computer. "However, with all that said, I've got a really good security system on my computer, Sid."

"Is it completely foolproof? No one could break it?"

Jeff laughed. "I don't know anyone in their right mind who could make that claim, Sidney."

Sidney looked at the disk, wishing she could just tear pages out of it and read them. "I'm sorry if I sound paranoid."

"No sweat. No offense, but most lawyers I know are borderline paranoid. They must have a class in law school on it or something. But we can at least do this." He unplugged the phone line from his CPU. "Now we're officially off-line. I have a first-rate virus sweeper on this system, in case anything got on previously. I just ran a check, so I think we're safe."

He motioned Sidney to sit down. She slid a chair around and they both studied the screen. Fisher hit a series of keys and a directory of the files on the disk appeared. He looked over at Sidney. "About a dozen files—from the number of bytes listed I'd say about four hundred or so pages if it's standard text. But if there are a lot of graphics there's really no way to gauge the length." Fisher hit some more keys. When the screen filled up with images, his eyes sparkled.

Sidney's face fell as she stared at the screen. It was all gibberish, high-tech hieroglyphics.

She looked at Fisher. "Is there something wrong with your computer?"

Fisher typed rapidly. The screen went blank and then reappeared with the same mess of digital images. Then at the bottom of the screen a box appeared with the command line requesting a password. "No, and there's nothing wrong with the disk either. Where'd you get it?"

"It was sent to me. By a client," she answered lamely.

Luckily, Fisher was too engrossed in the high-tech conundrum to question her further about the origin of the disk.

His fingers flew across the keyboard for several more minutes as he tried all the other files. The gibberish on the screen always reappeared. So did the message requesting a password. Finally he turned to her, a smile on his face.

"It's encrypted," he said simply.

Sidney stared at him. "Encrypted?"

Fisher continued to stare at the screen. "Encryption is a process whereby you take readable form text and put it into a nonreadable form before you send it out."

"What good is it if the person you sent it to can't read it?"

"Ah, but they can if they have the key that allows you to decrypt the message."

"How do you get the key?"

"The sender has to forward it to you, or you have to already have it in your possession."

Sidney slumped back in the chair. Jason would have had the damned key. "I don't have it."

"That doesn't make any sense."

"Would someone send an encrypted message to himself?" she asked.

Fisher looked over at her. "He wouldn't. I mean, ordinarily he wouldn't. If you have the message already in hand, you wouldn't encrypt it and then send it across the Internet to yourself at another location. It would just give someone the opportunity to intercept it and then maybe break it. But I thought you said a client sent you this?"

Sidney suddenly shivered. "Jeff, do you have any coffee? It seems chilly in here."

"Actually, I've got a fresh pot made. I keep this room a little cooler than the rest of the house because of the heat thrown off by the equipment. I'll be back in a minute."

"Thanks."

When Fisher returned with two cups of coffee, Sidney was staring at the screen.

Fisher took a sip of the hot liquid while Sidney sat back in the chair and closed her eyes. Fisher hunched forward and studied the screen. He returned to his last train of thought. "Yeah, you wouldn't encrypt a message you meant to send to yourself." He took another sip of coffee. "You'd only do it if you were sending it to someone else."

Sidney's eyes flew open and she jolted upright. The image of the e-mail flashing across Jason's computer screen like an electronic phantom swept through her memory. It was there and then gone. The key. Was it the key? Was he sending it to her?

She gripped Fisher's arm. "Jeff, how is it possible for an e-mail to appear on your computer screen and then vanish? It's not in your mailbox. It's nowhere on the system. How can that happen?"

"Pretty easily. The sender has a window of opportunity to cancel the transmission. I mean, he couldn't do it once the mail was opened and read. But on some systems, depending on their configuration, you can recall a message up until it's opened by the receiver. In that regard it's better than the U.S. mail." Fisher grinned. "You know, you get pissed off at someone and you write them a letter and mail it, and then you regret having done it. Once it's in the metal box, you cannot get it back. No way, nohow. With electronic mail, you can. Up to a point."

"How about outside a network? Like across the Internet?"

Fisher rubbed his chin. "It's more difficult to do because of the travel chain the message has to go through. Sort of like the monkey bars on the playground." Sidney again stared at him with a blank face. "You know, you climb up one side, swing yourself across and then climb down the other side. That's a rough analogy of how mail travels over the Internet. The parts are fluid per se, but they don't necessarily form a single cohesive unit. The result is, sometimes information sent cannot be retrieved."

"But it's possible?"

"If the e-mail was sent using one on-line service through the whole route—like, for example, America Online—you can retrieve it."

Sidney thought quickly. They had American Online at home. But why would Jason have sent her the key and then taken it back? She shuddered. Unless he wasn't the one who had canceled the transmission.

"Jeff, if you're sending the e-mail and you want it to go through, but someone else doesn't, could they stop it? Cancel the transmission like you said, even if the sender wants it to go through?"

"That's kind of a weird question. But the answer is yes. All you have to do is have access to the keyboard. Why do you ask?"

"I'm just thinking out loud."

Fisher looked at her quizzically. "Is something wrong, Sidney?"

Sidney ignored the question. "Is it possible to read the message without the key?"

Fisher looked at the screen and then turned slowly back to Sidney. "There are some methods one can employ." He sounded hesitant, his tone much more formal.

"Could you try to do it, Jeff?"

He looked down. "Look, Sidney, right after you called today, I phoned the office just to check on some ongoing projects. They told me . . ." He paused and looked at her with troubled eyes. "They told me about you."

Sidney stood up, her eyes downcast.

"I also happened to read the paper before you came over. Is that what this is all about? I don't want to get into trouble."

Sidney sat back down and looked directly at Fisher, gripping his hand with one of hers. "Jeff, an e-mail came across my computer at home. I think it was from my husband. But then it vanished. I think it might have been the key for this message because Jason mailed that disk to himself. Whatever is on that disk I've got to be able to read. I haven't done anything wrong, despite what my firm or the paper or anyone says. I have no way of proving that. Yet. All you have is my word."

Fisher looked at her for a long moment and then finally nodded. "Okay, I believe you. You happen to be one of the few attorneys at the firm I like." He turned back to the screen with a determined air. "You might want to get some more coffee. If you're hungry, there's some sandwich stuff in the fridge. This could take a while."

CHAPTER FORTY-THREE

The dinner with Frank Hardy had been an early one and it was only about eight o'clock when Sawyer pulled up to the curb in front of his apartment. When he climbed out of the car, his stomach felt immensely comfortable. His brain, however, didn't share that pleasant feeling. This case seemed to have so many angles, he wasn't quite sure where to start grabbing.

When he slammed the car door shut, he noticed the vintage Silver Cloud Rolls-Royce high-stepping down the street toward him. His neighborhood was seldom, if ever, witness to that sort of spectacular wealth. Through the windshield Sawyer could see a black-capped chauffeur at the wheel. Sawyer had to look twice and then it hit him what was odd. The driver was on the right side—it was a British-built car. It slowed down and came to a quiet stop next to him. Sawyer couldn't see in the back of the car because the glass was tinted. He wondered if that was an original production item or had been added later. He didn't have time to wonder past that. The rear window came down and Sawyer was staring into the countenance of Nathan Gamble. In the meantime the chauffeur had exited the car and stood ready by the passenger door.

Sawyer's eyes swept the length of the massive vehicle before coming to rest on the Triton chairman again. "Nice set of wheels. How's the gas mileage?"

"Like I care. You into basketball?" Gamble used a cutter to snip off the back end of his cigar and took a moment to light up.

"Excuse me?"

"NBA. Tall black guys running around in little shorts in return for shitloads of money."

"I catch it on the tube when I get a chance."

"Well, hop in, then."

"Why?"

"You'll see. I promise you won't be bored."

Sawyer looked up and down the street and shrugged. He jostled his car keys in his pocket and then looked at the chauffeur. "I got it, buddy." Sawyer pulled open the door and climbed in. When he settled back against the leather he noted Richard Lucas in the rear-facing seat. Sawyer inclined his head slightly. Triton's security chief returned the bare gesture. The Rolls pulled swiftly away.

"You want one?" Gamble held out a cigar. "Cuban. It's against the law to import them into this country. I think that's why I like them so much."

Sawyer took the offered cigar and snipped off the end with the cutter Gamble handed him. He looked surprised when Lucas held out a butane lighter, but accepted the service.

He took a few quick puffs and then a long one as he got it going. "Not bad. Guess I'll have to give you a break on the illegal smokes."

"Thanks tons."

"By the way, how'd you know where I lived? I hoped you weren't following me. I get real jumpy when people do that."

"I got better things to do than follow you, believe me."

"So?"

"So what?" Gamble eyed him.

"So how'd you know where I live?"

"What's it to you?"

"Actually, it's a lot to me. In my line of work you don't broadcast the place you call home."

"Okay, let me see, then. What did we do? Look you up in the phone book?" Gamble abruptly shook his head and his eyes flickered amusement at Sawyer. "No, that wasn't it."

"Good thing, since I don't happen to be listed."

"Right. Well, I guess we just knew." Gamble blew a pair of perfect smoke rings to the ceiling. "You know, all our computer technology. We're Big Brother, we know everything." Gamble chuckled while he puffed on his cigar and looked over at Lucas.

Lucas caught Sawyer's eye. "Actually, Frank Hardy told us. In confidence, of course. We don't intend to spread that information around. I understand your concern." Richard Lucas paused. "Just between us," he added, "I was with the CIA for ten years."

"Ah, Rich, I just had him going too." The smell of liquor on Gamble's breath permeated the car. He reached across and opened a small door built into the wood paneling of the Rolls. A well-stocked bar was revealed. "You look like a scotch and soda man."

"I had my fill at dinner."

Gamble filled up an etched china glass with the contents of a bottle of Johnnie Walker. Sawyer glanced over at Lucas, who looked on calmly enough. Apparently this was fairly routine.

"Actually, I didn't think I'd be hearing from you after our little chat the other day," said Sawyer.

"The simple answer to that is you took me down a peg and I probably deserved it. Actually, I *was* testing you with my big-shot asshole routine and you passed with flying colors. As you can imagine, I don't meet that many people with the balls big enough to do that. When I do, I like to get better acquainted. Plus in light of recent developments I want to talk to you about the case."

"Recent developments?"

Gamble took a sip of his drink. "You know what I'm talking about. Sidney Archer? New Orleans? RTG? I just got off the horn with Hardy."

"You work pretty fast. I just left him not more than twenty minutes ago."

Gamble pulled a tiny portable phone from a receptacle on the

Rolls's rear console. "Remember, Sawyer, I operate in the private sector. You don't move fast, you don't move at all, get it?"

Sawyer pulled on his cigar before answering. "I'm beginning to. By the way, you never did say where we're going."

"Didn't I? Well, sit tight. We'll be there shortly. And then we can have ourselves a nice little talk."

USAir Arena was home to the NBA Washington Bullets and the NHL Washington Capitals, at least until the new downtown stadium was completed. The arena was packed for the Bullets-Knicks game. Nathan Gamble, Lucas and Sawyer rode the private elevator to the second floor of the arena, where the corporate luxury boxes were located. When Sawyer stepped down the hallway and through the door marked TRITON GLOBAL, he felt as if he had boarded a luxury liner. These weren't merely seats to a ball game; the place was about the size of his apartment.

A young woman was tending bar and a hot and cold buffet was laid out on a long side table. There was a private bath, closet, overstuffed sofas and chairs and a giant-screen TV in one corner with the basketball game on. From up a flight of stairs leading to the viewing section, Sawyer could hear the crowd cheering. He looked at the TV. The home-team Bullets were up by seven over the heavily favored Knicks.

Sawyer took off his hat and coat and followed Gamble over to the bar area.

"You've gotta have something now. Can't watch a ball game without a drink in your hand."

Sawyer nodded toward the bartender. "Bud, if you've got it."

The young woman reached in the refrigerator, popped open a can of Budweiser and started to pour it in a glass.

"Can's good enough. Thanks."

Sawyer looked around the spacious room again. No one else was there. He strayed over to the buffet. He was still full from dinner, but some chips and salsa were calling to him.

"Place usually this empty?" he asked Gamble while he grabbed up a handful. Lucas assumed a hovering presence against the wall.

"Usually it's packed," Gamble replied. "Damn good perk for the employees. Keeps 'em happy and hardworking." The bartender handed Gamble his drink. In response, Gamble flushed a wad of hundred-dollar bills out of his pocket, pulled a glass off the counter and stuffed the bills in the glass. "Here, bartender's got to have a tip jar. Go buy some growth stocks." The young woman almost fainted with joy as Gamble walked over to join Sawyer.

Sawyer pointed his beer toward the TV. "Looks like a great game. I'm surprised there aren't Triton people packed in here."

"I'd be real surprised if they were, since I instructed that no tickets be given out for tonight's game."

"Why'd you do that?" Sawyer took a sip of his beer.

Gamble hooked Sawyer's arm with his free hand. "Because I wanted to talk to you in private."

Sawyer was led up the stairs to the viewing area. From up here the view was pretty much straight down onto the playing floor. Sawyer watched with a twinge of envy as two groups of tall, muscular and very rich young men ran up and down the court. The seating area he was in was closed in on three sides by Plexiglas. On either side were the occupants of other luxury boxes. However, with the glass shield, one could conduct a very private conversation amid a crowd of fifteen thousand.

The two men settled in. Sawyer jerked his head toward where they had just come from. "Rich doesn't like basketball?"

"Lucas is on duty."

"Is he ever off duty?"

"When he's sleeping. I occasionally let him do that." Gamble sat back in the comfortable chair and gulped his drink.

Sawyer looked around curiously. He had never been in one of these things before, and after the fancy dinner with Hardy he was feeling a little out of his depth. At least he'd have some stories to tell Ray. When he glanced over at Gamble, he stopped smiling. Nada in life was free. Everything had its cost. He decided it was time to check the price tag.

"So, what'd you want to talk about?"

Gamble stared down at the sports contest without really seeing any of it. "The fact is we need CyberCom. We need it badly."

"Look, Gamble, I'm not your business consultant, I'm a cop. I don't give a damn if you get CyberCom or not."

Gamble sucked on an ice cube. He seemed not to have heard. "You work hard building something and it's never enough, you know? Always somebody trying to take it away from you. Always somebody trying to screw you."

"If you're looking for sympathy, look someplace else. You can't spend all the money you've already got. What the hell do you care?"

Gamble exploded. "Because you damn well get used to it, that's why." He calmed down quickly. "You get used to being on top. Having everybody measure themselves against you. But a lot of it is about the money." He looked over at Sawyer. "You want to know what my total income is per year?"

Despite himself Sawyer was curious. "If I say no, why do I feel like you're going to tell me anyway?"

"One billion dollars." Gamble unceremoniously dropped the ice cube from his mouth into his glass.

Sawyer swallowed a mouthful of beer as he absorbed this stunning information.

"My federal income tax bill alone this year will come to about four hundred million dollars. With that you'd think I'd qualify for a little TLC from you Feds."

Sawyer glared at him. "If you're looking for TLC, try the hookers down on Fourteenth Street. They're a lot cheaper."

Gamble stared over at him. "Shit, you guys just don't get the big picture, do you?"

"Why don't you enlighten me as to what exactly that is."

Gamble put down his glass. "You treat everybody the same." His tone was one of disbelief.

"Excuse me—are you saying that's wrong?"

"It's not only wrong, it's stupid."

"I guess you never bothered to read the Declaration of Independence—you know, that warm, fuzzy part about all men being created equal."

"I'm talking reality. I'm talking about business."

"I don't make distinctions."

"Like I'm gonna treat the chairman of Citicorp the same as I would the janitor in the building. One guy can loan me billions of dollars and the other can scrub out my toilet."

"My job is to hunt down criminals, rich, poor, in-between. It doesn't make any difference to me."

"Yeah, well, I'm not a criminal. I'm a taxpayer, probably the biggest damned taxpayer in this whole country, and all I'm asking for is a little favor that I'd get in the private sector without even asking for it."

"Hooray for the public sector."

"That's not funny."

"Not for one second was it supposed to be." Sawyer stared him down. When Gamble finally looked away, Sawyer glanced down at his hands and then took another swallow of beer. Every time he was around this guy his heartbeat seemed to double.

Down on the court a slam dunk by the home team brought the crowd to its feet.

"By the way, you ever think there's something wrong with you being richer than God?"

Gamble laughed. "Like those guys down there?" He pointed at the basketball court. "Actually, based on the world's present condition, I think I had a better year than God." He rubbed at his eyes. "Like I said, it's not the cash anymore. You're right, I have more than I'll ever need. But I like the respect being on top brings. Everybody waits to see what you'll do."

"Don't confuse respect with fear."

"In my book they go hand in hand. Look, I got where I am by being one tough sonofabitch. You hurt me I'll hurt you back, only better. I grew up poorer than dirt, took a bus to New York when I was fifteen, started on Wall Street as a courier making a few bucks a day, worked my way to the top and I never looked back. Made fortunes, lost fortunes and then made them back. Hell, I got a half dozen bullshit honorary degrees from Ivy League colleges and I never finished the tenth grade. All you have to do is make donations." He arched his eyebrows and grinned.

"Congratulations." Sawyer prepared to stand up. "I guess I'll be heading on, then."

Gamble grabbed his arm and then immediately let it go. "Look, I read the paper. I've talked to Hardy. And I can feel RTG breathing down my neck."

"Like I said before, that's not my problem."

"I don't mind playing on a fair field, but I'll be damned if I'm gonna lose out because an employee sold me down the river."

"*Allegedly* sold you down the river. We haven't proven anything yet. And whether you like it or not, that's all that matters in a court of law."

"You saw the videotape. What more proof do you need? Hell, all I'm really asking you to do is your job. What's wrong with that?"

"I saw Jason Archer giving some documents to some people. I have no idea what the documents were or who the people are."

Gamble sat up. "See, the problem here is that if RTG knows my deal and outbids me for CyberCom, I'm screwed. I need you to prove they ripped me off. Once they get CyberCom, it's not going to matter how they got the deal, it's theirs. You hear where I'm coming from?"

"I'm working as hard as I can, Gamble. But there's no way in hell I'm going to tailor my investigation to fit your business agenda. The murder of a hundred and eighty-one innocent people means a lot more to me than how much you pay in income taxes." Gamble didn't answer. "You hear where *I'm* coming from?" Gamble finally shrugged. "If it turns out RTG was behind it, then you can rest assured that I'll spend every waking moment making sure I bring them down."

"But couldn't you put the screws hard to them right now? The FBI investigating them would probably knock them right out of the running for CyberCom."

"We are looking into it, Gamble. These things take time. Bureaucracy with a capital *B,* remember?"

"Time is something I don't have a lot of," he growled.

"Sorry, the answer's still no. Now, is there anything else I *can't* do for you?"

The two men watched the game in silence for a few minutes. Sawyer picked up a pair of binoculars from the table in front of him. As he watched the action up close he said, "So what's up with Tyler, Stone?"

Gamble grimaced. "If we weren't so far into the CyberCom deal, I'd fire their ass right now. But the fact is I need their legal exper-tise and institutional memory. For now, anyway."

"But not Sidney Archer's."

He shook his head. "Never would've figured that lady to do some-thing like that. Helluva lawyer. A real babe on top of it too. What a waste."

"How's that?"

Gamble looked at him, amazed. "Excuse me, did we read the same newspaper? She's in it up to her nice-looking ass."

"You think so?"

"Don't you?"

Sawyer shrugged and finished his beer.

"Lady takes off after her husband's memorial service," Gamble continued. "Hardy tells me she tried to give your guys the slip. You followed her all over New Orleans. She's acting suspicious, comes right home after getting a phone call. Hardy also said you thought somebody may have gone through her house while she drew all you guys off the scent. Brilliant how you let that happen, by the way."

"I'm gonna have to be careful what I tell Frank in the future."

"I pay him a hell of a lot of money. He better keep me informed."

"I'm sure he's worth every penny."

"Pennies, right! That's a joke."

Sawyer gave Gamble a sidelong glance. "For all he's done for you, you don't seem to hold Frank in very high regard."

Gamble chuckled. "Believe it or not, I have really high stan-dards."

"Frank was one of the best agents the bureau ever produced."

"I have a short memory for good work. You have to keep showering me with it." Gamble's smile quickly turned to a glare. "On the other hand, I never forget screwups."

They watched the game in silence. Finally Sawyer stirred. "Quentin Rowe ever screw anything up for you?"

Gamble looked surprised by the question. "Why do you ask that?"

"Because the guy's your golden egg and from all accounts you treat him like crap."

"Who said he's my golden egg?"

"You saying he's not?" Sawyer sat back and crossed his arms.

Gamble didn't answer right away. He brooded over his glass of liquor. "I've had a lot of golden eggs in my career. You don't get to where I am off one racehorse."

"But Rowe is valuable to you."

"If he wasn't, I wouldn't have much use for his company."

"So you tolerate him?"

"So long as the dollars keep pouring in."

"Lucky you."

Gamble's look was ferocious. "I took an ivory tower geek who couldn't raise a damned dime on his own and turned him into the country's richest thirty-something. Now, who do you think's the lucky one?"

Sawyer inclined his head toward the man. "I'm not trying to take anything away from you, Gamble. You chased a dream and made it come true. I guess that's what America's all about."

"Coming from a Fed, I'll have to really savor that compliment." Gamble once again focused on the basketball game.

Sawyer stood and crumpled his beer can.

Gamble stared up at him. "Where you going?"

"Home. It's been a long day." He held up the squashed can. "Thanks for the beer."

"I'll have my driver take you home. I'll be here awhile."

Sawyer looked around the luxury box. "I think I've had enough of the high life for one day. I'll take the bus. But thanks for the invite."

"Yeah, I really enjoyed it too," Gamble said with the heaviest of sarcasm.

The agent had started up the stairs, but Gamble's "Hey, Sawyer?" turned him around.

Gamble was looking squarely at him, and then he let out a deep sigh. "I hear where you're coming from, okay?"

Sawyer stared at him a moment before answering. "Okay."

"I wasn't always this rich. I remember real well what it's like to be penniless and powerless. Maybe that's why I'm such an asshole when it comes to business: I'm terrified of going back there."

Sawyer considered this for a moment. "Enjoy the rest of the game." He left Gamble staring into his glass, deep in thought.

As Sawyer walked down the steps, he almost bumped into Richard Lucas, who had assumed a position there. Sawyer wondered if Lucas had overheard any part of the conversation with Gamble. He nodded at Lucas and stepped down into the bar area, where he launched a hook shot and the beer can sailed through the air and neatly into the trash can.

The bartender looked at him with admiration. "Hey, maybe the Bullets should sign you up," she said with a cute smile.

"Yeah, I can be the token over-the-hill white guy."

Sawyer turned back before exiting the room. "Keep smiling, Rich."

CHAPTER FORTY-FOUR

Jeff Fisher stared humbly at the screen; a weary Sidney Archer sat beside him. She had given him all the personal information she could think of about Jason in order to fathom a proper password. Nothing had worked.

Fisher shook his head. "Well, we've gone through all the easy possibilities and all variations thereof. I've run a brute-force assault and got nothing. I've tried a partial random letter and number approach, but there are just too many possibilities to conduct in our lifetime." He turned to Sidney. "I'm afraid your husband really knew what he was doing. I figure he's probably got a random number-letter combo of about twenty or thirty characters. We're not going to crack it."

Sidney's hopes plummeted. It was maddening to have a disk full of information in her hand—presumably information that would explain a lot about her husband's fate—and be absolutely unable to read it.

She stood up and paced the room while Fisher continued to peck at the keyboard. Sidney crossed the room and stopped in front of a window. On a table next to the window was a stack of mail. On top was a *Field & Stream* magazine. Sidney idly glanced down at the stack of mail, eyed the magazine and then looked over at Fisher. He hardly seemed the outdoor type, she thought. Then she looked at the address label on the front cover. It was addressed to a Fred Smithers, but the address was that of the house she was standing in. She picked up the magazine.

Fisher looked over at her while he finished his Coke. When he saw the magazine in her hands, he scowled. "I keep getting that guy's mail. A bunch of companies somehow have my address on their system for this guy. I'm 6215 Thorndike and he's 6251 Thorn-drive, which is clear on the other side of Fairfax County. That whole stack is his. And that's just this week. I've told the mailman who handles this route, called the Postal Service a million times, called all the companies who have been erroneously sending his mail here. Still happens."

Sidney slowly turned toward Fisher. An improbable idea was taking shape in her head.

"Jeff, an e-mail address is like any other address or phone number, right? You type in the wrong address and it can go to someone you never intended it to go to. Like this magazine." She held up *Field & Stream.* "Right?"

"Oh, sure," Fisher replied. "That happens all the time. I have most of my frequently used e-mail addresses programmed in so I just have to point and click. That cuts down on the error rate."

"But if you had to *type* in a full e-mail address?"

"Well, there's a lot more room for error in that scenario. The addresses can get rather lengthy."

"So if you hit a wrong key, the message you intended for someone could go to God knows who?"

Fisher nodded as he munched on a potato chip. "I get misad-dressed e-mail all the time."

Sidney looked at him with a puzzled expression. "What do you do when that happens?"

"Well, what happens most often is pretty simple. I only have to click on my reply-to-sender command and I send a standard message saying they got the wrong address and I send the e-mail back so they know what message I'm talking about. That way I don't need to know the address. It automatically sends it back to the originator."

"Jeff, you mean if my husband sent an e-mail to the wrong location, the person receiving the e-mail by mistake could simply reply back to Jason's e-mail address to let him know the mistake?"

"Right. I mean, if you're on the same service, say America Online, it's relatively simple."

"And if that person did reply back, the e-mail would be in Jason's computerized mailbox right now, right?"

Fisher looked up at her, a slightly fearful look in his eyes at the tone in her voice. "Well, yes."

Sidney collected her purse.

Fisher looked at her. "Where are you going?"

"To check our computer at home for the e-mail. If the password is on there, I can read this disk." Sidney popped the disk out of the floppy drive and put it in her purse.

"Sidney, if you give me your husband's user name and password, I can access his mail from right here. I have AOL on my system. It's not hardware-specific. I'll just log you on as a guest. If the key to the encryption *is* in the mailbox, we can read the disk here."

"I know, Jeff. But would your access of Jason's mail from this location be traceable?"

Fisher's eyes narrowed. "It's possible. If whoever was looking knew what they were doing."

"I think we have to assume these people know what they're doing, Jeff. It'll be a lot safer for you if no one can trace that e-mail being accessed from here."

Fisher turned a shade paler. He spoke slowly, the nervousness evident in his tone and features. "What have you gotten involved in, Sidney?"

She turned away from him as she spoke. "I'll be in touch."

After she left, Fisher sat at the screen for a few more minutes and then plugged in the phone line to his computer.

Sawyer sat down in the recliner and looked once again at the *Post* story on Jason Archer and shook his head. He flipped the paper over and as his eyes hit the other headline, he almost gagged. It took him two minutes to devour the story. He jumped on the phone and made a series of calls. That finished, he tore down the stairs. A minute later his sedan shot down the street.

Sidney parked the Ford in the driveway, hurried into her house, threw off her coat and went straight to her husband's office. She was about to access her AOL mailbox when she suddenly jumped up. "Oh, God!" She couldn't do it from here, not with whatever was on there. She thought quickly. Tyler, Stone had AOL software on its computers; she could access the mailbox from there. She grabbed her coat, raced to the front door and flung it open. Her scream was easily heard up and down the street.

Lee Sawyer was standing there, looking less than pleased.

She caught her breath and grabbed at her chest. "What are you doing here?"

In response, Sawyer held up the newspaper. "You happen to catch this story?" Sidney stared at Ed Page's picture, recognition all over her features. "I . . . I haven't, no, just—" she stammered.

Sawyer stepped inside the house and slammed the door. Sidney retreated into the living room. "I thought we had a deal. You remember? Exchange of information? Well, we're gonna talk. Right now!" he bellowed.

She pushed past him toward the door. He grabbed her arm and flung her on the couch. She jerked back up. "Get out of here!" she screamed.

He shook his head and held up the paper. "You want to go it alone out there? Then your little girl better get another mommy."

She hurtled forward, slapped him across the face and wound up to do it again. He grabbed both her arms and put her in a bear squeeze. She struggled furiously.

"Sidney, I'm not here to fight you. Whether your husband did anything wrong or not, I will still help you. But dammit, you've gotta be straight with me."

They struggled across the room and fell onto the couch, she awkwardly on his lap, trying her best to slug him. He held her tightly until the tension in her arms finally faded away. He released her and she immediately pulled away to the far end of the couch and put her face in her lap. He slumped back and waited. Sitting up, Sidney wiped away the tears with her sleeve. Licking her lips, she looked over at the newspaper on the floor. The photo of Ed Page beckoned to her.

"You talked with him on the plane from New Orleans, didn't you?" Sawyer asked the question very quietly. He had watched Page get on the plane in New Orleans. The passenger manifest revealed Page had sat right next to Sidney. That fact had not been important, until now. "Didn't you, Sidney?" She slowly nodded. "Tell me about it. And this time I mean everything."

And she did, including Page's story of Jason's switch at the airport, and Page following her and tapping her phone.

"I talked to the medical examiner's office," Sawyer said when she was finished. "Page was killed, by someone who knew exactly what he was doing. One puncture wound to each lung. A precision cut through the carotid artery and jugular vein. Page died in under a minute. Whoever did it was not your typical street vermin wielding a pocketknife looking for some crack money."

Sidney took a deep breath. "That's why I almost shot you in the garage. I thought they were coming for me."

"You have no idea who 'they' are?"

Sidney shook her head and rubbed at her face again. She sat back and looked at him. "I really don't know anything other than the fact that my life has sunk far past hell."

Sawyer gripped one of her hands. "Well, let's see if we can get you back to the surface." He stood and picked up her coat from where it had fallen on the floor. "The investigative firm of Private Solutions has its headquarters in Arlington, across from the courthouse. I'm going to pay it a visit. And right now, I'd prefer to have you where I can keep an eye on you. You game?"

Sidney Archer swallowed hard as she guiltily felt the diskette in her pocket. That was one secret she could not bring herself, as yet, to reveal. "I'm game."

*   *   *

Edward Page's office was located in a nondescript low-rise office building opposite the Arlington County Circuit Court building. The security guard on duty could not have been more accommodating after seeing Lee Sawyer's credentials. The guard led the way to the elevators and in another minute, after being deposited on the third floor and walking down the dimly lit corridor, they stopped in front of a solid oak door with the name PRIVATE SOLUTIONS engraved on a metal plate next to it. The guard pulled out his key and tried to open the door.

"Damn!"

"What is it?" Sawyer asked.

"Key doesn't work."

"Isn't your master key supposed to open any door in the place?" Sidney asked.

" 'Supposed to' is right. We've had a problem with this guy before."

"How's that?" Sawyer asked.

The guard looked at them. "He changed the lock. Management jumped all over him. So he gave them another key that he said fit the new lock. Well, I can tell you right now it doesn't."

Sawyer looked up and down the corridor. "Any other way in?"

The guard shook his head. "Nope. I can try calling Mr. Page at his home. Tell him to come on down here and open it up. I'll ream his butt good too for pulling this crap. What if there was ever a problem and I needed to get in there?" The guard slapped his holster importantly. "You know what I mean?"

"I don't think calling Page will do any good," Sawyer said calmly. "He's dead. Murdered."

The blood slowly drained from the young man's face. "Jesus Christ! Omigod!"

"Police haven't been here, I take it?" Sawyer asked. The guard shook his head.

"How're we going to get in?" the guard asked, his voice barely above a whisper as, wide-eyed, he looked up and down the hallway for possible killers lurking there.

In response, Lee Sawyer hurled his massive bulk against the door, which splintered under the battering. One more thrust and the lock gave way and the door burst open, slamming against the inner wall of the office. Sawyer looked back at the stunned young guard while he brushed off his overcoat. "We'll check in with you on the way out. Thanks a lot."

The guard stood openmouthed for several seconds as the two moved into the office. Then he slowly walked back toward the elevator, shaking his head.

Sidney looked at the broken door and then over at Sawyer. "I can't believe he didn't even ask you for a search warrant. By the way, do you have one?"

Sawyer looked over at her. "What's it to you?"

"As an attorney, I'm an officer of the court. I just thought I'd ask."

He shrugged his thick shoulders. "I'll make a deal with you, *Officer:* We find something, you hold on to it and I'll go get a search warrant." Under different circumstances, Sidney Archer would have burst out laughing, and as it was, Sawyer's response drew a smile out of her. That perked up his own spirits.

The office was plain but neatly and efficiently furnished. For the next half hour they searched the small space, finding nothing out of place or extraordinary. They did find some stationery with Ed Page's home address on it. An apartment over in Georgetown. Sawyer perched on the side of the desk and surveyed the small area. "I wish my office was this tidy. But I don't see anything that's going to help us." Sawyer looked around the room, his expression glum. "I'd feel better if the place were ransacked. Then at least we'd know someone else was interested."

While he was talking, Sidney had made another pass around the room. She abruptly came back to one corner of the office where a row of gunmetal-gray filing cabinets stood in a row. She looked down at the floor, which was carpeted in a decidedly dull beige. "That's odd." Sidney got down on her knees, her face almost resting on the carpet. She looked at a small gap between the two filing cabinets nearest the spot she was examining. The other cabinets were butted together. She put her shoulder against one of the cabinets and shoved. The heavy cabinet didn't budge. "Can I get some help over here?" She looked back at Sawyer. He lurched over, motioned her out of the way and shoved the cabinet clear. "Hit that light over there," Sidney said excitedly.

Sawyer did so and then joined her. "What is it?"

Sidney moved aside so the FBI agent could see. On the floor where the cabinet had been was a rust spot, not very large but now clearly visible. Perplexed, Sawyer looked at her. "So? I can show you about a dozen of these in my office. Metal rusts, leaches into the carpet. Presto. Rust spots."

Sidney's eyes twinkled. "Really?" She pointed triumphantly. There were faint but discernible indentations on the carpet, which showed that the cabinet had originally butted up against the one next to it. There should have been no gap.

She motioned to the cabinet Sawyer had moved. "Lean it over and check the bottom.

Sawyer did so. "No rust spots," he said, then looked back at her. "So somebody moved this cabinet to cover the rust spot. Why?"

"Because that rust spot came from *another* filing cabinet. A filing cabinet that isn't here anymore. Whoever took it vacuumed out as best they could the indentations the missing cabinet made on the rug but couldn't get the rust spot out. So they did the next best thing. They covered it up with another filing cabinet and hoped no one paid any attention to the gap."

"But you did," Sawyer said, more than a trace of admiration in his tone.

"I couldn't figure why a guy obviously as neat as our Mr. Page would have a gap in a wall of filing cabinets. Answer: Someone else did it for him."

"And that means someone *is* interested in Edward Page and what he had in that file cabinet. Which means we're heading in the right direction." Sawyer picked up the phone on Page's desk. In a succinct request he instructed Ray Jackson to find out everything he could about Edward Page. He hung up and looked over at Sidney. "Since his office didn't yield all that much, what do you say we pay a visit to the late Edward Page's humble abode."

CHAPTER FORTY-FIVE

Page's residence was on the ground floor of a large turn-of-the-century home in Georgetown that had been transformed into a series of quaint apartments. The sleepy owner of the property had not questioned Sawyer's desire to view the premises. The man had read of Page's death and expressed dismay over it. Two detectives had been to the apartment and interviewed the landlord and several tenants. The landlord had also received a phone call from Page's daughter in New York. The private investigator had been a model tenant. His hours were somewhat irregular, and he would sometimes be gone for days at a time, but the rent was always paid on the first of the month and he had been quiet and orderly. He had no close friends of whom the owner was aware.

Using a key provided by the owner, who lived on the premises, Sawyer unlocked the front door of the apartment and he and Sidney stepped inside; he hit the light switch and then shut the door behind them. He was hoping to at least get a base hit here, although a homer would be nice.

They had checked the security log before leaving Page's office. The filing cabinet had been removed the day before by two guys in

movers' uniforms bearing a legit-looking work order and the keys to
the office door. Sawyer figured the moving company was certainly a
phony and the contents of Page's filing cabinet, which probably held
a treasure trove of interesting info, was probably no more than a pile
of ash at the bottom of some incinerator by now.

The interior of Page's residence resembled the man's office in its
simplicity and neatness. Sawyer and Sidney walked through the various rooms, surveying the basic layout of the apartment. A nice fireplace with a large Victorian-style mantel dominated the living
room. Bookshelves filled one wall. Edward Page had been a vora-
cious and eclectic reader, if his collection of books was any indica-
tion. There were not, however, any journals or records or receipts
that might have shown where Page had been lately or whom he
might have been following other than Sidney and Jason Archer.
After methodically searching the living and dining rooms, Sawyer
and Sidney moved on.

The kitchen and bathroom yielded nothing of interest. Sawyer
tried the usual places like the tank behind the toilet and in the refrigerator, where he checked Coke cans and heads of lettuce to make
certain they were real and not actually hiding places for clues as to
why Ed Page had been murdered. Sidney entered the bedroom,
where she undertook a thorough search, starting under the bed and
mattress and ending with the closet. The few pieces of luggage there
had no old airline tags. The wastebaskets were empty. She and
Sawyer sat down on the bed and scanned the room. He looked over
at the small stand of photographs on the side table. Edward Page
and family, obviously in happier times.

Sidney picked up one of the photos. "A nice-looking family." Her
thoughts were suddenly fixated on the photos residing in her house.
It seemed like a long time since that phrase had applied to her family. She handed the photo over to Sawyer.

The wife was real good-looking, he thought, the son a miniature
image of the old man. The daughter was very pretty. Red-headed
with long coltish legs, she looked about fourteen in the photo. The
date stamp showed it was taken five years ago. She must be a real

heartbreaker now, Sawyer figured. And yet according to the landlord they were all in New York and Page was down here. Why?

As Sawyer started to put the photo of the Page family back, he felt a slight bulge on the photo's backing. He opened up the back. Several photos about half the size of the framed one fell out. Sawyer picked them off the floor and studied them. They were all of the same person. A young man, mid-twenties. Good-looking, too handsome for Sawyer's taste—a pretty boy, was the FBI agent's first thought. The clothes were too fashionable, the hair too perfect. He thought he noted a trace of Ed Page along the jawline and around the deep brown eyes. Sawyer turned over all the photos. All except one were blank: "Stevie" was penned on the photo. Possibly Page's brother. If so, why were the photos hidden?

Sidney looked at him. "What do you think?"

He shrugged. "Sometimes I think this whole case is going to require more thinking than I can give it." Sawyer put all the photos back except the one with the name on the back. That one he put in his coat pocket. They looked around the room once more, then rose and left, locking the door securely behind them.

Sawyer walked Sidney to her house and then, out of an abundance of caution, conducted a search of the premises, making sure the house was empty and that every window and door was secure. "Day or night, you hear anything, you have a problem, you just want to talk, you call me. Understand?" Sidney nodded. "I've got two men outside. They can be in here in seconds." He walked to the front door. "I'm going to run some things down and I'll be back in the morning." He turned to look at her. "You going to be okay?"

"Yes." Sidney wrapped her arms around herself.

Sawyer sighed and leaned back against the door. "I hope one day I can deliver this case to you in one neat little ball, Sidney. I truly do."

"You . . . you still believe Jason is guilty, don't you? I guess I can't blame you. Everything . . . looks that way, I know." Her eyes searched Sawyer's troubled features. The big man sighed and looked away for a moment. When his eyes returned to her face, she saw a glimmer of something there.

"Let's just put it this way, Sidney," he said. "I'm starting to have some doubts."

She looked confused. "About Jason?"

"No, about everything else. I can promise you this: My top priority is finding your husband safe and sound. Then we can sort out everything else. Okay?"

She trembled slightly and then nodded at him. "Okay." When he turned to go, she touched his arm. "Thank you, Lee."

She watched Sawyer from the window. He walked over to the black sedan carrying the two FBI agents, looked back at the house, spotted her and waved. She made a feeble attempt at a wave back. She was feeling rather guilty right now, for what she was about to do. She left the window, turned out all the lights, grabbed her gray blazer and purse and raced out the back door seconds before one of Sawyer's men appeared to guard that area. Slipping through the woods at the edge of the backyard, she came out onto the road on the next block. After five minutes of brisk walking she had reached a pay phone. The cab picked her up within ten minutes.

Thirty minutes later she slipped her key in the security slot of her office building and the heavy glass door clicked open. She raced to the elevator bank. A minute later Sidney stepped out onto her floor. Inside the semidarkened space of Tyler, Stone, Sidney made her way quietly down the hallway. The library was at the end of the main hall on her floor. The double doors of frosted glass were open. Beyond this portal Sidney could plainly see shelf after shelf of books making up the firm's impressive law library. The area comprised a huge open space with a series of cubicles and adjacent enclosed work areas. Behind one partition stood a row of computer terminals, which attorneys and paralegals used for computerized legal research.

Sidney looked around the darkened interior of the library before venturing in. She heard no sound, saw no movement. Thankfully no junior associate was pulling an all-nighter. Walls of windows on two adjacent sides of the library overlooked the city streets; however, the blinds were pulled all the way down. No one could see in.

Sidney sat down in front of one of the darkened terminals and risked turning on a small lamp that sat on the computer table next to the terminal. She took the disk out of her purse and laid it on the table. In a minute the computer was warmed up. She clicked on the necessary commands to start America Online and jerked slightly as the screechy modem kicked in. After the connection was made, she typed in her husband's user name and password, silently thanking him for making her memorize them when they had signed on a couple of years ago. She stared anxiously at the screen, her breathing shallow, her features taut and her stomach queasy as though she were a defendant awaiting a verdict from a jury. The computerized voice made her jump slightly, but it was what she was hoping for. "You have mail," it said.

Down the hallway two pairs of legs quietly made their way toward the library.

Sawyer looked up at Jackson. They were in the FBI conference room. "So what'd you find out on Mr. Page, Ray?"

Jackson sat down and opened his notebook. "Had a nice chat with NYPD. Page used to be a cop up there. I also spoke with Page's ex-wife. Got her out of bed, but you said it was important. She still lives in New York. She hasn't had much to do with him since their divorce. However, he was very close to his kids. I talked with his daughter. She's eighteen, in her freshman year at college, by the way, and now she has to bury her father."

"What she have to say?" Sawyer asked.

"A lot. Like her father was nervous the last couple weeks. Didn't want them to visit him. He had started to regularly carry a gun. Hadn't done that in years. In fact he had taken a gun with him to New Orleans, Lee. It was found in a bag next to his body. Poor bastard never had a chance to use it."

"Why the move from New York down here, especially if his family stayed up there?"

Jackson nodded his head. "That's interesting. The wife wouldn't say one way or another. Just said the marriage was kaput and that was it. Page's daughter was of a different mind, though."

"She give you a reason?"

"Ed Page's younger brother also lived in New York. He committed suicide about five years ago. He was a diabetic. Gave himself a serious insulin overdose after a drinking binge. Page was close to his kid brother. His daughter said her dad was never the same after that."

"So he just wanted to get away from the area?"

Jackson shook his head. "I gather from talking to his daughter that Ed Page was convinced his brother's death wasn't a suicide or an accident," said Jackson.

"He thought he was murdered?"

Jackson nodded.

"Why?"

"I've requested a copy of the file from NYPD. There might be some answers in there, although I spoke briefly with the detective who worked the case and he says all the evidence points to either suicide or an accident. The guy was drunk."

"If he did kill himself, anybody know why?"

Jackson sat back. "Steven Page was a diabetic, like I said, so his health wasn't the greatest in the world. According to Page's daughter, her uncle could never get his insulin regulated. Although he was only twenty-eight when he died, his internal organs were probably much older." Jackson stopped talking and looked down at his notes for a moment. "On top of that, Steven Page had very recently tested positive for HIV."

"Shit. That explains the drinking binge," said Sawyer.

"Probably."

"And maybe the suicide."

"That's what NYPD thinks."

"How'd he contract it?"

Jackson shook his head. "No one knows. Officially, at least. I mean, the coroner's report wouldn't have been able to determine the origin. I asked the ex-wife. She wasn't any help. The daughter, however, tells me her uncle was gay. Not openly, but she was pretty sure about it and she thinks this is how he contracted HIV."

Sawyer rubbed his head and blew out a mouthful of air. "Is there some connection between the possible murder of a gay man in New York five years ago, Jason Archer ripping off his employer and a plane going down in Virginia?"

Jackson pulled at his lip. "Maybe, for some reason we don't know, Page knew that Archer didn't get on that plane."

Sawyer felt guilt for a moment. From his conversation with Sidney—a conversation he hadn't shared with his partner—Sawyer *knew* that Page had been aware that Jason hadn't been on the plane. "So Jason Archer disappears," he said, "and Page looks to pick up the trail through the wife."

"Makes sense as far as it goes. Hey, maybe it was Triton who hired Page to check on leaks, and he sniffed out Archer."

Sawyer shook his head. "Between their in-house staff and Frank Hardy's company, they have more than enough bodies to do the job."

A woman entered the room carrying a file. "Ray, this just came in over the fax from NYPD."

Jackson accepted the file. "Thanks, Jennie." After she had gone, Jackson scrutinized the file while Sawyer made a couple of calls.

"Steven Page?" Sawyer finally asked, pointing at the file.

"Yep. Real interesting stuff."

Sawyer poured a cup of coffee and sat down next to his partner.

"Steven Page was employed by Fidelity Mutual in Manhattan," said Jackson. "It's one of the biggest investment houses in the country. He lived in a nice apartment building; place was filled with antiques, original oil paintings, closet full of Brooks Brothers; Jag in the garage down the street. He also had an extensive investment portfolio: stocks, bonds, mutual funds, money markets. Well over a million dollars' worth."

"Pretty good for a twenty-eight-year-old. But I guess those investment bankers make killings. You hear all the time about these punks making truckloads of money for doing who the hell knows what. Probably screwing the likes of you and me."

"Yeah, but Steven Page wasn't an investment banker. He was a financial analyst, a market watcher. Strictly salaried position; not big bucks either, according to this report."

Sawyer's brow furrowed. "So where did the investment portfolio come from? Embezzlement from Fidelity?"

Jackson shook his head. "NYPD checked that angle. There were no funds missing from Fidelity."

"So what did NYPD conclude?"

"I don't think NYPD ever concluded anything. Page was found alone in his apartment, door and windows locked from the inside. And once the medical examiner's report came back as a probable suicide via insulin overdose, they pretty much lost interest. In case you didn't know, they've got a bit of a backlog on homicides in the Big Apple, Lee."

"Thanks for enlightening me, Ray, on New York City's corpse problem. So who inherited?"

Jackson sifted through the report. "Steven Page didn't leave a will. His parents were dead. He had no kids. His brother, Edward Page, as his only sibling, got everything."

Sawyer took a swallow of coffee. "That's interesting."

"But I don't think Ed Page popped his younger brother to fund his kids' college education. From what I could find out, he was as surprised as anyone else that his brother was a millionaire."

"Anything in the autopsy report catch your eye?"

Jackson picked out two pages from the file and handed them across to Sawyer. "As I said, a massive insulin overdose killed Steven Page. He injected himself in the thigh. It's a typical area of administration for diabetics. Other hypodermic entry sites around the thigh region showed it was his normal area of injection as well. Toxicology report showed a point-one-eight blood alcohol level. That didn't help his cause any when he took the overdose. *Algor mortis* indicated he had been dead about twelve hours when he was found; body temp was about eighty degrees. He was also in full rigor; that corroborates the time of death indicated by the body temperature and puts his check-out time at between three and four in the morning. Postmortem lividity was fixed. Guy died right where they found him."

"Who did find him?"

"Landlady," said Jackson. "Probably wasn't a real pretty sight."

"Death rarely is. Any note left behind?"

Jackson shook his head.

"Page make any calls before he kicked the bucket?"

"The last phone call Steven Page made from his apartment was at seven-thirty that evening."

"Who'd he call?"

"His brother."

"Did the police talk to Ed Page?"

"You bet they did. Especially after they found out about the bucks Steven Page had."

"Ed Page have an alibi?"

"A pretty damn good one. As you know, he was a police officer back then. He was working a drug bust with a squad of officers on the Lower East Side when his little brother was dying."

"The police ask Ed Page about the earlier phone conversation?"

"He said his brother was distraught. Steven told him about having HIV. Ed Page said his brother sounded like he had already been drinking."

"He didn't try to go see him?"

"He said he wanted to, but his brother wanted no part of that. Finally hung up on him. Ed Page tried calling back, but there was no answer. He had to go on duty at nine. He said he'd thought he'd let his brother alone for the night and then try to talk to him the next day. He didn't get off duty until ten A.M. He grabbed a few hours' sleep and then went to his brother's office downtown around three. When he found out Steven had never come to work, he went directly over to his brother's apartment. He got there about the time the police did."

"Jesus. I bet he was feeling some heavy-duty guilt."

"If that had been my little brother . . ." Jackson said. "Damn. Anyway, they ruled it a suicide. All the facts sure point that way."

Sawyer rose and started pacing. "And yet with all that, Ed Page didn't think it was suicide. I wonder why."

Jackson shrugged. "Wishful thinking. Maybe he was really feeling guilty and made himself think that so he'd feel better. Who knows? NYPD didn't find any evidence of foul play, and looking at this report, neither do I."

Sawyer didn't answer. He was in deep thought.

Jackson took the report on Steven Page and put it back in the file. He looked over at Sawyer. "Find anything at Page's office?"

Sawyer focused absently on his partner. "No. But I did find something interesting at his house." He put a hand inside his suit pocket and extracted the photograph labeled "Stevie." He handed the photograph to Jackson. "Interesting, because it was kind of hidden behind some other photo. I'm pretty sure it's a picture of Steven Page."

As soon as Jackson's eyes came to rest on the photo, his mouth dropped open. "Oh, my God!" He rose from his chair. "Oh, my God!" he said again, his voice rising, his hands violently shaking as they clasped the photo. "This can't be—it's not possible."

Sawyer grabbed his shoulder. "Ray, Ray? What the hell is it?"

Jackson ran to another table in the room. He frantically grabbed files, scanned them before tossing them down and snatching up others, his movements becoming more and more frenetic. Finally he stopped, a file open in his hand, his eyes glued to something in the mass of papers within.

Sawyer was beside him in an instant. "Dammit, Ray, what is it?" he said fiercely.

In response, Jackson handed over to his partner an object from the file. Sawyer stared down at the photo in disbelief. In a different pose, the too-handsome face of Steven Page looked back at him.

Sawyer grabbed the photo he had taken from Ed Page's apartment off the table where Jackson had dropped it and looked at the picture again. His eyes swung back to the file photo. There was no doubt, it was the same man in both photos.

A wide-eyed Sawyer looked at Jackson. "Where did you get this photo, Ray?" he asked very slowly, his voice hardly above a whisper.

Jackson licked his lips nervously; his head swayed from side to side. "I can't believe this."

"Where, Ray, where?"

"Arthur Lieberman's apartment."

CHAPTER FORTY-SIX

Subj: Fwd: Not me.
Date: 95-11-26 08:41:52 EST
From: ArchieKW2
To: ArchieJW2

Dear Other Archie: Watch your typing. By the way do you often send mail to yourself? Message a little melodramatic but a nice password nonetheless. Maybe we can talk encryption techniques. Heard one of the best around is the Secret Service's racal-milgo. See you in Cyberspace. Ciao.

Forwarded Message:
Subj: Not me
Date: 95-11-19 10:30:06 PST
From: ArchieJW2
To: ArchieKW2

sid all wrong all backwards/disk in mail099121.19822.
29629.295111.39614 seattlewarehouse-gethelphurryI

Sidney stared at the computer screen; her mind alternated between racing out of control and threatening to shut down. She had been right, though. Jason had mistyped, had hit the k instead of the j. Thank you, ArchieKW2, whoever you are. Fisher had also been right about the password—almost thirty characters long. She assumed that's what the numbers represented: the password.

Her heart sank as she looked at the date of the original message. Her husband had implored her to hurry. There was nothing she could have done about it, and yet she had an overwhelming sense of having let him down. She printed out the single page and put it in her pocket. At least she would finally be able to read what was on the disk. Her adrenaline soared with the thought.

It abruptly went even higher as the sound of someone entering the library reached her ears. She carefully exited the program and turned off the computer. Her hands were shaking as she put the disk back in her purse. She waited for additional sounds, her breath coming in shallow bursts, one hand on the butt of her pistol.

When a sound came from her right, she slipped out of the chair, bent low and proceeded to move quietly to her left. She rounded a corner and stopped. Staring her in the face was a bookshelf of *F.2d,* volumes she had spent much of law school and her first years in practice poring over. She looked through a gap in their ranks at the man in the shadows. She could not make out his face. She didn't dare move farther for fear of making any noise. Then the man started to come directly toward her. Her grip tightened on the Smith & Wesson; her index finger clicked off the safety. She pulled it from the holster as she backed away. Crouching low, she made her way behind a partition, her ears straining for any sound as she desperately tried to think of a way out. The problem was there was only one doorway leading into the library. Her only chance was to circle around, trying to keep a little ahead of whoever was out there until she reached the doorway and could run like hell. A bank of elevators was right down the hallway. If she could make it.

She proceeded to move a few feet and wait, then repeated the process. She had to assume she was making enough noise for the man to hear her but not in a manner, she felt, for him to gauge her strategy. The footsteps from behind matched her maneuvers almost perfectly. That should have been enough to set off alarm bells in her head. She was almost at the doorway and could actually see the frosted glass in the dim light. She gathered her strength and nerve to take a few more steps, and then she would make her run. Five more feet. Now she was almost at the exit. Flattened against the wall, she slowly began to count to three.

She never made it past one.

The bright lights blinded her. By the time she refocused, the man was right next to her. Pupils dilating, she instinctively swung the pistol in his direction.

"My God, have you lost your mind?" Philip Goldman blinked rapidly to adjust to the new level of brightness.

Sidney gaped at him.

"What the devil do you mean, sneaking in here like this? With a gun, no less?"

Sidney stopped shaking and straightened up. "I'm a partner in this firm, Philip. I have every right to be here." Her voice was trembling, but she met his gaze forcefully.

Goldman's voice was sneering. "Not for long, though." He withdrew an envelope from his inner pocket. "Actually, this will save the firm the cost of a messenger." He held out the envelope to Sidney. "Your termination from the firm. If you would kindly just sign it now, it would save everyone a great deal of trouble and rid the firm of an enormous embarrassment."

Sidney did not take the envelope but kept her eyes and the pistol on Goldman.

Goldman fingered the envelope before glancing at the pistol. "Would you mind putting away that gun before you add additional crimes to your résumé?"

"I haven't done a damn thing, and you know it." She spat the words out.

Goldman rolled his eyes. "Of course. I'm sure you were entirely ignorant of your loving husband's nefarious schemes."

"Jason hasn't done anything wrong either."

"Well, I'm not going to argue with you while you have a firearm pointed at me. Would you *please* put it away?"

Finally Sidney began to lower the 9mm. Then something occurred to her. Who had turned on the lights? Goldman hadn't been anywhere near a switch.

Before she had time to react, a strong hand gripped her arm and the pistol was violently jerked from her. A powerful force slammed into her and she was thrown up against a wall. She sank down to the floor, her head splitting with pain from the impact. When she looked up, a burly man dressed in a black chauffeur's uniform stood over her, pointing her own pistol at her head. From behind the gunman, another man appeared.

"Hello, Sid. Gotten anymore phone calls from dead husbands lately?" Paul Brophy laughed.

Shaking, Sidney managed to stand up and lean against the wall while she tried to get her breath back.

Goldman looked over at the burly man. "Good work, Parker. You can go get the car. We'll be down in a few minutes."

Parker nodded and put Sidney's pistol in his coat pocket. She noted that he carried a holstered gun of his own. Much to her dismay, he picked up her purse from the floor where it had fallen during the brief struggle and strode off.

"You've been following me!"

"I like to know the after-hours comings and goings at the firm: an electronic tap on the entry system to the building. I was quite pleased when I saw your name come over the log at one-thirty A.M." He looked at the shelves of legal tomes. "Doing some legal research, or perhaps following your husband's example and trying to steal some secrets?" Sidney would have hit Goldman flush in the face with her fist if Paul Brophy hadn't been too quick for her.

Goldman was unruffled. "Perhaps now we can get down to business." Sidney made a move to lunge through the doorway; Brophy blocked her way, however, pushing her back into the library. Sidney stared a hole through him. "Going from partner in a major firm to burglary in a New Orleans hotel is a big swing, Paul." Brophy's smile disappeared.

Sidney looked over at Goldman. "If I scream right now, someone might hear me."

Goldman responded coolly. "Actually, Sidney, you may have forgotten, but all attorneys and paralegals left earlier today for the firm's annual conference in Florida. They won't be back for several days. Unfortunately, I was called away on unexpected business and have to take an early morning flight down. Paul had a similar predicament. Everyone else is in attendance." He glanced at his watch. "Thus you can scream all you want. However, actually you have every reason to work with us."

Her eyes turned to slits, Sidney looked at both men. "What are you talking about?"

"This conversation might best be carried on in my office." Goldman motioned toward the door and then produced a small-caliber revolver of his own to reinforce the request.

Brophy closed and locked the office door. Goldman handed the gun to him and sat down behind his desk. He motioned for Sidney to sit across from him. "It's certainly been an exciting month for you, Sidney." He produced the termination letter again. "However, I'm afraid your recent excesses have resulted in your tenure at this firm coming to an end. I wouldn't be surprised if the firm and Triton Global instituted civil litigation against you. Possibly criminal action as well."

Sidney's eyes now bored in on Goldman. "You're holding me against my will at gunpoint and you're telling *me* to worry about criminal action?"

"Paul and I, both partners in this firm, observe someone, an intruder, in the firm's library doing God knows what. We attempt to apprehend said suspect and what does she do? She pulls a gun on us.

We're able to wrestle the gun away, fortunately, before anyone is hurt, and now we are detaining that intruder until the police arrive."

"Police?"

"Oh, that's right, I haven't called the police yet, have I? How absentminded of me." Goldman reached for the phone, lifted the receiver and then sat back in his chair without dialing. "Oh, now I remember why I haven't called them." His tone was goading. "Would you like to know the reason?" Sidney didn't answer. "You're a deal lawyer, Sidney. Well, what if I were to propose a deal to you? A way for you to not only remain at liberty but also derive some economic gain, since you now happen to be unemployed."

"Tyler, Stone isn't the only firm in town, Phil."

Goldman winced at the abbreviation of his name. "Well, actually, in your case that's not quite correct. You see, as far as you're concerned, there are no firms left. Not here, not anywhere in this country, perhaps the world."

Sidney's face betrayed her confusion.

"Let's be rational, *Sid.*" Goldman's eyes gleamed momentarily as he returned the verbal joust. "Your husband is suspected of sabotaging a plane, resulting in the murder of almost two hundred people. On top of that it's clear he stole money and secrets worth hundreds of millions of dollars from a client of this firm. Obviously these crimes were planned over a long period of time."

"I haven't heard you mention my name yet in this ridiculous scenario."

"You had high-level access to Triton Global's most important records, perhaps records to which even your husband wasn't privy."

"That was part of my job. That doesn't make it criminal."

"As they are fond of saying in legal circles, and as is embodied in the Canon of Ethics, even the 'appearance of an impropriety' must be avoided. I think that you long ago overstepped that boundary."

"How? By losing my husband? By being railroaded out of my job without a scintilla of proof? Why don't we talk about lawsuits for a minute? Like Sidney Archer versus Tyler, Stone for wrongful termination?"

Goldman looked over at Brophy and nodded slightly. Sidney

turned her head to look at him. Her chin began to tremble when she saw the minicassette recorder emerge from his pocket.

"These things come in so handy, Sid," said Brophy. "Record so clear it's as if you were right there in the same room." He hit the play button.

After a minute of listening to her conversation with her husband, Sidney whirled back around to face Goldman. "What the hell do you want?"

"Well, let's see. I suppose we must first establish market price. What is that tape worth? It establishes that you lied to the FBI. A felony in itself. Then there's aiding and abetting a felon. Accessory after the fact. Another nasty one. The list goes on from there. Neither of us is a criminal lawyer, but I think you get the picture. Father gone, mother in jail. Your little girl is how old? Tragic." He shook his head in mock sympathy.

Sidney jumped out of her chair. "Fuck you, Goldman. *Fuck you both*." Sidney screamed the words in uncontrollable fury. Then she lunged across the desk, gripped Goldman's throat with both hands and would have done him serious damage had Brophy not come once again to the older man's rescue.

Goldman, coughing and gagging, looked furiously at Sidney as soon as she was pulled off. "You ever touch me again, you'll rot in jail," he sputtered.

Breathing hard, Sidney stared wildly at the man. She flung off Brophy's restraining hand but did not move as he kept the gun trained on her. Goldman smoothed down his tie and ruffled shirt and reassumed his confident tone. "Despite your crude reaction, I am actually prepared to be quite generous with you. If you would look at the matter rationally, you would be compelled to accept the offer I'm about to make to you." He cocked his head at her and glanced down at the chair.

Shaking and breathing irregularly, Sidney finally sat back down.

"Good. Now, as succinctly as possible, here is the situation: I know that you have spoken with Roger Egert, who is now in charge of the CyberCom matter. You are privy to Triton's latest proposal regarding the CyberCom acquisition. This I also know to be fact. Now you are also still in possession of the password to the master computer file for the CyberCom transaction." Sidney looked dully at Goldman as her thoughts jumped ahead of his words. "I want both the latest terms of the proposal and the password to the computer file, just in case there are any last-minute changes in Triton's negotiation position."

Sidney's tone was slow, deliberate, her breathing now returned to normal. "RTG must really want CyberCom if they're paying you something other than your hourly rate to violate attorney-client privilege, not to mention stealing corporate secrets."

Goldman merely continued: "In return we are prepared to pay you ten million dollars, tax-free, of course."

"Ensuring my economic stability now that I'm unemployable? And my silence?"

"Something like that. You disappear to some nice little foreign country, raise your little girl in luxury. The CyberCom deal is consummated. Triton Global will continue on. Tyler, Stone will remain a viable firm. No one is the worse off. The alternative? Well, it's something considerably less pleasant. For you. However, time is of the essence. I need your answer in one minute." He stared at his watch, counting the seconds off.

Sidney sat back in her chair, her shoulders slumped as she swiftly thought through the few possibilities left to her. If she agreed, she would be rich. If she didn't, she could and probably would go to jail. And Amy? She thought of Jason and all the terrible events of the past month. More than enough for several lifetimes. She suddenly stiffened as she looked at Goldman's triumphant features, felt the sneering presence of Paul Brophy behind her.

She knew what course of action she would take.

She would accept their terms and then she would play her own cards. She would give Goldman the information he wanted and then she would go straight to Lee Sawyer and tell him everything, including the existence of the disk. She would hope for the best deal she could get and she would expose Goldman and his client for what they were. She wouldn't be rich and she might be away from her little girl if she did any prison time, but she wasn't going to raise Amy with Goldman's extortion money. And, most important, she could live with herself.

"Time," Goldman announced.

Sidney didn't speak.

Goldman shook his head slowly and lifted up the phone receiver once more. Finally, almost imperceptibly, Sidney nodded her head. Goldman rose from behind the desk, a broad smile on his face. "Excellent. What are the terms and the password?"

Sidney shook her head. "My bargaining position is a little fragile. First the money, then the information. Or you can just go ahead and dial 911."

Goldman hesitated for a moment. "Well, as you say, your position is precarious. However, precisely because of that fact, we can be somewhat flexible. Shall we?" He stood up and motioned to the door. Sidney looked confused. "Now that we've reached agreement, I want to fully implement the deal before I let you go. You may be difficult to find later," Goldman explained.

As Sidney rose and turned, Brophy put the revolver into the back of his waistband and intentionally brushed lightly against her with his shoulder, his lips near her ear. "After you get settled down into your new life, you may want some company. I see myself having a lot more free time and more money than I know what to do with. Think about it."

Sidney's knee slamming into his groin sent Brophy to the floor. "I just did, Paul, and I'm trying hard not to be sick to my stomach. Stay away from me if you want to keep what little manhood you've got left."

Sidney walked briskly down the hallway, Goldman right behind her. Brophy finally managed to pull himself up. Clutching his privates, his face pale, he staggered after them.

The limo was waiting for them on the lowest level of the garage next to the elevator bank, its engine running. Goldman held the door while Sidney climbed in. Brophy, still trying to catch his breath and painfully bent over, entered last and sat across from Goldman and Sidney; the darkened glass partition was fully raised behind him.

"It won't take long to make arrangements. You may find it's in your best interests to maintain your present domicile until things cool down a bit. Then we'll fly you to an interim destination. You can send for your daughter and live happily ever after." Goldman's tone was openly jovial.

Sidney's response was all business. "What about Triton and the firm? You mentioned lawsuits?"

"I think that can all be taken care of. Why would the firm want to immerse itself in such embarrassing litigation? And Triton really can't prove anything, can it?"

"So why should I deal?"

Brophy held up the minicassette recorder, his face still flushed. "Because of this, you little bitch. Unless you want to spend the rest of your life in prison."

Sidney's manner remained calm. "I'll want that tape."

Goldman shrugged. "Impossible for now. Perhaps later, when things have returned to normal."

Goldman looked at the glass partition. "Parker?"

The partition slid down.

"Parker, we can go now."

The arm coming through the now open space between the front and back of the limo held a gun. Brophy's head exploded and he fell face down onto the floor of the limo. Goldman and Sidney were both splattered with his blood, among other things. Goldman's mouth dropped open and he yelled in disbelief as the pistol turned in his direction. "Oh, God. No! Parker!"

The bullet slammed into his forehead and Philip Goldman's long career as an exceedingly arrogant attorney came to a decisive end. He jolted backward in the seat from the bullet's impact, blood covering his face as well as the rear glass of the limo. Then he slumped over against Sidney, who screamed as the gun now swiveled in her direction. Her fingernails dug into the soft leather seat in her panic. For an instant she stared at the face that was covered by a black ski mask and then her eyes zeroed in on the gleaming muzzle that hovered barely five feet from her face. Every detail of the pistol was seared into her memory as she awaited her death.

Then the gun was pointed toward the right-side door of the limo. As Sidney sat frozen, the arm motioned more firmly toward the door. Trembling and unable to understand what was happening other than the fact that she apparently was not going to die, Sidney managed to push Goldman's limp form off her and started to climb over Brophy's body. While she awkwardly made her way across the dead lawyer, her hand slipped on a patch of blood and she fell on top of him. She instantly jerked back. As her fingers clawed for a solid grip, she felt the hard object under Brophy's shoulder. Her fingers instinctively closed around the metal. With her back to the gunman, she was able to tuck Brophy's revolver into her coat pocket without being observed.

When she opened the door, something hit her in the back. Frightened out of her mind, she managed to turn around and eyed her purse where it had fallen on top of Brophy's body after bouncing off her. Then her eyes caught hold of the computer disk Jason had sent her as the hand holding it disappeared back through the partition. With trembling hands she picked up her purse, pushed open the heavy door all the way and fell out of the car. Then she staggered up and raced away with every ounce of energy in her possession.

Back in the limo the man leaned through the partition. Next to him in the front seat, Parker was slumped over, a bullet hole in his right temple. The man carefully picked up the minicassette recorder where it had fallen on the seat of the limo and played a few seconds of it. He nodded to himself when he heard the voices and then carefully moved Brophy's body slightly to the side, slid the recorder several inches under his body and let him slump back to his original position. The disk was put away in the man's fanny pack. His last act was to carefully pick up the three shell casings ejected from the pistol. He couldn't make it too easy for the cops. Then the man exited the limo, the gun he had used to murder three people carried in a baggie for deposit in an out-of-the-way place, but not so out of the way that the police would fail to uncover it.

Kenneth Scales took off the ski mask. Under the bright lights of the empty garage the deadly blue eyes twinkled with deep satisfaction. Another night's work successfully completed.

*   *   *

Sidney punched the elevator button again and again until finally the doors opened. She slumped against the wall of the elevator car. She was covered in blood. She could feel it on her face, her hands. It was all she could do not to start shrieking at the top of her lungs. She just wanted to get it off her. With an unsteady hand she hit the button for the eighth floor.

As soon as she got to the ladies' room and saw her bloody image in the mirror, she threw up in the sink, then dropped to the floor, where she lay moaning, the dry heaves pounding her unmercifully. Finally she managed to pull herself up and wash off the blood as best she could. She continued to pour hot water over her face until its sting began to calm the shakes; she kept raking shaky fingers through her hair, probing for things that did not belong there.

Leaving the rest room, she ran down the hallway to her office and grabbed a spare trench coat that she kept there. It effectively covered the remnants of blood that had refused to come off. Then she picked up the phone and prepared to dial 911. She gripped the .32 with her other hand. She could not shake the feeling that at any moment that gleaming pistol would be pointed in her direction again. That the man behind the black mask would not let her live a second time. She had keyed two of the numbers. Then her hand froze as the vision hit her. In the limo: the barrel of the gun staring her in the face. Then its image as it swung toward the door. That's when she saw it.

The grip. The cracked grip. Cracked when she had dropped the gun back at her home. The man had her gun. Two men had just been murdered with her 9mm.

Another vision burned into her brain. The tape of her and Jason's conversation. That too was back there, with the dead men. The reason why she had been left alive became abundantly clear to Sidney Archer: She had been allowed to live so that she could rot in jail for murder. Like a terribly frightened child, she scrambled back into the far corner of her office and slumped across the floor, her body quivering uncontrollably, tears and moans spilling out of her, with absolutely no sign of ever stopping.

CHAPTER FORTY-SEVEN

Sawyer was still staring at the photo of Steven Page, the dead man's face looming larger and larger in his mind until he finally had to drop the picture and turn away before it completely engulfed him.

"I just assumed it was a photo of one of Lieberman's kids. They were all on his desk together. I never thought to connect up that he has *two,* not three children." Jackson slapped his forehead. "It just didn't seem all that important. Then when the investigation shifted away from Lieberman to Archer—" Jackson shook his head in obvious misery.

Sawyer sat on the edge of the table. Only those closest to him would realize that the veteran FBI agent was more stunned than he had ever been in his professional life.

"I'm sorry, Lee." Jackson snatched another look at the photo and cringed. Sawyer softly patted his partner on the back. "It's not your fault, Ray. Under the circumstances it wouldn't have seemed important to me either." Sawyer stood up and started pacing. "But now it sure as hell is. We'll need to verify that it is Steven Page, although I really don't have any doubt about it." He abruptly stopped pacing.

"Hey, Ray, NYPD could never figure out where Steven Page got all that money, right?"

Jackson's mind clicked into high gear. "Maybe Page was blackmailing Lieberman. Perhaps over his affair. They were both in finance, same professional circles. That would explain the money Page had."

Sawyer shook his head. "A number of people seemed to know about the mistress—not much opportunity for blackmail there. Besides, most people don't keep photos of their blackmailers on display, Ray." Jackson looked sheepish. "No, I think it cuts deeper than that." Sawyer leaned against the wall of the conference room, folded his arms and sunk his head on his chest. "By the way, what did you ever get on our elusive mistress?"

Jackson took a minute to consult a file. "A lot of nothing. I found a number of people who had heard rumors. Unsubstantiated rumors, they were quick to point out. They were terrified of being named or involved. I had to do some quick soft-shoe to calm them down. It was the damnedest thing, though: They had all heard about her, could describe her pretty well, although each description I got was a little different than the last. But—"

"But nobody could tell you definitively that they had ever actually met the mystery lady."

"Jackson's face scrunched up. "Yeah, that's right. How'd you know that?"

Sawyer took a deep breath. "You ever play that game as a kid, Ray, where somebody tells you something and you tell somebody else and they tell somebody else? By the time it gets to the end of the line, the information is nothing like it started out to be. Or how a rumor gets started and spreads and everybody believes it to be the gospel, could almost swear they had personally seen whatever it was, and none of it is true."

"Hell, yes. My grandmother reads the *Star*. She believes everything in it and talks like she actually saw Liz Taylor getting it on with Elvis on the space shuttle."

"Right. It's not true, not one bit of it, but people will tell you it is, fervently believe that it is, simply because they've read about it or heard it, especially if they've heard it from more than one person."

"Are you saying . . ."

"I'm saying that I don't think the blond mistress ever existed, Ray. More to the point, I think she was created for a specific purpose."

"Like what?"

Sawyer took a very deep breath before answering. "To cover the fact that Arthur Lieberman and Steven Page were lovers."

Jackson dropped into a chair as he stared at Sawyer. "Are you serious?"

"The photo of Page at his apartment, next to his kids? Those love letters you found at the apartment? Why not sign them? A week's pay says the handwriting matches Steven Page's. And last but not least, Page being a millionaire on a working man's salary? Very doable if you're by chance *sleeping* with a guy who's made lots of people millionaires."

"Yeah, but why invent a story about a mistress? It could've blown Lieberman's chairmanship bid."

Sawyer was shaking his head. "In this day and age, Ray, who knows? If that were the criterion, a big chunk of the political leadership in this country would have to pack up and go home. And the fact is it didn't stop him from getting the Fed's top post. But do you think the outcome would've been the same if it was discovered Lieberman was homosexual and had a male lover less than half his age? Keep in mind that the financial community in this country is one of the most conservative you'll find anywhere."

"Okay, he would've been screwed, that's for damned sure. But talk about your double standards. It's okay to commit adultery, so long as it's with someone of the opposite sex."

"Right, you invent a phony heterosexual affair to cover the true homosexual one. They used to do that out in Hollywood with leading men who weren't attracted to the opposite sex. The studios would orchestrate phony marriages. All a complicated sham to preserve a lucrative career. Lieberman's scam wasn't a perfect fix, but it gets him the brass ring. His wife may or may not have known the truth. But she gets paid off big-time, so she's not going to talk. And she's six feet under now. So no loose lips there."

Jackson wiped his brow. "Jesus." He looked at Sawyer, puzzled. "If that's the case, then Steven Page's death *was* a suicide; there would be no reason to kill him."

Sawyer was shaking his head. "There would be every reason to kill him, Ray."

"Why?"

Sawyer paused for a moment, looked down at his hands and spoke quietly. "Want to make an educated guess as to how Steven Page contracted HIV?"

Jackson's eyes bulged. "Lieberman?"

Sawyer looked up. "I'd be real interested to find out whether Lieberman was HIV-positive."

Jackson's confusion suddenly cleared. "If Page knows he might be terminal, he'd have no reason to keep quiet."

"Right. Getting a terminal illness from one's lover doesn't normally inspire loyalty. Steven Page held Arthur Lieberman's professional future in his hands. I think that equals sufficient homicidal motive, in my book."

"So it looks like we need to approach this case from an entirely new angle."

"Agreed. Right now we have a lot of speculation, but not really a damn thing we can take to a prosecutor."

Jackson got out of his chair, started to tidy up the files. "So you really think Lieberman had Page killed?"

When Sawyer didn't answer, Jackson turned to find him staring off into space.

"Lee?" Sawyer finally looked over at him.

"I never said that, Ray."

"But—"

"I'll see you in the morning. Get some sleep, you're going to need it." Sawyer got up and walked to the door leading out of the conference room. "I've got somebody I need to speak to," Sawyer said.

"Who?"

Sawyer turned back momentarily. "Charles Tiedman, president of the San Francisco Federal Reserve Bank. Lieberman never got a chance to talk to him. I think it's about time somebody did."

Sawyer left Jackson bent over the stacks of files, his mind reeling.

CHAPTER FORTY-EIGHT

Sidney Archer picked herself up off the floor. As the twin feelings of hopelessness and fear faded away, they were slowly replaced with an even stronger impulse: survival. She unlocked one of her desk drawers and pulled out her passport. She had been called overseas on a moment's notice more than once in her legal career. But now the reason would be about as personal as one could get: her life. She went to the office next to hers. It belonged to a young associate who happened to be a rabid Atlanta Braves fan; a good portion of one of his shelving units mirrored that loyalty. She snatched the baseball cap off the shelf, bobby-pinned her long hair up, and pulled the cap down tight over her head.

She thought to check her purse. Amazingly, her wallet was still full of hundred-dollar bills from the New Orleans trip. The killer hadn't touched those. Exiting the building, she hailed a cab, gave the driver her destination and slid appreciatively into the seat as the vehicle sped away. She carefully slid the late Philip Goldman's .32 revolver out of her pocket, inserted it into the belt holster Sawyer had given her, and then buttoned up her trench coat.

The cab pulled in front of Union Station and she got out. She never would have gotten through airport security with her handgun, but she had no such worry traveling on Amtrak. Her plan, at the outset, was simple: Run to a safe place and try to figure things out. She planned on contacting Lee Sawyer, but she didn't want to be in the same country as the FBI agent when she did. The problem was she *had* tried to help her husband. She *had* lied to the FBI. A stupid act in retrospect, but at the time it was the only thing she could do. She had to help her husband. She had to be there for him. Now? Her gun was at a murder scene; the tape of her conversation with Jason was there as well. Despite her coming partially clean with Sawyer, what would he think now? Now, she was certain, the handcuffs would come out. She started to sink into despair again, but she gathered her courage, turned up her collar in the face of the icy wind and entered the railway terminal.

She bought a coach ticket on the next Metroliner train bound for New York City. The train would leave in about twenty minutes and would deposit her at Penn Station in midtown New York at about five-thirty in the morning. A cab ride would take her to JFK Airport, where she would buy a one-way plane ticket on an early morning flight to some country, she wasn't sure which one yet. She went to the ATM machine on the lower level of the train station and withdrew some more cash. As soon as an APB was put out on her, the plastic would be useless. It suddenly occurred to her that she had no other clothes and that she would have to travel as much as possible incognito. The problem was that none of the innumerable clothing shops were open in the terminal at this time of night. She would have to wait until she got to New York.

She stepped inside a phone booth and consulted her small address book; Lee Sawyer's card tumbled out. She stared at it for a long moment. *Dammit!* She had to, she owed the man. She dialed Sawyer's home number. After four rings the answering machine came on. She hesitated and then slammed the phone down. She dialed another number. It seemed to ring indefinitely until a sleepy voice answered.

"Jeff?"

"Who's this?"

"Sidney Archer."

Sidney could hear Fisher fumbling in his bedcovers, probably looking for the clock. "I waited up to hear from you. Must've fallen asleep."

"Jeff, I don't have much time. Something terrible has happened."

"What? What's happened?"

"The less you know, the better." She paused and struggled through her thoughts. "Jeff, I'm going to give you the number where I can be reached right now. I want you to go to a pay phone and call me back."

"Christ, it's . . . it's after two A.M."

"Jeff, please, just do what I ask."

After a little grumbling, Fisher assented. "Give me about five minutes. What's the number?"

Barely six minutes later, the phone rang. Sidney snatched it up. "You're at the pay phone. You swear?"

"Yes! And I'm freezing my ass off. Now talk to me."

"Jeff, I've got the password. It was in Jason's e-mail. I was right, it was sent to the wrong address."

"That's fantastic. Now we can read the file."

"No, we can't."

"Why not?"

"Because I lost the disk."

"What? How did you do that?"

"It doesn't matter. It's gone. I can't get it back." Sidney's misery was evident in her voice. She collected her thoughts. She was going to tell Fisher to leave town for a while. He could be in danger, serious danger, if her experience in the parking garage was any indicator. She froze at Fisher's words.

"Well, you're in luck, lady."

"What are you talking about?"

"I'm not only security conscious, I'm anal as hell. I've lost too many files over the years that weren't backed up properly, Sid."

"Are you saying what I think you are, Jeff?"

"While you were in the kitchen when we were working on trying to decrypt the file . . ." He paused somewhat dramatically. "I made a couple copies of the files on the disk. One on my hard drive and one on another floppy."

Sidney couldn't speak at first. When she did, her response made Fisher blush. "I love you, Jeff."

"When do you want to come over so we can finally see what's on that sucker?"

"I can't, Jeff."

"Why not?"

"I have to go out of town. I want you to send the disk to an address I'm about to give you. I want you to FedEx it. Drop it off first thing in the morning. First thing, Jeff."

"I don't understand, Sidney."

"Jeff, you've been a big help, but I don't want you to understand it. I don't want you involved any more than you already are. I want you to go home, get the disk and then go stay at a hotel. The Holiday Inn in Old Town is near your place. Send me the bill."

"Sid—"

"As soon as the FedEx office opens in Old Town, I want you to drop the package off," she repeated. "Then call in to the office, tell them you're extending your vacation for a few more days. Where does your family live?"

"Boston."

"Fine. Go to Boston and stay with them. Send me the bill for your transportation. Fly first class if you want. Just go."

"Sid!"

"Jeff, I have to get off in a minute so don't argue with me. You have to do everything I've just told you. It's the only way you can be reasonably safe."

"You're not kidding, are you?"

"Do you have something to write with?"

"Yes."

She flipped through her address book. "Write down this address. Send the package there." She gave him her parents' mailing address and phone number in Bell Harbor, Maine. "I'm truly sorry I had to involve you in this at all, but you're the only one who could help me. Thank you." Sidney hung up.

Fisher put the phone back in its cradle, looked warily around the darkened area, ran to his car and drove home. He was about to park his car at the curb when he noticed a black van about a block behind him. As he squinted in the dark light, Fisher was able to discern two figures in the front seat of the van. His breathing immediately accelerated. He did a slow U-turn in the middle of the street and headed back toward the heart of Old Town. He didn't look at the driver as he passed by the van. When he checked his mirror again, the van was following him.

Fisher pulled his car to a stop in front of the two-story brick building. He looked up at the sign: CYBER@CHAT. Fisher was good friends with the owner and had even helped set up the computer systems offered at Cyber@Chat.

The bar stayed open all night and with good justification. Even at this hour it was three-quarters full, mostly with a college-age crowd who didn't have to get up and go to work the next morning. However, instead of blaring music, rowdy patrons and a smoky atmosphere (because of the sensitive computer equipment, no smoking was allowed) the interior was filled with the sounds of computer games and low, often intense discussions about whatever was tripping its way across the abundance of computer monitors in the place. The age-old art of flirting still took place, and men and women roamed the room in search of companionship, however brief.

Fisher found his friend, the owner, a young man in his twenties, behind the bar and struck up a friendly conversation. Explaining enough of his situation to enable his friend to assist him, Fisher discreetly handed across the piece of paper containing the address in Maine Sidney had given him. The owner disappeared into the back room. Within five minutes Fisher was entrenched behind one of the computers. As he briefly peered out the window of the bar, the black van came to a stop in an alleyway across the street. Fisher turned back to the computer.

A waitress brought over a bottle of beer and a glass, and a plate of munchies. As she set the plate down next to the computer, she put a linen napkin next to it. Inside the carefully folded napkin was a blank three-and-a-half-inch disk. Fisher nonchalantly unfolded the napkin and quickly slid the disk into the computer's floppy drive. He typed in a series of characters and the high-decibel dialing of a phone modem could be heard. Within a minute, Fisher was connected to his computer at home. It took about thirty seconds for him to download the computer files he had copied from Sidney's disk onto the blank disk. He looked out the window again. The van had not moved.

The waitress came over to his table. Obviously privy to his plan, she asked if he needed anything else. On her tray was a padded FedEx envelope with the Bell Harbor address typed on the mailing label. Fisher looked out the window again. Then down the street he noticed two policemen standing next to their patrol cars shooting the breeze. When the waitress reached for the disk, which had been part of the plan hastily fleshed out with the bar's owner, Fisher shook his head. Sidney's warning had come back to him. He didn't want to involve his friends unnecessarily in any of this and now maybe he didn't have to. He whispered to the waitress. She nodded and took the FedEx envelope into the back room, returning barely a minute later. She handed another padded envelope across to Fisher. He looked down at it and smiled when he saw the metered postage label on the envelope. His friend had been very liberal in his estimation of what it would cost to mail the small package, even certified, return receipt requested. It was definitely not going to be returned for insufficient postage. It wasn't as fast as FedEx, but it would have to do under the circumstances, Fisher concluded. He slipped the disk into the envelope, sealed it and put it in his coat pocket. He then paid his bill, leaving a healthy tip for the waitress. He dabbed some of the beer on his face and clothes and then tipped the glass back and finished it in one gulp.

As he exited the bar and walked toward his car, the van's headlights came on and Fisher could hear the engine start up. The van headed toward him. Fisher started staggering and then singing loudly. The two cops down the street turned their heads in his direction. Fisher gave them an exaggerated salute and a bow before he collapsed into his car, started the engine and drove off toward the cops on the wrong side of the street.

As he hurtled by the police, his squealing tires doing at least twenty over the speed limit, the cops jumped in their cruisers. The van followed at a safe distance but then turned off when the police cruisers caught up to Fisher. His hazardous driving and the smell of beer on his breath earned Fisher a pair of handcuffs and a quick trip to the police station.

"I hope you know a good lawyer, fella," the cop barked from the front seat.

Fisher's response was completely lucid and tinged with more than a trace of humor. "Actually, I know a number of them, Officer."

At the police station he was fingerprinted and his possessions inventoried. He was allowed to make one phone call. Before he did so, however, he politely asked the desk sergeant to do him a favor. A minute later Fisher watched gleefully as the padded envelope was dropped into the police station's U.S. mail chute. The "snail mail." If his techie friends could only see him now. On his way to the holding cell, Jeff Fisher actually broke into a cheerful whistle. It wasn't wise to screw around with an MIT man.

To his pleasant surprise, Lee Sawyer did not have to travel to California to speak with Charles Tiedman. After a phone call to the Federal Reserve, Sawyer learned that Tiedman was actually in Washington for a conference. Although it was almost three in the morning, Tiedman, still operating on West Coast time, had quickly agreed to speak to the agent. In fact, it seemed to Sawyer that the San Francisco Federal Reserve Bank president was very eager to talk to him.

At the Four Seasons Hotel in Georgetown where Tiedman was staying, Sawyer and Tiedman sat across from each other in a private room adjacent to the hotel restaurant, which had closed several hours earlier. Tiedman was a small, clean-shaven man in his early sixties who had a habit of nervously clasping and unclasping his hands. Even at this hour of the night, he was dressed in a somber gray pinstripe with a vest and bow tie; a tasteful gold watch chain spanned the vest. Sawyer could envision the dapper little man wearing a soft felt cap and tooling around in a roadster with the top down. His conservative appearance smacked much more of the East Coast than the West, and Sawyer learned quickly in the preliminary conversation that Tiedman had spent a good many years in New York before heading to California. For the first few minutes of their meeting he would only occasionally seek direct eye contact with the FBI agent, usually keeping his watery gray eyes, which were covered with a fragile pair of wire-rimmed spectacles, squarely on the carpeted floor.

"I take it you knew Arthur Lieberman quite well," said Sawyer.

"We attended Harvard together. We both started out at the same banking firm. I was the best man at his wedding, and he at mine. He was one of my oldest and dearest friends."

Sawyer took advantage of the opening. "His marriage ended in divorce, right?"

Tiedman eyed the agent. "That's right," he replied.

Sawyer consulted his notebook. "In fact, that was right about the time he was being considered to head the Fed?"

Tiedman nodded.

"Lousy timing."

"You could say that." Tiedman poured out a glass of water from the carafe on the table next to his chair and took a long drink. His thin lips were dry and chafed.

"I understand the divorce started out being really nasty but was soon enough settled and really didn't affect his nomination. Guess Lieberman lucked out."

Tiedman's eyes blazed. "You want to call that lucky?"

"All I meant was he got the Fed job. I assume that as a close personal friend of Arthur's you probably know more about it than just about anyone." Sawyer looked at Tiedman with frank, questioning eyes.

Tiedman didn't say anything for a full minute, then he let out a deep breath, put his glass down and settled back in his chair. Now he looked directly at Sawyer.

"While it's true that he became chairman of the Fed, it cost Arthur just about everything he had worked for over the years to make his 'nasty' little divorce go away, Mr. Sawyer. It wasn't fair after a career such as his."

"But the chairmanship paid good money. I looked up the salary. A hundred thirty-three thousand six hundred dollars per year. He was much better off than most."

Tiedman laughed. "That may be true, but before Arthur joined the Fed he earned hundreds of millions of dollars. Consequently, he had expensive tastes, and some debt."

"A lot of debt?"

Tiedman's eyes again went to the floor. "Let's just say the debt was somewhat more than he could afford on his Fed salary, despite its relatively large size."

Sawyer let that information sink in while he asked another question. "What can you tell me about Walter Burns?"

Tiedman looked sharply at Sawyer. "What do you want to know?"

"Just general background stuff," Sawyer replied innocently.

Tiedman rubbed at his lip in a distracted manner and eyed Sawyer's notebook. Sawyer caught the glance and abruptly closed the pad. "Off the record."

Tiedman looked resignedly at Sawyer. "I have no doubt Burns will succeed Arthur as chairman. It's quite fitting. He was a follower of Arthur's. However Arthur voted, Walter did too."

"Was that a bad thing?"

"Not usually."

"What does that mean?"

The little man's expression became astonishingly sharp when he focused on the agent's face. "It means that it is never wise to follow placidly along when good judgment should dictate otherwise."

Sawyer leaned back in his chair. "Meaning you didn't agree with Lieberman all the time."

Tiedman was not looking at the agent now. His features betrayed what he was thinking, however. It was clear that he now intensely regretted ever allowing this interview.

"Meaning that members of the Federal Reserve Board are placed on that board to exercise their own minds and their own judgments and not to blindly succumb to arguments that have little basis in reality and could lead to disastrous consequences."

"That's a pretty big statement."

"Well, it's a pretty big job we have."

Sawyer referred to his notes from the conversation with Walter Burns. "Burns said Lieberman took the bull by the horns early on, to get the market's attention, to shake it up. I take it you thought that wasn't such a good idea."

"Ludicrous would be a better term."

"If it was so off-the-wall, why did a majority go along?" Sawyer was a little skeptical.

"There's a phrase that critics of economic forecasting like to use: Give an economist a result you want, and he'll find the numbers to justify it. This entire city is filled with number crunchers who look at the exact same data and interpret it in widely disparate ways on everything from the federal budget deficit to the Social Security surplus."

"Meaning that data can be manipulated."

"Of course it can, depending on who's paying the meter and whose political agenda is being furthered," Tiedman said with asperity. "You've no doubt heard the principle that for every action there is an equal and opposite reaction?" Sawyer nodded. "Well, I'm convinced its genesis is political rather than scientific."

"No disrespect, but could it be they thought your views were wrong?"

"I am not omniscient, Agent Sawyer. However, I have been intimately involved in the financial markets for the last forty years. I have seen up and down markets. I have seen robust economies and ones teetering on collapse. I have seen Fed chairmen take prompt, effective action when confronted with crisis and I have seen others flounder badly, with the result that the economy gets tipped on its head. An ill-advised half-percent increase in the Fed Funds Rate can cost hundreds of thousands of jobs and absolutely devastate whole sectors of the economy. It is an enormous power that must not be exercised lightly. Arthur's zigzagging with the Fed Funds Rate placed every American citizen's economic future in serious jeopardy. I was not wrong."

"I thought you and Lieberman were close. Didn't he ask for your advice?"

Tiedman fingered his coat button nervously. "Arthur had previously sought out my counsel. Often. For a period of about three years he stopped doing that."

"Was that the period during which he played roller-coaster with the rates?"

Tiedman nodded. "I finally concluded, as did others on the board, that Arthur was punching a lazy financial market flush in the face. But that is not the board's mission, it's far too dangerous. I lived through the last stages of the Great Depression. I have no desire to do so again."

"I guess it never occurred to me how much power the board wields."

Tiedman looked sternly at him. "Do you know that when we decide to raise rates we can tell fairly precisely how many businesses will declare bankruptcy, how many people will lose their jobs, how many homes will be foreclosed? We have all that data, neatly bound, carefully studied. To us it's only numbers. We never, officially, look behind those numbers. If we did, I don't think any of us would have the stomach for the job. I know that I wouldn't. Perhaps if we started tracking suicide, murder and other criminal statistics, we would be more understanding of the vast powers that we hold over our fellow citizens."

"Murder? Suicide?" Sawyer looked at him warily.

"Surely you would be the first to admit that money is the root of all evil. Or perhaps more accurately stated, the *lack* of money is the root of all evil."

"Jesus, I never really thought of it that way. You sort of hold the power of . . ."

"God?" Tiedman's eyes sparkled. "Do you know how much money the Fed wire-transfers out to maintain its policies and to insure that the commercial banking system operates smoothly?" Sawyer shook his head. "One trillion dollars per day."

Sawyer sat back, stunned. "That's a lot of money, Charles."

"No, that's a lot of power, Agent Sawyer. We're one of this country's best-kept secrets. Indeed, if average citizens were fully aware of what we can do and have often done in the past, I believe they'd storm the walls and cast us all into dungeons, if not worse. And maybe they would be right."

Sawyer looked down at his notes. "Do you know the dates those rate changes occurred?"

Tiedman retreated from his musings. "Not offhand. An astonishing admission for a banker, but my memory isn't all that good with numbers anymore. I can get you the answer, though."

"I'd appreciate it. Could there have been another reason why Lieberman went nuts with the rates?" Now Sawyer clearly saw the twinge of anxiety mixed with fear in the man's features.

"What do you mean?"

Sawyer leaned back in his chair. "You said it was out of character for him. And then he abruptly returned to normal. Doesn't that sound mysterious to you?"

"I guess I never thought about it in that light. I'm afraid I still do not understand your point."

"Let me put this as clearly as I can. Maybe Lieberman was manipulating the rates against his will."

Tiedman's eyebrows shot up. "How could anyone make Arthur do that?"

"Blackmail," Sawyer said simply. "Any theories?"

Tiedman regrouped and began speaking nervously. "I had heard rumors that Arthur was having an affair, years ago. A woman—"

Sawyer broke in. "I don't buy that and neither do you. Lieberman paid off his wife to avoid a scandal so he could run the Fed, but it wasn't over a woman." Sawyer leaned forward so that his face was within inches of Tiedman's. "What can you tell me about Steven Page?"

Tiedman's face froze, but only for an instant. "Who?"

"This might jog your memory." Sawyer reached in his pocket and pulled out the photo Ray Jackson had found in Lieberman's apartment. He held the photo up in front of Tiedman.

Tiedman took the photo in quivering hands. His head bent low, his long brow a sea of creases. However, Sawyer could see the recognition in the man's eyes.

"How long have you known about this?" Sawyer asked quietly.

Tiedman's mouth moved, but no words came out. He finally handed the photo back to Sawyer and took another drink of water. He didn't look at Sawyer when he spoke, which seemed to make the words come a little easier. "I was actually the one who introduced them," was Tiedman's surprising reply. "Steven worked at Fidelity Mutual as a financial analyst. Arthur was still president of the New York Fed at that time. I was introduced to Steven at a financial symposium. Many colleagues whom I respected sang his praises loudly. He was an exceptionally bright young man with some intriguing ideas on the financial markets and the Fed's role in the evolving global economy. He was personable, cultured, attractive; he'd graduated near the top of his college class. I knew that Arthur would find him a welcome addition to his circle of intellectual acquaintances. He and Arthur quickly struck up a friendship." Tiedman faltered.

"A friendship that eventually blossomed into something else?" Sawyer prompted.

Tiedman nodded.

"Were you aware at the time that Lieberman was homosexual, or at least bisexual?"

"I knew that his marriage was troubled. I did not know, at the time, that the trouble stemmed from Arthur's sexual . . . confusion."

"He seemed to solve that confusion. He divorced his wife."

"I don't think that was Arthur's idea. I believe Arthur would have been perfectly happy keeping intact at least the facade of a happy heterosexual marriage. I know that more and more people 'come out' these days, but Arthur was an intensely private man and the financial community is very conservative."

"So the missus wanted the divorce. Did she know about Page?"

"His specific identity? No, I don't think so. But I believe she knew Arthur was having an affair, and that it wasn't with a woman. I believe that was why the divorce was so acrimonious and so one-sided. Arthur had to act quickly, lest his wife tell her attorneys, even, about her suspicions. It cost him every penny he had. Arthur only disclosed this information to me as the most personal secret one friend could tell another. And I only tell it to you under those same strict, confidential terms."

"I appreciate that, Charles," Sawyer said. "Only you have to understand if Lieberman was the reason that plane went down, I have to explore every possibility to solve that crime. However, I can promise you that I won't use the information you've just given me unless it directly impacts on my investigation. If it turns out Lieberman's affair is not connected, then no one will ever learn from me what you've just disclosed. Fair enough?"

"Fair enough," Tiedman finally said. "Thank you."

Sawyer noted Tiedman's exhaustion and decided to move forward quickly. "You're familiar with the circumstances of Steven Page's death?"

"I read about it in the paper."

"Did you know that he had tested positive for HIV?"

Tiedman shook his head.

Sawyer sat back. "A couple more questions. Did you know that Lieberman had terminal pancreatic cancer?" Tiedman nodded. "How did he feel about it? Devastated? Hurt?"

Tiedman didn't answer immediately. He sat quietly, his hands clasped in his lap. Then he looked at Sawyer. "Actually, Arthur seemed happy."

"The guy was terminal and he seemed happy?"

"I know it sounds strange, but it's the only way I can describe it. Happy and relieved."

The puzzled FBI agent thanked Tiedman and left, his head swimming with an entirely new set of questions and no way, as yet, to answer them.

CHAPTER FORTY-NINE

Sidney sat alone in the dining car as the train rumbled through the night on its way to New York. While darkened images flew past the windows, she distractedly sipped at a cup of coffee and nibbled on a microwave-warmed muffin. The steady clicking of the train wheels and the car's gentle swaying as it headed up the much-traveled northeast corridor soothed her.

For a good part of the train trip her mind focused on her daughter. It seemed like an eternity since she had held her little girl. Now she had no idea when she would see her again. The only thing keeping her away was the certainty that if she tried to see Amy, she would bring harm to her little girl. She would never do that, not even if it meant never seeing her again. She would call, though, as soon as she got into New York. She wondered how she could explain to her parents the next nightmare that awaited them: the headlines proclaiming their overachieving, cherished daughter a murderer now on the run. She could do nothing to shield them against the onslaught of attention that would be hurtling their way. That attention would find its way to Bell Harbor, Maine, she was sure, but perhaps her parents' trip north would buy them some precious time away from the hideous spotlight.

Sidney knew she had only one shot to unravel whatever it was that had come and blasted her life to hell. That opportunity lay in the information in the hard plastic shell that would soon be speeding its way north as fast as Federal Express could ship it. The disk was all she had. Jason seemed to think it vitally important. If he was wrong? She shuddered and forced her thoughts away from that potential nightmare. She had to trust her husband on that one. She peered out the window as a blur of trees, modest homes with crooked TV antennas and the cracked, ugly cinder blocks of abandoned businesses raced by. She huddled into her coat and lay back in the seat.

As the train rolled into the dark caverns of Penn Station, Sidney stood by the exit door. Her watch proclaimed it was five-thirty in the morning. She didn't really feel tired, although she couldn't remember the last time she had slept. Penn Station was fairly crowded for that hour of the morning. Sidney waited in the cab line and then decided to make a quick phone call before she went to JFK. She planned to dump the gun before leaving for the airport. However, the cold metal gave her a feeling of security she desperately needed right now. She still had not decided where she was traveling, but at least the cab ride to the airport would give her time to think of a destination.

On her way to the pay phone, she grabbed a copy of the *Washington Post* and scanned the headlines. Nothing about the murders had appeared yet; however, the bodies could have been found and the reporters might simply not have had time to file their stories before deadline. If her two former partners hadn't been found yet, it would not be long now. The parking garage opened to the public at seven A.M. but it could be accessed at any time by tenants of the building.

She dialed her parents' number in Bell Harbor. An automated message greeted her and announced that the number was not in service. She groaned as she suddenly remembered why. Her parents always had the phone turned off during the winter. Her father had probably forgotten to turn the service back on. He would certainly do so once he got up there. Since it wasn't back on, that meant they probably hadn't arrived yet.

Sidney swiftly calculated travel times. When she had been a child, her father would drive all the way through, about thirteen hours, stopping along the way only for food and gas. As he had grown older, though, he had become more patient. Ever since his retirement, he would stop along the way for the night, break the trip up into two days. If they had left early yesterday afternoon, as planned, that would put them in Bell Harbor at about midafternoon today. *If* they had left as planned. It suddenly occurred to Sidney that she had not verified her parents' departure yet. She decided to correct that oversight immediately. The phone rang three times and then the answering machine picked up. She spoke into the phone to let her parents know it was she. They often screened their calls. However, no one picked up the phone. She put the phone receiver back. She would try again from the airport. She checked her watch and decided to make one more phone call. Now that she knew of Paul Brophy's involvement with RTG, something didn't make sense to her. There was only one person she could think of to ask about it. And she had to do it before news of the murders reached the public.

"Kay? It's Sidney Archer."

The voice on the other end of the line was sleepy at first and then wide awake as Kay Vincent sat up in bed. "Sidney?"

"I'm sorry to call so early, but I really need your help on something." Kay didn't answer. "Kay, I know what all the papers have been saying about Jason."

Kay's voice cut her off. "I don't believe any of that stuff, Sidney. Jason could never have been involved in any of that."

Sidney breathed a sigh of relief. "Thank you for saying that, Kay. I was beginning to think I was the only one who hadn't lost the faith."

"Not by a long shot, Sidney. How can I help you?"

Sidney took a moment to calm her nerves, to keep her voice from shaking too much. She eyed a police officer walking down the hallway of the train station. She turned her back to him and hunched against the wall. "Kay, you know Jason never really talked to me about his work."

Kay snorted. "It's no small wonder. It's beaten into our heads here: Everything's one big secret."

"Right. But now secrets don't do me any good. I need to know what Jason was working on the last few months. Were there any big projects he was on?"

Kay shifted the phone to her other ear. Her husband was snoring on the other side of the bed. "Well, you know he was working on organizing the financial records for the CyberCom deal. That took a lot of his time."

"Right, I knew something about that one."

Kay chuckled. "He'd come back from that warehouse looking like he'd just mud-wrestled an alligator, filthy from head to toe. But he kept at it and did a great job. In fact, he really seemed to enjoy it. The other thing he spent a lot of time on was the integration of the company's tape backup system."

"You mean the computer system storing automatic copies of e-mails and documents and such?"

"Right."

"Why did they need an *integration* of the tape backup system?"

"Well, as you probably could've guessed, Quentin Rowe's company had a first-rate system before it was bought out by Triton. But Nathan Gamble and Triton didn't. Between you and me, I don't think Nathan Gamble knows what a tape backup is. Anyway, Jason's job was to integrate Triton's previous backup systems into Quentin's more sophisticated one."

"What exactly would the integration entail?"

"Going through all of Triton's backup files and formatting them into a shape that would be compatible with the new system. E-mails, documents, reports, graphs—anything created on the computer system. He finished that one too. The whole system is now fully integrated."

"Where were the old files kept? At the office?"

"Oh, no. At the storage facility over in Reston. Boxes stacked ten high. Same place where the financial records were stored. Jason spent a lot of time there."

"Who authorized those projects?"

"Quentin Rowe."

"Not Nathan Gamble?"

"I don't think he even knew about it initially. But he does now."

"How can you be sure?"

"Because Jason got an e-mail from Nathan Gamble commending him on the job he had done."

"Really? That doesn't sound like Nathan Gamble."

"Yeah, it surprised me too. But he did."

"I suppose you don't recall the date of that e-mail, do you?"

"Actually, I do, for a terrible reason."

"What do you mean?"

Kay Vincent sighed deeply. "It was the day of the plane crash."

Sidney jerked upright. "You're sure?"

"There was no way I could forget that, Sid."

"But Nathan Gamble was in New York on that day. I was there with him."

"Oh, that doesn't matter. He has his secretary send out his e-mails on a preset schedule regardless of whether he's in the office or not."

That didn't make any sense to Sidney. "Kay, I suppose there's been no more news on the CyberCom deal, has there? The records issue is still hanging things up?"

"What records issue?"

"Gamble didn't want to turn over the financial records to Cyber-Com."

"I don't know anything about that. I do know that the financial records have already been turned over to CyberCom."

"What?" Sidney almost screamed out the word. "Did any attorneys at Tyler, Stone look them over first?"

"I don't know about that."

"When did they go out?"

"Ironically, same day as Nathan Gamble sent Jason that e-mail."

Sidney's head was spinning. "The day of the plane crash? You're absolutely sure of that?"

"I'm real good friends with one of the mail-room clerks. They recruited him to help transport the records to the copy department and then he helped deliver them to CyberCom. Why? Is that important for some reason?"

Sidney finally spoke. "I'm not sure if it is or not."

"Oh, well, do you need to know anything else?"

"No, Kay, you've given me plenty to think about." Sidney thanked her, hung up the phone and headed for the cab stands.

Kenneth Scales looked down at the message he was holding in his hands, his eyes narrowing. The information on the disk was encrypted. They needed the password. He looked over at the one individual who they now knew had to be the recipient of that precious e-mail. Jason wouldn't have sent the disk to his wife without sending the password as well. That had to be the e-mail message Jason had sent from the warehouse. The password. Sidney stood in the cab line outside Penn Station. He should have just taken care of her in the limo. It was neither his practice nor to his liking to leave anyone alive. But orders were orders. At least she had been kept on a short leash until they knew where the e-mail had gone. Now he had marching instructions he could truly sink his deadly blade in. He moved forward.

When Sidney's cab pulled up, she caught a reflection in the window of the vehicle. The man was only focused on her for an instant, but with her nerves set on high, it was long enough. She whirled around and their eyes locked for one terrifying moment. The same devilish eyes from the limo. Scales cursed and raced forward. Sidney jumped in the cab and it roared off. Scales pushed several people waiting ahead of him in line aside, threw the protesting cab stand attendant to the pavement and leaped into the next available cab. It sped after Sidney.

Sidney looked behind her. Through the darkness and driving sleet she couldn't make out much. However, traffic was relatively light at this time of the morning and she saw a pair of headlights swiftly approaching. She turned back around. "I know this is going to sound crazy, but we're being followed." She gave the driver another destination. He made a hard left, then a sharp right and roared down an empty side street and then back out onto Fifth Avenue.

Sidney's cab pulled to a stop in front of a skyscraper. She jumped out and raced toward the entrance, pulling something out of her purse as she did so. She stuck the access card into the slot in the wall and the door clicked open. She went inside, pulling the door closed behind her.

The security guard at the granite console in the lobby looked up sleepily. Sidney dug once more in her bag and produced her Tyler, Stone ID card. The guard nodded and slumped back in his chair. Sidney glanced back once more as she hit the elevator button. Only one elevator car was activated this early in the morning. The second cab screeched to a stop in front of the building and a man jumped out and raced over to the glass doors and pounded on them. Sidney watched as the guard got up from his chair.

Sidney called to him. "I think that man was following me. He might be a nut. Please be careful."

The guard eyed her for a minute and then nodded. He looked back over at the doorway. One hand slipped down to the pistol in his holster as he strode over to the doorway. Sidney glanced back once more before she got on the elevator. The guard was looking up and down the street. Sidney breathed a sigh of relief and got on the elevator, hitting the button for the twenty-third floor. Moments later she entered the darkened Tyler, Stone suite and hurried into an office. She hit a light, pulled out her address book, consulted a phone number and dialed.

She was calling her parents' longtime neighbor and family friend, seventy-year-old Ruth Childs. Ruth answered the phone on the first ring, and from her brisk tone it was clear, despite it being a little after six in the morning, that she had been up for a while. Ruth tenderly commiserated with Sidney over her recent loss and then, in response to Sidney's query, reported that the Pattersons and Amy had left yesterday around two o'clock after hastily packing for their trip. She knew Bell Harbor was the destination, but that was all.

"I saw your father put his shotgun case in the trunk, Sidney," Ruth said provocatively.

"I wonder why," was Sidney's weak response. She was about to say good-bye when Ruth said something that made Sidney's heart skip a beat.

"I have to admit I was kind of worried the night before they left. There was a car driving by at all hours. I don't sleep much, and when I do, it doesn't take much to wake me up. It's a quiet neighborhood, you know that. Nothing out here unless you're going to see someone for a visit. The car was back yesterday morning."

"Did you see anyone in the car?" Sidney's voice was trembling.

"No, my eyes aren't what they used to be, even with trifocals."

"Is the car still there?"

"Oh, no. It left right after your parents did. Good riddance, I say. I've got my baseball bat by the door, though. Just let somebody try to break in my house. They'll wish they hadn't."

Before hanging up, Sidney told Ruth Childs to be careful and to call the police if the car showed up again, which Sidney was certain it wouldn't. The car was far away from Hanover, Virginia. It was, she was almost positive, on its way to Bell Harbor, Maine. And now, so was she.

She hung up the phone and turned to leave. That's when she heard the ding of the elevator car arriving at the floor she was on. She didn't stop to wonder who might be arriving this early. She immediately assumed the worst. She pulled out the .32 revolver and ran out of the office in the opposite direction from the elevator. At least she had the advantage of knowing the office layout.

Flying feet behind her confirmed her worst suspicions. She ran as hard as she could, her purse flapping against her side. She could hear the person's breath as he turned onto the darkened corridor she was on. He drew closer. She ran faster than she had since her college basketball days, but it clearly wasn't going to be fast enough. She would have to try a different tactic. She rounded a corner, stopped, spun around and knelt down in a shooting stance, the revolver pointed straight ahead. The man, charging hard, hurtled around the corner and stopped dead barely two feet from her. She glanced at the knife in his hand, the blood still gleaming on its blade. His body seemed to tense for an all-out attack. As if sensing that, Sidney sent a round sailing just past his left temple.

"The next one hits your brain." Sidney stood up, her eyes glued to his face, and motioned for him to drop the knife, which he did. "Move," she barked, pointing behind him with the gun. She backed him down the hallway until they reached a metal door.

"Open it."

The man's eyes bore into her. Even with the gun pointed right at his head, she felt like a kid with a slender stick confronting a rabid dog. He opened the door wide and looked inside. The lights automatically came on. It was the copy room, a large operation with massive machines, stacks of paper and all the other mundane items required by a busy law firm. She motioned through the doorway to another door at the far end of the copier room. "In there." He moved through the doorway. Sidney caught the door and held it open as she watched him move across the room. He looked back at her as he opened the other door. It was a storage closet for office supplies.

"That door opens, you're dead." Holding the door open with her shoulder, the gun still trained directly on him, she reached across to a counter just inside the room and made a show of picking up a telephone. As soon as the man closed the door, Sidney put down the phone, quietly closed the copier room door and raced down the hallway to the elevators. She hit the button and the door immediately opened. Thank God it had remained on the twenty-third floor. She jumped on and pushed the button for the first floor, all the time listening for the man coming for her. She kept the revolver trained on the opening, but the office remained quiet. As soon as she reached the first floor, she hit all the buttons up to the twenty-third floor and jumped off the elevator. She let out her breath and allowed herself a small smile. It quickly turned to horror as she rounded the corner and almost fell over the security guard's body. Forcing herself not to scream, she raced out of the building and down the street.

*   *   *

It was seven-fifteen in the morning and Lee Sawyer had just closed his eyes when the phone rang. He flopped a big hand over and picked it up.

"Yeah?"

"Lee?"

Sawyer's groggy brain snapped into high gear and he sat up. "Sidney?"

"I don't have much time."

"Where are you?"

"Just listen!" She was once again standing at a pay phone in Penn Station.

He switched the phone to his other ear as he threw the bedcovers off. "Okay, I'm listening."

"A man just tried to kill me."

"Who? Where?" Sawyer sputtered as he grabbed a pair of pants off the bed and started to shove them on.

"I don't know who he is."

"Are you okay?" he asked anxiously.

Sidney looked around at the crowded train station. A number of New York's finest were in attendance. Problem was, they were the enemy now too. "Yes."

Sawyer let out a deep breath. "Okay, what's going on?"

"Jason sent an e-mail to our house after the plane crash. There was a password in that e-mail."

"What?" Sawyer started to sputter again. "Jesus Christ, an e-mail, you said?" Sawyer's face was now blood-red. He stamped around the room, throwing on a shirt, socks and shoes while holding the cordless phone.

"I don't have time to tell you how I eventually received the e-mail, only that I now have it."

With a massive effort at self-control, Sawyer managed to calm down. "Well, what the hell did it say?"

From the pocket of her coat, Sidney pulled out the single sheet of paper containing the e-mail. "Do you have something to write with?"

"Hold on."

Sawyer ran into the kitchen and snatched a piece of paper and pen from a drawer. "Go ahead. But make sure you give it to me exactly as it appears."

Sidney did so, including the absence of spaces between certain words and the decimal points segregating portions of the password exactly as they appeared on the printed page she was holding. Sawyer stared down at what he had written. He went back through it again with her for accuracy.

"Do you have any idea what this message means, Sidney?"

"I haven't had much time to focus on it. I know that Jason said it was all wrong, and I believe him. It is all wrong."

"But what about this disk? Do you know what's on it?" He quickly read the message again. "Did you get it in the mail?"

Sidney hesitated and then said, "I haven't yet."

"Is the password for the disk? Is it an encrypted file?"

"I didn't know you were such a computer expert."

"I'm just full of surprises."

"Yes, I believe it is."

"When do you expect to get it?"

"I'm not sure. Look, I have to go."

"Wait a minute. The guy who tried to kill you. What'd he look like?"

She gave him a description. The thought of the maniacal blue eyes made her shudder. Sawyer wrote it down. "I'll run it through the system and see what comes up." He jolted upright. "Wait a minute, I've got you under surveillance. What the hell happened to my guys? Aren't you at your house?"

Sidney swallowed hard. "I'm not exactly under surveillance right now. At least not by your people. And no, I'm not at my house."

"Then would you mind telling me where you are?"

"I've got to go."

"The hell you do. Some creep just tried to punch your clock, my guys are nowhere on the scene. I want to know what's going on," he raged.

"Lee?"

He calmed down slightly. "What?" he said gruffly.

"Whatever happens, whatever you encounter, I want you to know that I haven't done anything wrong. Nothing." She choked back some tears and added softly, "Please believe that."

"What are you talking about? What the hell's that supposed to mean?"

"Good-bye."

"No! Wait!" The phone clicked in his ear and he angrily slammed it down. He looked at the message and then put it down on the table next to the phone. He bent over. His knees felt wobbly, his stomach more upset than normal. He went into the bathroom and gulped down some liquid Maalox. Wiping his mouth with the back of his hand, he returned to the kitchen, picked up the piece of paper he had written the e-mail down on and sat down at the small table. He silently mouthed the words as he read them. *Watch your typing.* The first portion of the message seemed to suggest that Archer had sent the message to the wrong person. Sawyer read the recipient's name and then the sender's. Sidney said Jason had sent the e-mail to their house. ArchieJW2. That had to be Jason Archer's e-mail name, his last name and initials. Then ArchieKW2 was the person the message had initially gone to. Jason Archer had hit the *K* instead of the *J*, that seemed clear enough. ArchieKW2 had sent the message back to the *sender* with a message about the mistake, but in doing so had actually delivered it to the intended *destination:* Sidney Archer.

The reference to the Seattle warehouse made sense. Jason had evidently run into some serious trouble with whomever he was meeting. The exchange had somehow gone bad. *All wrong?* Obviously, Sidney had pounced on it as proof of her husband's innocence. Sawyer wasn't so sure about that. *All backwards?* That seemed to be an awkward phrase. Next, Sawyer stared at the password. Jesus, Jason was truly a brain if he could pull that long a password off the top of his head. Sawyer could make no sense out of it. He squinted and parked his face closer to the paper. Jason obviously had not had the opportunity to finish the message.

Sawyer stretched his kinked neck from side to side and leaned back in his chair. The disk. They had to get the disk. Or, more accurately, Sidney Archer would have to get it. His thoughts were interrupted by the ringing phone. Certain it was Sidney calling back, he snatched it up.

"Yeah?"

"Lee, it's Frank."

"Christ, Frank, can't you ever call during normal business hours?"

"It's bad, Lee. Real bad. Law firm of Tyler, Stone. The underground garage."

"What is it?"

"Triple homicide. You better get down here."

Sawyer put the phone down. Sidney's last words to him had just taken on real meaning. *Sonofabitch!*

The street leading into the underground parking garage was a sea of red and blue lights as police and emergency vehicles parked everywhere. Sawyer and Jackson flashed their badges at the security line. A concerned-looking Frank Hardy met them just inside the entrance and led them to the lowest level of the garage, four stories underground, where the temperature in the garage was well below freezing.

"Looks like the murders took place very early this morning, so the trail's reasonably fresh. The bodies are in good shape, too, except for some extra holes in them," Hardy said.

"How did you find out about it, Frank?"

"The firm's managing partner, Henry Wharton, was notified by the police in Florida, where he's on firm business. He called Nathan Gamble; Gamble, in turn, immediately informed me."

"So I take it whoever got bumped was affiliated with the law firm?" Sawyer asked.

"You can see for yourself, Lee. Everybody's still here. But let's say Triton has a particular interest in these murders. That's why Warton called Gamble so fast. We also just found out that the security guard at Tyler, Stone's office in New York was murdered early this morning."

Sawyer stared at him. "New York?"

Hardy nodded.

"Anything else on it?"

"Not yet. But there were reports of a woman running out of the building about an hour before the body was discovered."

Sawyer digested this new development as the men walked through the throng of police and forensics personnel to the driver's side of the sleek limo. Both doors were open. Sawyer observed the print technicians completing their dusting of the limo's exterior. A crime scene photographer was snapping away, while another technician was filming the area with a video camera. The medical examiner, a middle-aged man wearing a white dress shirt with shirtsleeves rolled up, tie tucked inside the shirt, and sporting plastic gloves and a surgical mask, was consulting with two men wearing dark blue trench coats. Then the two men walked over to join Hardy and the FBI agents.

Hardy introduced Sawyer and Jackson to Royce and Holman, a pair of D.C. homicide detectives. "I've briefed them on the bureau's interest in the case, Lee."

"Who found the bodies?" Jackson asked Royce.

"Accountant who worked in the building. Arrived a little before six. His parking space is down here. He thought it was odd to see a limo here at this hour, particularly since it was blocking a bunch of other parking spaces. The glass on the vehicle is all tinted, as you can see. He tapped on the door, got no response. So he opened the passenger door. Bad decision. I think he's still upstairs puking. At least he managed to call it in."

The men moved over to the limo. Hardy motioned for the FBI agents to have a look. After peering inside the front and back, Sawyer looked up at Hardy. "Guy on the floor looks familiar."

"He should be: Paul Brophy."

Sawyer looked over at Jackson.

"Gentleman in the backseat with the third eye is Philip Goldman," Hardy stated.

"RTG's counsel," Jackson said.

Hardy nodded. "Victim in the front seat is James Parker, an employee of the local RTG subsidiary; the limo is registered to RTG, by the way."

"Hence, Triton's interest in the case," Sawyer said.

"You got it," Hardy said.

Sawyer leaned back in the limo and studied the wound on Goldman's forehead before scanning Brophy's body. Over his shoulder, Hardy continued, his tone calm and methodical. He and Sawyer had worked innumerable homicides together. At least here all body parts were intact. They had viewed many where that was not the case. "All three died from gunshot wounds. Appears to be heavy-caliber, fired from close proximity. Parker's wound is a contact one. Brophy's looked to be a near-contact, the little I was able to see of it. Goldman probably bought it from about three feet, maybe more, considering the burn pattern on the forehead."

Sawyer nodded in agreement. "So the shooter may have been in the front seat. Took out the driver first, Brophy next, and then Goldman last," he ventured.

Hardy didn't look convinced. "Maybe, although the killer could have been sitting next to Brophy, facing Goldman. Popped Parker through the partition opening, shot Brophy and then Goldman, or vice versa. We'll have to wait for the autopsy to get the exact trajectory of the shots. That may give us a better idea of the order." He paused and then added, "Along with some other residue." The interior of the limo was indeed a grisly sight.

"Got an approximate time of death yet?" Jackson asked.

Royce checked his notes. "Rigor hasn't peaked yet—far from it, actually. Lividity isn't fixed either. They're all in similar stages of postmortem, so it looks like they all bought it at roughly the same time. Coupled with the body temp, ME just gave me a preliminary of four to six hours."

Sawyer checked his watch. "Eight-thirty now. So anywhere between two and four this morning."

Royce nodded.

Jackson shivered as a cold draft swept down on them when the elevator doors opened to emit additional police. Sawyer grimaced as he watched clouds of breath floating everywhere. Hardy smiled. "I know what you're thinking, Lee. Nobody screwed with the air-conditioning like with your last corpse, but as cold as it is down here—"

"I'm not sure how accurate that time of death is going to be,"

Sawyer finished for him. "And I feel pretty certain that every minute we're off is gonna be real significant."

"Actually, we've got an exact time of entry for the limo into the garage, Agent Sawyer," Royce volunteered. "Access is limited to those having valid key cars. The garage's security system records who enters by the individual card used to access the premises. Goldman's card was entered at one-forty-five this morning."

"So he wouldn't have been here long before it all went down," Jackson ventured. "At least it gives us a benchmark."

Sawyer didn't answer. He rubbed his jaw as his eyes continued to dart around the crime scene. "Weapon?"

Detective Holman pulled out an object enclosed in a large sealed plastic bag. "One of the uniforms found this in a nearby sewer drain. Luckily it had gotten hung up on some debris lodged in there or we might never have found it." He handed the baggie to Sawyer. "Smith & Wesson nine-millimeter. Hydra-Shok rounds. Serial numbers intact. Shouldn't be much trouble tracing it. Three rounds short of a full clip. And we've preliminarily accounted for a total of three wounds in the victims." All of the men could easily see the traces of blood on the pistol, which was natural enough if it had been used to perpetrate a contact wound. "Sure looks to be the murder weapon," Holman continued. "Shooter picked up the ejected shell casings, but the slugs appear to still be in all the victims, so we'll get a definitive match from ballistics depending on projectile deformity."

Even before he was handed the pistol, Sawyer had already noted it. So had Jackson. They looked at each other with a sinking feeling: the cracked grip.

Hardy noticed the exchange. "You got something?"

Sawyer sighed. "Shit," was all he could think to say at the moment. He shoved his hands deep in his pockets, looked over at the limo and then back at the murder weapon. "I'm ninety-nine percent sure this gun belongs to Sidney Archer, Frank."

"What was that name again?" Both homicide detectives piped in almost simultaneously.

Sawyer filled the detectives in on Sidney's identity and connection to the law firm.

"Right, the paper ran a story on her and her husband. I knew the name was familiar. That explains a hell of a lot," Royce said.

"How's that?" Jackson asked.

Royce consulted his notebook. "The front entrance to the building also tracks who enters and leaves after hours. One-twenty-one this morning, guess whose security card was entered?"

"Sidney Archer's," Sawyer said with a weary tone.

"Bingo. Damn, husband *and* wife. Nice couple. We'll get her, though. Bodies are fresh, not too much of a head start." Royce sounded confident. "We've already lifted a slew of partials from the limo. We'll run them against the dead men for elimination purposes and then focus on the remaining ones."

"I wouldn't be surprised if Archer's prints turned up all over the place," Holman said. He cocked his head at the limo. "Particularly with all the blood in there."

Sawyer turned to the detective. "Got a motive?"

Royce held up the recorder. "Found this under Brophy. It's already been dusted." The detective hit the play button. They all listened to the tape until it stopped a few minutes later. Sawyer's face flushed.

"That's Jason Archer's voice," Hardy said. "Know it well." He shook his head. "Now if we just had a body to go along with the voice."

"And that's Sidney's voice," Jackson added. He looked over at his partner, who was leaning against a support column, looking miserable.

Sawyer assimilated the new information and plugged it into the mutating landscape this case had become. Brophy had taped the conversation the morning they had gone to interview Sidney. That's why the sonofabitch had looked so pleased with himself. That also explained his trip to New Orleans and his little frolic and detour through Sidney's hotel room. Sawyer grimaced. He never would have disclosed voluntarily what Sidney had told him about the phone call. Only now the secret was out. She had lied to the FBI.

Even if Sawyer testified—which he would do in a minute—that she had later disclosed to him the details of the phone call, she had still made plans to aid and abet a fugitive. Now she was looking at throw-away-the-key prison time. Amy Archer's tiny face intruded on his thoughts and his shoulders slumped even farther.

As Royce and Holman drifted away to continue their investigation, Hardy walked over to Sawyer. "You want my two cents?"

Sawyer nodded. Jackson joined them.

"I probably know a couple things that you don't. One being that Tyler, Stone was terminating Sidney Archer," Hardy said.

"Okay." Sawyer's eyes remained fixed on Hardy.

"Ironically, the letter of termination was found on Goldman's person. It could've gone down like this: Archer comes down to the office on her own for some reason. Maybe it's innocent, maybe it's not. She meets up with Goldman and Brophy, either by accident or arrangement. Goldman probably made Sidney Archer very familiar with the contents of the termination letter, and then they spring the tape on her. That's pretty heavy blackmail material."

"I agree the tape is very damaging, but what would they blackmail her for?" Sawyer's eyes were still fixed on his friend.

"Like I told you before, up until the plane crash, Sidney Archer was lead counsel on the CyberCom deal. She was privy to confidential information. Information that RTG would be dying to get their hands on. The price for that information is the tape. She either gives them the deal info or she goes to prison. The firm is terminating her anyway. What the hell does she care?"

Sawyer looked confused. "But I thought her husband had delivered that information to RTG already. The exchange on the videotape."

"Deals change, Lee. I know for a fact that since Jason Archer's disappearance the terms of Triton's offer for CyberCom have changed. What Jason gave them was old news. They needed fresh stuff. Ironically, what the husband couldn't give them, the wife could."

"Sounds like they would've made a deal, then. So how does the killing part come in, Frank? Just because it was her gun doesn't mean she fired it." Sawyer was now being argumentative.

Hardy ignored the tone, continuing on with his analysis. "Maybe they couldn't agree to terms. Maybe things turned ugly. Maybe they decided the best way was to get the information they needed and then dispose of her. Maybe that's why they ended up in the limo. Parker was carrying a gun; it was still in his holster, unfired. There might have been a struggle. She pulls her piece, fires and kills one of them in self-defense. Horrified, she decides not to leave any witnesses."

Sawyer was shaking his head vigorously. "Three able-bodied men against one woman? Doesn't make sense that the situation would've gotten out of their control. Assuming she was in the limo, I can't believe she would've been able to kill all three and just walk away."

"Maybe she didn't just walk away, Lee. She might've been wounded, for all we know."

Sawyer looked at the concrete floor beside the limo. There were several bloodstains, but none readily visible farther away from the limo. Inconclusive at best, but Hardy's scenario was plausible.

"So, she kills all three and then leaves without the tape. Why?"

Hardy shrugged. "Tape was found under Brophy. The guy was big, at least two hundred pounds of literally dead weight. It took two heavyweight cops to move the body when they were trying to I.D. him. That's when they spotted the tape. The simple answer may be that she physically couldn't get to it. Or maybe she didn't know it was under there. From the looks of it, it fell out of his pocket when he went down. Then she panicked and just ran. She tosses the gun in the sewer and gets the hell out of Dodge. How many times have we both seen that happen?"

Jackson looked at Sawyer. "Makes sense, Lee."

Sawyer, however, was doubtful. He walked over to Detective Royce, who was signing off on some paperwork.

"You mind if I call some of our forensics people in to check out a few things?"

"Hell, be my guest. I rarely turn down an assist from the FBI. You guys got all those federal dollars. Us? We're lucky if we have gas in the cars."

"I'd like to run a few tests on the interior of the limo. I'll have my team here within twenty minutes. I'd like them to do the exam with the bodies still in place. Then I'd like to do a more thorough search—minus the bodies, of course—back at the lab. Tow's on us."

Royce considered the request for a moment and then said, "I'll get the necessary paperwork in order." He looked suspiciously at Sawyer. "Look, I'm always glad of the bureau's help, but this *is* our jurisdiction. I'd be more than a little ticked to see credit misplaced when this one gets solved. You hear what I'm saying?"

"Loud and clear, Detective Royce. It's your case. Whatever we learn is yours to use in solving the crime. I sincerely hope it earns you a promotion and a nice raise."

"You *and* my wife."

"Can I ask a favor?"

"You can always ask," Royce replied.

"You mind having one of your techs get gunshot residue samples from each of the three corpses? We're running out of time on that one. I can have my people analyze the samples."

"You think one of them might have fired the gun?" Royce looked highly doubtful.

"Maybe, maybe not. We can pretty much tell one way or another, though."

Royce shrugged and motioned for one of his techs to come over. After instructing her on what was wanted, they watched as she lugged over a battered, bulky crime scene kit, opened it and began preparations to perform a gunshot residue test, a GSR. However, time was running out: Samples optimally had to be collected within six hours of the gun having been fired, and Sawyer was afraid they were about to miss that deadline.

The tech dipped a number of cotton swabs in a diluted nitric acid solution. Separate swabs were rubbed over the front and back of each corpse's hands. If any of them had fired a gun recently, then testing would reveal deposits of barium and antimony, primer charge components used in the manufacture of virtually all ammo. It wasn't conclusive. If a positive result came back, it wouldn't necessarily mean any of them had fired the murder weapon, only *some* firearm within the last six hours. In addition, they could have merely handled the firearm after it had been fired—for instance, in a struggle—and gotten the residue from the exterior of the weapon after it had just been fired. But a positive GSR result could conceivably help Sidney Archer's cause, Sawyer figured. Even though all the evidence seemingly pointed to her involvement in the homicides, Sawyer was dead certain she hadn't pulled the trigger.

"One more favor?" Sawyer asked Detective Royce. Royce's eyebrows shot up. "I'd like a copy of that tape."

"Sure. Whatever."

Sawyer rode the elevator back up to the lobby, walked to his car and phoned in for the FBI's forensics team. While he waited for them to arrive, one thought beat relentlessly through Sawyer's head. *Where the hell was Sidney Archer?*

CHAPTER FIFTY

Usually eschewing any except the most modest makeup, Sidney now took great pains to stencil in her face with considerable detail, holding up her compact as she stood in the stall in the women's rest room at Penn Station. She had concluded that the man pursuing her wouldn't have figured her to come back here. She then put on a tan leather cowboy hat, pulling the brim down low over her forehead. With enough artificial color on her face to almost qualify for hooker status and her bloody clothes in a shopping bag destined for a Dumpster, she walked out of the rest room attired in an assortment of garments she had spent the better part of the day acquiring: tight stone-washed blue jeans, pointy beige cowboy boots, thick white cotton shirt and a heavily insulated black leather bomber jacket. She looked nothing like the conservative Washington, D.C., attorney she had recently been and whom the police would soon be hunting down for murder. She made certain the .32 was carefully hidden away in an inner pocket. New York's gun laws were among the stiffest in the country.

A half-hour ride northeast on the commuter train took her to Stamford, Connecticut, one of a string of bedroom communities feeding the working New Yorker's desire to live outside the hyper-kinetic metropolis. A taxicab ride of twenty minutes took her to a lovely white brick home with black shutters nestled in a quiet neighborhood of similarly high-priced residences. The name PAT-TERSON was stenciled on the mailbox. Sidney paid the cabdriver, but instead of going to the front door she walked around back to the garage area. Next to the garage door hung a large, ornate wooden bird feeder. Sidney looked around and then stuck her hand into the feed, pushing through the rough particles until she got to the bot-tom of the feeder. She pulled out the set of keys buried there, went over to the back door, put a key in the lock and the door opened. Her brother, Kenny, and his family were in France. He was incredibly bright, ran a very successful independent publishing business, but was also absentminded as hell. He had locked himself out of every home he had ever owned, hence the keys in the bird feeder, a fact well known to every member of his family.

The home was old, solidly built and beautifully decorated, with large rooms and comfortable furnishings. Sidney did not have time to enjoy the surroundings. She went into a small study. Against one wall was a large enclosed oak cabinet. Using another key from the key ring, Sidney opened the heavy double doors and viewed the con-tents of the cabinet: An impressive array of shotguns and pistols loomed in front of her. She settled on a Winchester 1300 Defender. The twelve-gauge shotgun was relatively light, weighing in under seven pounds. It chambered three-inch Magnum shells that would stop anything on two legs, and, perhaps most important, sported an eight-shot magazine. She put several boxes of Magnum shells into one of her brother's ammo bags she had pulled from a drawer in the cabinet. Next she looked over the pistols hanging on special hooks mounted into the wall of the cabinet next to the shotgun collection. She had little confidence in the stopping force of the .32. She picked up several of the pistols, testing them for weight and comfort. Then she smiled as her hand closed around an old familiar: a Smith & Wesson Slim Nine complete with unblemished grip. She grabbed the pistol and a box of 9mm ammo, stuffed it in the same bag with

the shotgun loads and locked the cabinet back up. Snagging a pair
of binoculars off another shelf, Sidney left the room.

She ran upstairs to the master bedroom and spent several minutes
going through her sister-in-law's clothing. Soon Sidney had assembled a suitcase full of warm clothing and footwear. A thought suddenly struck her. She switched on the small TV in the bedroom. She
channel-surfed until she found an all-news station. The top story of
the day was being recounted, and though she had been expecting it,
her heart sank when her face appeared on the screen next to a picture of the limo. The news story was brief but devastating in portraying her inescapable guilt. Sidney received another shock as the
screen split into two and she was joined by a photo of Jason. He
looked tired in the photo, which she instantly recognized as the one
on his Triton security badge. Apparently the media were finding the
husband-wife master criminal angle an engaging one. Sidney studied her own face on the screen. She too looked tired, her hair plastered down on either side of her head. She and Jason looked . . .
guilty, she concluded. Even if they weren't. But right now, most of
the country would believe them to be villains, a modern-day Bonnie
and Clyde.

She rose on unsteady legs and on a sudden impulse went into the
bathroom, where she stripped off her clothes and climbed in the
shower. The sight of the limo had reminded her that she still carried
vestiges on her person of those horrible few moments. She had closed
and locked the bathroom door upon entering. Keeping the shower
curtain wide open, she never left her back exposed to the door. The
loaded .32 revolver lay within easy reach. The hot water took the
chill off her bones. By accident she glimpsed her exhausted, gaunt
face in the small mirror affixed to the shower wall and shuddered at
the sight. She felt tired and old. Emotionally and mentally spent,
her body was giving way on her. She could feel the physical decline
inch by miserable inch. Then she gritted her teeth and slapped herself in the face. She couldn't give up now. She was an army of one,
but a damned determined one. She had Amy. That was something
no one would ever take away from her.

Finished with her shower, she dressed warmly and raced to the mudroom, where she grabbed a heavy-duty flashlight off a hook. It had suddenly occurred to her that the police would be checking with all of her family and friends. She carried everything out to the garage, where she eyed the dark blue Land Rover Discovery, one of the sturdiest vehicles ever built. She put her hand under the left fender and pulled out a set of car keys. Her brother really was something. She turned off the sophisticated car security system by punching the tiny button on the car key, slightly wincing at the weird birdlike sound made by the deactivation. She was careful to place the shotgun on the floorboard of the backseat with a heavy blanket over it. The pistols were placed in the ammo bag, which was shoved under the front seat.

The V-8 engine roared to life. Sidney hit the door opener that was clipped to the visor and backed the Land Rover out of the garage. Carefully searching the street for any people or vehicles and finding none, Sidney eased the two-ton truck out of the driveway and onto the road, rapidly gathering speed as she left the quiet Stamford neighborhood.

Within twenty minutes she had reached Interstate 95. Traffic was heavy and it took her a while before she left Connecticut behind. She sliced her way through Rhode Island and made the loop around Boston by one in the morning. The Land Rover was equipped with a cellular phone; however, after her informative talk with Jeff Fisher, Sidney was reluctant to use it. Besides, who would she call? She stopped once, in New Hampshire, to grab some coffee and a candy bar and to fill the gas tank. The snow was now coming down full-tilt, but the Land Rover easily plowed through it, and the flapping sound of the windshield wipers at least was keeping her awake. By three in the morning, however, she was nodding off at the wheel so frequently that she had to pull over finally at a truck stop. She wedged the Land Rover in between two Peterbilt OTR semis, locked the doors, slid into the backseat, gripped the loaded 9mm with one hand and fell asleep. The sun was well up by the time she awoke. She grabbed a quick breakfast at the truck stop and within a few hours was well past Portsmouth, Maine. Two hours later she saw the exit she was seeking and turned off the highway. She was now on

U.S. Route 1. At this time of year, Sidney had the road pretty much to herself.

In the blur of heavy snow she passed the small sign announcing her arrival into the town of Bell Harbor, population 1,650. While she was growing up, her family had spent many wonderful summers in the peaceful town: private, wide beaches, ice-cream sundaes and juicy sandwiches at the innumerable eateries in the resort town, a show at the town's very own playhouse, long bike rides and walks along Granite Point, where one could observe, up close, the ominous power of the Atlantic on a windy afternoon. She and Jason had planned one day to buy a beach house near her parents. They both had looked forward to spending summers up here, watching Amy run along the beach and dig pools in the sand much as Sidney had done twenty-five years before. It was a nice thought. She hoped it was still capable of becoming reality. Right now none of it seemed even remotely possible.

Sidney made her way toward the ocean, finally turning south onto Beach Street, where she slowed down. Her parents' house was a large, two-story affair of gray weathered board with dormer windows and a deck running the width of the house on both the upper-level ocean side and the street side. A garage occupied the basement level of the house. The ocean wind funneling in between the close-together beach houses managed to rock even the tanklike Land Rover. Sidney could not remember ever being in Maine at this time of year. The sky looked particularly unfriendly. When she glimpsed the endless darkness of the Atlantic, it occurred to her that she had never seen snow falling into the ocean before.

She slowed down slightly as her parents' house came into view. All of the other beach homes on the street were uninhabited. In winter, Bell Harbor was akin to a ghost town. Added to that, the Bell Harbor Police Department numbered all of one during off-season months. If the man who had calmly killed in a stretch limo in Washington and tracked her to New York decided to come after her again, he would be more than a match for Bell Harbor's finest of one. She grabbed the ammo bag from under the seat and put a clip in her 9mm. She pulled into her parents' snow-covered drive and got out.

There was no sign that her parents had arrived. They must have stopped along the way because of the weather. She pulled the Land Rover into the garage and shut the door. She unloaded it and carried the items up the interior stairs leading from the garage to the house.

She had no way of knowing that the heavy snow had covered up very recent tire tracks in her parent's yard. Nor did she venture into the back bedroom, where numerous pieces of luggage were neatly stacked. As she entered the kitchen, she couldn't see the car passing slowly by the house and then continuing on.

The interior of the FBI testing facility was going full steam. The white-coated FBI technician walked around the exterior of the limo, motioning Sawyer and Jackson to follow her. The left-side rear passenger door was open. Fortunately, the limo's recent occupants had been since transported to the morgue. Set up next to the limo was a PC with a screen a full twenty-one inches across. The tech stepped in front of it and began keying in commands as she was speaking. Wide of hip, with lovely olive skin and a mouth that showed many smile lines, Liz Martin was one of the bureau's best and hardest-working lab rats.

"Before we physically removed any trace, we hit the entire interior, both front and back, with the Luma-lite, as you requested, Lee. We found some things of interest. We also videotaped the interior of the vehicle while we were conducting the exam and fed that video into the system. Makes it a lot easier for you to follow along." She handed each of the two agents a pair of goggles while she donned a pair herself. "Welcome to the theater; these are for your viewing pleasure." She smiled. "Actually, they block out different wavelengths that may have occurred during the exam and which may otherwise obscure what was captured on the film." As she spoke, the screen came alive. They were looking at the inside of the limo. It was very dark, the conditions under which a Luma-lite exam was conducted. Using a powerful laser of particularly high wattage, the test was designed to make a wide range of otherwise invisible items lurking at a crime scene visible.

Liz manipulated a mouse connected to the PC and the two agents watched as a large white arrow made its way across the screen. "We started out using a single light source, no chemicals applied. We were looking for inherent fluorescence, then we moved on to a series of dyes and powders."

"You said you found some items of interest, Liz?" Sawyer's tone was a touch impatient, his eyes glued to the screen even as he asked the question.

"Hard not to in such a contained space as that, considering what happened there." Her eyes flickered briefly over at the limo. As her fingers expertly manipulated the mouse, the white arrow came to rest on what looked to be the rear seat of the limo. Liz hit some additional keys and the area was blocked off on a series of grids appearing on the screen and magnified until it was readily visible. However, being readily discernible to the human eye and being readily identifiable were not the same thing.

Sawyer turned to Liz. "What the hell is that?" It looked like a string of some kind, but magnified and enlarged as it was, it had taken on the thickness of a pencil.

"Simply speaking, a fiber." Liz pressed another key on the computer and the fiber took on a three-dimensional shape. "From the looks of it, I'd say wool, animal, the real thing, not synthetic, gray in color. Sound familiar to either of you?"

Jackson snapped his fingers. "Sidney Archer was wearing a blazer that morning. It was gray."

Sawyer was already nodding. "That's right."

Liz looked back at the screen and nodded thoughtfully. "Wool blazer. That would fit the bill."

"Where exactly did you find it, Liz?" Sawyer asked.

"Left rear seat, more towards the middle really." Using the mouse, Liz drew a line across the screen measuring from the spot the fiber was found to the far left side of the rear seat. "Twenty-seven inches from the end of the left-side rear seat, seven inches up from the seat. With that location it would seem logical that it came from a coat. We also picked up some synthetic cloth fibers right next to the left-side door. They matched the clothing found on the deceased male sitting in that position."

She turned back to the screen. "We didn't need the laser to find these next samples. They were plainly visible." The screen changed and Liz used the arrow to point out several single strands of hair.

"Let me guess," Sawyer said. "Long and blond. Natural, not bleached. Found very near the fiber."

"Very good, Lee, we'll make a scientist out of you yet." Liz smiled pleasantly. "Next we used leucocrystal violet to test for blood. Found a ton of it, as you can imagine. Spray patterns are pretty evident and actually very demonstrative in this case, again probably due to the tight parameters of the crime scene." They looked at the computer screen, where the interior of the limo was now glowing brightly in numerous places. For a moment it looked like they were deep in a mine and bits of gold blazed out at them from every nook and cranny. Liz marked several spots with the pointer. "My conclusion is that the gentleman found on the floor of the backseat was either sitting facing the rear or with his face partially toward the right-hand side window. Gunshot wound was near the right temple. Blood, bone and tissue throw-off was considerable. You can see the rear seat is covered with the debris."

"Yeah, but there's an evident gap there." Sawyer pointed to the left side of the rear seat.

"Good eye, that's absolutely right," Liz said. She used her measuring device again. "We found samples pretty uniformly distributed on the rear seat. That's what makes me think the victim"—she glanced at some notes next to the computer—"Brophy, had turned away, toward his left. That would leave the area of the gunshot, the right temple, facing directly at the rear seat, which accounts for the considerable trace coverage on the rear seat."

"Sort of like a cannon firing," Sawyer said dryly.

"Not exactly a technical term, but not bad for a layman, Lee." Liz arched her eyebrows and then continued. "However, the left half of the rear seat is virtually absent of any trace, no blood, no tissue, no bone fragments for approximately forty-five inches, almost four feet. Why is that?" She looked at the two agents like a schoolmarm waiting for her students to start waving their hands.

Sawyer answered. "We know one of the victims was sitting on the far left side: Philip Goldman. He was found there. But he was an average-size guy. There's no way he could account for that width. From the size of the gap, and the hair and fiber trace you already picked up, another person was sitting right next to Goldman."

"That's how I read it," Liz answered. "Goldman's wound would have thrown off quite a bit of residue as well. Again, nothing on the seat next to him. That reinforces the conclusion that someone else was seated there and took the full brunt of it. Not a pleasant business, to say the least. I'd be soaking in a bath for a week if it had happened to me, knock on wood."

"Wool coat, long, blond hair—" Jackson began.

"And this," Liz broke in, and pointed at the screen. They all stared as the scene changed once more. It was the rear seat again. The leather had been torn in several spots. Three parallel jagged lines ran from front to back at a spot very near where Goldman had been found. In the middle of the damage a solitary object rested. The agents looked at Liz.

"That's part of a fingernail. We haven't had time to run a DNA typing analysis, of course, but it's definitely female."

"How do you know that?" Jackson asked.

"It's not always so complicated, Ray. Long nail, professionally manicured, fingernail polish. Men rarely put themselves through that."

"Oh."

"The parallel lines on the leather—"

"Scratches," Sawyer said. "She scratched the seat and broke a nail."

"Right. She must've been really panicked," Liz noted.

"Not surprising, is it?" Jackson added.

"Anything else, Liz?" Sawyer queried her.

"Oh, yes. Lots of goodies. Prints. We used MDB, a compound which is particularly good at fluorescing latent prints under laser light. Also used a deep blue lens on the Luma-lite. Got really good results. We did elimination typing on the three victims. Their prints were everywhere. Understandably. Found a number of other partials, though, including one that coincided with those scratches, which seems natural enough. We also found one that was of particular interest."

"What's that?" Sawyer's nose was almost quivering with anticipation.

"Brophy's clothes were heavily spotted with blood and other human residue from his wound. His right shoulder, in particular, was covered in blood. Makes sense, since his right temple would have been bleeding heavily. We found a number of prints, thumb, index, pinkie, really examples of the entire hand, in the blood on his right shoulder."

"How do you account for that? Someone trying to turn him over?" Sawyer looked puzzled.

"No. I wouldn't say that, although I don't have firm evidence to support it. My gut is, judging from the palm print I was able to pull up, it was more like—and I know this sounds pretty bizarre under the circumstances—but it was like someone was trying to climb over him, or at least was straddling the guy. But the close placement of the fingers, the angle of the palm and so on, really strongly suggest that's what happened."

Sawyer looked highly skeptical. "Climb over him? That's kind of a stretch, isn't it, Liz? You can't really tell that from the prints, can you?"

"I'm not basing my conclusion simply on that. We also found this." She pointed at the screen again. A strange object appeared there. A shape or pattern of some sort. In fact, a couple of them. The dark background around the objects they were looking at made it difficult to understand what they were really observing.

"This was a shot taken of Brophy's body," Liz explained. "He's face down on the floorboard. We're looking at his back. You see in the middle of his back this shape pattern. Again, it's made possible by a patch of blood."

Jackson and Sawyer squinted and leaned close to the screen, trying to discern what the image was. They finally gave up and looked at Liz.

"A knee." She magnified the image until it spanned the entire screen. "The human knee does make a very unique shape, especially when you have a malleable background such as blood." She clicked another button and another image sprang to life. "We also have this."

Sawyer and Jackson again looked at the screen. This time the pattern was readily identifiable. "A shoe print, the heel," Jackson said.

Sawyer looked unconvinced. "Yeah, but why climb all the way over the dead guy, get blood and who knows what else all over you, leave trace of yourself behind, when you could just open the left-side passenger door and step out? I mean, the person we're probably talking about was seated right next to Goldman on the *left* side."

Jackson and Liz looked at each other. Neither one had a ready answer for that. Liz shrugged and smiled. "That's why they pay you the big bucks, guys. I'm just a lab rat."

Jackson smiled. "I'd love fifty more just like you, Liz."

She smiled at the compliment. "I'll have a written report on all this for you later today."

They all took off the goggles.

"I'm assuming you've already run the prints?" Sawyer looked at her.

"Jesus, I'm sorry, talk about leaving out the main course. All of the prints—the one we looked at on the screen, from the probable murder weapon, and all of the ones in the limo and leading from the limo and on to the eighth floor and back down—were from one person."

"Sidney Archer." Jackson said.

"That's right," Liz responded. "The office where the blood trail took us was hers as well."

Sawyer stepped over to the limo and peered inside. He motioned for Liz and Jackson to join him.

"Okay, based on what we know right now, can we assume that Sidney Archer was sitting about right there?" He pointed to a spot slightly left of the middle of the rear seat.

"Seems reasonable enough, based on the trace we've uncovered so far. The blood spray patterns, fiber and print evidence would certainly support that conclusion," Liz said.

"Okay, looking at where the body ended up, Brophy was most

likely sitting facing the rear. You say he may have turned his head and that accounted for the heavy residue on the rear seats. Right?"

"That's right." Liz was nodding her head as she followed Sawyer's reconstruction.

"Now, Brophy's wound was of the contact variety, there's little doubt of that. How far would you say that it?" Sawyer was pointing to the space between the front and rear seats of the passenger area.

"We don't have to guess," Liz said. She walked over to her desk, pulled out a tape measure and came back over. With Jackson's assistance she measured the space. Liz looked at the result on the tape and then frowned as she now saw where Sawyer was headed with his analysis. "Six feet six inches from the middle of one seat to the other."

"Okay, based on the absence of residue on the rear seats, Archer and Goldman were sitting there, their backs flush against the seats, you agree?" Liz nodded, as did Jackson. "All right, is it possible for Sidney Archer, if she was sitting with her back *flush* against the rear seat, to have perpetrated a contact wound on Brophy's right temple?"

Liz answered first. "No, not unless her arms dragged the ground when she walked."

Sawyer was eyeing Liz carefully. "How about Brophy was leaning toward Archer, very close, and she pulls the gun and fires. His body falls on her, let's say, but she pushes him off and he lands on the floor. What's wrong with that picture?"

Liz thought for a moment. "If he was leaning forward—and he really would have had to almost leave his seat—then given the distance, the shooter would still have to be doing about the same thing: They would sort of meet in the middle, so to speak, for the contact wound to be possible. But if the shooter is leaning forward, then the spray patterns would be different, more than likely. The shooter's back is not flush with the seat. Even if her body caught most of the residue, it would be highly unlikely for some not to have ended up on the seat behind her. For her to remain flush against the seat when she fired, Brophy would most likely had to have been almost in her lap. That doesn't seem too probable, does it?"

"Agreed," Sawyer said. "Let's talk about Goldman's wound for a minute. She's sitting next to Goldman on his left side, okay? Wouldn't you think his entry wound would have been to the right temple and not in the middle of the forehead?"

"He could've turned to face her—" Liz started to say, and then stopped. "But then the blood spray patterns wouldn't make sense. Goldman was definitely looking toward the front of the limo when the bullet hit him. But it could still be possible, Lee."

"Really?" Sawyer pulled up a chair, sat down in it, held an imaginary gun in his right hand, coiled it around and pointed it backward as though he were about to shoot someone sitting on his left, in the forehead as that person stared directly ahead. He looked at Liz and Jackson. "Pretty awkward, isn't it?"

"Very," Jackson said, shaking his head.

"It gets even more awkward, guys. Sidney Archer is left-handed. Remember, Ray, her drinking coffee, handling the pistol? Left-handed." Sawyer repeated his performance, this time holding the imaginary firearm in his left hand. The result was almost laughable as the bulky agent contorted his body.

"That would be impossible," Jackson said. "She'd have to turn and face him to inflict a wound like that. Either that or she pops her arm out of the socket. Nobody would fire a pistol in that manner."

"So, if Archer is the shooter, she somehow shoots the driver in the front seat, jumps across to the rear seat, blows away Brophy, which we've already shown she couldn't have done, and then supposedly nails Goldman using a completely unnatural—in fact impossible— firing angle." Sawyer got up from the chair and shook his head.

"You've made some good points, Lee, but there's still a lot of indisputable trace tying Sidney Archer to the crime scene," Liz rejoined.

"Being *at* a crime scene and being the perpetrator of said crime are two different things, Liz," Sawyer said heatedly. Liz looked pained at the agent's sharp rebuff.

As they were leaving the lab, Sawyer had a final question. "You get an answer on the gunshot residue test yet?"

"I hope you realize the bureau's firearms section doesn't really do the GSR tests anymore, since the findings weren't typically turning up anything relevant. However, since it was you requesting the test, of course no one balked. Give me one minute, Agent Sawyer, and I'll check." Liz's tone was plainly antiseptic now. Sawyer didn't seem to notice as he moodily studied the floor.

Liz went back to her desk and picked up a phone. Sawyer was staring over at the limo, looking for the world like he wanted to make it disappear. Jackson watched his partner carefully, a trace of concern filtering through his eyes.

Liz walked back over. "Negative. None of the victims had either fired a gun or handled a recently fired weapon with their bare hands in the six hours before their death."

"You're sure? No mistake?" Sawyer asked, his brow laced with furrows.

Liz's usually pleasant face quickly turned to a scowl. "My people know how to do their job, Lee. A GSR test is not that complicated, although, as I said, it's not routinely done anymore because a positive finding may not always be that accurate; there are so many substances out there that could, in practice, give a false positive. However, that nine-millimeter would have thrown off a good deal of residue, and the test result was *negative*. I'd say the confidence level in that finding should be very high. However, just in case you didn't catch it, I did add a disclaimer about their bare hands. They could have worn gloves, of course."

"But none were found on the dead men," Jackson pointed out.

"That's right," Liz said, looking at Sawyer triumphantly.

Sawyer ignored the look. "Were there any other prints found on the nine-millimeter?" he asked.

"One thumb print, partially obscured. It belonged to Parker, the chauffeur driver."

"No one else's?" Sawyer asked. "You're sure." Liz said nothing. Her expression plainly answered the question.

"Okay, you said Parker's print was partially obscured. What about Archer's prints? How clean were they?"

"From what I recall, fairly clean. Although there was some smudging. I'm talking about the grip, trigger and trigger guard. Her prints on the barrel were very clear."

"The barrel?" Sawyer said this more to himself. He looked at Liz.

"We have a report on the ballistics yet? I'm real interested in the trajectory patterns."

"The autopsies are being performed as we speak. We'll know soon enough. I've asked to be advised of the results. They'll probably call you first, but in case they don't, as soon as I hear, I'll buzz you." She added with a trace of sarcasm, "You'll want to make sure they didn't make any mistakes, of course."

Sawyer looked at her for a moment. "Thanks, Liz. You've been a big help." His sarcastic tone was not lost on either Liz or Jackson. Lost deep in thought, his massive shoulders sagging, Sawyer trudged away slowly.

Jackson stayed behind for a moment with Liz. She watched Sawyer leave and then looked over at Jackson. "What the hell's eating him, Ray? He's never treated me like that before."

Jackson didn't answer right away. He finally shrugged and turned to leave. "I'm not sure I can answer that right now, Liz. Not sure at all." He quietly followed his partner out.

CHAPTER FIFTY-ONE

Jackson climbed in the car and looked over at his partner. Sawyer was sitting there, his hands on the wheel, staring off into the darkness. Jackson looked at his watch. "Hey, Lee, how about some grub?" When Sawyer didn't reply, he added, "My treat? Don't pass that offer up. It may not be repeated in your lifetime." Jackson gripped Sawyer's shoulder and gave it a friendly squeeze.

Sawyer finally looked over at him. For an instant a smile appeared on his lips and then was gone. "Springing for a meal, huh? You think I'm seriously screwed up over this case, don't you, Raymond?"

"I just don't want you to get too skinny," said Jackson.

Sawyer laughed and put the car in gear.

Jackson attacked his meal with vigor while Sawyer merely played with a mug of coffee. The diner was in close proximity to the headquarters building and was thus a popular one for FBI personnel. The pair greeted a number of colleagues either grabbing a bite before heading home or fortifying themselves before going on duty.

Jackson eyed Sawyer. "That was a nice piece of work you did back at the lab. But you could've cut Liz some slack. She was just doing her job."

Sawyer's eyes suddenly burned into his partner. "You cut some slack when your kid misses curfew or puts a ding in your car. If somebody wants slack, then I would strongly suggest they don't seek employment with the FBI."

"You know what I mean. Liz is damned good at her job."

Sawyer's face softened. "I know, Ray. I'll send her some flowers. Okay?" Sawyer looked away again.

Between bites Jackson said, "So what's our next move?"

Sawyer looked over at him. "I'm not really sure. I've had cases change on me in midstream before, but not quite to this degree."

"You don't believe Sidney Archer killed those guys, do you?"

"Aside from the fact that the physical evidence says she couldn't have, no, I don't believe she did."

"But she did lie to us, Lee. The tape? She was helping her husband. You can't get around that."

Sawyer felt the guilt seep in again. He had never withheld information from a partner before. He looked over at Jackson and then decided to tell him what Sidney had revealed. Five minutes later, Jackson sat back stunned. Sawyer glanced at him anxiously. "She was scared. Didn't know what to do. I'm sure she wanted to tell us from the get-go. Damn, if we only knew where she was. She could be in real danger, Ray." Sawyer smacked a fist into his palm. "If she would only come to us. Work together. We could bust this whole case, I know it."

Jackson leaned forward, a determined expression on his face. "Look, Lee, we've done a lot of cases together. But, despite it all, you kept your distance. You saw things for what they were."

"And you think this case is different?" Sawyer's tone was steady.

"I *know* it's different. You've been sticking up for this lady almost from the start. And you've damn sure been treating her differently than you ordinarily would a major suspect in a case like this. Now you tell me she spilled to you about the tape and her talking to her husband. And you kept that info to yourself. Jesus Christ, Lee, that's grounds to get your butt kicked right out of the bureau."

"If you feel you need to report it, Ray, I'm not stopping you."

Jackson grunted and shook his head. "I'm not pissing away your career. You're doing a good enough job of that."

"This case isn't any different."

"Bullshit!" Jackson hunched forward even more. "You know it is and it's messing you up. All the evidence points, at minimum, to Sidney Archer being involved in some serious crimes, and yet you go out of your way at every opportunity to put a positive spin on it. You did it with Frank Hardy, with Liz, and now you're trying to do it with me. You're not a politician, Lee, you're a law enforcement officer. She may not be in on everything, but she's no angel either. That's for damned certain."

"You disagree with my conclusions on the triple homicide?" Sawyer shot back.

Jackson shook his head. "No. I think you're probably right. But if you expect me to believe that Archer is just an innocent babe caught up in some Kafkaesque nightmare, then you're talking to the wrong FBI agent. Remember what you said about slack? Well, I'd have to cut you a ton of it to even begin to believe that Sidney Archer, beautiful and intelligent as she might be, shouldn't spend a considerable part of her remaining years in prison." Jackson sat back.

"So that's what you think it's all about? Beautiful, brainy babe turns veteran agent to mush?" Jackson didn't respond, but the answer was clearly painted on his face. "Old, divorced fart wants to jump in her panties, Ray? And I can't do that if she's guilty. Is that what the hell you think?" Sawyer's voice was rising.

"Why don't you tell me, Lee?"

"Maybe I should throw your ass through that window over there instead."

"Maybe you should goddamn try," Jackson shot back.

"You sonofabitch." Sawyer's voice shook.

Jackson reached across and grabbed his shoulder. "I want you to get your head on right. You want to sleep with her, fine. Wait until after the case is over and she's proved not guilty!" Jackson shouted at him.

"How dare you!" Sawyer shouted back, ripping Jackson's hand away. Sawyer then jumped up and cocked a very large fist, a fist that stopped in midair as Sawyer realized what he was about to do. Several of the other restaurant patrons stared in shock at the scene. Sawyer's and Jackson's eyes remained locked until finally Sawyer, his chest heaving, his bottom lip trembling, lowered his fist and sat back down.

Neither of them spoke for several minutes. Finally Sawyer looked embarrassed and sighed. "Shit, I knew I was going to regret giving up the smokes one day." He closed his eyes. When he reopened them, he was looking squarely at Jackson.

"Lee, I'm sorry. I'm just worried about—" Jackson abruptly stopped as Sawyer held up his hand.

Sawyer began speaking slowly and softly. "You know, Ray, I've been with the bureau half my life. When I first started out, it was easy to tell the good guys from the bad. Back then, kids didn't go around killing people like they were yesterday's lunch. And you didn't have smooth-running drug empires worth hundreds of billions of dollars, enough money that just about anybody will do just about anything. They had revolvers, we had revolvers. Pretty soon they'll be toting surface-to-air missiles as standard equipment.

"While I'm at the grocery trying to decide what lousy TV dinner to eat and looking for which beer's on sale, about twenty new corpses are created for no better reason than somebody turning down the wrong street or a bunch of unemployed kids going at each other over a block-long piece of drug turf with more firepower than an Army battalion used to carry around. We play catch-up every day, but we never gain any ground."

"Come on, Lee, the thin blue line is still around. As long as there are bad guys."

"That thin blue line is a lot like the ozone layer, Ray. It's got mountain-size holes punched all through it. I've been walking that line for a long time. What do I have to show for it? I'm divorced. My kids think I'm a lousy father because I was out running down a plane bomber, or hauling in some slick-smiling butcher who likes to line his trophy case with human specimens, instead of helping them blow out candles on their birthday cakes. You know what? They were right. I was a lousy dad. Especially to Meggie. I worked ungodly hours, never around, and when I was, I was either sleeping or so zoned out on a case I probably never heard half of what they were trying to tell me. Now I live all alone in a crummy apartment and most of my paycheck I don't even see. My stomach feels like it's got a bunch of meat cleavers stuck in it and while I'm sure that's just my imagination, I do happen to have several pieces of real lead permanently embedded in me. On top of that, lately I find it real hard to go to sleep unless I've had a six-pack of beer."

"Jesus, Lee, you're always the rock at work. Everyone respects the hell out of you. You go into an investigation and see stuff I never do. Wrap the whole picture together while I'm still getting my notebook out. You've got the best instincts of any one I've ever seen."

"Good thing, Ray. Considering it's really the only thing I have left. But don't shortchange yourself. I've got twenty years on you. You know what instinct is? Seeing the same thing over and over again until you start to get a feel for things. A little extra step. You're way ahead of where I was with just a half dozen years under my belt."

"I appreciate that, Lee."

"But don't misinterpret this little episode of venting. I don't feel sorry for myself and I'm sure as hell not looking for any pity from anybody. I had choices and I made them. Just me. If my life's screwed up, it's because *I* screwed it up, nobody else."

Sawyer got up, walked over to the counter and exchanged a few words with a skinny, wrinkled waitress. In a moment he was striding back, cupping his hands together, a thin line of smoke floating up. He sat back down and held up the cigarette. "For old times' sake." Slowly grinding out the match in the ashtray, he sat back and took a long pull on the cigarette, a barely audible chuckle escaping his lips.

"I go into this case, Ray, thinking that I had it pretty much nailed from the get-go. Lieberman's the target. We figure out how the plane went down. We got a lot of motives, but not so many we can't follow up, sift through until we nail the sonofabitch responsible.

Shit, we get the actual bomber gift-wrapped and delivered to us, even if he's not breathing anymore. Things are looking pretty damn good. Then the floor falls out from under us. We find out Jason Archer pulled off this incredible heist and turns up in Seattle selling secrets instead of being in a hole in the ground in Virginia. Is that his plan? Seems pretty likely.

"Only the bomber turns out to be a guy who somehow slipped right through the Virginia State Police's computer system. I get hoodwinked into going to New Orleans and something happens at Archer's house that I'm still in the dark about. Then, when you least expect it, Lieberman gets thrown back into the picture chiefly because of Steven Page's apparent suicide five years ago that doesn't seem to fit into the puzzle except for the fact that his big brother, who can probably tell us a lot, gets his throat handed to him in a parking lot. I talk to Charles Tiedman and maybe, just maybe, Lieberman is being blackmailed. If true, how the hell does that tie into Jason Archer? Do we have two unconnected cases seemingly connected through a coincidence: namely, Lieberman gets on a plane Archer has paid someone to blow up? Or is it all one case? If it is, what the hell is the connection? Because if there is one, it sure as hell has escaped yours truly."

Sawyer shook his head in unconcealed frustration and took another drag on his cigarette. He exhaled smoke up to the grimy ceiling and then put his elbows on the table and looked over at Jackson. "Now two other guys we figure are trying to rip off Triton Global check into the hereafter. And the common denominator in a hell of a lot of it is Sidney Archer." Sawyer slowly rubbed a finger across his cheek. "Sidney Archer. . . . I know I respect the woman. But maybe my judgment is getting a little clouded. You're probably right to kick me in the ass over it. But I'll let you in on a little secret, friend." Sawyer tapped the end of his cigarette into the ashtray.

"What's that?"

"Sidney Archer *was* in that limo. And whoever killed those three guys let her walk. Her pistol ends up with the police." Sawyer made an imaginary gun with his left hand and pointed at various parts of it with his cigarette as he continued to speak. "Smudged prints on the part she would've held if she had fired it. Clear prints on the barrel only. What do you make of that?"

Jackson thought quickly. "We know she handled the gun." The truth suddenly dawned on him. "If somebody else fired it, and they were using gloves, her prints would've been smudged on those areas but not the barrel."

"Right. The tape gets left behind. They probably did use it to blackmail her, I'm not arguing with you over that. She would've known they had it, they would've had to play it for her to make her know the threat was real. You think she would've left something like that behind? That's slam-dunk evidence of enough felonies to keep her in prison until she's a hundred. I'm telling you, she or anyone else in that situation would've lifted that damn limo clear up in the air to get to that tape. No, they let her go for one reason only."

"To set her up for the killings." Jackson slowly put his coffee cup down.

"And maybe to make sure our focus doesn't wander again."

"That's why you wanted the GSR test done."

Sawyer nodded. "I needed to be sure that one of the dead guys wasn't the shooter. You know, there could have been a struggle. From the looks of it, the wounds were all instantly fatal, but who the hell really can be sure? Or one of them could have done it and then committed suicide, for all we know. Freaked out over what he'd done and decided to blow his own brains out. Then Sidney, in a panic, grabs the gun and throws it down a sewer drain. But that didn't happen. None of the stiffs fired that weapon."

They sat in prolonged silence before Sawyer stirred. "I'll let you in on another secret, Ray. I'm gonna figure this sucker out, even it if takes me another twenty-five years walking that thin line. And when that day comes, you're going to find out something really enlightening."

"Such as?"

"That Sidney Archer has no more of a clue to what the hell is going on than you or I do right now. She's lost her husband, she's lost her career, she stands a better than even chance of standing trial for murder and about a dozen other felonies and spending the rest of her life in prison. Right now she's scared out of her wits and running for her life, not knowing who to trust or believe. Sidney Archer is in fact something that, if you just looked at the evidence in a superficial manner, you would conclude she couldn't possibly be."

"What's that?"

"Innocent."

"You really think that?"

"No. I *know* it. I wish I knew something else."

"What's that?"

Sawyer stabbed out his cigarette at the same time he let out a final mouthful of smoke. "Who really killed those three guys." Sawyer's mind drifted away as he said the words. *Sidney Archer might know. But where the hell is she?*

As the two rose to leave, Jackson put a hand on Sawyer's shoulder. "Hey, Lee, for what it's worth, I don't care how long the good guy/bad guy odds ever get to be. As long as you're willing to walk the line, I will too."

CHAPTER FIFTY-TWO

Looking through her binoculars, Sidney surveyed the street in front of her parents' house and then checked her watch. Dusk was rapidly gathering. She shook her head in disbelief. Could the FedEx shipment have been delayed because of weather? Snowfall in coastal Maine was usually heavy, and because of its proximity to the ocean, it was usually very slushy. That often made for hazardous driving conditions when the slush froze. And where were her parents? The problem was she had no way to communicate with them while they were traveling. Sidney hurried to the Land Rover, dialed information on the cellular phone and got the 800 number for Federal Express. She gave the operator the names and addresses of the sender and recipient of the package. After Sidney listened to computer keys clicking, the operating delivered her astonishing answer.

"You mean you have no record of the package?"

"No, ma'am, I mean, according to our records, we didn't receive the package."

"But that's impossible. You *had* to get it. There must be some mistake. Please check again." Sidney listened with growing impa-

tience to the sounds, once again, of the keyboard. The response was
the same.

"Ma'am, perhaps you should check with the sender to make sure
the package was actually sent out."

Sidney hung up, got Fisher's number from her purse in the house,
went back out to the Land Rover and dialed it. There was little
chance that Fisher would be there—he had undoubtedly taken Sidney's warnings to heart—but he would most likely call in for messages. Her hands were shaking. What if Jeff had been unable to send
out the package? The vision of the gun pointed at her in the limo
blasted into her mind. Brophy and Goldman. Their heads exploding. All over her. For a moment, in her despair, she rested her head
on the steering wheel, then picked up the phone and dialed.

The phone rang and then was answered. Sidney prepared to leave
a message on the machine when a voice said hello.

Sidney started to speak until she realized the voice on the other
end was a live one.

"Hello?" The voice said again.

Sidney hesitated and then decided to go ahead. "Jeff Fisher,
please."

"Who is this?"

"I'm . . . I'm a friend of his."

"Do you know where he is? I really need to find him," said the
voice.

The hackles on the back of Sidney's neck went up. "Who is this?"

"Sergeant Rogers of the Alexandria Police Department."

Sidney quickly cut off the call.

The interior of Jeff Fisher's townhouse had seen drastic changes
since Sidney Archer had been there, chief of which was that not one
single piece of computer equipment or files was left in the place. In
the middle of the day, neighbors had seen the moving truck. One of
them had even talked to the movers. Thought it was all legitimate.
Fisher hadn't mentioned that he was moving, but the movers had
been so open about it, took their time, boxed things up, had paperwork on a clipboard, had even taken a smoke break in the middle of

the job. Only after they had left did the neighbors get suspicious. When Fisher's next-door neighbor had gone inside to check on things, he had noticed that none of the furniture was gone, only Fisher's extensive computer system. That's when the police had been called.

Sergeant Rogers scratched his head. The problem was, nobody could find Jeff Fisher. They had checked at his job, with his family up in Boston, with his friends locally. No one had seen him in the last couple of days. Sergeant Rogers had received another shock during his investigation. Fisher had actually been in custody at the Alexandria Police Station on a reckless driving charge. He'd posted bail, been given a court date and been released. That was the last anyone apparently had seen of Jeff Fisher. Rogers finished writing up his report and left.

Sidney ran up the stairs and slammed and locked the bedroom door. She grabbed the shotgun off the bed, racked the action of the weapon, backed into the far corner and sat down on the floor, the gun pointed straight at the door. Tears streamed down her cheeks as she shook her head in disbelief. *Oh, God!* She should never have gotten Jeff involved.

Sawyer was at his desk at the Hoover Building when Frank Hardy called. He briefly filled Hardy in on the most recent developments, chief of which was Sawyer's conclusion, based on his examination of the forensics evidence, that Sidney Archer had not killed Goldman and Brophy.

"You think it could have been Jason Archer?" Hardy asked.

"That doesn't make any sense."

"You're right. Too big a risk for him to come back here anyway."

"Plus I can't believe he'd set up his wife for the murders." Sawyer paused as he considered his next question. "Any word from RTG?"

"I was just about to tell you. The president, Alan Porcher, is unavailable for comment. Big surprise there. The company's PR person gave the standard line vigorously denying the allegations, of course."

"How about the CyberCom deal?"

"Well, there we finally have some good news. This latest development with RTG has thrown CyberCom firmly into Triton's camp. In fact, a news conference is scheduled for later this afternoon announcing the deal. You want to attend?"

"Maybe. Nathan Gamble should be a happy camper."

"You got that right. I'll leave a couple of visitor badges for the press conference if you and Ray want to come see the show. It's at Triton's headquarters."

Sawyer considered the request for a moment. "I think you'll see us there, Frank."

Sawyer and Jackson, their yellow visitor badges riding brightly on their lapels, walked into the auditorium-sized room, which still managed to be crowded.

"Damn, this *must* be a big event." Jackson eyed the sea of reporters, industry people, financial analysts and other investment types.

"Money always is, Ray." Sawyer snagged two cups of coffee from the hospitality table and handed one to his partner. Sawyer stretched his six-foot-three-inch frame to its maximum height as he looked over the crowd.

"Looking for somebody?" Frank Hardy appeared behind the pair.

Jackson smiled. "Yeah, we were looking for some poor people. But I think we're in the wrong place."

"That you are. Gotta admit, you can feel the excitement, can't you?"

Jackson nodded and then pointed at the army of reporters. "But is one company buying out another really all that newsworthy?"

"Ray, it's a little more than that. I would be hard put to name any other company in America whose potential exceeds CyberCom."

"But if CyberCom is so special, why do they need Triton?" Jackson asked.

"With Triton they can partner with a world leader and have the billions of dollars needed to produce, market and expand their product base. The result will be that in a couple of years, Triton will dominate like GM and IBM used to—even more so, really. The flow of ninety percent of the world's information will be through hardware, software and other technology created by the business combination being formed today."

Sawyer shook his head as he gulped his coffee down. "Damn, Frank," he said, "that doesn't leave much room for everybody else. What happens to them?"

Hardy smiled weakly. "Well, that's capitalism for you. Survival of the fittest comes from the law of the jungle. You've probably watched those *National Geographic* shows. Animals eating each other, struggling to survive. It's not a pretty sight."

Hardy looked up at the small elevated stage where a podium had been situated. "It's about to start, guys. I've got us seats near the front. Come on." Hardy herded them through the crowds, entering a special roped-off section that encompassed the first three rows from the stage. Sawyer looked over the occupants of a short line of chairs to the left of the podium. Quentin Rowe was there. He was a little more dressed up today, but despite his hundreds of millions of bucks in the bank the guy apparently didn't own any neckties. He was engaged in an animated conversation with three men in low-key business suits who Sawyer assumed were the CyberCom people.

Hardy seemed to be reading his mind. "From left to right, CEO, CFO and COO of CyberCom."

"And SOL, shit outta luck, for everybody else," Sawyer said.

Hardy pointed at the stage. From the right side Nathan Gamble, nattily dressed and smiling, marched across and settled in at the podium. The crowd quickly took their seats and abruptly quieted down as if Moses had just strolled down Mount Sinai with those tablets. Gamble took out a prepared speech and launched into it with considerable vigor. Sawyer didn't hear most of it. He was busy watching Quentin Rowe. The young man was looking at Gamble. Whether he was conscious of it or not, his expression was not amicable. From the little Sawyer did hear of Gamble's words, the main import was money, big money that came with market domination. After Gamble finished with a flourish—he was quite the glib salesman, Sawyer had to admit—there was a huge wave of applause.

Then Quentin Rowe took his place at the podium. As Gamble passed him on his way to sit down, the two men exchanged smiles that were about as phony as Sawyer had ever seen outside a B movie.

In comparison to Gamble, Rowe's emphasis was on the limitless positive potential the two companies, Triton and CyberCom combined, could offer the planet. The issue of money never came up. At least from Sawyer's point of view, Gamble had pretty much covered that issue anyway. Now he looked over at Gamble, who was not looking at Rowe at all. He was engaged in a friendly discussion with the CyberCom acronyms. Rowe apparently noticed the exchange at one point as he glanced over, lost his train of thought for a moment and then carried on. His talk received, Sawyer thought, polite applause. The good of the world apparently took a distant backseat to Mother Green. At least with this crowd.

When the CyberCom people finished up the presentation, all of the men engaged in a handshaking, ringed-arm photo opportunity. Sawyer noted that Gamble and Rowe never actually touched flesh. They kept the CyberCom boys between them. Maybe that's why they were so excited about the deal; they'd have a buffer zone now.

Everyone from the stage made his way into the crowd and was instantly besieged by questions. Gamble was smiling, quipping and playing the moment for all it was worth. The CyberCom people followed in his wake. Sawyer watched as Rowe broke rank and headed over to the hospitality table, where he fixed a cup of tea and moved quickly over to a secluded corner.

Sawyer tugged on Jackson's sleeve and they headed in Rowe's direction. Hardy went over to listen to Gamble's pontificating.

"Nice speech."

Rowe looked up to see Sawyer and Jackson standing in front of him.

"What? Oh, thank you."

"My partner, Ray Jackson."

Rowe and Jackson exchanged hellos.

Sawyer looked over at the large group surrounding Gamble. "He seems to like the limelight."

Rowe sipped his tea and wiped his mouth delicately with his napkin. "His bottom-line approach to the business and limited knowl-edge of what we actually do makes for good sound bites," he said disdainfully.

Jackson sat down next to Rowe. "Personally, I liked what you were saying about the future. My kids are really into computers. It's true what you were saying: Better educational opportunities for everyone, especially the poor, translates into better jobs, less crime, better world. I really believe that."

"Thank you. I believe it too." Rowe looked up at Sawyer and smiled. "Although I don't think your partner shares that view."

Sawyer, who had been scanning the crowds, looked down at him with a hurt look on his face. "Hey, I'm for all that positive stuff. Just don't take away my pencil and paper. That's all I'm saying." Sawyer pointed his coffee cup over at the group of CyberCom people. "You seem to get along with those guys all right."

Rowe brightened. "I do. They're not as liberal-thinking as I am, but they're a long way from Gamble's money-is-everything position. I think they might bring a nice equilibrium to the place. Although now we have to endure at least two months of the lawyers taking their pound of flesh while the final documents are negotiated."

"Tyler, Stone?" Sawyer asked.

Rowe looked at Sawyer. "That's right."

"You gonna keep them as your counsel after the CyberCom deal is put to bed?"

"You'll have to ask Gamble that. It's his call. He *is* the head of the company. Excuse me, gentlemen, but I have to go." Rowe quickly got up and left them.

"What bee's up his bonnet?" Jackson asked Sawyer.

Sawyer shrugged his thick shoulders. "More like a hornets' nest. If you were partners with Nathan Gamble, you'd probably under-stand."

"So what now?"

"Why don't you grab another cup of coffee and mingle, Ray. I want to talk to Rowe some more." Sawyer disappeared into the crowd. Jackson looked around and then went over to the hospitality table.

By the time Sawyer had made his way through the crowd, he had lost sight of Rowe. As he swept his head back and forth, he saw Rowe go out the door. Sawyer was about to follow him when he felt a tug at his sleeve.

"Since when is a government bureaucrat interested in the goings-on of the for-profit sector?" Nathan Gamble asked.

Sawyer cast one more look in Rowe's direction, but he was already out of sight. The FBI agent turned to Gamble.

"I'm all for making a buck. Nice speech you gave, by the way. Left me kind of tingling all over."

Gamble let out a belly laugh. "Like hell it did. You want something stronger?" He pointed at Sawyer's Styrofoam cup.

"Sorry, I'm on duty. Besides, it's a little early for me."

"We're celebrating here, FBI man. Just announced the biggest damn deal of my life. I'd say that's worth getting drunk over, wouldn't you?"

"If you want to. It's not *my* deal."

"You never know," he said provocatively. "Let's take a walk."

Gamble led Sawyer up across the stage, down a short corridor and into a small room. Gamble plopped down in a chair and pulled a cigar from his coat pocket. "If you don't want to get drunk, at least have a smoke with me."

Sawyer put out his hand and the two men lit up.

Gamble slowly waved his match back and forth like a miniature flag before crumpling it under his foot. He eyed Sawyer intently through the twin walls of cigar smoke. "Hardy tells me you're thinking about joining up with him."

"To tell you the truth, I really haven't given it much thought."

"You could do a hell of a lot worse for yourself."

"Frankly, Gamble, I don't think I do all that bad for myself right where I am."

Gamble grinned. "Shit! What do you make a year?"

"That's none of your damned business."

"Jesus, I told you what I pull in. Come on, just a ballpark."

Sawyer cradled the cigar in his hand before clenching it between his teeth. There was now mild amusement in his eyes. "Okay, it's less than what you make. That narrow it down enough?"

Gamble laughed.

"Why do you care what my paycheck says?"

"The point is, I don't. But from what I've seen of you and knowing the government's way of doing business, I gotta believe it's not nearly enough."

"So? Even if it isn't, that's not your problem."

"I'm not into problems so much as I'm into problem solving. That's what chairmen do, Sawyer. They look at the big picture, or at least they're supposed to. So how about it?"

"So how about what?"

Gamble puffed on his cigar, a small twinkle in his eye.

It finally dawned on Sawyer what the man was getting at.

"Are you offering me a job?"

"Hardy says you're the best. I only hire the best."

"Exactly what position are you looking to fill?"

"Head of security, what else?"

"I thought Lucas already had that job."

Gamble shrugged. "I'll take care of him. He's more of my personal guy anyway. I *quadrupled* his government salary, by the way. I'll do better than that for you."

"I take it you blame Lucas for what happened with Archer."

"Hey, it's somebody's responsibility. So what do you say?"

"What about Hardy?"

"He's a big boy. Who says I can't bid for your services? I get you on board, maybe I don't need as much of him."

"Frank's a good friend of mine. I'm not doing anything that would screw him. That's not how I operate."

"It's not like the guy's gonna be reduced to going through trash cans. He's already made a hell of a lot of money. Most of it off me." Gamble shrugged. "But suit yourself."

Sawyer stood up. "To tell you the truth, I'm not sure you and I could ever survive each other."

Gamble eyed him steadily. "You know, you're probably right about that."

Sawyer left Gamble sitting there. When he exited the room, he came face-to-face with Richard Lucas, who had been standing outside the door.

"Hey, Rich, you certainly get around."

"It's part of my job," Lucas said brusquely.

"Well, in my book, you qualify for sainthood." Sawyer nodded toward the room where Nathan Gamble was puffing on his cigar and walked off.

Sawyer had just gotten back to his office when his line buzzed.

"Yes?"

"Charles Tiedman, Lee."

"I'll sure take that one." Sawyer hit the flashing red light on his phone. "Hello, Charles."

Tiedman's manner was brisk and businesslike. "Lee, I was getting back to you on your question."

Sawyer flipped back through his notebook until he reached the section on his previous discussion with Tiedman. "You were going to check on the dates Lieberman had raised the rates."

"I didn't want to mail or fax them to you. Even though they are technically publicly known . . . well, I wasn't certain who might see them other than yourself. No need to stir things up unnecessarily."

"I understand." *God, these Fed guys never stop with the secrecy, do they?* Sawyer thought. "Why don't you give them to me now."

Tiedman cleared his throat and began. "There were five such instances. December nineteenth, 1990, was the first change. The others occurred on February twenty-eighth of the following year, September twenty-sixth, 1992, November fifteenth of the same year, and finally April sixteenth, 1993."

Sawyer wrote them down. "What was the net effect? After all five changes?"

"The net effect was to add one-half a percentage point to the Fed Funds Rate. However, the first reduction was one percentage point. The last increase was three-quarters."

"I take it that's a lot at one time."

"If we were in the military discussing weapons systems, one percentage point would easily equate to a nuclear bomb."

"I know if early word leaked out about the Fed's decision regarding interest rates, then people could make enormous profits."

"Actually," said Tiedman, "advance notice of the Fed's action on interest rates is, for all intents and purposes, worthless."

Mother of God. Sawyer closed his eyes, slapped his forehead and leaned back in his chair so far he almost toppled over. Maybe he should just plant his trusty ten-millimeter against his temple and save himself additional misery. "So, excuse my French, but why all the goddamned secrecy?"

"Don't misunderstand me. Unscrupulous people could certainly profit in innumerable ways from learning inside information about the Fed's deliberations. However, advance information of Fed action is not typically one of them. The market has an army of Fed watchers who are so adept at their job that the financial community usually knows well in advance whether the Fed is going to lower or raise interest rates and by how much. In effect, the market already knows what we'll do. Is that clear enough for you?"

"Very." Sawyer exhaled audibly. Then he jerked up in his chair. "What happens if the market is wrong?"

Tiedman's tone showed he was very pleased with the question. "Ah, that is an entirely different matter. If the market is wrong, then you could have enormous swings on the financial landscape."

"So if somebody knew ahead of time that one of these unexpected changes was coming down the pike, he could make some nice profits?"

"That's considerably understating it. Anyone with advance information of an unanticipated Fed change in interest rates could potentially make *billions* of dollars seconds after the Fed action was announced." Tiedman's response left Sawyer momentarily speechless. He wiped his brow and whistled under his breath. "There are innumerable vehicles in which to do so, Lee, the most lucrative probably being Eurodollar contracts trading on the International Monetary Market in Chicago. The leverage is thousands to one. Or the stock market, of course. Rates go up, the market goes down, and vice versa, it's that simple. You can make billions if you're right, lose billions if you're wrong." Sawyer was still silent. "Lee, I believe there is one more question you want to ask me."

Sawyer cupped the phone receiver under his chin while he hurriedly wrote down some notes. "Only one? I was just getting warmed up."

"I think this query may make unimportant anything else you may want to know." Although Tiedman seemed on the surface to be toying with him, the agent sensed a true grimness behind the tone. He pushed himself to think. He almost yelled into the phone when it hit him. "The dates you just gave me, when the rates changed— were they all 'surprises' to the market?"

Tiedman paused before answering. "Yes." Sawyer could almost feel the electricity coming over the phone line. "In fact, they were the worst kind of surprises for the financial markets, because they did not occur as the result of regularly scheduled Fed meetings, but by Arthur's unilateral actions as Fed chairman."

"So he can raise rates by himself?"

"Yes, the board can give the chairman that power. It's often been done over the years. Arthur lobbied hard for it and got it. I'm sorry I didn't tell you that before. It didn't seem important."

"Forget it," Sawyer said. "And with those rate changes, maybe somebody made more money than there are stars?"

"Yes," Tiedman said very quietly. "Yes," he said again. "There's also the reality that others *lost* at least an equal amount of money."

"What do you mean?"

"Well, if you're correct that Arthur was being blackmailed to manipulate rates, the extreme steps he took—adjusting the Fed Funds Rate by as large as a percentage point at a time—leads me to conclude that damage to others was intended."

"Why?" Sawyer asked.

"Because if your goal was merely to profit from the adjustment in rates, you wouldn't need much in the way of movement to do so, so long as the direction, up or down, was a surprise to the markets. However, to the investments of others who anticipated a change in the other direction, a point adjustment *the other way* is catastrophic."

"Jesus. Any way to find out who took those kinds of hits?"

Tiedman smiled. "Lee, with the complexities of money movement today, neither you nor I would have enough years left to do that."

Tiedman didn't speak for at least another minute, and Sawyer really couldn't think of anything else to say. When Tiedman finally broke the silence, his voice was suddenly bone tired. "Until we had our earlier discussion, I never had considered the possibility that Arthur's relationship with Steven Page could have been used to coerce him into doing it. Now it seems rather obvious."

"You understand, though, that we don't have any proof that he was being blackmailed?"

"We'll probably never know the answer to that, I'm afraid," said Tiedman. "Not with Steven Page dead."

"Do you know whether Lieberman ever met Page at his apartment?"

"I don't believe that he did. Arthur mentioned to me once that he leased a cottage in Connecticut. And he cautioned me about mentioning it in front of his wife."

"You think that was the rendezvous spot for Page and Lieberman?"

"It could've been."

"I'll tell you where I'm going with this. Steven Page left behind a considerable estate when he died. Megabucks."

Tiedman's tone was one of complete shock. "I don't understand. I remember Arthur telling me more than once that Steven was always complaining about money."

"Nonetheless, it's undisputed that he died a very rich man. I'm wondering, could Lieberman have been the source of that wealth?"

"Highly unlikely. As I just said, Arthur's conversations with me indicated that he believed Steven to be far from affluent. In addition, I think it quite impossible that Arthur could have transferred that kind of money to Steven Page without his wife knowing about it."

"Then why take a risk with leasing a cottage? Couldn't they have met at Page's apartment?"

"All I can say is he never mentioned to me that he had visited Steven Page's apartment."

"Well, maybe the cottage was Page's idea."

"Why do you say that?"

"Well, if Lieberman didn't give Page the money, someone else had to. Don't you think Lieberman would've been suspicious if he had walked into Page's apartment and saw a Picasso on the wall? Wouldn't he have wanted to know where the funds came from?"

"Absolutely!"

"Actually, I'm certain Page wasn't blackmailing Lieberman. At least not directly."

"How can you be sure?"

"Lieberman kept a picture of Page at his apartment. I don't think he would keep a blackmailer's photo around. On top of that, we also found a bunch of letters at Lieberman's apartment. They were unsigned, romantic in content. Lieberman obviously valued them highly."

"You think Page was the author of those letters?"

"I know a way to tell for sure. You were friends with Page. Do you have a sample of his writing?"

"Actually, I've kept several handwritten letters he wrote me while he was working in New York. I can send them to you." Tiedman paused. Sawyer could hear him scribbling a note. "Lee, you've adeptly pointed out ways Page could *not* have reaped his millions. So where did he get his wealth?"

"Think about it. If Page and Lieberman were having an affair, that's plenty of ammo to blackmail him with, you agree?"

"Certainly."

"Okay, what if someone else, a third party, encouraged Page to have an affair with Lieberman."

"But I introduced them. I hope you're not accusing me of perpetrating this ghastly conspiracy."

"You may have been the one to introduce them, but that's not to say Page and whoever was funding him couldn't have helped that introduction occur. Moving in the right circles, helping publicize Page's financial brilliance to the right people."

"Go on."

"So Page and Lieberman hit it off. The third party may believe that Lieberman may one day run the Fed. So Page and his backer bide their time. The backer pays Page to keep up the romance. They would've documented the relationship every which way from Sunday—taped phone calls, video, still photos—you can believe that."

"Then Steven Page was all part of a setup. He never actually cared for Arthur. I . . . I can't believe this." The little man sounded terribly depressed.

"Then Page gets HIV and allegedly commits suicide."

"Allegedly? You have doubts about his death?"

"I'm a cop, Charles, I have doubts about the Pope. Page is gone, but his accomplice is still out there. Lieberman becomes Fed chairman, and bam, the blackmail begins."

"But Arthur's death?"

"Well, your comment about him seeming almost happy that he had cancer tells me one thing."

"Which is?"

"That he was about to tell his blackmailer to take a flying leap and was going to go public with the scheme."

Tiedman rubbed his brow nervously. "It all makes perfect sense."

Sawyer lowered his voice. "You haven't mentioned any of what we've discussed to anyone, have you?"

"No, I haven't."

"Well, stick to that habit, and never let your guard down."

"What exactly are you suggesting?" There was a sudden catch in Tiedman's voice.

"I'm just recommending in the very strongest possible terms that you be very careful and do not tell anyone—not any of the Fed members, including Walter Burns, your secretary, your assistants, your wife, your friends—anything about this."

"Are you saying that you think *I'm* in danger? I find that very hard to believe."

Sawyer's tone was grim. "I'm sure Arthur Lieberman thought that too."

Charles Tiedman gripped a pencil on his desk so hard that it snapped in half. "I'll certainly follow your advice to the letter." Thoroughly frightened, Tiedman hung up.

Sawyer leaned back in his chair and longed for another cigarette as his mental engine went into overdrive. Somebody had obviously been paying off Steven Page. Sawyer thought he had a reasonable answer for why: setting up Lieberman. The question nagging at him now was who? And then the biggest question of all: Who had killed Steven Page? The FBI agent was now convinced, despite evidence to the contrary, that Steven Page had been murdered. He picked up the phone. "Ray? It's Lee. I want you to give Lieberman's personal physician another call."

CHAPTER FIFTY-THREE

Bill Patterson looked at the dashboard clock and stretched out his large body. They were traveling *southbound* about two hours north of Bell Harbor. Next to him, his wife was sound asleep. It had been a far longer trip to the market than they were expecting. Sidney Archer had been incorrect. They had not stopped on the drive up to Bell Harbor, and had reached the beach house barely ahead of the storm. Having piled their luggage in the back bedroom, they headed out for food before the storm worsened. The market in Bell Harbor was sold out, so they were compelled to drive north to the far larger grocery in Port Vista. On the way back, their route had been closed off by a jackknifed tanker truck. Last night had been spent very uncomfortably in a motel.

Patterson now checked the backseat; Amy was also napping, her little mouth forming a perfect circle. Patterson looked at the heavily falling snow and grimaced. Fortunately, he had not been privy to the latest news flashes proclaiming his daughter to be a fugitive from justice. He was sick enough with worry as it was. In his anxiety he had chewed his fingernails until they had bled and his gut was full of acid. He wanted to be protecting Sidney now, as he had dutifully done when she was a little girl. Ghosts and bogeymen had been his chief foes back then. The current ones were far more deadly, he had to assume. At least he had Amy with him. God help the person who tried to harm his granddaughter. *And God be with you, Sidney.*

Ray Jackson stood silently in the doorway of Sawyer's cramped office. Behind his desk, Lee Sawyer was immersed in a file. A full pot of coffee was on a hot plate in front of him, a half-eaten meal next to it. Jackson could not remember the last time the man had failed at his job. However, Sawyer had been taking increasing heat—internally from the director of the FBI on down, in the press and from the White House to Capitol Hill. Jackson grimaced. Hell, if they thought it was so damn easy, why didn't they hit the streets and try to solve the case?

"Hey, Lee?"

Sawyer jerked up. "Hey, Ray. Fresh pot of coffee on the hot plate, help yourself."

Jackson poured himself a cup and sat down. "Word is you've been taking some grief from upstairs on this case."

Sawyer shrugged. "Goes with the territory."

"You want to talk about it?" Jackson settled down in a chair next to him.

"What's there to talk about? Fine, everybody wants to know who was behind that plane going down. I do too. I also want to know a hell of a lot more than that. I want to know who used Joe Riker for target practice. I want to know who killed Steve and Ed Page. I want to know who blew away those three guys in the limo. I want to know where Jason Archer is."

"And Sidney Archer?"

"Yeah, and Sidney Archer. And I'm not gonna find out by listening to all the people who just have a bunch of questions and no answers. Speaking of which, have you got any for me? Answers, that is?"

Jackson got up and closed the door to Sawyer's office.

"According to his doctor, Arthur Lieberman did not have the HIV virus."

Sawyer exploded. "That's impossible. The guy's lying his ass off."

"Don't think so, Lee."

"Why the hell not?"

"Because he showed me Lieberman's medical file." Sawyer sat back, stunned. Jackson continued. "When I asked the guy, I thought it was going to be like you and I talked about—his expression would have to tell us, because the man sure as hell wasn't going to show me any records without a subpoena in hand. But he did, Lee. No harm in his doctor proving that Lieberman *didn't* have the virus. Lieberman was some kind of health fanatic. Had yearly physicals, all sorts of preventive measures and testing. As part of the physicals, Lieberman was routinely tested for HIV. The doctor showed me the results from 1990 until last year. They were all negative, Lee. I saw them myself."

Sidney closed her bloodshot eyes for a moment, lay back on her parents' bed and took a deep breath. Wearily she made a decision. She pulled out the card from her purse and stared at it for some minutes. She felt the overpowering need to talk to someone. For a number of reasons, she decided it had to be him. She went down to the Land Rover and carefully dialed the number.

Sawyer had just opened the door to his apartment when he heard the phone start to ring. He grabbed up the phone, taking off his overcoat as he did so.

"Hello?"

The line was silent for a moment and Sawyer was just about to hang up. Then a voice came on the other end. Sawyer gripped the receiver with both hands and let his coat fall on the floor. He stood rigidly in the middle of his living room.

"Sidney?"

"Hello" The voice was small, but firm.

"Where are you?" Sawyer's question was automatic, but he instantly regretted it.

"Sorry, Lee, this is not a geography lesson."

"Okay, okay." Sawyer sat down in his battered recliner. "I don't need to know where you are. But are you safe?"

Sidney almost laughed. "Reasonably so, I guess, but it's still just a guess. I'm heavily armed, if that makes a difference." She paused for a moment. "I saw the TV news."

"I know you didn't kill them, Sidney."

"How——"

"Just trust me on that one."

Sidney let out a deep breath as the memory of that horrific night settled back down on her. "I'm sorry I didn't tell you when I called before. I . . . I just couldn't."

"Tell me what happened that night, Sidney."

Sidney was silent, debating whether to hang up or not. Sawyer sensed her deliberations. "Sidney, I'm not at the Hoover Building. I can't trace your call. And I happen to be on your side. You can talk as long as you want."

"Okay. You're the only one I happen to trust. What do you want to know?"

"Everything. Just start from the beginning."

It took Sidney about five minutes to recount the events of that night.

"You didn't see the shooter?"

"He was wearing a ski mask that covered his face. I think it was the same guy who tried to kill me later. At least I hope there aren't two guys walking around with eyes like that."

"In New York?"

"What?"

"The security guard, Sidney. He was murdered."

She rubbed at her forehead. "Yes. In New York."

"But definitely a man?"

"Yes, from his build and what I could see of his facial characteristics through the mask. And the bottom of his neck was exposed. I could see beard stubble."

Sawyer was impressed with her observations and said so.

"You tend to remember the smallest details when you think you're about to die."

"I know what you mean. I've actually been in that situation myself. Look, we found the tape, Sidney. Your talk with Jason?"

Sidney looked around the darkened interior of the Land Rover and the garage beyond. "So, everyone knows—"

"Don't worry about that. On the tape your husband sounded jumpy, nervous. Answered some of your questions but not all."

"Yes, he was distraught. Panicked."

"How about when you talked to him on the pay phone in New Orleans? How did he sound then? Different or the same?"

Sidney narrowed her eyes as she thought back. "Different," she said finally.

"How? Give it to me as exactly as you can."

"Well, he didn't sound nervous. In fact, it was almost a monotone. He told me I couldn't say anything, that the police were watching. He just gave me instructions and hung up. It was a monologue rather than a conversation. I never said anything."

Sawyer sighed. "Quentin Rowe is convinced that you were in Jason's office at Triton after the plane crash. Were you?"

Sidney was silent.

"Sidney, I really don't give a tinker's dam if you were there. But if you were, I just want to ask you one question about something you might have done while you were in there."

Sidney remained silent.

"Sidney? Look, *you* called me. You said you trust me, although at this point I can understand you not wanting to trust anyone. I wouldn't recommend it, but you can hang up now, try going it alone."

"I was there," she said quietly.

"Okay, Rowe mentioned a microphone on Jason's computer."

Sidney sighed. "I accidentally hit it; it bent. I couldn't get it back straight."

Sawyer sat back in the recliner. "Did Jason ever use the microphone feature of the computer? Did he, for instance, have one at home?"

"No. He could type much faster than he could speak. Why?"

"So why did he have a microphone on his computer at work?"

Sidney thought about it for a moment. "I don't know. I think it was fairly recent. A few months or so, maybe a little longer. I've noticed them in other offices at Triton, if that helps. Why?"

"I'm getting there, Sidney, just bear with an old, tired G-man." Sawyer tugged at his top lip. "When you talked to Jason, both times, you're sure it was him?"

"Of course it was him. I know my own husband's voice."

Sawyer's tone was deliberate and steady, as though he were trying to graft those traits onto Sidney. "I didn't ask you if you were sure it was your husband's *voice*." He stopped momentarily, took a slow breath and then continued. "I asked you if you were sure it was your *husband* both times."

Sidney froze. When she finally found her own voice, it came out in a furious whisper. "What are you suggesting?"

"I listened to your first conversation with Jason. You're right, he did sound panicked, breathing heavy, the works. You guys had a real conversation. But now you tell me the second time around, he sounded far different, that it really wasn't a conversation. He talked, you listened. No panic. Now, we know about this microphone in Jason's office, something that he never uses. If he never uses it, why is it really there?"

"I . . . What other reason would it be there?"

"A microphone, Sidney, is for recording things. Sounds . . . Voices."

Sidney gripped the cell phone so hard her hand turned red. "Are you saying . . ."

"I'm saying that I believe that you heard your husband's voice over the phone both times, all right. But I think what you heard the second time was a compilation of your husband's words derived from the recordings taken by the microphone, because that was its real purpose, I'm fairly certain. A recorder."

"That can't be possible. Why?"

"I don't know why, yet. But it seems clear enough. That explains why your second conversation with him was so different. The second time around I gather the vocabulary was pretty ordinary?" Sidney didn't answer. "Sidney?" Sawyer heard a sob come over the line.

"Then you think . . . you believe that Jason is . . . dead?" Sidney fought back the tears. She had already lived through one episode of believing her husband dead, only to suddenly encounter him alive. Or so she thought. The tears started to slide down her cheeks as she contemplated having to grieve again for Jason.

"I have no way of knowing that, Sidney. The fact that I believe Jason's recorded voice was used rather than the real thing leads me to think that he was not around to speak himself. Why, I don't know. Let's leave it at that for now."

Sidney put down the phone and clutched her head. Every limb was now shaking like a slender elm in a windstorm.

Alarmed, Sawyer spoke earnestly into the phone. "Sidney? *Sidney?* Don't hang up. Please! Sidney?"

The line went dead.

Sawyer slammed down the receiver. "Dammit! Sonofabitch!"

A minute went by. Sawyer stomped around the small room. Working himself into a rage, he finally slammed a heavy fist right through the wall. He leaped for the phone when it rang again.

"Hello?" His voice was shaking with anticipation.

"Let's not talk anymore about whether Jason is . . . is alive, all right?" Sidney's voice was devoid of any emotion.

"All right," Sawyer said quietly. He sat down and paused for a moment, deciding what line of questioning to pursue.

"Lee, why would someone at Triton want to record Jason's voice and then use it to communicate with me?"

"Sidney, if I knew the answer to that, I'd be doing cartwheels down the hallway. You said a number of offices had them installed recently. That means that it could have been anyone at the company who could have jerry-built his mike into a recording device. Or maybe one of Triton's competitors could have done it somehow. I mean, if *you* knew he didn't use the microphone, other people would as well. I do know that it's no longer in his office. Maybe it has something to do with the secrets he sold RTG." Sawyer rubbed his scalp as he sorted through the additional questions he wanted to ask her.

She beat him to it. "Only Jason selling secrets to RTG doesn't make any sense now."

Amazed, Sawyer stood up. "Why not?"

"Because Paul Brophy was working on the CyberCom deal too. He was present at all the strategy sessions. He even made an attempt to take over the lead role in the transaction. Brophy, I now know, was working with Goldman and RTG to learn Triton's final negotiating position and beat them to the punch. He would've known far more about Triton's bargaining position than Jason ever would. The precise deal terms were physically maintained at Tyler, Stone, not at Triton."

Sawyer's eyes grew wide. "You're saying—"

"I'm simply saying that since Brophy was working for RTG, they wouldn't have needed Jason."

Sawyer sat down and swore under his breath. He had never made that connection. "Sidney, we both saw a video of your husband passing information to a group of men in a warehouse in Seattle on the day of the plane crash. If he wasn't giving them information on the CyberCom deal, then what the hell was it?"

Sidney shook in frustration. "I don't know! I do know that when Brophy was cut out of the final rounds of the deal, they tried to blackmail me for it. I pretended to go along. My actual plan was to go to the authorities. But then we got in the limo." Sidney shuddered. "You know the rest."

Sawyer stabbed a hand into his pocket and pulled out a cigarette. He cradled the phone under his chin while he lit up. "You find out anything else?"

"I spoke with Jason's secretary, Kay Vincent. She said the other major project Jason was working on other than CyberCom was an integration of Triton's backup files."

"Tape backups? Is that important?" Sawyer asked.

"I don't know, but Kay also told me that Triton had delivered financial records to CyberCom. On the very day of the plane crash." Sidney sounded exasperated.

"So what's unusual about that? They're involved in a deal."

"On that same day I got my butt chewed out in New York by

Nathan Gamble because he didn't want to turn those very same records over to CyberCom."

Sawyer rubbed at his forehead. "That doesn't make any sense. Do you think Gamble knew the records were turned over?"

"I don't know. I mean, I can't be sure about that." Sidney paused. The damp cold was starting to become painful. "In fact, I thought the CyberCom deal might blow up because of Gamble's refusal."

"Well, I can tell you for a fact that it didn't. I attended the press conference today announcing the deal. Gamble was smiling like the Cheshire cat."

"Well, with CyberCom in the fold I can understand him being very happy."

"Can't say the same for Quentin Rowe."

"They certainly are an odd pair."

"Right. Like Al Capone and Gandhi."

Sidney breathed deeply into the receiver but said nothing.

"Sidney, I know you're not going to like this, but I'm going to say it anyway. You'd be a lot better off if you came in. We can protect you."

"You mean imprison me, don't you?" she said, a bitter edge in her voice.

"Sidney, I know you didn't kill anyone."

"Can you prove it?"

"I think I can."

"You *think*? I'm sorry, Lee. I really appreciate the vote of confidence, but I'm afraid that's not quite good enough. I know how the evidence stacks up. And the public's perception of things. They'd throw away the key."

"You could really be in danger out there." Sawyer slowly fingered the FBI shield pinned to his belt. "Listen, tell me where you are and I'll come. No one else. Not my partner, nobody, just me. To get you, they go through me first. Then, meanwhile, we can try to figure this thing out together."

"Lee, you're an FBI agent. There's a warrant for my arrest. It's your official duty to take me into custody the moment you lay eyes on me. On top of that, you've already covered for me once."

Sawyer swallowed with difficulty. In his mind a pair of captivating emerald eyes blended together into the light of a train bearing right down on him. "Then let's just call it part of my unofficial duty."

"And if it's found out, your career is over. On top of it, *you* could go to prison."

"I'm a big boy, I'll take my chances about that. I give you my word it'll just be me coming." His voice trembled with suppressed excitement. Sidney could not speak. "Sidney, I'm shooting straight with you. I . . . I really want you to be okay, all right?"

There was a catch in Sidney's throat. "I believe you, Lee. And I can't tell you how much that means to me. But I'm not going to let you throw your life away either. I'm not having that on my conscience too."

"Sidney—"

"I have to go now, Lee."

"Wait! Don't."

"I'll try to call back."

"When?"

Sidney stared straight ahead through the windshield, her face suddenly rigid, her eyes widening. "I'm . . . I'm not sure," she said vaguely. Then the line went dead.

Sawyer put the phone down and fumbled in his pants pocket for the pack of Marlboros and lit another cigarette. He used his cupped hand for an ashtray while he paced around the room. He stopped and fingered the fist-sized hole in the wall and seriously contemplated giving it a twin. Instead he stepped to the window and looked out in complete despair at a frosty winter night.

As soon as Sidney had gone back into the house, the man stepped from the dark shadows of the garage. His breath frosted in the freezing environment. He opened the door to the Land Rover. As the car's interior dome light came on, the deadly blue eyes shimmered like hideously carved jewels in the soft light. Kenneth Scales's gloved hands expertly searched the car but found nothing of interest. He then picked up the cell phone and hit the redial button. The phone rang only once before Lee Sawyer's excited voice came on the line. Scales smiled as he listened to the urgent tones of the FBI agent, who evidently thought Sidney Archer had called him back. Then Scales disconnected the call, quietly closed the car door and made his way up the stairs to the house. From a leather sheath on his belt he pulled the stiletto blade he had used to kill Edward Page. He would have taken care of Sidney Archer as she stepped from the Land Rover except he was uncertain whether she was armed. He had already seen her skill with a gun. Besides, his method of killing was based on the total surprise of his victims.

He made his way through the first floor looking for the leather jacket Sidney had been wearing, but did not find it. Her purse was on the counter, but what he wanted wasn't in there. He proceeded over to the stairs leading up to the second floor. He paused at that point and cocked his head. Over the rush of the wind, the sound reaching his ears from the second floor made him smile once again. Water running in the tub. On this bitterly cold winter's night in rustic Maine, the sole occupant of the house was preparing to take a nice, hot, soothing bath. He made his way silently up the stairs. The bedroom door at the top of the landing was shut, but he could clearly hear the water running in the adjoining bathroom. Then the water was turned off. He waited a few more seconds as he envisioned Sidney Archer climbing into the tub, letting the hot water comfort her weary body. Then he stepped to the door of the bedroom. Scales would get the password first and then occupy himself for a while with the lady of the house. If he could not find what he wanted, he would promise to let her live in exchange for her secret and then he would kill her. He wondered briefly what the attractive lawyer would look like naked. From what he had seen of her, Scales concluded she would look very good indeed. And it wasn't as though he was in a rush. It had been a long, weary trip up the East Coast to Maine. He deserved a little R&R, he thought as he contemplated the upcoming event.

Scales stood to the side of the door, his back against the wall, his knife at the ready, and placed one hand on the knob, turning it virtually noiselessly.

The shotgun blast that disintegrated the door and embedded several pieces of the weapon's Magnum load in his left forearm was not nearly so quiet. He screamed and threw himself down the stairs, athletically rolling and landing virtually upright, gripping his bloody arm. He jerked his eyes upward as Sidney Archer, fully dressed, charged out of the bedroom. She racked the action of the shotgun again and Scales barely managed to throw himself out of the way before another blast hit the very spot where he had been standing. The house was almost totally dark, but if he moved again she would be able to zero in on his location. He crouched down behind the sofa, his predicament evident. At some point Sidney Archer would risk turning on a light and the deadly power of the shotgun would quickly devastate everything in the small room, including him.

Breathing quietly, he gripped his knife with his good hand, looked around the confines of the living room and waited. His arm stung terribly; Scales was far more used to inflicting pain than receiving it. He listened to Sidney's footsteps as she proceeded cautiously down the stairs. He was sure the shotgun was making wide sweeps of the area. From out of the darkness, he cautiously raised his head an inch or so above the top of the sofa. His eyes instantly riveted on her. She was halfway down the stairs. So intent was she on locating her quarry, she did not see a piece of the bedroom door that had landed on the stairs. When she unwittingly placed her weight fully on it, the piece slipped free and both her feet flew out from under her. With a scream, she tumbled down the stairs, the shotgun smashing against the railing. In an instant he pounced. As the pair rolled along the hardwood floor, he pounded her head against it. She kicked furiously against his chest and ribs with her heavy boots. Then she twisted away just as he struck savagely with his knife. The blow missed barely, tearing through the inside of her jacket instead of her flesh. A white object that had been in Sidney's pocket was dislodged from the impact of the blow and floated to the floor.

Sidney managed to grab the shotgun and delivered a terrific blow to Scales's face with the butt of the solid Winchester, breaking his nose and knocking out several front teeth. Stunned, Scales dropped his knife and fell back for an instant. Then, furious, he wrenched the shotgun free, turning it on a dazed Sidney Archer. In a panic she hurled herself several feet away but was still easily in range. His finger pulled the trigger, but the muzzle remained silent. The fall down the stairs and the ensuing struggle had jammed the weapon. Sidney, her head bursting with pain from the earlier blow, desperately crawled away. With a vicious snarl, Scales threw the useless shotgun away and stood up, blood streaming down his shirt from his torn mouth and rearranged nose. He picked up his knife where it had fallen and advanced with murderous eyes toward Sidney. When he lifted the blade to strike, Sidney whirled around, the 9mm pointed right at him. A split second before she fired, however, he exploded into an acrobatic leap that carried him over the dining room table. She held the trigger down, throwing the 9mm into full automatic fire, the Hydra-Shok slugs tracing an explosive pattern across the wall as she tried desperately to follow the path of his impromptu flight. Scales hit the polished wood floor hard, his momentum sending him headlong into the wall. As his torso whiplashed sideways from the impact with the wall, he crashed into the legs of an ornate mahogany sideboard. The slender mahogany legs snapped like matchsticks and the heavy piece collapsed right on top of him, spewing its contents across the room as drawers flew open from the fall. Scales did not move after that.

Sidney jumped up, ran through the kitchen, grabbed her purse off the counter and fled down the stairs to the garage. A minute later the garage door splintered and erupted outward and the Land Rover careened through the savaged opening, did a 180-degree spin in the driveway and disappeared into the snowstorm.

As Sidney looked in her rearview mirror, she saw a pair of headlights. Her heart skipped a beat as she watched the big Cadillac pull into the driveway of the house she had just left. The blood drained from her face. Omigod! Her parents were finally here and the timing could not have been worse. She swung the truck around, plowing through a snowdrift, and raced back toward her parents' house. Then her problem was suddenly compounded as she caught sight of another pair of headlights coming down the road from the same di-

rection her parents had come. She watched in steadily growing fear
as the black sedan moved down the street, its tires slowly crunching
over the path just left by the Caddie. The people who had dogged
her parents from Virginia. With everything else happening, she had
forgotten about them. Sidney slammed the Land Rover's accelerator
to the floor. Slipping in the snow for a moment, the four-wheel drive
system kicked in and the massive V-8 took hold, propelling the little tank forward like a cannonball. As she bore down on the sedan,
Sidney saw the driver react. His hand went inside his coat. But he
was a millisecond too late. She flew past her parents' house, veered
across the road and, with a crush of metal, slammed into the smaller
vehicle, pushing it across the slippery road and depositing it in a
steep ditch. The air bag in the truck inflated. With a furious effort,
Sidney ripped it off the steering column and slammed the truck into
reverse. The sound of metal wrenching free was clearly heard as the
two vehicles uncoupled.

Sidney turned the truck around and then stared in disbelief. Her
swift attack had taken care of whoever was following her parents. It
also had another result. She watched in dismay as the Cadillac
turned off Beach Street and roared off back to Route 1. Sidney
rammed the accelerator down and headed after them.

The man struggled out of the car and stared in shock at the
rapidly disappearing truck.

Sidney saw the taillights of the Cadillac just ahead. At this point,
Route 1 was a two-lane road. She pulled up behind her parents and
blew her horn repeatedly. The Cadillac immediately accelerated. Her
parents were by now probably so scared they wouldn't even stop for
a state trooper in a marked car, much less a lunatic blowing her horn
in a smashed-up truck. Sidney momentarily held her breath and
then careened onto the wrong side of the road, mashed the gas pedal
to the floor and pulled alongside her parents' car. She saw her father
react to the Land Rover appearing on his left. The Caddie shimmied
from side to side as it sped up, and Sidney had to keep the accelerator close to the floor to keep up, as the damaged Land Rover was
sluggish to respond. As Sidney steadily gained ground, Bill Patter-

son planted the bulky Caddie squarely in the middle of the two-lane road, daring their pursuer to overtake them. Sidney rolled down her window and steered her vehicle halfway onto the dirt-and-gravel shoulder. Thank God the roads hadn't been plowed yet or she would have had no shoulder to travel on. As she inched up to the passenger side of the Cadillac, her father swung back onto the right side, forcing Sidney to go off the road entirely. As the Land Rover bounced and swayed over the rough terrain, Sidney looked at her speedometer; it hovered near eighty. Fear rattled through every nerve in her body. She looked up ahead. They were coming to a steep curve. She was about to run out of road. She smashed the accelerator flat to the floor. She only had seconds left. "Mom!" She screamed over the fury of the wind and the wall of pouring snow. "*Mom!*" Sidney leaned as far out the driver's window as she could while maintaining some control over the truck. She took one deep breath and screamed as loud as she ever had in her life. "MMMOOOMM!"

She saw her mother peering through the whipping snow, her eyes wide with terror, and then Sidney finally saw recognition and then relief in them. Her mother quickly turned to her father. The Cadillac slowed down immediately and allowed Sidney to move back onto the road ahead of them. Her face and hair covered with snow, Sidney motioned with one hand for them to follow her. In the near-blinding swirl of white, the two cars raced down the road.

About an hour later, they veered off at an exit. Within ten minutes the Land Rover and the Cadillac pulled into the parking lot of a motel. The first thing Sidney Archer did was jump out of the truck, race to her parents' car, throw open the rear door and grab up her daughter in her arms. Tears were pouring down Sidney's face as fiercely as the snow. She gripped her sleepy daughter with fingers that promised never to let go again. Amy had no way of knowing how close she had come to losing her mother this night. If the blade had veered one inch the other way? If Sidney's mother had recognized her daughter a second too late? But the little girl would never know that. Sidney Archer certainly did, however, and it made her squeeze her daughter to her breast as tightly as she possibly could as her own body painfully convulsed. Bill Patterson came around the car and planted a bear hug around his daughter. The big man was shaking severely too after this latest nightmare. His wife joined them and they stood in a small circle, clutching each other tightly, each of them silent. Though the snow soon covered their clothes, they didn't budge; they were just holding on.

The man had managed to free his vehicle and then ran over to the Pattersons' house, where it was still quiet. A minute later the house was quiet no more as the sideboard was slowly raised off the floor and then violently hurled away with another crash and splintering of wood. Scales painfully stood up with the aid of his colleague. The look on his battered face made it abundantly clear that it was indeed fortunate for her that Sidney Archer was not presently within his deadly reach. As he went back to retrieve his knife he noticed the piece of paper Sidney had dropped—Jason's e-mail message. Scales picked it up, studying it momentarily. In another five minutes he and his associate had made their way to the damaged car. Scales picked up his cellular phone and punched in a speed-dial number. It was time to bring in reinforcements.

CHAPTER FIFTY-FOUR

At two-thirty in the morning, a highly agitated Lee Sawyer drove to the office through a snowstorm that threatened to hit blizzard status by that afternoon. The whole East Coast was being assaulted by a major winter storm system that threatened to hang around until Christmas.

Sawyer went directly to the conference room, where he spent the next five hours going over every aspect of the case, from the files, his notes and memory. His main goal was assembling the case as he now understood it into some semblance of logic. The problem was that not much made sense, chiefly because he was not certain whether he was confronted with one case or two: Lieberman and Archer together, or Lieberman and Archer separately. That's really what it boiled down to. He jotted down some new angles that occurred to him, but none of them seemed all that promising. Then he picked up the phone and dialed the lab asking for Liz Martin, the technician who had performed the Luma-lite exam on the limousine.

"Liz, I owe you an apology. I've been letting this case get to me a little bit and I took it out on you. I was out of line and I'm sorry."

Liz smiled. "Apology accepted. We're all under pressure. What's up?"

"I need your resident computer expert skills. What do you know about computer tape backup systems?"

"Funny you should ask. My boyfriend's a trial lawyer and he was just telling me the other day it's the hottest topic in the legal sector right now."

"Why's that?"

"Well, tape backups are potentially discoverable in litigation. For example, an employee writes an interoffice memo or e-mail that contains damaging information about the company. The employee later erases the e-mail and destroys all hard copies of the memo. You'd think it was gone for good, right? Nope, because with tape backup, the system might well have saved it before it was erased. And under the rules of discovery, they may have to turn it over to the other side. My boyfriend's firm advises clients that with documents created via computer, if you don't want someone else to ever read it, then don't create it."

"Hmmm." Sawyer thumbed through the papers in front of him. "Good thing I still opt for invisible ink."

"You're a relic, Lee, but at least you're a nice relic."

"Okay, Professor Liz, I've got another one for you." Sawyer read her the password.

"That's a pretty good password, isn't it, Liz?"

"Actually, it's not."

"What?" That was the absolute last response Sawyer had expected to hear.

"It's so long that it would be easy to forget a portion of it or otherwise get it incorrect. Or if you were communicating it to someone else orally, they could easily get it wrong in the transmission, transpose a number, that sort of thing."

"But because it's so long, it wouldn't be capable of being broken, right? I thought that was the beauty of it."

"Certainly. However, you don't have to use *all* those numbers to accomplish that goal. Ten would've been ample for most purposes. With fifteen numbers you're pretty much invulnerable."

"But these days you've got computers that could crank those combos through."

"With fifteen numbers you're looking at well over a trillion combos and most encryption packages come with a shut-down feature if too many combos are tried at one time. Even if it didn't have the shut-down feature, the fastest computer in the world doing a numbers crunch still wouldn't pop this password because the presence and placement of those decimal points make the possible combinations so high that a traditional brute-force assault wouldn't work."

"So you're saying—"

"I'm saying whoever put together this password went way overboard. The negatives far outweigh its imperviousness to being cracked. It simply didn't need to be this complex to avoid being penetrated. Maybe whoever put it together was a novice about computers."

Sawyer shook his head. "I think this person knew exactly what he was doing."

"Well, then it wasn't solely for protection purposes."

"What else could it be?"

"I'm not sure, Lee. I've never seen one like this before."

Sawyer didn't say anything.

"Anything else?"

"What? Uh, no, Liz, that's it." Sawyer sounded very depressed.

"I'm sorry if I wasn't much help."

"No, you were. You gave me a lot to think about. Thanks, Liz." He brightened. "Hey, I owe you a lunch, okay?"

"I'm going to hold you to that one and this time I get to pick the place."

"Fine, only make sure they take the Exxon card. That's about the only plastic I have left."

"You really know how to show a girl a good time, Lee."

Sawyer hung up and looked down at the password again. If half of what he had heard about Jason Archer's mental prowess was true, then the complexity of the password had been no accident. He looked at the numbers again. It was driving him nuts, but he couldn't shake the feeling that they somehow seemed familiar. He poured himself another cup of coffee, took out a scratch piece of paper and started doodling, a habit that helped him think. This case seemed to have been with him for years. With a start he looked at the date on the e-mail message Archer had sent his wife: 95-11-19. He wrote the numbers down on the scratch paper: 95-11-19. He smiled. Figures a computer would kick it out like that, more confusing than anything else. Then he found himself staring at the numbers more intently. His smile faded. He quickly wrote them down another way: 95/11/19 then, finally, 951119. He quickly scribbled again, made a mistake, scratched it out and kept going. He looked at the finished product: 599111.

Sawyer's face turned whiter than the paper he was writing on. *Backwards*. He read the e-mail from Jason Archer again. All backwards, Archer had said. But why? If Archer were under so much pressure that he had mistyped the address and not finished the message, why take the time to type two phrases—"all wrong" and "all backwards"—if they meant the same thing? The truth suddenly dawned on Sawyer: unless the two phrases had entirely different meanings, both quite literal. He looked at the numbers comprising the password one more time and then started to write furiously. After several mistakes he finally finished. He numbly drained the last of his coffee as he took in the numbers in their true (unbackward) order: 12-19-90, 2-28-91, 9-26-92, 11-15-92 and 4-16-93. Archer had been very precise in his selection of passwords. It had actually been a clue within the password itself. Sawyer didn't need to consult his notes. He knew what the numbers represented. He took a deep breath.

The calendar dates of the five times Arthur Lieberman had changed interest rates on his own. The five times somebody out there had made enough money to buy a country or maybe lost that much.

Sawyer's question had finally been answered. He had one case, not two. There *was* a connection between Jason and Lieberman. But what was it? Another thought struck him. Edward Page had told Sidney he hadn't been following Jason Archer at the airport. The other person he could have been dogging was Lieberman. Page could have been shadowing the Fed chairman and walked right into Archer's switch. But why follow Lieberman? With a scowl, Sawyer finally put the message aside and looked at the videocassette recording of Archer's exchange at the warehouse, which was sitting on the table. If Sidney was right about Brophy knowing far more than Jason Archer, what the hell had been passed off in that warehouse? Could that be the connection to Arthur Lieberman? He hadn't looked at the tape in a while. He decided to fix that oversight right now.

He popped the tape in a VCR that rested under a large-screen TV in one corner of the room. He poured some more coffee and hit the control; the tape started. He watched the scene twice through. Then he watched it a third time, in slow motion. A frown spread over his features. When he had watched the tape for the very first time in Hardy's office, something had made him frown then too. What the hell was it? He rewound the tape again and then hit the start button. Jason and the other man were waiting, Jason's briefcase was visible. The knock on the door, the other men came in. The old guy, the other two in sunglasses. Real cute. Sawyer looked at the two burly men again. They looked oddly familiar, but he couldn't . . . He shook his head and continued to watch. Here came the exchange, Jason looking extremely nervous. Then the plane going over. The warehouse was on a flight path to the airport, he had learned. Everyone in the room looked up at the thundering sound. Sawyer jerked so hard he spilled most of his coffee on his shirt. Only this time it wasn't from the sound of the plane.

"Holy shit!" He froze the tape. Then he planted his face a bare inch from the screen. He grabbed the phone. "Liz, I need your magic, and this time, Professor, it'll be dinner." He quickly told her what he wanted.

It took Sawyer two minutes, running flat out, to reach the lab. The equipment was all set up, a smiling Liz standing next to it. Sawyer, puffing hard, handed her the tape, which she put into another VCR. She sat down at a control panel and the tape began to play. The screen it appeared on was a good sixty inches across.

"Okay, okay, get ready, Liz. There! Right there!" Sawyer almost jumped off the floor in his excitement.

Liz froze the tape and then hit some buttons on her panel. The human figures on the screen grew until they spanned the whole screen. There was only one person Sawyer was looking at. "Liz, can you blow this part up right here?" His thick finger stabbed at a specific section of the screen. Liz did as he asked.

Sawyer shook his head in silent amazement. Liz joined him in looking at the startling scene. She looked up at him. "You were right, Lee. What does it mean?"

Sawyer stared at the man who had identified himself to Jason Archer as Anthony DePazza on that fateful November morning in drizzly Seattle. More specifically, Sawyer zeroed in on DePazza's neck, which was clearly visible, since he had jerked his head up when the plane had gone over. In fact, Sawyer and Liz were both staring at a clear break in the neckline, real and false skin.

"I'm not sure, Liz. But why the hell is the guy with Archer wearing some sort of a disguise?"

Liz stared wistfully at the screen. "I used to be into that when I was a thespian in college."

"Into what?"

"You know, costumes, makeup, masks. For when we put on a performance. I'll have you know I was one wicked Lady Macbeth."

Sawyer looked at the screen, his mouth wide open as the word she had just uttered pounded through his head: *Performance?*

Chewing on this new information, Sawyer hustled back to the conference room. Ray Jackson was sitting there with several documents in his hand, which he waved at his partner. "By fax from Charles Tiedman. Page's handwriting samples. I've got copies of the letters I found in Lieberman's apartment. I'm no expert, but I think we've got a match."

Sawyer sat down and looked over the letters comparing the writing. "I agree with you, Ray, but get the lab to give us a definite."

"Right." Jackson started off to perform that task, but Sawyer abruptly stopped him. "Hey, Ray, let me look at those letters one more time."

Jackson handed them over.

Sawyer only really wanted to look at one of them. The letterhead was impressive: Columbia University Alumni Association. Tiedman hadn't mentioned that Steven Page had attended Columbia. Page had evidently, at some point, been active in alumni affairs. Sawyer did some rough arithmetic in his head. Steven Page was twenty-eight when he had died five years ago. That would make him thirty-three or thirty-four today, depending on his birthdate. So he probably would have been a 1984 graduate. Another thought suddenly flared into Sawyer's head.

"Go ahead, Ray. I've got some calls to make."

After Jackson went off with the documents, Sawyer dialed information and got the number for Columbia University's information office. Within a couple of minutes he got through. He was told that Steven Page had indeed been a 1984 graduate of the university, in fact a magna cum laude graduate. Sawyer looked down at his hands as he prepared to ask his next question. Every finger was quivering. He did his best to keep his emotions under control as he waited for the woman on the other end of the line to consult her records. Yes, Sawyer was told. The other student was also an '84 grad; indeed, this one had graduated summa cum laude. Quite impressive, the voice said, to achieve that at Columbia. He asked another question and was told he would have to talk to Student Housing for the answer. He waited, his nerves humming with electricity. When he finally got someone at Student Housing, the question was answered within a minute. Sawyer quietly thanked the person for his help and then slammed down the phone. The veteran FBI agent jumped out of his chair and yelled "Fucking bingo!" to the empty room. Under the circumstances, Sawyer's excitement was quite natural.

Quentin Rowe was also a 1984 graduate of Columbia University. And, far more importantly, Steven Page and Quentin Rowe had shared the same residence during their last two years in college.

When it occurred to Sawyer a few seconds later why the two guys in sunglasses on the videotape looked so familiar, his happiness quickly faded into complete disbelief. There was just no damned way. But, yes, it did make sense. Particularly if you looked at it for what it was: a performance, all a sham. He picked up the phone. He had to find Sidney Archer as fast as possible and he knew where he wanted to start looking. *Jesus, Joseph, Mary, has this case just taken one big U-turn,* he thought.

CHAPTER FIFTY-FIVE

Traveling in a rental car, Mrs. Patterson and Amy were on their way to Boston, where they would stay for a few days. Despite arguing about it until the early morning hours, Sidney had been unable to persuade her father to accompany them. He had sat up all night in the motel room cleaning every speck of dirt and grit from his Remington twelve-gauge, his jaw clenched tight and his eyes staring straight ahead as Sidney had marched back and forth in front of him pleading her case.

"You know you really are impossible, Dad!" She said this as they were heading back toward Bell Harbor in her father's car; the battered Land Rover had been towed to a service shop for repairs. She breathed a quiet sigh of relief, though, as she leaned back against the seat. Right now she didn't want to be alone.

Her father looked stubbornly out the window. Whoever was after his daughter would have to kill him in order to get to her. Ghosts and bogeymen beware: Papa was back.

The white van trailing them was a good half mile behind and yet had no trouble mirroring the Cadillac's movements. One of the eight men in the van was not in particularly high spirits. "First you let Archer send an e-mail and then you let his wife get away. I can't believe this shit." Richard Lucas shook his head and angrily eyed Kenneth Scales, who sat beside him. His mouth and forearm were heavily bandaged and his nose, although reset by his own hands, was crimson-red and swollen.

Scales looked over at Lucas. "Believe it." The low voice coming through the damaged mouth carried with it enough pure menace to make even the tough-as-nails Lucas blink and quickly change tack.

Triton's internal security chief hunched forward in his seat. "All right, no good talking about what's past," he said hurriedly.

"Jeff Fisher, the computer guy from Tyler, Stone, had a copy of the contents of the disk on his hard drive. The file directory on Fisher's computer shows that it was accessed at the same time he was in the bar. He must've gotten another copy that way. Smart little sonof-abitch. We had a few words with the waitress from the bar last night. She gave Fisher a certified-mail envelope addressed to Bill Patterson, Bell Harbor, Maine, Sidney Archer's father. It's on its way here, that's for sure, and above all else, we've got to get it. Understood?" The six other grim-faced men in the van nodded. Each sported a tattoo of a star with an arrow through it on the back of his hand, the insignia of a veteran mercenary group to which they all belonged—a group that had been formed from the vast dregs of the defunct Cold War. As a former CIA operative, Lucas had found it easy to rekindle the old ties with the allure of U.S. dollars. "We'll let Patterson pick up the package, wait for them to get to an isolated area and then we hit them, hard and fast." He looked around. "A million-dollar bonus per man when we get it." The men's eyes gleamed. Then Lucas looked over at the seventh man. "Do you understand, Scales?"

Kenneth Scales didn't look at him. He pulled out his knife and pointed the tip toward the front of the van and spoke slowly through his wounded mouth. "You can get the disk. I'll take care of the lady. And I'll throw in her old man for no extra charge."

"*First* the package, then you can do whatever the hell you want," Lucas said angrily. Scales didn't answer him. His eyes stared straight ahead. Lucas started to speak again and then thought better of it. He sat back and put one hand nervously through his thinning hair.

During the twenty minutes it took to drive to Alexandria, Jackson tried Fisher's number three times from the car phone, but there was no answer.

"So you think this guy was helping Sidney with the password?" Jackson watched the Potomac River meandering by as they scooted down the GW Parkway.

Sawyer glanced over at him. "According to the surveillance log, Sidney Archer came here the night of the murders at Tyler, Stone. I checked with them. Fisher is Tyler, Stone's resident computer geek."

"Yeah, but it looks like the gent's not at home."

"Lotta things in one's home that may help us out, Ray."

"I don't recall that we have a search warrant, Lee."

Sawyer turned off Washington Street and shot through the heart of Old Town Alexandria. "Details, Ray, you always get hung up on the details." Jackson snorted and fell silent.

They pulled to a stop in front of Fisher's townhouse, got out and quickly headed up the steps. A young woman, her dark hair blowing in the whirling snow, called to them as she got out of her car.

"He's not home."

Sawyer looked back at her. "You wouldn't happen to know where he is, would you?" He walked down the steps and over to the woman, who was hauling a couple of grocery bags out of her car. Sawyer helped her and then held out his official credentials. Jackson did likewise.

The woman looked confused. "FBI? I didn't think they called in the FBI for burglary."

"Burglary, Ms. . . . ?"

"Oh, I'm sorry—Amanda, Amanda Reynolds. We've lived here for about two years and it's the first time we had the police on the block. They stole all of Jeff's computer equipment."

"You've already talked to the police, I take it?"

She looked sheepish. "We moved down from New York City. There, you don't chain your car to an anchor it's gone in the morning. You're on your guard. Here?" She shook her head. "Still, I feel like an idiot. I thought for sure it was all on the up and up. I just didn't think stuff like that happened in an area like this."

"Have you seen Mr. Fisher recently?"

The woman's brow wilted into furrows. "Oh, three or four days ago, at least. So miserable outside this time of the year, everyone stays indoors."

They thanked her and drove over to the Alexandria Police Station. When they inquired about the burglary at Jeff Fisher's house, the desk sergeant punched some keys on his computer.

"Yeah, that's right. Fisher. In fact, I was on duty the night they brought him in." The desk sergeant stared at the screen, scrolling down some of the text with his skinny fingers while Sawyer and Jackson exchanged puzzled looks. "Came in on a reckless endangerment spewing this story about some guys following him. We thought he'd had a few too many. Did a sobriety test; he wasn't drunk but he reeked of beer. Kept him overnight just to be sure, he posted bail the next day, got his court date and left."

Sawyer stared at the man. "You're saying Jeff Fisher was arrested?"

"That's right."

"And the next day his home was burglarized?"

The desk sergeant nodded his head and leaned against the counter. "Quite a run of bad luck, I'd say."

"Did he describe the people following him?" Sawyer asked.

The sergeant looked at the FBI agent as if he wanted to smell his breath as well. "There wasn't anybody following him."

"You're sure?"

The sergeant rolled his eyes and smiled.

"Okay, you said he wasn't drunk and yet you kept him overnight?" Sawyer put his hands on the counter.

"Well, you know some of these folks, those tests don't work on them. Down a twelve-pack and the breathalyzer comes back a point-oh-one. Fisher was driving crazy and *acting* drunk, anyway. We thought it best to keep him overnight. If he was intoxicated, he could at least sleep it off."

"And he didn't object?"

"Hell, no, said he'd never spent a night in jail before. Thought it might be refreshing." The sergeant shook his bald head. "Doesn't that take the cake? Refreshing, my ass!"

"You don't have any idea where he is now?"

"Hell, we couldn't even find him to tell him his place was broken into. Like I said, he posted his bail and got his court date. Only gets to be my concern if he doesn't show."

"Anything else you can think of?" Sawyer's face was full of disappointment.

The sergeant drummed his fingers on the counter, staring off into space. Finally Sawyer looked at Jackson and they started to leave. "Well, thanks for your help."

They were halfway to the door before the man broke out of his trance. "The guy gave me a package to mail for him, can you believe that crap? I mean, I know I wear a uniform, but do I *look* like a mailman?"

"A package?" Sawyer and Jackson bolted back to the counter.

The sergeant was shaking his head as he recalled the event. "I tell him he can make a phone call and he says, before he does that could I just pretty please drop this in the mail chute for him? Postage is already on it, he says. He'd really appreciate it." The sergeant laughed.

Sawyer stared at the man. "The package—did you mail it?"

The sergeant stopped chuckling and blinked at Sawyer. "What? Yeah, I put it in that chute right over there. I mean, it wasn't any trouble. I figured I'd help the guy out."

"What'd it look like? The package?"

"Well, it wasn't a letter. It was in one of those brown puffy packages, you know."

"The ones with the bubble packing inside," Jackson suggested.

The sergeant pointed at him. "That's right, I could feel it through the outside."

"How big was it?"

"Oh, well, not big, about yea wide and yea long." The sergeant made an eight-by-six-inch shape with his bony hands. "It was going first-class mail, return receipt requested."

Sawyer again put both hands flat on the counter and looked across at him, his heart racing at a fever pitch. "Do you remember the address on the package? Who it was sent from or going to?"

Again the man resumed his drumming. "Don't remember who sent it; just assumed it was Fisher. But it was going up to, uh, Maine, that's right. Maine. I know because the wife and I just went up in that part of the country, fall a year ago. If you ever get a chance, you should go, absolutely breathtaking. You'll wear out your Kodak, that's for darn sure."

"Where in Maine?" Sawyer was trying his best to be patient.

The man shook his head. "Something Harbor, I think," he finally said.

Sawyer's hopes plummeted. Off the top of his head he could think of at least a half dozen towns in Maine with that word in the name.

"Come on, think!"

The sergeant's eyes popped wide open. "Were there drugs in that package? That Fisher fellow a dealer? I thought something was funny. That why the Feds are interested?"

Sawyer shook his head wearily. "No, no, it's nothing like that. Look, do you at least remember who it was sent to?"

The man thought for another minute and then shook his head. "I'm sorry, fellows, I just don't."

Jackson said, "How about Archer? Was it going to anyone with that last name?"

"Nope, I'd remember that one. One of the deputies here has that last name."

Jackson handed him his card. "Well, if you think of anything else, anything, give us a call immediately. It's very important."

"I'll sure do that. Right away. Count on it."

Jackson touched Sawyer on the sleeve. "Let's go, Lee."

They headed toward the exit. The sergeant went back to his work. Suddenly Sawyer whirled around, his thick finger pointing across the room like a pistol directly at the sergeant, the vision of a MAINE

VACATIONLAND bumper sticker on a Cadillac firmly planted in his mind. "Patterson!"

The sergeant looked up, startled.

"Was it going to someone named Patterson in Maine?" Sawyer asked.

The sergeant brightened and then snapped his fingers again. "That's right. Bill Patterson." His smile was cut short as he watched the two FBI agents sprint out of the police station.

CHAPTER FIFTY-SIX

Bill Patterson looked over at his daughter as they drove through the snow-covered streets. The snow had grown much heavier in the last half hour. "So you're saying this guy from your office was supposed to send a package up to me to hold for you? A copy of something on a computer disk Jason sent you?" Sidney nodded. "But you don't know what it is?"

"It's in code, Dad. I have the password now, but I had to wait for the package."

"But it never came? You're sure?"

Sidney sounded exasperated. "I called FedEx. They have no record of the package being picked up. Then I called his house and the police answered. Oh, God." Sidney shuddered as she thought of Jeff Fisher's possible fate. "If anything's happened to Jeff . . ."

"Well, have you tried your answering machine at home? He might have called and left a message."

Sidney's mouth dropped open at the brilliant simplicity of her father's suggestion. "Christ! Why didn't I think of that?"

"Because you've been running for your life the last two days, that's why." Her father's voice was gruff. He reached down and gripped the shotgun that lay on the floorboard.

Sidney pulled the Cadillac into a gas station and stopped near a phone booth. She ran over to the phone. The snow was pouring down so fast she didn't notice the white van that drove past the station, turned down a side road, made a U-turn and awaited her return to the highway.

Sidney punched in her calling card and phone numbers. It seemed an eternity before the machine picked up. There was a slew of messages. From her brothers, other family members, friends who had seen the news and called with questions, outrage, support. She waited with growing impatience as the messages plodded on. Then she sucked in her breath as the sound of a familiar voice reached her ears.

"Hello, Sidney, this is your Uncle George. Martha and I are up in Canada this week. Enjoying it very much, although it's very cold. I sent your and Amy's Christmas presents early like I said I would. But it's coming in the mail instead because we missed the damn Federal Express and didn't want to wait. Be on the lookout for it. We sent it first-class, certified mail so you have to sign for it. I hope it's what you wanted. We love you very much and look forward to seeing you soon. Kiss Amy for us."

Sidney slowly put the phone down. She didn't have an Uncle George or an Aunt Martha, but there was no mystery about the phone call. Jeff Fisher had impersonated the voice of an old man pretty well. Sidney raced back to the car and got in.

Her father looked sharply at her. "Did he call?"

Sidney nodded as she gunned the car and drove off with a squeal of tires, throwing her father back against the seat. "Where the hell are we going so damned fast?"

"The post office."

The Bell Harbor Post Office was located in the middle of the town center, its United States flag whipping back and forth in the punishing wind. Sidney pulled up to the curb and her father jumped out. He went in and then came out again a couple of minutes later, ducking his head to get back in the car. He was empty-handed. "The day's mail shipment isn't in yet."

Sidney stared at him. "You're sure?"

He nodded. "Jerome's been the postmaster up here ever since I can remember. He said to check back around six. He'll stay open for us. You know, it may not be in today's bundle if Fisher only mailed it two days ago."

Sidney banged the steering wheel fiercely with both hands before laying her head wearily down on it. Her father put a big hand gently on her shoulder. "Sidney, it'll get here eventually. I just hope whatever's on that disk will clear up this nightmare."

Sidney looked up at him, her face pale and her eyes jumpy. "It has to, Dad. It has to." Her voice cracked painfully. *If it didn't? No, she couldn't think like that.* Brushing the hair out of her face, she put the car in gear and headed out.

The white van waited a couple of minutes and then pulled out of an alleyway and followed them.

"I can't friggin' believe this," Sawyer roared.

Jackson looked at him with clear frustration. "What can I tell you, Lee, it's a blizzard out there. National, Dulles and BWI are all shut down. Kennedy, La Guardia and Logan are closed too. So are Newark and Philly. It's tied up flights all across the country. The whole East Coast looks like Siberia. And the bureau won't release a plane to fly in this weather."

"Ray, we have got to get to Bell Harbor. We should've been there by now. How about the train?"

"Amtrak's still clearing track. Besides, I checked—the train doesn't go all the way through. We'd have to take a bus the last leg. And in this weather sections of the Interstate are bound to be down. Plus it's not all highway. We'd have to take some back roads. We're talking fifteen hours at least."

Sawyer looked as if he were about to explode. "They could all be dead in one hour, much less fifteen."

"You don't have to tell me that. If I could spread my arms and fly, I would, but dammit, I can't," Jackson angrily retorted.

Sawyer calmed down rapidly. "Okay, I'm sorry, Ray." He sat down. "Any luck getting the locals rounded up?"

"I made calls. The closest field office is Boston. Well over five hours away. And in this weather? Who knows? There are small resident agencies in Portland and Augusta. I've left messages, but I haven't heard back yet. The state police might be a possibility, although they've probably got their hands full with traffic accidents."

"Shit!" Sawyer shook his head in despair and drummed his fingers impatiently on the table. "A plane's the only way. There's got to be someone willing to fly in this crap."

Ray shook his head. "Maybe a fighter pilot. Know any?" he asked sarcastically.

Sawyer jumped up. "I sure as hell do."

The black van pulled to a stop near a small hangar at the Manassas county airport. The snow was falling so hard that it was difficult to see more than a few inches ahead. A half dozen black-clad members of the heavily armed Hostage Rescue Team, each carrying assault rifles, followed by Sawyer and Jackson, filed out rapidly and ran toward the plane that awaited them on the tarmac, engines running. The agents quickly boarded the Saab turboprop. Sawyer settled in next to the pilot while Jackson and the HRT members strapped themselves in the rear seats.

"I was hoping to see you again before this was over, Lee," George Kaplan shouted over the noise of the engines, and smiled at the big man.

"Hell, I don't forget my friends, George. Besides, you're the only sonofabitch I know crazy enough to fly in this." Sawyer looked out the windshield of the Saab. Staring back at him was a blanket of white. He looked over at Kaplan, who was working the controls as the plane taxied to the runway. A bulldozer had just finished clearing the short strip of tarmac, but the runway was rapidly being covered again. No other planes were operating because officially the airport was closed. All sane people had heeded that edict.

In the back, Ray Jackson rolled his eyes and gripped the seat as he stared through the window at the near-whiteout conditions. He looked at one of the HRT members. "We're all crazy; you know that, don't you?"

Sawyer turned around in his seat and grinned. "Hey, Ray, you know you can stay here. I can tell you about all the fun when I get back."

"Then who the hell would look after your sorry ass?" Jackson shot back.

Sawyer chuckled and turned back around to look at Kaplan. The agent's smile was replaced with a sudden look of apprehension. "You gonna be able to get this baby off the ground?" Sawyer asked.

Kaplan grinned. "Try flying through napalm for a living."

Sawyer managed a weak smile, but he also noted how focused Kaplan was on the controls, how he continually looked at the driving snow. Finally Sawyer's eyes came to rest on the throbbing vein located on the NTSB man's right temple. Sawyer let out a deep breath, hitched his safety belt as tight as he could and held on to his seat with both hands as Kaplan pushed the throttle forward. The plane rapidly gathered speed, bumping and swaying along the snowy runway. Sawyer stared ahead. The plane's headlights illuminated a dirt field that signaled the end of the airstrip; it hurtled toward them. As the plane struggled against the snow and wind, Sawyer again looked over at Kaplan. The pilot's eyes constantly scanned ahead and then skipped briefly across his instrument panel. When Sawyer looked back ahead, his stomach went into his throat. They were at the end of the runway. The Saab's twin engines were at their loudest pitch. It didn't look as if it was going to be enough.

In the back, Ray Jackson and all the HRT members simultaneously closed their eyes. A silent prayer escaped Ray Jackson's lips as he thought back to another dirt field where a plane had ended its existence along with that of everyone on board. Suddenly the nose of the plane jerked skyward and it lifted off the ground. A grinning Kaplan looked over at Sawyer, who was two shades paler than he had been a minute before. "See, I told you it would be easy."

As they rose steadily through the skies, Sawyer touched Kaplan's sleeve. "This question might seem a little premature, but when we get up to Maine, do we have a place to land this thing?"

Kaplan nodded. "There's a regional airport in Portsmouth but that's several hours from Bell Harbor by car. That's in good weather. I checked the maps when I filed our flight plan. There's an abandoned military airfield ten minutes outside of Bell Harbor. I verified with the state police that transportation will be waiting for us."

"Did you say 'abandoned'?"

"It's still usable, Lee. The good thing is there's no air traffic to worry about because of the weather. We've got a pretty straight shot all the way."

"You mean nobody else is this crazy?"

Kaplan grinned. "Anyway, the bad news is there's no operating tower at the airstrip. We'll be on our own for landing purposes, although they're going to put lights out for us outlining the runway. It's okay, I've gone solo like that plenty of times."

"In weather like this?"

"Hey, there's a first time for everything. Seriously, this plane is solid as a rock, and the instrumentation is first-rate. We'll be okay."

"If you say so."

Through several thousand feet the plane bumped and swayed sickeningly as the snow and high winds pummeled it. One sudden blow seemed to halt the Saab in its tracks. All on board gasped collectively as the plane shuddered from the assault and then suddenly dropped a few hundred feet before being hit by another gust. The aircraft turned sideways, almost stalled and then dropped again, this time even farther. Sawyer looked out the window. All he saw was white: snow and clouds, he really couldn't tell which was which. His senses of direction and elevation were completely gone. For all he knew, terra firma was about six feet away and coming at them way too fast. Kaplan looked over at Sawyer. "Okay, I admit, this is pretty bad. Hang on, guys, I'm going to take us up to ten thousand feet. This storm system is really strong but not that deep. Let's see if I can get us a smoother ride."

The next few minutes were more of the same as the plane lurched up and down and occasionally to the side. Finally, they broke through the cloud cover and emerged into a rapidly darkening, clear sky. Within a minute the plane assumed a level, smooth flight pattern due north.

From a private airstrip in a rural area forty miles west of Washington, D.C., a private jet had rocketed into the sky about twenty minutes ahead of Sawyer and his men. Flying at thirty-two thousand feet and at over double the speed of the Saab, the jet would arrive in Bell Harbor in less than half the time it would take the FBI to get there.

At a few minutes past six Sidney and her father pulled in front of the Bell Harbor Post Office. Bill Patterson went in and this time he exited carrying a package. The Cadillac sped off. Patterson pulled open one end of the package and peered inside. He hit the interior light so he could see better.

Sidney looked over at him. "Well?"

"It's a computer disk, all right."

Sidney relaxed slightly. She reached her hand in her pocket to pull out the paper with the password on it. Her face turned pale as her finger probed through the large hole in her pocket and, for the first time, she noted that the inside of her jacket, including the pocket, was slashed open. She stopped the car and frantically searched all of her other pockets. "Oh, my God! I don't believe this." She smashed her fists into the seat. "Dammit."

"What's wrong, Sid?" Her father grabbed one of her hands.

She slumped back in the seat. "I had the password in my jacket. Now it's gone. I must've lost it back at the house, when that guy was doing his best to carve me up."

"Can't you remember it?"

"It's too long, Dad. All numbers."

"And nobody else has it?"

Sidney nervously licked her lips. "Lee Sawyer does." She automatically checked the rearview mirror as she put the car back in gear. "I can try him."

"Sawyer. Isn't he the big guy who came to the house?"

"Yes."

"But the FBI's looking for you. You can't contact him."

"Dad, it's okay. He's on our side. Hang on." She turned into a gas station and pulled up to a phone booth. While her father held sentinel in the car with his shotgun, Sidney dialed Sawyer's home. As she waited for Sawyer to answer, she watched as a white van pulled into the gas station. It bore Rhode Island license plates. She eyed the van suspiciously for a moment and then completely forgot about it as she watched a car carrying two Maine state troopers pull into the station. One got out of the car. She froze as he glanced in her direction. Then he went inside the small gas station building, which also sold snacks and drinks. Sidney quickly turned away from the remaining trooper and put the collar of her coat up. A minute later she got back in the car.

"Jesus, I thought I was going to have a stroke when I saw the police pull in," Patterson said, his chest heaving.

Sidney put the car in gear and very slowly pulled out of the lot. The trooper was still in the gas station. Going for coffee, she surmised.

"Did you reach Sawyer?"

Sidney shook her head. "God, I can't believe it. First I have the disk and no password. Then I get the password and I lose the disk. Now I have the disk back and I've lost the password again. I'm losing my mind." She pulled at her hair.

"Where did you get the password in the first place?"

"From Jason's electronic mailbox on America Online. Omigod!" She sat straight up in the seat.

"What?"

"I can access the message again from Jason's mailbox." Sidney slumped back down again. "No, I'd need a computer to do that."

A smile slid across her father's face. "We've got one."

She jerked her head in his direction. "What?"

"I brought my laptop up with me. You know how Jason got me hooked on computers. I've got my Rolodex, investment portfolio, games, recipes, even medical information on there. I also have an AOL account, software all loaded on. My laptop's equipped with a phone modem."

"Dad, you're beautiful." She kissed him on the cheek.

"There's only one problem."

"What's that?"

"It's back at the beach house with all our other stuff."

Sidney slapped her forehead. "Dammit!"

"Well, let's go get it."

She shook her head violently. "Uh-uh, Dad. That's way too risky."

"Why? We're armed to the teeth. We lost whoever was following you. They probably think we're long gone from the area. It'll take me one minute to get it and then we can drive back to the motel, plug it in and get the password."

Sidney was wavering. "I don't know, Dad."

"Look, I don't know about you, but I want to see what's on this sucker." He held up the package. "Don't you?"

Sidney looked over at the package, bit her lip. Finally she clicked on her turn signal and headed back to the beach house.

The jet broke through the low cloud cover and skidded to a stop on the private airstrip. The sprawling resort on the Maine shoreline had once been a robber baron's summer retreat. It was currently a popular destination for the well-heeled. Now, in December, it was deserted except for weekly maintenance checks by a local firm. Because there was nothing within several miles, its seclusion was one of its chief attributes. Barely three hundred yards from the runway the Atlantic pitched and bellowed. A group of very grim-looking people alighted from the plane, were met by a waiting car and driven over to the resort located about a minute away. The jet turned around and taxied to the opposite end of the runway, where its door reopened and another man climbed off and walked quickly toward the resort building.

Sidney, struggling with the Cadillac, burrowed down the snowy road. The plows had made several passes over the hard surface but Mother Nature clearly had the upper hand. Even the big Cadillac pitched and swayed over the uneven surface. Sidney turned to her father. "Dad, I don't like this. Let's just drive down to Boston. We can be there in four or five hours. We'll hook up with Mom and Amy and find another computer tomorrow morning."

Her father's face assumed a very stubborn look. "In this weather? The highway's probably closed. Hell, most of the state of Maine closes down this time of year. We're almost there. You stay in the car, keep it running and I'll be back before you can count to ten."

"But Dad—"

"Sidney, there's nobody around. We're all alone. I'll take my shotgun. You think somebody would try anything? Just wait by the side of the road. Don't pull in the driveway, you'll get stuck."

Sidney finally gave in and did as she was told. Her father got out of the car, leaned back in and, with a grin on his face, said, "Start counting to ten."

"Just hurry, Dad!"

She anxiously watched as he trudged through the snow, shotgun in hand. Then she began to scan the street. Her father was probably right. As she glanced down at the package containing the disk, she picked it up and put it in her purse. She wasn't going to lose it again. She jerked up suddenly as a light came on in the house. Then she caught her breath. Her father needed to see where he was going. They were almost there. A minute later she looked over at the house as the front door closed and footsteps approached the car. Her father had made good time.

"*Sidney!*" She jerked her head upward and stared in horror as her father burst onto the second-story deck. "*Run!*"

In the blinding white of the snow, she could see hands grabbing her father, pulling him roughly down. She heard him scream again over the wind and then she didn't hear him anymore. Headlights hit her in the face. As she whirled around to stare out the windshield, the white van was almost on her. It must have been driving before without its lights on.

Then she saw the shadowy figure next to the car and watched in horror as the muzzle of a machine gun started its ascent toward her head. All in one motion she hit the automatic door locks, slammed the car in reverse and hit the accelerator. As she threw herself down sideways in the seat, a burst from the machine gun strafed the front of the Cadillac, shooting out the passenger-side window and shattering half the windshield. The front end of the heavy vehicle slid sharply sideways under the sudden surge, thudded into human flesh and sent the gunman flying into a snowdrift. The wheels of the Caddie finally burned through the layers of snow, hit asphalt and leaped backward. Covered with bits of glass, Sidney sat back up, fighting to get control of the spinning car as she watched the van bearing down on her. She backed down the street until she had just passed the intersection leading away from the beach. Then she slammed the car in drive, punched the gas and fishtailed through the intersection. The car flew forward, kicking snow, salt and gravel in its wake. The next minute she was hurtling down the road; snow and wind screamed into the Cadillac's new multiple openings. She looked in the rearview mirror. Nothing. Why weren't they following her? She almost immediately answered her own question as her mind began to function again. Because now they had her father.

CHAPTER FIFTY-SEVEN

Here we go, guys, hang on." Kaplan cut the airspeed, manipulated the plane's controls, and the aircraft, rocking and swaying, suddenly burst through the low cloud cover. A few miles ahead, lit wands, stuck in the hard ground, signaled the outlines of the airstrip. Kaplan eyed the illuminated path to safety and a proud grin spread across his face. "Damn, I'm good."

The Saab landed barely a minute later in a swirl of snow. Sawyer had the door open before the plane had even stopped rolling. He sucked in huge amounts of the frigid air and his nausea quickly passed. The HRT members stumbled off, several of them sitting down on the ice-sheathed tarmac, breathing deeply. Jackson was the last off. A recovered Sawyer eyed him. "Damn, Ray, you almost look white." Jackson started to say something, then pointed a shaky finger at his partner, covered his mouth with his other hand and silently headed off with the HRT members to the vehicle waiting nearby; a Maine state trooper stood next to it, waving his flashlight at them as a guidepost.

Sawyer leaned his head back in the plane. "Thanks for the ride,

George. You gonna hang tight here? I don't know how long this is gonna take."

Kaplan couldn't hide the grin. "Are you kidding? And miss the opportunity to chauffeur you guys back home? I'll be right here waiting."

Grunting in response, Sawyer closed the door and hurried over to the vehicle. The others were gathered around waiting for him. When he saw what their transport vehicle was, he stopped dead in his tracks. They all eyed the paddy wagon.

The state trooper looked over at them. "Sorry, guys, it's all we had on such short notice to accommodate eight of you."

The FBI agents climbed into the back of the paddy wagon.

The vehicle had a small window of chicken wire and glass communicating with the front. Jackson slid it open so the trooper could hear him. "Can you turn some heat on back here?"

"Sorry," the man said, "a prisoner we were transporting went nuts and busted the vents; they haven't been fixed yet."

Huddled on the bench, Sawyer watched clouds of breath so thick it looked like a fire had broken out. He laid his rifle down and rubbed his stiff fingers together to warm them. A cold draft from some invisible crevice in the truck's body hit him right between the shoulder blades. Sawyer shivered. *Christ,* he thought, *it's like someone turned the air-conditioning on full-blast.* He hadn't been this cold since investigating Brophy's and Goldman's deaths in the parking garage. At that instant, Sawyer recalled his other recent encounter with the frigid effects of air-conditioning—the slain plane fueler's apartment. The look on his face became one of utter disbelief as he made the mental connection. "Oh, my God."

Sidney figured there was only one way for the men who had abducted her father to contact her. She pulled in to a convenience store, got out and hurried over to the phone. She dialed her home in Virginia. When the answering machine came on, she tried her best to recognize the voice, but she didn't. She was given a number to call. She assumed it was a cellular phone rather than a fixed location. She took a deep breath and dialed the number. The phone was immediately answered. It was a different voice than the one on the answering machine, but again she couldn't place it. She was to drive twenty minutes north of Bell Harbor along Route 1 and take the exit for Port Haven. Then she was given detailed directions that took her to an isolated stretch of land between Port Haven and the larger town of Bath.

"I want to talk to my father." The request was refused. "Then I'm not coming. For all I know, he's already dead."

She was met with an eerie silence. Her heart thumped against her rib cage. The air rushed out of her as she heard the voice.

"Sidney, sweetie."

"Dad, are you all right?"

"Sid, get the hell out of he—"

"Dad? Dad?" Sidney screamed into the phone. A man coming out of the convenience store carrying a cup of coffee stared at her, looked over at the heavily damaged Cadillac and then back at her. Sidney stared back at him as her hand dipped instinctively to the 9mm in her pocket. The man hurried to his pickup truck and drove off.

The voice came back on. Sidney had thirty minutes to get to her destination.

"How do I know you'll let him go if I give it to you?"

"You don't." The tone of voice brooked no opposition.

The attorney in Sidney, however, stomped to the surface. "That's not good enough. You want this disk so bad, then we're going to have to agree to terms."

"You've gotta be kidding. You want your old man back in a body bag?"

"So we meet in the middle of nowhere, I give you the disk and you let him and me go out of the goodness of your heart? Right! Under that proposal you'll have the disk and my father and I will be somewhere in the Atlantic providing nourishment for sharks. You'll have to do a lot better than that if you want what I've got."

Though the man had covered the receiver, Sidney heard voices on the other end of the line, a couple of them raised in anger.

"It's our way or nothing."

"Fine, I'm on my way to state police headquarters. Be sure to stay tuned to the evening news. I'm sure you don't want to miss anything. Good-bye."

"Wait!"

Sidney didn't say anything for a minute. When she did, she spoke with far more confidence than she was feeling at the moment. "I'll be at the intersection of Chaplain and Merchant Streets smack in the center of Bell Harbor in thirty minutes. I'll be sitting in my car. It should be easy to spot—it's the one with all the extra air-conditioning. You blink your headlights twice. You let my father out. There's a diner right across the street. I see him go in there, I open the car door, place the disk on the sidewalk and drive off. Please keep in mind that I'm heavily armed and more than prepared to send as many of you as I can straight to hell."

"How do we know it's the right disk?"

"I want my father back. It'll be the right disk. I hope you choke on it. Do we have a deal?" Now *her* tone of voice brooked no opposition.

She waited anxiously for the answer. *Please, God, don't let them call my bluff.* She let out a sigh of relief when it finally came. "Thirty minutes." The line went dead.

Sidney got back in the car and gripped the dashboard in frustration. How the hell had they tracked her and her father? It was impossible. It was as if they had been watching Sidney and her father the entire time. The white van had also been at the gas station. The attack probably would have occurred there except for the timely arrival of the state troopers. She lay down across the front seat as she fought to keep her nerves in check. She moved her purse out of the way and then opened it, just to make sure the disk was still there. The disk for her father. But once the disk was gone, she would spend the rest of her life running from the police. Or at least until they caught her. Quite a choice. But there was really no choice about it.

As she sat back up she started to close her purse. Then she stopped, her thoughts drifting back to that night, the night in the limo. So much had happened since her terrifying escape. And yet it hadn't really been an escape, had it? The killer had let her go and also had courteously let her keep her purse. In fact, she would have forgotten it entirely except for him tossing it to her. She had been so happy to get out alive, she had never really considered why he would have done something so remarkable. . . . She started to claw through the contents of her purse. It took a couple of minutes, but she finally found it, at the very bottom. It had been inserted through a slit in the lining of the purse. She held it up and stared at it. A tiny tracking device.

She looked behind her as a shiver thudded up her spine. Putting the car in gear again, she sped off. Up ahead, a dump truck converted into a snowplow had pulled to the curb. She looked in her mirror. There was no one behind her. She rolled down the driver's-side window, pulled up to the truck and cocked her hand back as she prepared to toss the tracking device into the back of the truck. Then, just as quickly, she stopped the swing of her arm and rolled her window back up. The tracking device was still in her hand. She hit the gas, leaving the truck quickly behind. She looked down at her tiny companion of the last few days. What did she have to lose? She quickly headed toward town. She had to get to the arranged drop-off spot as early as possible. But first she needed something from the grocery store.

The diner Sidney had mentioned in her telephone conversation was filled with hungry patrons. Two blocks over from the pre-arranged drop-off spot, the Cadillac, lights out, was parked at the curb next to the impressive bulk of an evergreen surrounded by a calf-high wrought-iron fence. The interior of the Cadillac was dark, the silhouette of the driver barely visible.

Two men walked quickly along the sidewalk, while another pair across the street paralleled their movements. One of the men looked down at a small instrument clutched in his hands; the small amber screen had a grid stamped on it. A red light burned brightly on the screen, pointing directly at the Cadillac. The men quickly moved in. One weapon flashed through where the passenger-side window had once been. At the same instant the driver's-side door was torn open. The gunmen looked in astonishment at the driver: a mop with a leather jacket over it, a baseball cap perched rakishly on top.

*   *   *

The white van was parked at the intersection of Chaplain and Merchant, its motor running. The driver checked his watch, scanned the street and then hit his headlights twice. In the back of the van, Bill Patterson lay on the floor, his feet and hands tied securely, his mouth taped shut. The driver jerked his head around as the passenger-side door was thrown open and a 9mm pistol was pointed at his head. Sidney climbed in the van. She cocked her head toward the back to make sure her father was okay. She had already seen him through the back window when she had spotted the van a minute earlier. She figured they had to be prepared to actually hand her father over. "Put your gun down on the floorboard. Take it out muzzle first. If your finger goes anywhere near the trigger, I will empty my entire clip into your head. Do it!"

The driver quickly did as he was told.

"Now get out!"

"What?"

She shoved the pistol into his neck, where it pushed painfully against a throbbing vein. "Get out!"

When he opened the door and turned his back to her, Sidney swung her legs up on the seat, coiled them back and kicked him with all her might. He sprawled on the pavement. She closed the door, jumped into the driver's seat and hit the gas. The van's tires turned the white snow black and then it rocketed off.

Ten minutes outside of town, Sidney stopped the van, jumped into the back and untied her father. The two sat for several minutes holding on to each other, their bodies quivering with a heavy mixture of fear and relief.

"We need to get another car to drive. I wouldn't put it past them to have bugged this one. And they'll be on the lookout for the van," Sidney said as they hurtled down the road.

"There's a rental place about five minutes away. But why don't we just go to the cops, Sid?" Her father rubbed his wrists. His swollen eyes and cracked knuckles testified to the struggle the old man had put up.

She breathed deeply and looked over at him. "Dad, I don't know what's on the disk. If it's not enough . . ."

Her father looked at her, the realization sinking in that he might lose his little girl after all.

"It will be enough, Sidney. If Jason took all the trouble to send it to you, it *has* to be enough."

She smiled at him and then her face went dark. "We have to split up, Dad."

"There's no way I'm leaving you now."

"Your being with me makes you an accessory. I'll tell you one thing: We're not both going to jail."

"I don't give a damn about that."

"Okay, then what about Mom? What would happen to her? And Amy? Who would be there for them?"

Patterson started to say something and then stopped. He frowned as he looked out the window. Finally he looked over at her. "We'll go to Boston together and then we'll talk about it. If you still want to split up then, so be it."

While Sidney sat outside in the van, Patterson went in to rent a car. When he came out a few minutes later and walked over to the van, Sidney rolled down the window.

"Did you rent a car?" Sidney asked.

Patterson nodded. "They'll have it ready in about five minutes. I got us a roomy four-door. You can sleep in the back; I'll drive."

"I love you, Dad." Sidney rolled the window back up and drove off. Her stunned father ran after her, but she was quickly out of sight.

"Christ!" Sawyer peered out the window into near-zero visibility. "Can't we go any faster?" he yelled through the window to the trooper. They had already seen the devastation of the Patterson beach house and were now desperately looking everywhere for Sidney Archer and her family.

The trooper yelled back, "We go any faster, we're going to end up dead in some ditch."

Dead. Is that what Sidney Archer is right now? Sawyer looked at his watch. He fumbled in his pocket for a cigarette.

Jackson was looking at him. "Damn, Lee, don't start smoking in here. It's hard enough to breathe as it is."

Sawyer's lips parted as he felt the slender object in his pocket. He slowly pulled the card out.

As Sidney headed out of town, she decided to keep her emotions in check and let longtime habits take over. For what seemed like forever, she had been merely reacting to a series of crises, without the opportunity to think things through. She was an attorney, trained to view facts logically, look at the details and then work them into an overall picture. She certainly had some information to work with. Jason had labored on Triton's records for the CyberCom deal. That she knew. Jason had disappeared under mysterious circumstances and had sent her a disk with some information on it. That, also, was a fact. Jason was not selling secrets to RTG, not with Brophy in the picture. That also was clear to her. And then there were the financial records. Apparently Triton had simply handed them over. Then why the big scene at the meeting in New York? Why had Gamble demanded to talk to Jason about his work on the records, particularly after he had sent Jason an e-mail congratulating him on a job well done? Why the big deal of getting Jason on the phone? Why put her in an impossible situation like that?

She slowed down and pulled off the road. Unless the intent all along was to put her in an impossible situation. Making it appear as though she had lied. Suspicion had followed her from that very moment. What exactly had been in those records in the warehouse? Was that what was on the disk? Something Jason had found out? That night Gamble's limo had whisked her to his estate, he had obviously wanted some answers. Could he have been attempting to find out if Jason had told her anything?

Triton had been a client for several years now. A big, powerful company with a very private past. But how did that tie in to all the other things? The deaths of the Page brothers. Triton beating out RTG for CyberCom. As Sidney thought once more of that horrible day in New York, something clicked. Ironically, she had the same thought Lee Sawyer had experienced earlier but for a different reason: *A performance.*

My God! She had to get in touch with Sawyer. She put the van in drive and got back on the road. A shrill ring interrupted her thoughts. She looked around at the interior of the van for the source until her eyes alighted on the cellular phone resting on a magnetized plate against the lower dashboard. She hadn't noticed it until just that moment. It was ringing? Her hand went instinctively down to answer it and then pulled back. Finally she picked it up. "Yes?"

"I thought you weren't interested in playing games." The voice was filled with anger.

"Right. And you just forgot to mention that you had a bug in my purse and were just waiting to jump me."

"Okay, let's talk about the future. We want the disk and you're going to bring it to us. Now!"

"What I'm going to do is hang up. Now!"

"If I were you, I wouldn't."

"Listen, if you're trying to keep me on the phone so you can lock on my location, it's not going—" Sidney's voice broke off and her entire body turned to putty as she listened to the small voice on the other end of the line.

"Mommy? Mommy?"

Her tongue as big as a fist, Sidney could not answer. Her foot went off the accelerator; her dead arms no longer had the strength to steer the van. The vehicle slowed down and drifted into a pile of snow on the shoulder.

"Mommy? Daddy? Come over?" The voice sounded frightened, pitiful.

Suddenly sick to her stomach, her entire body swaying uncontrollably, Sidney managed to speak. "AA-Amy. Baby."

"Mommy?"

"Baby, it's Mommy. I'm here." An avalanche of tears poured down Sidney's face.

Sidney heard the phone being taken away.

"Ten minutes. Here are the directions."

"Let me talk to her again. Please!"

"Now you have nine minutes and fifty-five seconds."

A sudden thought occurred to Sidney. What if it was a tape? "How do I know you really have her? That could be just a recording."

"Fine. If you want to take that chance, don't come." The voice sounded very confident. There was no earthly way Sidney would ever take that chance. The person on the other line knew that too.

"If you hurt her—"

"We're not interested in the kid. She can't identify us. After it's over, we'll drop her at a safe place." He paused. "You won't be joining her, though, Ms. Archer. Your safe places have just run out."

"Let her go. Please just let her go. She's only a baby." Sidney was trembling so much she could barely keep the phone pressed against her mouth.

"You better write down these directions. You don't want to get lost. If you don't show, there won't be enough left of your kid to identify."

"I'll be there," she said in a hushed voice and the line went dead. She pulled back on the road. A sudden thought leaped across her mind. Her mother! Where was her mother? Her blood seemed to be pooling in her veins as she gripped the steering wheel. Another ringing sound invaded the interior of the van. With a shaking hand, Sidney picked up the phone, but there was no one there. In fact, the ringing sound was different. She pulled off the road again and desperately searched everywhere. Her eyes finally stopped on the seat right next to her. She looked at her purse, slowly put her hand inside and pulled the object out. Written across the small screen on her pager was a phone number she didn't recognize. She turned off the pager's ringer. It was probably a wrong number. She couldn't imagine that someone from her law firm or a client was attempting to call her; she was fresh out of legal advice. She was about to erase the message, but her finger stopped. Could it be Jason? If it was Jason, then it would qualify as the worst timing in the history of the world. Her finger remained poised over the erase button. Finally she put the pager in her lap, picked up the cellular phone and dialed the number on the pager's screen.

The voice that came on the other end of the line was enough to take her breath away. Apparently, miracles did happen.

The main house of the resort was dark, its seclusion made all the more stark by a wall of bulky evergreens in front. When the van pulled down the long driveway, two armed guards emerged from the entryway to meet it. The snowstorm had lightened considerably in the last few minutes. Behind the house the dark, foreboding waters of the Atlantic assaulted the land.

One of the guards jerked back as the van continued to roll toward them without any sign of slowing down. "Shit," he yelled as both men hurled themselves out of the way. The van tore past them, crashed right through the front door and came to an abrupt halt, its wheels still spinning, when it struck a four-foot-thick interior wall. A minute later, several heavily armed men surrounded the van and wrenched the damaged door open. No one was inside. The men's eyes passed over the receptacle where the cellular phone would normally be kept. The phone was completely under the front seat, the phone cord pretty much invisible under the weak illumination of the dome light. They believed the phone had probably been dislodged upon impact rather than that it had deliberately been placed there.

Sidney entered the house through the rear. When the man had given her directions to the place, she had instantly recognized it. She and Jason had stayed at the resort several times, and she was very familiar with the interior layout. She had taken a shortcut and arrived in half the time her daughter's captors had alloted her. She had used those precious extra minutes to rig the van's steering wheel and accelerator with rope she had found in the back of the vehicle. She clutched her pistol, her finger resting lightly on the trigger as she stole through the dark rooms of the resort. She was ninety percent certain that Amy was not on the premises. The ten percent of doubt had led her to use the rigged van as a diversion so that she could attempt a rescue, however improbable, of her daughter. She was under no delusions that these men would let Amy go free.

Up ahead she heard the sounds of raised voices and feet running toward the front of the house. She cocked her head to the left as a pair of footsteps echoed down the hallway. This person was not running; the tread was slow and methodical. She shrank back into the shadows and waited for the person to pass by. As soon as he did, she pressed the muzzle of her pistol directly against his neck.

"Make any sound at all, and you're dead," she said with a cold finality. "Hands over your head."

Her prisoner complied. He was tall, with broad shoulders. She felt for his gun and found it in a shoulder holster. She crammed the man's pistol in her jacket pocket and pushed him forward. The large room up ahead was well lit. Sidney could not hear any noise emanating from the space, but she didn't think that silence would last long. They would soon figure out her ploy, if they hadn't already. She prodded the man away from the light and down a darkened hallway.

They came to a doorway. "Open it and move inside," she told him.

He opened the door and she pushed him inside. One of her hands felt around for the light switch. When the lights came on, she shut the door behind her and looked at the man's face.

Richard Lucas stared back at her.

"You don't look surprised," Lucas said, his voice even and calm.

"Let's just say nothing surprises me anymore," Sidney replied. "Sit." She motioned with her gun to a straight-backed chair. "Where are the others?"

Lucas shrugged. "Here, there, everywhere. There are a lot of them, Sidney."

"Where's my daughter? And my mother?" Lucas kept silent. Sidney put both hands on her gun and pointed it directly at his chest. "I'm not screwing around with you. Where are they?"

"When I was a CIA operative, I was captured and tortured by the KGB for two months before I escaped. I never told them anything and I'm not telling you anything," Lucas said calmly. "And if you're thinking about using me to exchange for your daughter, forget it. So you might as well pull the trigger, Sidney."

Sidney's finger quivered on the trigger as she and Lucas engaged in a staring contest. Finally she swore under her breath and lowered the pistol. A smile cracked Lucas's lips.

She thought quickly. *All right, you sonofabitch.* "What color is the hat Amy was wearing, Rich? If you have her, you should know that."

The smile disappeared from Lucas's lips. He paused for a second and then answered. "Like a beige."

"Good answer. Neutral, could apply to lots of different colors." She paused as an enormous wave of relief washed over her. "Only Amy wasn't wearing a hat."

Lucas started to bolt out of the chair. A second faster than he, Sidney smashed her pistol across his head. Lucas went down in a heap, unconscious. She towered over his prostrate form. "You're a real asshole."

Sidney exited the room and stole down the corridor. From the direction of where she had entered the house, she heard men approaching. She changed course and once again headed toward the lit room she had spied earlier. She peered around the corner. The light from inside was enough to let her check her watch. She said a silent prayer and edged into the room, keeping low behind a long, carved wooden-backed sofa. She looked around, her eyes taking in a wall of French doors that was visible on the ocean side. The room was huge, with ceilings that soared at least twenty feet high. An interior second-story balcony ran across one side of the room. Another wall held a collection of finely bound books. Comfortable furnishings were placed throughout.

Sidney shrank back as far as she could when a group of armed men, all dressed in black fatigues, entered the room through another doorway. One of them barked into a walkie-talkie. By listening to his words, she knew they were aware of her presence. It was only a matter of time before they found her. Blood pounding in her eardrums, she made her way out of the room, keeping well out of sight behind the sofa. Once in the corridor, she walked swiftly back toward the room in which she had left Lucas, with the intent of using him as her exit card. Maybe they would not care about killing Lucas to get to her, but right now it was the only option she had.

Her plan ran into an immediate problem when she discovered Lucas was no longer in the room. She had hit him very hard, and she briefly marveled at his recuperative powers. Apparently he hadn't been kidding about the KGB. She ran out of the room and toward the door where she had entered the house. Lucas would most certainly raise the alarm. She probably only had seconds to make her getaway. She was a few feet from the door when she heard it.

"Mommy, Mommy."

Sidney jerked around. Amy's wails continued down the hallway.

"Oh, my God!" Sidney turned and sprinted toward the sound.

"Amy? *Amy!*" The doors to the large room she had earlier been in were closed. She hurled them open and burst into the room, her chest heaving, her eyes wildly searching for sight of her daughter.

Nathan Gamble stared back at her as Richard Lucas appeared behind him. He wasn't smiling. The side of his face was heavily swollen. Sidney was quickly disarmed and held by Gamble's men. The disk was taken from her purse and handed to Gamble.

Gamble held up a sophisticated recording device and Amy's voice was heard once again: "Mommy? Mommy?"

"As soon as I found out your husband was on to me," Gamble explained, "I had your house bugged. You get lots of goodies that way."

"You sonofabitch." Sidney glared at him. "I knew it was a trick."

"You should have gone with your first instinct, Sidney. I always do." Gamble shut off the tape and strolled over to a desk situated against one wall. For the first time Sidney noticed that a laptop computer was set up there. Gamble took the disk and popped it in. Then he pulled a piece of paper from his pocket and looked over at her. "Nice touch your husband had on the password. All backwards. You're sharp, but I bet you didn't figure that one out, did you?" His face crinkled into a smile as he looked from the paper to Sidney. "Always knew Jason was a smart guy." Using one finger, Gamble punched a number of keys on the keyboard and studied the screen. While doing so, he lit up a cigar. Satisfied with the contents of the disk, he sat down in the chair, folded his arms across his chest and flicked cigar ash on the floor.

She kept her eyes fixed on him. "Brains run in the family. I know it all, Gamble."

"I think you don't know shit," he calmly replied.

"How about the billions of dollars you made trading on changes in the Fed Funds Rate? The very same billions you used to build Triton Global."

"Interesting. How did I do that?"

"You knew the answers before the tests were given out. You were blackmailing Arthur Lieberman. The mighty businessman who couldn't make a dime without cheating." She spat out the last words. Gamble's eyes glittered darkly at her. "Then Lieberman threatens to expose you and his plane crashes."

Gamble got up and advanced slowly toward Sidney; his hand an anger-laden fist. "I made billions *on my own*. Then some jealous competitors paid off a couple of my traders to secretly tank me. I couldn't prove anything, but they ended up with cushy jobs down the street and I lost everything I had. You call that fair?" He stopped walking and took a deep breath. "You're right, though. I caught on to Lieberman's little secret life. Scraped enough cash together to set up my little mole in luxury and bided my time. But it wasn't that simple." His lips curled into a wicked smile. "I waited until the people who had screwed me took their investment positions on interest rates and then I took the opposite one and told Lieberman which way to swing it. After it was over, I'm back on top and those guys couldn't afford a cup of spit. Nice and clean, and damn sweet."

His face gleamed as he recalled his personal triumph. "People mess with me, I pay them back. Only a lot worse. Like Lieberman. Nice guy that I am, I paid the sonofabitch over a hundred million dollars for doing his thing with the rates. How does he show his gratitude? He tried to take me down. Was it my fault he got cancer? He thought he could outsmart me, the big Ivy League legend. Didn't think I knew he was dying. I do business with somebody, I find out everything about him. Everything!" Gamble's face flushed for an instant and then he broke into a sly grin. "Only thing I regret is not having a picture of his face when that plane hit."

"I didn't think you were into genocide, Nathan. Men, women, babies." Gamble suddenly looked troubled and took a nervous puff on his cigar. "You think I *wanted* to do it like that? My business is making money, not killing people. If I could have come up with another way, I would have. I had two problems: Lieberman and your husband. They both knew the truth, so I had to get rid of them both. The plane was the only way to tie them together: Kill Lieberman and blame your husband. If I could have bought every ticket on that plane except Lieberman's, I would have." He paused and looked at her. "If it makes you feel any better, my charitable foundation has already donated ten million dollars to the victims' families."

"Great, you score PR points off your own dirty work. You think money is the answer to everything?"

Gamble exhaled smoke. "You'd be surprised how often it is. And the fact is, I didn't *have* to do anything for them. It's like I told your buddy Wharton: When I go after somebody who screwed me, I don't care who gets in the way. Too bad."

Sidney's face suddenly hardened. "Like Jason? Where is he? Where is my husband, you sonofabitch?" She screamed the words in an out-of-control fury and would have pounced on Gamble if his men hadn't held her back.

Gamble stepped directly in front of her. His fist slammed into her jaw. "Shut up!"

Sidney swiftly recovered, ripped her arm free and slashed Gamble's face with her fingernails. Shocked, he stumbled back, clutching his torn skin. "Damn you!" he yelled. Gamble pressed his handkerchief against his face, his eyes blazing at her. Sidney stared back at him, her entire body shaking with more anger than she had felt in her entire life. Gamble finally motioned to Lucas. Lucas left the room for a minute, and when he returned, he was not alone.

Sidney instinctively jerked back as Kenneth Scales stepped into the room. He stared at Sidney Archer with eyes that bespoke intense hatred. She looked over at Gamble. He looked down and sighed while he stuffed his handkerchief back in his pocket, touching his face gingerly. "I guess I deserved that. You know, I had no intention of killing you, but you just couldn't leave it alone, could you?" He ran a hand through his hair. "Don't worry, I'll set a big trust fund up for your kid. You should be grateful I think everything through." He waved Scales forward.

Sidney shouted at him. "Oh, really? Did you think through the fact that maybe if I could figure it out, so could Sawyer?" Gamble stared blankly at her. "Like the fact that you blackmailed Arthur Lieberman by setting him up with Steven Page. But just when Lieberman was up for the Fed nomination, Page contracted HIV and threatened to blow the whole thing. What did you do? Just like you did with Lieberman. You had Page killed."

Gamble's response stunned her. "Why the hell would I have him killed? He was working for me."

"He's telling the truth, Sidney." She jerked her head around and stared at the source of those words. Quentin Rowe walked into the room.

Gamble stared at him, his eyes wide. "How the hell did you get up here?"

Rowe barely glanced at him. "I guess you forgot that I have my *own* private suite on the corporate jet. Besides, I like to see projects through to their completion."

"Is she right? You had your own lover boy killed?"

Rowe looked at him calmly. "It's not any of your concern."

"It's my company. Everything concerns me."

"Your company? I don't think so. Now that we have CyberCom, I don't need you. My nightmare is finally over."

Gamble's face grew red. He motioned toward Richard Lucas. "I think we need to show this little prick some respect for his superior."

Richard Lucas pulled out his weapon.

Gamble shook his head. "Just rough the little sucker up some," he said, his eyes glowing maliciously. The glow quickly ebbed as Lucas swung the pistol in his direction and the cigar fell out of the Triton chief's mouth. "What the hell. You sonofabitch traitor—"

"Shut up!" Lucas roared back. "Shut your mouth or I'll blow you away right here and now. I swear to God I will." Lucas's eyes tore into Gamble's face and Gamble quickly closed his mouth.

"Why, Quentin?" The words floated softly across the room. "Why?"

Rowe turned to find Sidney's eyes on him. He took a deep breath. "When he bought into my company, Gamble drew up legal documents so that he technically controlled my ideas, everything. In essence, he owned me." For a moment he stared at the now docile Gamble with ill-concealed disgust. Rowe looked back at Sidney, reading her mind. "The oddest couple in the world. I know."

He sat down at the desk in front of the computer. He stared at the screen as he continued to talk. The proximity of the high-tech equipment seemed to soothe Quentin Rowe even more. "But then Gamble lost all his money. My company was going nowhere. I pleaded with him to let me out of the deal, but he said he'd tie me up in court for years. I was stuck. Then Steven met Lieberman and the plot was hatched."

"But you had Page killed. Why?"

Rowe didn't answer.

"Did you ever try to find out who gave him HIV?"

Rowe didn't answer. Tears spilled down onto the laptop.

"Quentin?"

"I gave it to him. I did it!" Rowe exploded out of his chair, staggered for a moment and then collapsed back into the chair. In a painful voice, he continued. "When Steven told me he had tested positive, I couldn't believe it. I had always been faithful to him and he swore the same to me. We thought it might have been Lieberman. We got a copy of his medical records; he was clean. That's when I took an examination." His lips started to quiver. "And that's when I was told I was HIV-positive. The only thing I could think of was a damn blood transfusion I'd had when I was in a serious car accident. I checked with the hospital and discovered that several other surgery patients had contracted the virus during the same time period. I told Steven everything. I cared for him so much. I never felt so much guilt in all my life. I thought he would understand." Rowe took a deep breath. "Only he didn't."

"He threatened to expose you?" Sidney asked.

"We had come too far, worked too damn hard. Steven wasn't thinking clearly, he . . ." Rowe shook his head in complete despondence. "He came to my apartment one night; he had been drinking very heavily. He told me what he was going to do. He was going to tell everything about Lieberman, the blackmail scheme. We'd all go to prison. I told him he had to do what he thought was right." Rowe paused, his voice breaking. "I often gave him his daily dosages of insulin, kept a supply at my place. He was always forgetful about it." Rowe looked down at the teardrops dropping onto his hands. "Steven passed out on the couch. While he was asleep, I gave him an overdose of insulin, woke him up, and put him in a cab for home." Rowe added quietly, "And he died. We kept our relationship since college a secret. The police never even questioned me."

He looked at Sidney. "You understand, don't you? I had to do it. My dreams, my vision for the future." His voice was almost pleading. Sidney didn't answer. Finally Rowe stood up and wiped the tears away. "CyberCom was the last piece I needed. But it all came with a price. With all the secrets between us, Gamble and I were wedded for life." Rowe grimaced, then suddenly smiled as he looked at Gamble. "Fortunately, I will outlive him."

"You double-crossing bastard!" Gamble tried his best to get to Rowe, but Lucas held him back.

"But Jason found out everything when he was going through the records at the warehouse, didn't he?" Sidney said.

Rowe exploded again and directed his tirade at Gamble. "You idiot! You've never respected technology, and it was your undoing. You never realized that the secret e-mails you sent Lieberman could be captured on tape backup even if you later deleted them. You were so damn anal about money, kept your own set of books documenting the profits trading on Lieberman's actions. And your enemy's losses. It was all buried in the warehouse. You idiot!" Rowe exclaimed again, and looked over at Sidney. "I never wanted any of this to happen, please believe me."

"Quentin, if you cooperate with the police—" Sidney began.

Rowe erupted in laughter and Sidney's hopes faded completely.

He went over to the laptop and popped out the disk. "I'm now the head of Triton Global. I just acquired the one asset that will enable me to accomplish a better future for us all. I don't intend to pursue that dream from a prison cell."

"Quentin . . ." She froze as he turned to Kenneth Scales.

"Make it quick. She is not to suffer. I mean it." He nodded in Gamble's direction. "The bodies go into the ocean, as far out as you can. A mysterious disappearance. In six months' time no one will even remember you," he said to Gamble. Rowe's eyes shone with that thought.

Gamble was slowly led away, struggling mightily and cursing.

"Quentin!" Sidney screamed as Scales came closer. Quentin Rowe didn't turn around.

"Quentin, please!" Finally he looked at her. "Sidney, I'm sorry. I really am." Holding the disk, he started to leave the room. As he passed by, he kindly patted her on the shoulder.

Her body and mind numb, Sidney's head dropped on her breast. When she looked back up, the cold, blue eyes were floating toward her, the face completely blank of emotion. She looked around. Everyone in the room was intently watching Scales's methodical advance, waiting to see how he would kill her. Sidney gritted her teeth and backed away until she was flat against a wall. She closed her eyes and did her best to hold the image of her daughter rigidly in her mind. Amy was safe. Her parents were safe. Under the circumstances, that was the absolute best she could do. *Good-bye, baby. Mommy loves you.* The tears spilled down her face. *Please don't forget me, Amy. Please.*

Scales lifted up his knife and a smile crept across his face as he looked down at the glistening blade. Light reflecting off it turned the metal a harsh reddish color, a color it had been many times in the past. Scales's smile receded as he looked down at the source of this colored light and saw the tiny red laser dot on his chest, and the barely visible, pencil-thin beam that emanated outward from the dot.

Scales backed away, his shocked eyes fixed on Lee Sawyer, who was pointing his assault rifle with attached laser scope directly at him.

Bewildered, the mercenaries looked at the weaponry pointed at them by Sawyer, Jackson, the HRT and a contingent of the Maine State Police. "Guns down, gentleman, or start looking for your brains on the floor," Sawyer bellowed, tightening his grip on the rifle. "Guns down! *Now!*" Sawyer took a few more steps into the room, his finger closing on the trigger. The men started to put down their weapons. Out of the corner of his eye, Sawyer spotted Quentin Rowe trying to discreetly disappear. Sawyer swiveled his gun in the computer man's direction. "Don't think so, Mr. Rowe. Sit down!"

A thoroughly frightened Quentin Rowe sat down in a chair, the disk gripped against his chest. Sawyer looked at Ray Jackson. "Let's get to it." Sawyer started toward Sidney. At that instant a shot rang out and one of the FBI agents went down. Gunfire erupted as Rowe's men used the opportunity to seize their weapons and open fire. The lawmen quickly dove for cover and returned the fire. Muzzle flashes popped up all over the room as instant death spewed forth from over a dozen locations. It took only seconds for every light in the room to be shot out by gunmen on both sides, plunging the room into total darkness.

Caught in the cross fire, Sidney threw herself to the floor, her hands over her ears as bullets whizzed overhead.

Sawyer dropped to his knees and scrambled toward Sidney. From the other direction, Scales, his knife between his teeth, slid on his belly along the floor toward her. Sawyer reached her first and took her by the hand to lead her to safety. Sidney screamed as she saw Scales's blade flash through the air. Sawyer swung his arm out and took the brunt of the blow, the knife cutting through his thick jacket and slicing his forearm. Grunting in pain, he kicked at Scales, losing his balance and toppling over on his back. Scales pounced on the FBI agent and struck at his chest twice. The blade, however, met the advanced-stage Teflon mesh in Sawyer's body armor head-on and lost decisively. Scales paid for that defeat with a mouthful of one of Sawyer's massive fists and one of Sidney's elbows slamming into the back of his neck. The man howled in pain as his already battered mouth and broken nose received an additional litany of injuries.

Furious, Scales violently threw Sidney off and she slid across the floor and crashed into a wall. Scales's fist repeatedly slammed into Sawyer's face and then he raised the knife, the center of the FBI agent's broad forehead his target. Sawyer clamped his hand around Scales's wrist and slowly but surely heaved himself up. Scales felt the amazing strength in Sawyer's bulk, raw strength the much smaller man could not hope to match. Used to his victims being dead before they ever had a chance to fight back, Scales abruptly discovered he had hooked a very much alive Great White Shark. Sawyer smashed Scales's hand against the floor until the knife went flying into the darkness. Then Sawyer hauled back and unleashed a haymaker that landed flush on Scales's face and Scales went backward across the room, screaming in agony, his nose now lying flat against his left cheek.

Ray Jackson was in one corner of the room exchanging fire with two of the mercenaries. Three of the HRT members had made their way to one of the balconies. With this tactical advantage they were quickly winning the shoot-out. Two of the mercenaries were dead already. Another was about to expire with a bullet wound in his leg that had severed the femoral artery. Two of the state troopers had been shot, one seriously. Two of the HRT members had taken hits but were still participating in the gun battle.

Stopping to reload, Jackson looked across the room and saw Scales get to his feet, knife raised, and sprint toward the very broad back of Lee Sawyer as the FBI agent again tried to pull Sidney to safety.

There was no time for Jackson to reload his rifle, his 9mm was empty and he was out of clips. If he tried to yell, Sawyer would be unable to hear him over the barrage of gunfire. Jackson jumped to his feet. As a star member of the University of Michigan Wolverines football team, he had rushed for thousands of hard-fought yards on the gridiron. Now he was about to make the run of his life. His thick legs exploded under him, and with bullets splattering all around Jackson reached maximum speed three steps into his sprint.

Scales was solid bone and muscle, but he carried about fifty fewer pounds on his frame than did the two-hundred-pound battering ram of an FBI agent. And despite being a very dangerous individual,

Kenneth Scales had never experienced the brutally violent world of Big Ten football.

Scales's blade was barely a foot from Sawyer's back when Jackson's iron shoulder collided with his breastbone. The resulting crack as Scales's chest collapsed could almost be heard over the gunfire. Scales's body was lifted cleanly off the ground and it didn't stop moving until it slammed against the solid oak wall almost four feet away. The second crack, while not as loud as the first, heralded Kenneth Scales's exit from the living as his neck snapped neatly in half. As he slumped to the floor and came to rest on his back, it was finally Scales's turn to stare blankly upward with a pair of dead eyes. By any yardstick, it was a long-overdue event.

Jackson paid a price for his heroics as he took a slug in his arm and another in his leg before Sawyer was able to ward off the shooter with multiple bursts from his 10mm. Sawyer grabbed Sidney's arm and hauled her to a corner behind a heavy table he had flipped on its side. He then raced over to Jackson, who was slumped against a wall breathing hard, and proceeded to drag him toward safety. A shot thudded against the wall within an inch of Sawyer's head. Then another hit him squarely in the rib cage. His pistol flew from his hand and slid across the floor as he slumped back against the wall, coughing up blood. The vest had done its job again, but he had heard the crack of some ribs upon impact. He started to pull himself up, but now he was very much a sitting duck.

Suddenly a string of shots erupted from near the overturned table. An abrupt scream from the direction of the shot that had hit Sawyer followed the lead barrage. Sawyer looked over at the table and his eyes widened in amazement as he saw Sidney Archer jam the still smoking 10mm pistol in her waistband. She raced out from behind the protective cover, and together she and Sawyer pulled Jackson safely behind the table.

They sat Jackson up against the wall.

"Damn, Ray, you shouldn't have done that, man." Sawyer's eyes quickly examined his partner, confirming that there were two wounds and no more.

"Right, and let you give me hell from the grave for the rest of my life? No way, Lee." Jackson bit his lip hard as Sawyer ripped off his tie and, using Scales's stiletto blade, made a crude tourniquet above the wound on Jackson's leg.

"Keep your hand right there, Ray." Sawyer guided his hand to the handle of the knife, pressing his fingers tightly against it.

He next tore his coat off, balled it up and stanched the bleeding on Jackson's arm wound. "Slug went right through, Ray. You're gonna be okay."

"I know, I could feel it exit." The sweat poured off Jackson's forehead. "You took a round, didn't you?"

"Nah, vest caught it, I'm okay." As he slumped back, Sawyer's savaged forearm started to pour blood again.

"Oh, God, Lee," Sidney stared at the crimson flow. "Your arm." Sidney took off her scarf and wound it around Sawyer's wounded limb.

Sawyer eyed her kindly. "Thanks. And I'm not talking about the scarf."

Sidney slumped against the wall. "Thank God we were able to fill in each other's blanks when you called. I regaled Gamble with my brilliant deductions to buy you some time. Even so, I didn't think it was going to be enough."

He sat down next to her. "For a couple of minutes, we lost the signal from the cell phone. Thank God we picked it back up again." He abruptly sat up, making the cracked rib even worse. He looked at her battered face. "You're okay, aren't you? Jesus, I didn't even think to ask."

She rubbed her swollen jaw gingerly. "Nothing that time and makeup won't help." She touched his swollen cheek. "How about you?"

Sawyer had another jolt. "Omigod! Amy? Your mother?"

She quickly explained about the voice recording.

"Those sonofabitches," he growled.

She looked at him wistfully. "I'm not sure what would have happened if I hadn't answered your page."

"Point is, you did. I'm just glad I had one of your business cards." He smiled. "Maybe this high-tech crap has its uses. In tiny doses."

*   *   *

In another corner of the room Quentin Rowe huddled behind the desk. His eyes were closed and his hands were over his ears as he tried to shield out the sounds exploding all around him. He did not notice the man come up behind him until the last instant. His ponytail was jerked violently backward, forcing his chin up farther and farther. The hands then twisted his head around, and just before he heard the snap of his spine, he was staring into the vicious, grinning countenance of Nathan Gamble. The Triton chief let the limp body go and Rowe dropped to the floor, dead. He had experienced his last vision. Gamble snatched the laptop off the desk and smashed it so hard over Rowe's body that it cracked in half.

Gamble hovered over Rowe's body for a moment longer, then turned to make his escape. The bullets hit him square in the chest. He looked, wide-eyed, at his killer, disbelief and then anger racing across his features. Gamble managed to grip the man's sleeve for an instant before toppling to the floor.

The killer took the disk from where it had fallen next to Quentin Rowe and made his way out.

Rowe had fallen on his side and his body had come to rest on its back, his head turned toward Gamble. Ironically, he and Gamble were bare inches from each other, far closer than the two men ever had been in life.

Sawyer inched his head above the table and surveyed the room. The remaining mercenaries had dropped their weapons and were coming out of hiding, their hands high. The HRT members moved in, and in a moment the men were down on the floor in handcuffs. Sawyer noticed the limp bodies of Rowe and Gamble. But then, outside the French doors he heard running feet. Sawyer turned to Sidney. "Take care of Ray. Show's not over yet." He hustled out.

CHAPTER FIFTY-EIGHT

The wind, snow and ocean spray assaulted Lee Sawyer on every front as he ran along the sand. His face was bloody and swollen, his injured arm and ribs throbbed like hell and his breath came in thudding fits and starts. He took a minute to strip off the heavy body armor, then he plunged on, pressing a hand firmly against his cracked ribs to hold them in place. His feet twisted and turned in the loose surface, slowing him down. He stumbled and fell twice. But he figured the person he was hunting was having the same problem. Sawyer had a flashlight, but he didn't want to use it, at least not yet. Twice he ran through frigid water as he strayed too close to the border of the pounding Atlantic. He kept his eyes straight down as he followed the set of deep footprints in the sand.

Then Sawyer was confronted with a massive outcropping of rock. It was a common enough formation along the Maine coast. For a moment he debated how to navigate the obstacle until he saw a rough path that cut through the middle of the miniature mountain. He headed up, pulling his gun out as he did so. Sawyer was hit with a wall of ocean spray as the waters beat relentlessly against the ancient stone. His clothes clung to his body like plastic. Still he pushed on; his breathing came in huge bursts as he struggled up the path, which was becoming more and more vertical. He looked out to the ocean for a moment. Black and endless. Sawyer rounded a slight bend in the path and then stopped. He shone his light ahead, out to the very edge of the cliff before it disappeared straight down into the Atlantic far below.

The light illuminated the man fully. He squinted back and he put up a hand to shield his eyes from the unexpected burst of light. Sawyer sucked in air. The other man was doing the same after the long chase. Sawyer put one hand on his knee to steady himself as he half bent over, his gut heaving.

"What are you doing up here?" Sawyer's voice was wheezy but clear.

Frank Hardy stared back at him, his breath also coming in deep gusts from weary lungs. Like Sawyer's, his clothes were drenched and dirty and his hair was a wind-ravaged mess.

"Lee? That you?" Hardy said.

"It sure as hell ain't Santa Claus, Frank," Sawyer wheezed back. "Answer my question."

Hardy took a last lengthy breath. "I came up with Gamble for a meeting. Right in the middle of it, he tells me to go upstairs, that he has some personal business to conduct. The next thing I know, all hell broke loose. I got out of there as fast as I could. You mind telling me what's going on?"

Sawyer shook his head admiringly. "You always could think fast on your feet. It's what made you a great FBI agent. By the way, did you kill Gamble *and* Rowe, or did Gamble beat you to Rowe?"

Hardy looked at him grimly, his eyes narrowed.

"Frank, take out the pistol, muzzle first, and toss it over the cliff."

"What gun, Lee? I'm not armed."

"The gun you used to shoot one of my men and start that little gun battle in there." Sawyer paused and tightened his grip on his own pistol. "I won't tell you again, Frank."

Hardy slowly took the pistol out and tossed it over the cliff.

Sawyer flushed a cigarette out of his pocket and clenched it between his teeth. He pulled out a lighter and held it up. "Ever seen one of these, Frank? These suckers will stay lit in a tornado. It's like the one they used to down the plane."

"I don't know anything about the plane bombing," Hardy said angrily.

Sawyer paused to light his cigarette and then took a long puff. "You *didn't* know anything about the plane bombing. That's true. But you were in on everything else. In fact, I bet you charged Nathan Gamble a nice little premium. Did you get a piece of the quarter billion you framed Archer for stealing? Duplicated his signature and everything. Nice work."

"You're crazy! Why would Gamble steal from himself?"

"He didn't. That money's probably spread over a hundred different accounts he's got all over the world. It was perfect cover. Who'd ever suspect the guy who got taken for all that money? I'm sure Quentin Rowe handled the BankTrust piece and also breaking into Virginia's AFIS database to monkey around with Riker's prints. Jason Archer had the evidence to the whole blackmail scheme with Lieberman. He had to tell someone. Who? Richard Lucas? Don't think so. He was Gamble's man, plain and simple. The inside guy."

"So who did he tell?" Hardy's eyes were now pinpoints.

Sawyer took a long drag on his cigarette before answering. "He told you, Frank."

"Right. Prove it," Hardy said with disgust.

"He went to you. The 'outside' guy. The former FBI agent with a list of commendations as long as his arm." Sawyer spat this last sentence out. "He went to you so you could help him expose the whole thing. Only you couldn't let that happen. Triton Global's your gravy train. Giving up private jets, the pretty ladies and nice clothes wasn't an option, was it?"

Sawyer continued, "Then you all took me through the dog and pony show, setting up Jason to be the bad guy. You guys must've been laughing your asses off at how you suckered me. Or *thought* you had. But when you saw I wasn't buying all of it, you got a little nervous. Was it your idea to have Gamble offer me a job? Between you and him I never felt so popular." Hardy remained silent. "But that wasn't your only performance, Frank."

Sawyer reached in his pocket and took out a pair of sunglasses and put them on. He looked quite ridiculous in the darkness. "You remember these, Frank? The two guys on the video in the warehouse in Seattle? They were wearing sunglasses, indoors, in a fairly dark room. Why would anybody do that?"

"I don't know." Hardy's voice was a mere whisper now.

"Sure you do. Jason thought he was handing over his proof . . . to the FBI. At least in the movies all Feds wear shades and the guys you hired to play the FBI agents must have liked going to the theater. You couldn't just kill Jason. You had to win his trust, make sure he hadn't told anyone. A top priority was getting back all the hard evidence he had. The videotape of the exchange had to be in pristine condition because you knew you'd be giving it to us as evidence of Jason's guilt. You only had one shot to get it right. But Archer was still suspicious. That's why he kept a copy of the information on another disk and later sent it to his wife. Did you tell him he'd get a big reward from the government? Was that it? Probably told him it was the biggest damned sting in the history of the FBI."

Hardy remained silent.

Sawyer looked at his old partner. "But unknown to you, Frank, Gamble had his own big problem. Namely that Arthur Lieberman was about to spill his guts. So he hires Riker to sabotage Lieberman's plane. I'm sure you didn't know about that part of the plan. On Gamble's orders you arrange for Archer to get ticketed on the flight to Los Angeles, and then you had him pull a switch and he gets on the flight to Seattle instead so you could film your little videotape of the exchange. Rich Lucas is ex-CIA, he probably had lots of ties to former Eastern European operatives with no families, no past. The guy who went down in Archer's place wouldn't be missed. You had no idea Lieberman was on the L.A. flight or that Gamble was going to kill him. But Gamble knew it was the only way the blame for Lieberman's death could be thrown on Archer. And with it, Gamble kills two birds with one stone: Archer and Lieberman. You bring me the video and I switch all my efforts to catching Jason and I forget all about poor old Arthur Lieberman. Except for Ed Page wandering into the picture, I don't think I would've ever picked up Lieberman's thread again.

"And let's not forget old RTG, who got blamed for everything, with Triton conveniently ending up with CyberCom. I told you about Brophy being in New Orleans. You found out he was actually connected to RTG and that they might actually accomplish what you'd set Jason up for: working with RTG. So you had Brophy and Goldman followed and when the opportunity arose, you took them both out and set up Sidney Archer to take the fall. Why not? You'd already done the same thing to her husband." Sawyer paused. "That's a hell of a transition, Frank: FBI agent to participation in a massive criminal conspiracy. Maybe I should take you on a visit to the crash site. You want to do that?"

"I didn't have anything to do with the plane bombing, I swear," Hardy yelled out.

"I know. But you were involved in one regard." Sawyer took off his sunglasses. "You killed the bomber."

"Would you care to prove that?" Hardy's eyes blazed at him.

"You told me, Frank." Hardy's face froze. "Down in the parking garage where Goldman and Brophy checked out. The place was freezing. I was concerned about the decomposition of the bodies, that the frigid temperatures might make ascertaining the time of death impossible. Remember what you said, Frank? You said it was the same problem with the bomber. That the air-conditioning had made the apartment freeze just like the outside air did to the parking garage."

"So?"

"I never told you the air-conditioning was turned on in Riker's apartment. In fact, I turned the heat back on right after we found the body. There was no mention of the A/C being turned on in any of the bureau reports—not that you would've been privy to them anyway." Hardy's face had turned ashen. "You knew, Frank, because you were the one who turned the A/C on. When you found out about the bombing, you knew Gamble had used you. Hell, maybe they planned to kill Riker all along. But you were more than willing to do the honors. It didn't hit me until I was freezing my ass off in a police paddywagon driving over here."

Sawyer moved forward. "Twelve shots, Frank. I admit, that one really puzzled me. You were so furious at the guy for what he'd done that you went a little berserk. Emptied your whole clip into him. I guess you still had a *little* bit of the cop left in you. But now it's over."

Hardy swallowed hard, struggling to keep his nerves under control. "Look, Lee, everybody who knows about my involvement is dead."

"What about Jason Archer?"

Hardy laughed. "Jason Archer was a fool. He wanted the money, just like all of us. Only he didn't have the nerve, you know, not like you and me. He kept having *bad dreams*." Hardy edged forward. "You look the other way, Lee. That's all I'm asking. You start work at my company next month. One million dollars a year. Stock options, the works. You'll be set for life."

Sawyer flicked his cigarette away. "Frank, let me make this real clear to you. I don't like ordering my food in foreign languages, and I wouldn't know a damned stock option if it jumped up and clamped me right on the balls." Sawyer raised his gun. "Where you're going, the only *option* will be top or bottom bunk."

Hardy snarled, "Not by a long shot, old *buddy*." He pulled the disk from his pocket. "You want this, then put your gun down."

"You've gotta be kidding me—"

"Put it down," Hardy screamed. "Or I throw your whole case into the Atlantic. You let me go, I'll mail it to you from parts unknown."

Hardy started to smile as Sawyer's pistol began dropping. Then, as Sawyer stared into the grinning countenance, he abruptly returned the pistol to its original position. "First, I want an answer to one question, and I want it now."

"What is it?"

Sawyer moved forward, his hand tightening on the trigger. "What happened to Jason Archer?"

"Look, Lee, what does it matter—"

"Where is Jason Archer?" Sawyer roared over the crash of the waves. "Because that is exactly what the lady back there wants to know, and dammit, you're going to tell me, Frank. By the way, you can throw that disk as far as you want. Rich Lucas is alive," Sawyer lied. He had seen Lucas lying dead in the middle of the battlefield the hotel lobby had become. The silent sentinel was now forever silent. "Want to bet how anxious he is to rat on your ass?"

Hardy's face went stone cold as he realized his exit option had just evaporated. "Take me back to the house, Lee. I want to call my lawyer." Hardy started forward and then suddenly stopped as Sawyer assumed a textbook shooting stance.

"Now, Frank. Tell me right now."

"Go to hell! Read me my rights if you want, but get out of my damned face."

Sawyer's response was to shift his pistol slightly to the left and fire one round. Hardy screamed as the slug took off skin and the top part of his right ear. Blood poured down the side of his face. He fell to the ground. "Are you crazy?" Sawyer now aimed the gun directly at Hardy's head. "I'll have your badge and your pension, and your ass will be in jail for more years than you've got left, you sonofabitch," Hardy screamed. "You'll lose everything."

"No I won't. You're not the only person who can manipulate a crime scene, *old buddy*." Hardy watched in growing astonishment as Sawyer popped open the gun bag riding above his belt and took out another 10mm. He held it up. "This will be the gun you'll have gotten away from me in the struggle. They'll find it clutched in your hand. It'll have several shots fired from it, evidencing your homicidal intent." He pointed toward the vast ocean. "Kind of hard to find the slugs out there." He held up the other pistol. "You used to be a first-rate investigator, Frank. Care to deduce what role this pistol will play?"

"Dammit, Lee, don't!"

Sawyer continued calmly. "This will be the pistol I use to kill you."

"Jesus, Lee!"

"Where is Archer?"

"Please, Lee. Don't!" Hardy wailed.

Sawyer moved the muzzle to within a few inches of Hardy's head.

When Hardy covered his face with his hands, Sawyer snatched the disk from Hardy's quivering fingers and looked at it. "Come to think of it, this might come in handy." He put it in his pocket. "Good-bye, Frank." His finger descended on the trigger.

"Wait, wait, please, I'll tell you. I'll tell you." Hardy gagged for a moment and then looked up into Sawyer's grim face.

"Jason is dead," he cried out.

The few words slammed into Lee Sawyer like lightning bolts. His big shoulders collapsed and he felt the last vestiges of energy leave his body. It was as though he had simply died. He had been almost certain of this result but had been hoping for a miracle, for Sidney Archer and her little girl's sake. Something made him turn and look behind him.

Sidney was standing at the top of the path, barely five feet from him, drenched and shivering. Their eyes met under soft moonlight suddenly revealed through the patchy clouds. They did not need to speak. She had heard the terrible truth: Her husband was not coming back.

A scream came from the cliffside. Gun ready, Sawyer whirled around just as Hardy went over the cliff. Sawyer made it to the edge in time to see his old friend and new nemesis bounce off the jagged rocks far below and disappear into the violent waters.

Sawyer stared down at the abyss and then with a furious thrust he hurled his pistol as far as he could into the ocean. The movement tore at his damaged ribs, but he didn't feel the pain. He closed his eyes and then opened them to stare at the savage outline of the Atlantic. "Dammit!" Sawyer's big body leaned heavily to one side as he fought to keep his fractured ribs immobile and his weary lungs functioning. His ripped arm and battered face started to bleed once again.

He stiffened as he felt the arm on his shoulder. Under the circumstances, Sawyer would not have been surprised to see Sidney Archer run as fast as she could from this place; who could've blamed her? Instead, she put one of her arms around his waist and one of his around her shoulder, and helped the injured FBI agent back down the path.

CHAPTER FIFTY-NINE

The funeral that finally laid Jason Archer to rest in peace occurred on a clear December day atop a quiet knoll about twenty minutes from his brick and stone home. During the graveside service Sawyer had stayed in the background as family and close friends attended the once again grieving widow. The FBI agent had stayed at the grave site after all of them had gone. As he stared at the newly etched tombstone, Sawyer rested his bulk on one of the folding chairs that had been used for the simple, brief burial ritual. Jason Archer had occupied the agent's every waking moment for over a month and yet the two men had never met. That was often the case in his line of work; however, this time the emotions wending their way through the veteran agent's psyche were far different. Sawyer knew he had been powerless to prevent the man's death. And yet he still felt crushed that he had let the man's wife and little girl down, that the Archer family had been irretrievably destroyed because of his inability to get at the truth in time.

He covered his face in his hands. When he removed them some minutes later, the tears still glimmered in his eyes. He had successfully completed the case of a lifetime, yet he had never felt like more of a failure. He stood up, put on his hat and headed slowly toward his car. Then he froze. The long black limo was parked at the curb. It had come back. Sawyer watched the face peering out from the limo's rear window. Sidney was looking at the fresh hump of dirt in the earth. She turned her head in Sawyer's direction as he stood there trembling, unable to move, his heart pounding, his lungs heaving, and wishing more than anything else on earth to be able to reach into that cold soil and return Jason Archer to her. The glass slid back up as the limousine drove away.

The night before Christmas Eve, Lee Sawyer rolled his sedan slowly down Morgan Lane. The houses along the street were beautifully decorated with lights, wreaths, all-weather Santa Clauses and their trusty reindeer. Down the block a group of bundled-up carolers was performing. The area was in a festive mood, all except for one house, which was dark but for one light on in the front room.

Sawyer pulled into the Archers' driveway and got out of his car. He was dressed in a new suit, his cowlick plastered down as much as it could be. He pulled a small gift-wrapped box out of the car and walked up to the house. His gait was a little stiff; his ribs were still on the mend.

Sidney Archer answered his knock. She was dressed in dark slacks and a white blouse, her hair flowing down over her shoulders. She had gained some weight back, but her features were still gaunt. The cuts and bruises had healed, though.

They sat in the living room in front of the fire. Sawyer accepted her offer of cider and looked around the room while she went to get it. On the side table was a box of computer disks with a red bow on top. He put the box he had brought with him on the coffee table, since there was no Christmas tree to put it under.

"Going somewhere for the holidays, I hope?" he asked as she sat down across from him. They each took a sip of the warm cider.

"My parents'. They've got the place fixed up for Christmas. Big tree, decorations. My father's going to dress up like Santa. My brothers and their families will be there. It'll be good for Amy."

Sawyer looked over at the box of disks. "I hope that's a gag gift."

Sidney followed his gaze and briefly smiled. "Jeff Fisher. He thanked me for the most exciting night of his life and offered me free computer advice in perpetuity." Sawyer then eyed the small, damp towel Sidney had brought back with her and placed on the coffee table. He slid the present across. "Slip this under the tree for Amy, will you? It's from me and Ray. His wife picked it out. It's a doll that does a bunch of stuff, you know, it talks and pee-pees—" He abruptly stopped and looked embarrassed. He took another sip of cider.

Sidney smiled. "Thank you very much, Lee. She'll love it. I'd give it to her now, except she's asleep."

"It's better to open presents on Christmas anyway."

"How is Ray?"

"Hell, you couldn't hurt him if you tried. He's already off the crutches—"

Sidney turned green and quickly reached for the towel. She held it against her mouth, got up and raced out of the room. Sawyer stood up but didn't follow. He sat back down. In a couple of minutes she had rejoined him. "I'm sorry, I must have caught a bug."

"How long have you known you were pregnant?" Sawyer asked. She sat back, stunned. "I've got four kids, Sidney. Believe me, I know morning sickness when I see it."

Sidney's voice was strained. "About two weeks. The morning Jason left . . ." She started to rock back and forth, one hand pressed across her face. "God, I can't believe this. Why did he do it? Why didn't he tell me? He shouldn't be dead. Dammit! He shouldn't!"

Sawyer looked down at the cup in his hands. "He tried to do the right thing, Sidney. He could've just ignored what he'd found, like most people would have. But he decided to do something about it instead. A real hero. He took a lot of risks, but I know he did it for you and Amy. I never had the opportunity to meet him, but I know he loved you." Sawyer was not about to disclose to Sidney that the hopes of a government reward had played a prominent role in Jason Archer's decision to gather evidence against Triton.

She looked at him through tear-filled eyes. "If he loved us so much, why did he choose to do something that was so dangerous, so . . . It doesn't make any sense. God, it's like I lost him twice. Do you know how that feels?"

Sawyer considered this for a minute, cleared his throat and started speaking very quietly. "I have this friend who's kind of contradictory. He loved his wife and kids so much he would've done anything for them. I mean anything."

"Lee—"

He held up a hand. "Please, Sidney, let me finish. Believe me, it took a lot to get to this point." She sat back as Sawyer continued. "He loved them so much he spent all his time trying to make the world a safer place for them. So much time, in fact, that he ended up hurting terribly the very people he loved so much. And he didn't see it until it was too late." He took a sip of the cider as a massive lump formed in his throat. "So you see, sometimes people do the dumbest things for the very best reasons." His eyes shimmered. "Jason loved you, Sidney. Hell, at the end of the day, that's all that really matters. That's the only memory you ever have to keep."

Neither broke the silence for several minutes as they both stared into the flames.

Finally Sawyer looked at her. "So what're you going to do now?"

Sidney shrugged. "Tyler, Stone lost its two biggest clients, Triton and RTG. However, Henry Wharton was very nice; he said I could come back, but I don't know if I'm up to it." She covered her mouth with the towel and then her hand dropped to her lap. "I probably don't have a choice, though. Jason didn't have much life insurance. We've pretty much run through our savings. With the new baby on the way . . ." She shook her head in misery.

Sawyer waited for a moment and then reached in his suit pocket and slowly took out an envelope. "Maybe this'll help."

She dabbed at her eyes. "What is it?"

"Open it."

She pulled out the slip of paper inside. She finally looked up at Sawyer. "What is this?"

"It's a check made out to you for two million dollars. I don't think it'll bounce, considering it was issued by the United States Treasury."

"I don't understand, Lee."

"There was a two-million-dollar reward from the government for information leading to the capture of the person or persons responsible for the plane bombing."

"But I didn't do anything. I haven't done anything to earn this."

"Actually, I'm absolutely certain it will be the only time in my life that I'll give anyone a check for that much money and then tell them what I'm about to tell you."

"What's that?"

"That it doesn't even come close to being enough. That there's not enough money in the whole world that could be enough."

"Lee, I can't accept this."

"You already have. The check itself is ceremonial. The funds have already been deposited into a special account set up under your name. Charles Tiedman—he's the president of the San Francisco Federal Reserve Bank—has already put together a team of top financial advisers to invest the funds for you. All gratis. Tiedman was Lieberman's closest friend. He asked me to convey to you his sincerest condolences and heartfelt thanks."

The United States government had initially been reluctant to give the reward to Sidney Archer. It had taken Lee Sawyer a full day with congressional and White House representatives to make them change their minds. Everyone was adamant that the full details of the deliberate manipulation of America's financial markets must not come out. Sawyer's less-than-subtle suggestion that he would join with Sidney Archer in auctioning off the disk he had taken from Frank Hardy while on the cliff in Maine to the highest bidder had caused them to abruptly change their minds on the reward. That and his flinging a chair the length of the attorney general's office.

"The funds are all tax-free," he added. "You're pretty much set for life."

Sidney wiped at her eyes and put the check back in the envelope. Neither one of them said anything for several minutes. The fire popped and crackled in the grate. Finally Sawyer looked at his watch and put down the cup of cider. "It's getting late. I'm sure you've got things to do. And I've got some work back at the office." He stood up.

"Don't you ever take a break?"

"Not if I can help it. Besides, what else am I gonna do?"

She stood up too and before he could say good-bye she wrapped her arms around his thick shoulders and pressed herself against him. "Thank you." He could barely hear the words, not that he needed to. The sentiments were emanating from Sidney Archer like the warmth from the fire. He put his arms around her, and for several minutes they stood there in front of the flickering firelight holding each other as the sounds of the carolers grew closer.

When they finally drew apart, Sawyer gently took her hand in his. "I'll always be there for you, Sidney. Always."

"I know," she finally said, her voice only a whisper.

As he started to the door, she called to him. "This friend of yours, Lee . . . you might want to tell him it's never too late."

Driving down the street, Lee Sawyer spotted a full moon planted against a clear black sky. He proceeded to hum quietly a Christmas carol of his own. He wasn't going back to the office. He'd go over and hassle Ray Jackson for a while, play with his kids and maybe drink some egg nog with his partner and his wife. Tomorrow he'd do some late shopping for presents. Max out the old plastic and surprise his kids. What the hell, it was Christmas. He unclipped the FBI badge from his belt and took his pistol out of its holster. He laid them both on the seat next to him. He allowed himself a weary smile as the sedan drifted down the road. The next case was just going to have to wait.

AUTHOR'S NOTE

The aircraft featured in the preceding pages, the Mariner L500, is fictitious, although some of the general specifications noted in the book are based on actual commercial airplanes. Given that acknowledgment, aircraft enthusiasts may quickly point out that the sabotage of Flight 3223 is rather far-fetched. My goal in writing this book was not to prepare an instructional manual for deranged persons.

With respect to the Federal Reserve Board, suffice it to say the idea of this country's economic destiny being, in large measure, controlled by a handful of people who meet in secrecy without much in the way of supervision by anyone was irresistible to me from a storytelling point of view. Truth be known, I've probably *understated* the Fed's iron grip on all our lives. To be fair, though, over the years, the Fed has navigated this country's economy extremely well through some very tough waters. Their job isn't easy, and it's far from an exact science. While the results of Fed action can be painful for many of us, we can be reasonably certain these actions are taken with the good of the country, as a whole, in mind. Still, with such enormous power concentrated in such a small, isolated sphere, the temptation to reap oceans of illegal profit can never be far from the surface. And the stories one can write!

Regarding the computer-technological aspects of *Total Control*, all of them, to the best of my research ability, are perfectly plausible if they are not already in full-scale use or perhaps even, if you can believe it, obsolete. The numerous benefits of computer technology are undeniably significant; however, with benefits of such scale, there is inevitably a downside. As the world's computers become increasingly linked into a global network, the risk that one person may one day exercise "total control" over certain important aspects of our lives also increases proportionately. And as Lee Sawyer queried in the novel, "What if he's a bad guy?"

David Baldacci
Washington, D.C.
January 1997